CROWNLESS

M. H. WOODSCOURT

True North Press

Copyright © 2021 by M. H. Woodscourt

2nd Edition Copyright © 2022 by M. H. Woodscourt

All rights reserved.

No part of this book may be reproduced in any form or by any electronic or mechanical means, including information storage and retrieval systems, without written permission from the author, except for the use of brief quotations in a book review.

This is a work of fiction. Names, characters, and places are products of the author's imagination.

www.mhwoodscourt.com

Cover designed by Getcovers

Paperback ISBN: 9798419911000

Hardcover ISBN: 9798419911451

To the unsung heroes in every era who stand for truth against despots, traitors, cynics, cowards, liars, and fools.

Your bravery astounds me.

CONTENTS

1. Wanderlust — 1
2. The Lady Queen — 9
3. The Dying King — 21
4. Rille — 27
5. The Dungeon — 39
6. The Holy Empire of KryTeer — 51
7. In Hiding — 57
8. Traveria — 67
9. Death — 73
10. The Vices of Men — 77
11. A Battle of Wits — 85
12. The Journey South — 89
13. Children of the Earth — 103
14. The Missing King — 115
15. The Honor of Blood — 123
16. The Hut in the Woods — 131
17. Threads of Freedom — 145
18. Where Deception Ends — 151
19. A Storyteller True — 159
20. The Lost Prince — 171
21. Fairy Wings — 187
22. Unfolding Visions — 193
23. The Curse — 199
24. The Drifting Sands — 209
25. Beyond the Arch — 227
26. The Second Prince of the Blood — 239
27. The Shepherd of Shing — 255
28. The Way of the Elders — 263
29. The Snake — 283
30. Within the Fortress — 293

31. A Thread of Smoke	315
32. Envy and Revenge	327
33. A Plea for Help	337
34. Sea Bells	345
35. Before the Emperor	355
36. Five Spears	367
37. Caught in a Trap	375
38. Almost Dawn	389
39. Between Two Pillars	393
40. The Man from Shing	401
Coming Soon	405
Dearest Reader	407
Addendum	409
Acknowledgments	419
About the Author	421
Also by M. H. Woodscourt	423

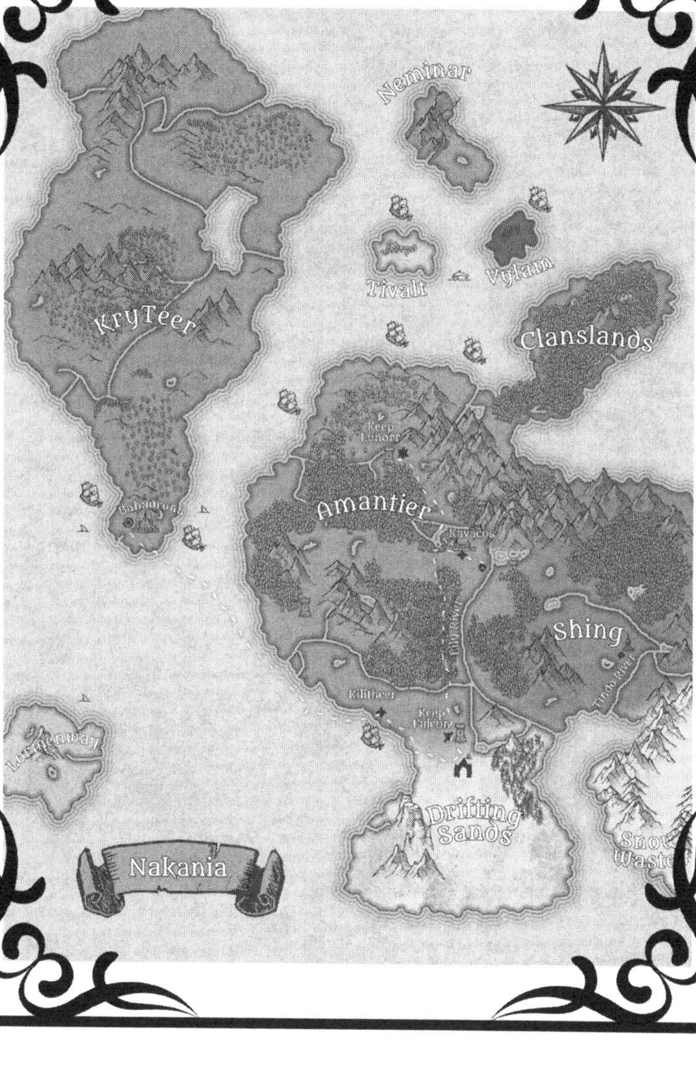

Neminar
KryTeer
Tivalt
Vylam
Clanslands
Amantier
Shing
Kilitheer
Keep
Falcon
Drifting
Sands
Nakania

1
WANDERLUST

There was nothing special about him.

He traveled with a satchel over one shoulder, his gait slow, ignorant of the world rushing on without him. His clothes; threadbare, vest open, every button gone, shoes worn out. The traveler didn't appear to mind, meandering as he was through tall meadow grass beside a trickling stream. He strolled with a full smile on his lips, eyes bright as he gazed all around. Rarely did he look ahead, yet his steps were certain, and he never stumbled. When he looked forward, there was a light in his face that left no room for doubt: He knew his destination, but he was in no hurry to get there.

Crouched against a hillside west of the stream, Yeshton watched the man. One hand gripped the pommel of his sword.

One thing Yeshton didn't understand: How could this man have a price on his head? Not that Yeshton would receive any reward for bringing the traveler in. As an Amantieran soldier under Duke Lunorr's banner, this was duty, not fortune. But by capturing the wanted man himself, no one else could claim the reward either. Two hundred gold kana was a lot of money.

Yeshton's eyes narrowed. *Is he from Shing?*

The black hair and short stature implied it. Was this simple man a spy for the KryTeer Empire? In that case, the price was too low.

But the Shingese weren't really of the KryTeer Empire. Shing had surrendered only five years ago. Odd that a loyal spy would come from there so soon. A paid informant, then? Not duty-bound but seeking profit or maybe a decent meal. The latter was probable, judging by his apparel.

You're a soldier, man. Do your job. Yeshton raised his hand, bracing to signal the other men stationed in the shadows around the point of ambush. The traveler approached the sloping path between two steep inclines. Yeshton had guessed right. This was the way toward Kavacos of Rose Province, the Royal City of His Majesty King Jetekesh the Fourth.

The rabbit strolled toward the snare.

Yeshton pressed against the slope. *Patience. No mistakes.*

The traveler stopped before he reached Yeshton's position and turned to study a large elm. Had he seen Brov hidden in the higher branches?

The traveler whistled up at a nesting bird. The bird trilled a reply. Hitching the satchel higher on his shoulder, the man continued walking.

Three more steps. Two. One.

Yeshton signaled and his men appeared around the hill, three wielding bows and arrows, the rest with their swords unsheathed. Yeshton stood tall and folded his arms as the traveler stopped to gaze up at the eight armed soldiers.

"Jinji Wanderlust," Yeshton said. "By order of Her Majesty Queen Bareene, you are under arrest."

The man turned to look up at him, a gentle smile on his lips. "What is my crime, sir?" His accent was faint. His eyes were a teal blue color. Perhaps not from Shing after all.

"Rabble-rousing," Yeshton said.

Jinji blinked. "I can't see how that is so."

"Contend with the queen if you dare. You're to come with us."

"I will come." Jinji hitched up his satchel again.

Yeshton nodded to Kivar, who slung his bow over his shoulder and moved down the slope. Near the bottom he stumbled. Jinji darted forward and grabbed the man's arm before his feet caught even ground.

"Take care. The dew is abundant this morning."

Kivar jerked from his grasp. "I don't need your help, spy."

Jinji held out one wrist. "Do I go in irons?"

Yeshton looked him up and down. Pale and thin, white threading through his hair, though he appeared little older than Yeshton; perhaps thirty years. "I doubt that will be necessary." He trotted down the hill and started along the path. His men followed, Jinji at their center until they cleared the hills and reached the horses tethered to several fallen trees. Yeshton untied his horse and swung up into the saddle. "Can you ride, Wanderlust?"

The man studied the horse. "I've never tried, but I can learn."

"We don't have time. Nallin, help him up behind me."

The young soldier helped Jinji to clamber onto the horse's back. He rested his hands against Yeshton's shoulders, his touch light as a breath. "I am ready."

"Move out!" They rode in single file, following the rough path to straighter, wider roads, where they spread into two columns. Twenty minutes later signs of civilization appeared along the King's Highway. Yeshton's eyes darted every which way. Amid the wagons and peddlers, he found several unsavory faces, but none looked ready to hinder an armed company; not even for a royal reward.

Jinji Wanderlust began to hum.

Yeshton glared back at him. "Stop that."

"Is something amiss?" asked Jinji.

"Yes, you. Are you so unconcerned with your fate?"

"What, pray, is my fate; do you know?"

"Sedition usually ends in death."

"Indeed, so do all things. But I am innocent of inciting crowds in Amantier." The man's tone was not the whiny protest of other condemned men. His smile remained.

"Say what you will. Queen Bareene feels otherwise."

"Her Majesty does not know me yet."

Yeshton snorted. "Will that make a difference?"

"I should think so. Is a man condemned before his trial?"

"You're a foreigner," Yeshton answered.

"My mother was of Shing," Jinji said. "My father, Amantieran."

"Then you had best hope your father appears at your trial."

"He won't."

That wouldn't help the man's case.

"What is your name?" asked Jinji.

"Why?"

"Because in my head I cannot help but call you 'the man who frowns,' and I think it would be better to call you by name."

"Fine. Yeshton."

"It's a pleasure to meet you, Yeshton. I am Jinji, as you know."

Yeshton tightened his fists over the reins. "Stop that."

"Stop what?"

"It's not a pleasure. Your situation is bleak. Don't hum, don't smile, don't exchange pleasantries. You're going to die. Do you understand, or are you mad?"

Jinji laughed. It was a soft sound, like water. "Such a dismal outlook. Of course I will die. Everyone will, someday. But today, in this moment, I am alive. That is enough for me."

Yeshton stared at the road ahead. "You *are* mad."

"Perhaps," Jinji said. "Or perhaps you are mad, not I. Who can say?" His voice was still smiling.

As the stone gates shut behind him, Yeshton let out a breath and pushed his shoulder-length, dark blond hair away from his face. After the hustle and bustle of Kavacos, the palace grounds were a welcome reprieve, frequented by only the handful of guards on duty. No incidents had occurred on the streets outside, but there had been a lot of inquisitive gazes.

The captain of the guard stood on the gravel drive. Was the heat too much or had he been born with that snarl? "*This* is the infamous Wanderlust?"

Yeshton helped Jinji stumble off the horse, then swung down. "It's him. He fits the description and he answers to the name."

The captain looked Jinji up and down, then turned his critical eye on Yeshton. "And you are…?"

"Yeshton of Duke Lunorr's militiamen. He sent us to confirm a report of Wanderlust's location, then bring him straight here, should the informant be truthful."

"Your orders?"

Yeshton pulled the crinkled parchment from under his hauberk and smoothed it before he handed it over.

The captain read through it as he sucked at something between his teeth. "All right. Wanderlust is now in the custody of Her Majesty the Queen."

Yeshton saluted and stepped back. He kept his gaze away from the prisoner.

The captain signaled with his hand. "Jinji Wanderlust, you are hereby under arrest for sedition."

The prisoner made no sound as two armed guards stepped from the shadows of the gate. One claimed his satchel. Yeshton moved beside his horse; its body heat wafted under the scorching sun. Sweat pricked Yeshton's brow. His eyes wandered to Rose Palace. Its sandstone towers stretched wide and tall across the green lawn, and the banner of Amantier limped in a half-hearted breeze.

The captain of the guard glanced his way. "Still here?"

"Duke Lunorr will want proof I've obeyed his orders."

The captain grunted and ran a hand through his short, coarse hair. "I bet he'll want the reward, too."

"His reward is the queen's smile."

The captain snorted. "Right. And yours?"

"Only proof I've done my lord proud."

With a sigh, the captain gestured, and a young boy scampered from the shade, paper and quill in hand. "Jot this down, boy: 'To Duke Lunorr of Sage Province. Your men did high service to Her Majesty the Queen this day by bringing in the notorious Wanderlust. He will stand trial for his crimes against the Crown. Her Majesty's smile is yours.' Got that?" The captain snatched the parchment and quill. He scrawled his name and rolled the parchment up. "Take it and begone. You're stinking up the royal gates."

Yeshton took the parchment with murmured thanks. He glanced toward Jinji as the captain turned away. The prisoner eyed Yeshton with an open smile, even as the two guards flanking him set hands on his shoulders to guide him to his fate.

"I am glad I met you, Yeshton. Farewell."

Yeshton turned away, but the man's eyes remained in his vision. Bright and unafraid. No accusation harbored there. Yeshton swallowed and looked at his waiting men, then swung up into his saddle. "Move out."

It was odd, Yeshton thought as he rode through the gates and entered the milling streets of Kavacos. Most traitors were heralded by angry mobs on their way to trial, but no one had tried to waylay Yeshton or his men, though they had a highly prized criminal in tow.

Why? Why was Jinji different?

He spotted a crowd of children staring at him and his companions with wide eyes.

"It's him," one whispered, "the lost knight."

"Nuh-uh," said another. "He's Prince Sharo."

A third shoved the second. "Does he look like a prince to you, you poxy oaf?"

The second boy shoved back. "Course not. Neither does Sharo though."

Yeshton turned away, hiding a smile. Even in these dangerous times when the world was at war, children played make-believe. He remembered long, long ago pretending to be Sharo, fabled prince of fairyland.

A woman darted into the street ahead of Yeshton. His horse reared as he yanked the reins. The woman danced out of the way.

"Watch it, wench!" Brov barked from his own startled mount.

She bobbed an apology as Yeshton laid a calming hand on his stallion's neck. "Terrible sorry, I am, honored sirs!"

"No harm done," Yeshton said. He shot Brov a look. The man held his tongue.

The woman bobbed again. "You're most kind, honored sir." She whirled on the children. "Hush, ye fools. Don't play near the palace." She swatted one boy's backside. "Get away. Y'know the queen hates fairy stories. Off with ye."

The children scattered, shouting and laughing. Yeshton frowned up at the high spires of the palace visible beyond the gates. It seemed silly to ban fairy stories because of a war, but then fear did strange things to people, even queens.

2
THE LADY QUEEN

Queen Bareene stretched out on the settee and kicked off her slippers to flex her toes. With a sigh she sank her head into the pillows, then glanced across the room to where her son sat in silence before the fire in the hearth.

She puckered her lips. "Do not fret, my dear boy. It isn't the end of the world."

Prince Jetekesh threw up his hands. "How am I ever to govern the land if you keep intervening, Mother?"

Bareene's smile stretched wider. "It was a sensitive issue, darling. You hesitated."

"I was thinking!" Jetekesh snatched up the poker and prodded at the burning wood. "For all of two seconds before you took over!"

"Please don't sulk, dearheart. It spoils your looks."

Jetekesh smoothed his face. He was a fine-looking young man, twice what his father had been even before his illness ravaged him. Straight golden hair framed the prince's face and fell past his shoulders in the present fashion of young men. His eyes, a beautiful teal blue shade, danced in the firelight. His cheekbones, high and delicate; frame lean, not yet a man's. He promised to be tall, but not gangling. A perfect specimen of good breeding.

Ah, yes. He would make a fine ruler, if only he learned to control his temper.

"Mother, next time I hesitate, count to five. Can you promise me that at least?"

"Whatever you wish, pet."

A scowl gathered at his brow, but he sighed and relaxed his face. He was learning, just…slowly. "Thank you, Lady Mother."

A knock hammered the door. Bareene sighed. "It had better not be about your father. He's so demanding these days."

Jetekesh started to rise, but Bareene waved him back down.

"Come in." She narrowed her eyes. "We never walk to a summons."

A servant poked her head inside. "Your Majesty, Captain Frebe of the Royal Guard seeks an audience. He comes with a gift."

"How *intriguing*." Bareene sat up and smoothed the layers of her full dress. She tucked her toes under the fabric and nodded. "Let him enter."

Frebe marched inside the ornate, wood-beamed chamber and bowed. Bareene's lip curled as the reek of sweat and stables wafted toward her. "This had better be important, Captain."

"I would not come otherwise, My Queen." He straightened and waved his hand. Two more pungent guards entered, a papery-looking wayfarer between them.

"What in the name of all the holy saints is *this*?" She eyed the threadbare apparel. The cut of his jaw and the fine lines of his cheeks. The upward slant of his eyes. "You bring a Shingese peasant to my private parlor, Captain?"

"Your Majesty, I present Jinji Wanderlust."

Her eyes darted up and down the frail frame before her. A smile tugged at her lips. "Oh really?" She rose with a rustle of cloth and approached, gathering her skirts to keep them back. "You are Jinji Wanderlust? You're the madman selling tales of sedition to my people?"

"I am named Jinji," the prisoner said. "But I do not claim the title Wanderlust."

"You really ought," she said, drawing as close as she dared to half-blood filth. "I gave it to you."

He inclined his head. "I thank you, Your Majesty, for the gift."

"You know why I gave it to you, I daresay. You're an elusive man, wandering from place to place, avoiding those sent to keep you from your foul purpose. It's poetic, perfect for the seditious storyteller who ignores my royal decrees, don't you think?"

"Are you a storyteller, truly?"

Bareene pursed her lips and turned to Jetekesh. The boy stood beside the fire now, his eyes flickering with light as he studied Jinji. "Two hundred gold kana just to catch a storyteller. Really, Mother?"

"Stay out of this, precious."

Jetekesh's eyes flashed. "Why should I? Am I not to

be king when my lord father dies? And won't you bow to me, your lord son?"

Bareene curled her hand into a ball, nails digging into flesh. "Not today, dearest. This man is not a toy, but an enemy."

"Honestly, Mother, you sound paranoid. He's one man, if that. How much harm can he do?"

"You might be surprised," Bareene said. "He came through Kavacos last Autumn, didn't you, Wanderlust? You stirred up a lot of trouble then, telling tales of pretend princes coming to claim what belongs to them. Oh, you might have fooled the masses, but you don't fool me. I know a KryTeer sympathizer when I hear one." She rested a finger under the prisoner's chin. "You thought to hide your heritage under that filthy Shingese face, but I smell KryTeer on your breath."

"I am not of KryTeer," Jinji said. "Perhaps you smell the onions I ate for breakfast."

Her eyes narrowed. Was he mocking her?

"Mother." Jetekesh rested a hand on her shoulder. "Let me have him. Please?"

She whirled on him. "Why?"

"Because he interests me. Let me have him, and when I'm bored, you can torture him, or boil him, or whatever else you had in mind."

She studied her son's face, the curiosity in his eyes, and she smiled. It might be a good teaching opportunity. "Very well, Jetekesh, but don't say I didn't warn you. He's a menace and a threat. Be careful and don't let him escape."

∽

Jetekesh waited until Mother was gone before he ordered the captain and his guards to depart. When they hesitated, he sighed. "Tifen is nearby. Leave us. I'm fine."

When the doors closed after the guards, he turned to Jinji. "What a fascinating figure you cut." He moved to the settee and threw himself against the pillows, then snapped his fingers. His protector stepped from the deepest shadows of the room and approached. He bowed. "This is Tifen, my bodyguard. If you try anything, Wanderlust, he won't hesitate to spread your guts across my courtyard. Do you understand?" He motioned to a decanter and Tifen poured him a goblet of bloodred wine.

"Yes," Jinji said, "I understand."

"I understand, *Your Highness* would be more respectful." Jetekesh sipped the wine and licked his lips. "But then, the Shingese aren't a respectful people, are they? Shing doesn't consider any of its conquerors to be worth respecting, so my tutors tell me. Odd, that. You would think that a people constantly trampled by other countries would understand their place in life."

"The people of Shing respect those who respect others," Jinji said.

Jetekesh swallowed a second sip of wine and chuckled. He sank deeper into his pillows. "Tell me a story."

Jinji smiled. "Your mother forbade the telling of stories."

"My mother isn't here. Besides, that law has been in effect for some time, and yet you seem to have a reputation for the trade just the same." He stretched out a foot and kicked a nearby chair. It wobbled before it settled back down. "Sit."

Jinji sat. "How old are you, Your Highness?"

"Fifteen. Why?"

"So young."

Jetekesh straightened with a scowl. "I am eligible to wed next spring."

"So you are."

"You don't seem very old yourself." Jetekesh studied the white in his hair and the light color of his eyes. "Or perhaps you are very old. I can't quite decide. How old are you?"

"Thirty-two," Jinji said.

"But your hair is turning."

Jinji fingered a snowy lock. "Yes, it is."

"What a meek creature you are." Jetekesh stretched across the settee. "You remind me of my mother's pet birds. Are you going to tell me a story or not?"

"What would you like to hear, Your Highness?"

"Oh, anything." Jetekesh waved a hand. "How about that pretend prince Mother mentioned? The one coming to claim what belongs to him. Is he meant to oust me?"

"He is not a prince of this land," Jinji said. "His name is Sharo of the land of Shinac."

Jetekesh laughed into his goblet. "Shinac? And where is that?"

"Nowhere and everywhere."

"How…evasive. What would it be like to rule a land such as that?" Jetekesh sat up and handed the goblet to Tifen. "Is it like Tifen here? So near, yet easily forgotten?"

Jinji met the prince's gaze with a smile. "You mock, and yet you almost understand."

Jetekesh shrugged. "I guessed; that is all. So, how did Sharo lose his kingdom?"

"He was exiled."

"By whom?"

"His father the king."

Jetekesh clicked his tongue. "Sounds like a foolish prince."

"No. His father was more the fool."

Jetekesh eyed Jinji through narrowing eyes. "Be careful what you say."

"I speak of the king of Shinac, not of Amantier."

Jetekesh folded his fingers over his flat stomach. "Why was his father a fool?"

"Because he feared his son and threw him out."

Jetekesh sighed. "We're going in circles. Why did the foolish king throw his son out?"

"He was afraid. You see, in the king's greed, he took whatever he pleased. He never cared about the consequences. But all actions carry weight, just as a stone plunging into a lake will cause ripples. One day as His Majesty King Darint returned from hunting in an ageless wood, he beheld a maiden fair above any in his kingdom. She disappeared into the woods, but he could not forget her beauty. He was already wedded, but his queen was barren. Seizing his chance, King Darint ordered the woman found and brought to his castle. By the time she arrived, the present queen had met with a horrible accident. King Darint commanded the fair maiden to wed him. She could hardly refuse. One year later Prince Sharo was born."

Jinji's eyes found the fire.

"Well, go on. Why did the king exile his own son when he had no other heir?"

Jinji stirred and met the prince's gaze. "You must understand something about Shinac. It is what most folk call fairyland, a realm of magical beings and magic itself."

Jetekesh chuckled. "I recall tales of Shinac, I think. I had a maid servant who often recited rhymes of fairies and dragons and other rubbish. Is this what you do, sell fairytales to my father's kingdom? And my mother actually thinks you a danger?" His gaze drifted across Jinji's face, then his clothes. "You appear ready to splinter. Can you even lift a sword?"

"I've never tried," Jinji said, a faint smile touching his eyes.

"Never mind. You were telling me of Shinac and its magical prince."

"Just so. And you are more right than you know. You see, Shinac was once part of this world. It was in the place now called the Drifting Sands."

"Shinac is a desert?"

"No. It disappeared years ago, leaving only desert behind."

"How?"

Jinji spread his hands. "Magic."

"Oh, yes. I forgot; this is a fairy story. Pray tell, why did Shinac leave our world?"

Jinji's smile faded. "Because we were greedy and wanted its magic for ourselves."

"And the people of Shinac wouldn't share?"

"They couldn't share. We aren't magical. We cannot wield magic unless certain conditions are met."

Jetekesh sniggered. "You almost appear to believe

Shinac is real. Indeed, you almost make me believe it's real. That's quite a gift you've got, Wanderlust."

"It is real." Jinji's smile was back, quiet and reflective and almost sad.

Jetekesh threw his head back and laughed. "Oh, you are something else! Utterly mad, aren't you? So, Shinac is real and it's…everywhere? And nowhere, so you said. Does it just float somewhere above our heads, invisible?" He leaned forward. "Are there fairies dancing around my head?"

"Magic is difficult to understand, even for those who believe in it."

"So, then, this prince of yours, this Sharo; his father threw him out. It seems to me your Shinac is no different from our world, even for all its magic."

"There were some who lived in Shinac who wielded no magic but vanished with the land just the same. King Darint's line was among those privileged few, but then his ancestors usurped the throne of Shinac's true kings."

"Oh, so he's an impostor king, like KryTeer's emperor. But how did non-magical people defeat magical creatures?"

"By very dark means, my prince. King Darint was aware that his line was not the true one, and he had been careful to silence any stirring whisper of the true king's return. But he was not as careful as he thought. Indeed, he brought his own undoing upon himself when he caught the forest maiden, a descendant of the fae kings of old. Through her—"

"Fae kings? What are they?"

"Magical beings."

"Like elves?"

"In a way."

"All right. Go on."

Jinji's eyes darted to the hearth. "If you please, Your Highness, I'm chilled from recent illness. Might I sit a little closer to the fire?"

"Tifen, move his chair."

"I can manage, Your Highness." Jinji took up his chair as Tifen moved toward him.

"Nonsense. You're my *guest*. Besides, I doubt you have the strength to carry it far."

Jinji allowed Tifen to take the chair, and they walked together to the hearth. Jinji sat and stretched out his hands to warm them near the flames. "King Darint first began to suspect his son was different when the boy kept vanishing from his lessons at an early age."

Jetekesh shrugged. "I vanished from mine all the time."

"He didn't hide, Your Highness. He disappeared. Into the air itself."

Jetekesh considered that. "Lucky boy."

"At first the king refused to believe his own eyes, but the boy became stranger and stranger with each passing year. In his early years, he was close to his father and, if you will allow, quite a spoiled child. His mother did not know what to do with him. Sharo bullied the servants, and whipped his horse, and did all the sorts of things refined young men shouldn't do."

"He's a prince," Jetekesh said. "He can do what he likes."

Jinji nodded. "So he felt. But remember what I said of ripples in a lake. There are consequences for every action."

"Please." Jetekesh slumped against his pillows. "Your stories were interesting at first, but now I see the truth of them. You're not telling tales; you're selling morals, which is altogether different and much less pleasant."

"Forgive me if I seem to preach. I mean only to tell stories, and you asked after Prince Sharo yourself."

Jetekesh snorted. "Don't think me a fool, Wanderlust. You tale-weavers always tweak the story to accommodate the present audience. What is your goal here? Teach the heir apparent to mind his manners? 'Say please and thank you and don't beat your horse, else the goblins will eat you.' So my tutors used to warn."

"It isn't a bad way to live," Jinji said, "but it isn't my purpose. I did not intend to come to the palace, Your Highness. Remember, I was arrested by your queen mother."

"It wasn't your plan, perhaps, but you're taking advantage of your misfortune as any sensible man would. However," Jetekesh leaned forward, "you would fare better to flatter me, rather than teach childish morals. I'm of half a mind to throw you in the dungeon."

"You may do as you wish, Your Highness."

Jetekesh snorted and ran a hand through his hair. "You don't know how to treat royalty. First you preach and then you patronize."

Jinji bowed his head. "My apologies if I offend. It is not my intention. Indeed, I didn't intend to tell any stories this day. I feel…rather weak."

The prince rose and paced the room, passing his hand over silken drapery. "What *is* your intention, Wanderlust? What is your purpose in coming to my kingdom and feeding lies to my people?"

"I only wish to give them some happiness."

"By telling them of a land that allegedly abandoned us because we weren't good enough? Such an inspiring thought!"

"I tell them of people who daily overcome struggles much like their own."

"You *are* a madman, Wanderlust." He stepped to the window and stared at the waning sun. "What changed the prince? What made him stop whipping his horse and bullying his servants?"

"He learned to care for others above himself," Jinji answered. "He learned that a leader serves his people, not the other way around."

Jetekesh turned a quiet sneer on the storyteller. "Mother was right. You are a danger. You bring your Shingese philosophies into my country, convincing the masses that they need a benevolent and weak-willed ruler to serve them. Well, we don't need that. We need strength. We need power. We need absolute fealty, and you are undermining everything my lady mother and I are working for. I hope you find my dungeons to your liking, Wanderlust. They certainly suit your purpose."

3
THE DYING KING

"Very good, Your Highness. That's enough for today."

Jetekesh set aside his rapier and mopped his brow with a handkerchief. His instructor, a willowy, aging man, bowed and strode off across the private courtyard to change clothes. Jetekesh turned to find his own quarters and change from his drenched fencing outfit. The trees surrounding the courtyard stood still, their leaves curled in the heat. Jetekesh glanced up at the sun. Not yet nine o'clock. Perhaps he should stay indoors today.

His boots slapped cobblestones as he trotted toward the eastward corridor, but as he lowered his head his steps faltered. Mother stood in the open doorway, arms folded, eyes narrowed. Her lips pulled in a pucker. She was draped in a pale gold gown and her long blonde hair twisted in a braid that fell past her knees.

Jetekesh inhaled, squared his shoulders, and imagined gliding.

"Good morrow, Lady Queen. How was your rest?"

"Until this moment I was in perfect repose, dearheart," came her smooth, watery tones. "But alas, when I came to wake you, I discovered you were *dueling* again."

Jetekesh throttled the handkerchief in his hand. "Yes, Mother. I've been carrying on my lessons in secret."

"But *why*, Jetekesh? Your hands." Mother caught his wrist to bring his palm up for inspection. "Look at those calluses! And see how damp you are with sweat. You *reek* and princes mustn't ever reek."

Jetekesh bit his lip. Best not mention battles or fox hunts or all the other times a prince, just as any other man, might break into a sweat. There was no point. She couldn't understand. She wouldn't let herself understand.

"Wash yourself." Mother dropped his hand. "Make yourself presentable. Your father has summoned you this morning."

Jetekesh's heart soared until his head grew light. "He wants to see me?"

"Only for a few moments. You mustn't excite him. He's delicate, dearest. Don't forget." She sighed. "I shall see to your instructor. He'll be sent away directly."

Jetekesh's heart stuttered and fell. "Mother?"

"No, darling, you shan't duel. I won't abide it."

"But Mother! Father is an excellent duelist. Kings for ages now—"

"Your father lies upon his deathbed, Jetekesh!" The queen's voice cracked like a whip. "I won't subject my son to the same weakness of body. You will *not* push yourself so cruelly."

He opened his mouth to argue. Her words were preposterous. Fencing would hardly wind him, let alone drive him to his death. It kept him active, graceful, healthy. But with the king's illness, Mother had become unreasonable. Jetekesh could do nothing that might mar his looks: not lose his temper, not run down the corridors, not ride a horse. And what could he do but submit? But only until he was king. After that, he would *not* indulge her mad requests any longer. Yet the very idea of becoming king horrified him, for it would signify the death of Jetekesh's hero.

"Fine." He stomped past her.

"Your posture, pet!"

He slowed until he turned the corridor, then sprinted to his rooms. After sponging himself off, Jetekesh found his way to Father's dark chambers.

The smell of death lingered close, as though the *Driodere*—grim death itself—hovered above the grand four-post bed, waiting to claim King Jetekesh the Fourth. Prince Jetekesh hated this close and dismal room and what it held. The king was not as he had always been. Rather than the strong arms and broad shoulders, the bright cunning eyes, the meticulous thinker, the lord and ruler of Amantier, here lay the papery ghost of a man: haggard, skeletal, with sunken eyes and harsh, clipped breaths.

Jetekesh squared his shoulders and dragged in a breath. He approached the bed, hands damp with sweat as he clenched his fingers into fists. His heart clattered in his ears.

Father slept, breaths rattling.

Jetekesh wet his lips. Lately, pain had made Father's rest difficult. Should Jetekesh leave him be and come on another day? It was so rare to see him, to hear him, to speak with him. The prince was no fool. Time was wearing down, and soon he must bid Lord Father farewell forever.

The putrid scent of rot washed over Jetekesh. He gagged. *I hate this. I want to leave!*

"My son…is that you?"

Jetekesh's heart took flight as he leaned across the bed. "Yes, sire. It is I."

Lord Father's eyes cracked open and caught fire in the candlelight. "I can…hardly see anything. Draw aside the curtains, Kesh."

"Should I, sire? Lady Mother said the sunlight is too harsh for you."

"Non…sense… A little sunlight won't harm anyone."

Jetekesh strode to the window and let in a crack of light. "Better?"

"Yes… Now stand…where I can see you…"

Jetekesh traced the light across the floor and stood in it, aware of the sun playing against his gold hair. Mother would love the effect if she saw it.

Father's ashen lips lifted in a broad smile. "You grow more every time I see you. How do you pass your days, my son?" A cough traced lines of pain across his sunken face. "Do you grow your mind…as your body grows…as a prince should?"

Jetekesh considered how to answer, but his frustrations were so near the surface, they just bubbled over. He blurted out how Mother was even now discharging the fencing master. How Jetekesh could no longer ride or hunt or enjoy any other traditional pastimes that might spoil his appearance.

The king listened, his mouth a grim line. He sighed as

Jetekesh finished. "I…feared this. I shall speak with the queen, I promise you, Kesh. Come."

Jetekesh gently crawled across the bed to kneel beside Father's ravaged body. If Jetekesh breathed too strong, Father might break apart and float away like embers in a hearth.

The king raised his emaciated fingers to stroke Jetekesh's cheek once. His hand fell to his side. "I'm told…you met the wandering…storyteller. How do you like the tales of Shinac?"

"Mother says they're meant to stir up unrest and rebellion among our people."

Father's bright eyes locked onto Jetekesh's. "Your lady mother also says you shouldn't fence or dream or think for yourself."

Jetekesh scowled. "That may be, but Jinji Wanderlust started to tell me one of his stories, and I found it distasteful. He thinks a prince should *serve* his people, when certainly it's the other way around."

"It seems to me…Jinji of Shinac may be wiser by far…than anyone here at court."

The door flew open.

Mother stood highlighted in the doorway, hazel eyes wide and raging. "I *told* you not to exhaust your father, yet here you are *still*. Your tutors are waiting, my son." Her eyes traveled to the window. "What have I said about sunlight? Jetekesh, useless, disobedient son! You'll be the very death of your king. Out. *Go*."

Jetekesh scrambled from the bed. Mother's lips pursed, but he hurried past her without a word and shut the door behind him. Guilt and loathing roiled in his stomach, struggling for victory over each other. He stalked to a suit of armor down the hall. The urge to kick it swept like a tremor through his frame, but Mother was so near. She would scold him for losing his temper. For letting emotion show on his face. For ruining his appearance. Jetekesh shut his eyes and breathed. He must conquer his temper.

Anger was his enemy. He must control himself. Must be in control.

Mother insisted on it.

Father would want it.

For Father.

He stormed down the corridor toward his study. For a wild moment, he considered changing course midway. Perhaps he would visit Jinji in the dungeon instead.

No. If he displeased Mother again, there would be no end to her fury.

4
RILLE

Keep Lunorr had fallen.
Word reached Yeshton by messenger as he sat in a tavern to wait out a storm. Sage Province had been overrun by the Imperial Forces of KryTeer. The soldier sat now in silence with his comrades at the tavern table, a tankard of ale gripped in his hand, untouched. The hastily scrawled report lay before him, a testament of Yeshton's high hopes dashed to bits. He couldn't read the bitter words, but Nallin could.

The tavern was half filled because of the storm, and those who sought shelter this night were grim. Sage Province lay thirty miles from here. So close. Too close.

"What'll we do, Yesh?"

Yeshton ignored Brov's soft murmur. Duke Lunorr was probably dead. KryTeer had no use for him. That vast empire needed no hostages or tools to plow its way through Amantier toward Kavacos. Most had assumed the Empire would march straight through Amantier by way of Ivy Province, the most direct *and* prosperous stretch of Amantier. Take that course and lay ruin to the wealth of the kingdom; surely then Amantier would buckle before the dread sword of KryTeer's Blood Prince.

So why Sage Province? It was small, indirect, even unpopular. Duke Lunorr had been out of favor with the court and gentry since his elder brother, King Jetekesh, had fallen ill several years before. Everyone knew Queen Bareene despised the duke, for he spoke his mind. By *his* way of thinking, the queen was a selfish, gluttonous hag who would sooner sell Amantier to its enemies than suffer for her country's sake, should the choice be laid before her. So he had accused her the last time he'd appeared at court.

Such a declaration would have meant death for any other man, but Duke Lunorr was third in line to the throne, and that lent the duke certain protections. Nevertheless, Duke Lunorr had essentially exiled himself to his home province, and there he seemed content to stay.

Even should KryTeer desire a bargaining chip, the duke was the worst candidate for it.

A secret suspicion tugged at Yeshton's mind as he swallowed a draught of ale. Was the queen behind it? Had she, *dared she*, sell her own countryman to the enemy? Might she strike a deal with the enemy to maintain her throne at the cost of her people?

Yeshton took another long drink as he struggled against the notion.

"D'you think the Blood Prince is after *her*?"

Yeshton glanced toward the youthful Nallin, just sixteen, who had been one of Duke Lunorr's household servants until he'd proved his uncanny skill with a blade. Nallin was plain faced, but brave and levelheaded. Respectful too. Yeshton studied him now.

"Her who, lad?" asked Brov over his tankard.

Nallin blushed a brilliant red. "Oh, uh, n-nothing. Just thinking aloud. S'all. It's nothing."

Yeshton pounded the table with his own tankard and looked hard at the youth. "Is it nothing, boy, or are you hiding something? If you've a thought of what the Blood Prince is after, you'd best spill it."

The boy lost that bright red blush along with the rest of the blood in his face. Though Yeshton was fond of Nallin, he'd never let on that he was. He pushed his men hard. Made them earn their keep. Had meant to make them indispensable to Lunorr until every last one of them was knighted...Yeshton kept his gaze rooted on Nallin now. Brave though he might be, Nallin wouldn't long hold up against Yeshton's will.

"W-well, sir." Nallin glanced around, but none of the other tavern patrons dared to approach the table where sat nine armed men bearing the heraldry of Sage Province. The droop of his shoulders told Yeshton the boy would hold nothing back. Nallin took a breath. "It's just, sir...well...I was thinking how KryTeer has no reason to storm Sage Province and destroy Keep Lunorr. E-except for one thing."

"And? So?" Brov leaned across the table, close enough Yeshton could smell the ale on his breath.

Nallin's face reddened again. "I swore I'd never tell." He glanced at Yeshton. "It's Rille, sir. Lord Lunorr's daughter."

Yeshton's eyes narrowed. Rille? That wisp of a girl, too sickly to leave her chambers within the keep? Barely ten, wasn't she? Not of marriageable age, not lauded for her beauty and wit. Chamber maids whispered sometimes that she was a halfwit, but the duke wouldn't admit it. He had no male heirs. His wife had died some years before in an accident on the road. Lunorr doted on Rille, but few ever saw her. Yeshton had glimpsed the child once from her window in the keep's tower. At the time he'd thought little of it, and never since, until now.

And now the poor girl is dead or captured. I've failed my lord.

"Why would the Blood Prince want young Rille?" asked Brov, as usual taking his place as Yeshton's voice for the group. Yeshton always let him.

Nallin ducked his head and sucked in a breath. "See, she's not normal. Not…not natural. She's different."

"All that means the same thing," piped up Kivar, elbowing the youth beside him. "Be more specific, lad." A mocking glint caught in his eye, but it flickered and died. The raucous drinking when Yeshton and his men had first reached the tavern had ended long ago, and mirth felt forced and foreign now. Unwelcome as the KryTeeran invaders. Not even the warmth of ale could lighten the mood.

Nallin shoved his tankard aside and leaned toward Yeshton. His voice lowered as he spoke. "Lady Rille… she's a witch."

Kivar whooped with laughter, but it was harsh and humorless. "Listen to the lad. Superstitious little fool! You sound like a sailor full of tales of merfolk and buried treasure. That ale's gone straight to your head."

Nallin flinched, cheeks red as blood.

"Ease up a mite," barked Brov. "There may be something there. But I think Nallin's only half right."

Kivar snorted and swigged his ale.

"Maybe there's no such thing as witches," said Brov, "but KryTeer's known for its magicians and such. They *believe* in magic. The Blood Prince too. Maybe he's heard tell of Lady Rille from those who think she's a witch, and he came to catch himself a prize."

"Not a witch," said Marder from the end of the table. His voice was soft but firm. "Rille's not a witch. She's something else. Not evil. She *sees* things."

Kivar's derisive smile fell away. The skeptical looks on Yeshton's men turned thoughtful. Marder never spoke unless he *must*. And he *never* spoke anything but the truth. Those in Yeshton's company held Marder in a strong regard bordering on reverence, for the man was battle-scarred, with a stub on the end of one arm and burns that covered half his face. He'd served Lunorr for many years, and he knew things—knew what other men spent a lifetime learning.

Yeshton looked between Nallin's hopeful glance in his direction and Marder's direct, calm eyes. Yeshton sighed. "What say you, Marder? Did the Blood Prince come looking for Rille?"

"It's just possible. Some say Rille's mother had the same gift. That's why she was killed."

Nallin made a sound, and when Yeshton looked toward him, the boy was nodding. "That's what I heard. And…and I met Rille once, before I joined this company. She spoke to me. Called me by name and I never told her my name. She inquired if I knew where someone was. I had no idea what she even meant."

"Who?" asked old Marder. "Who was she looking for?"

Nallin shrugged. "A storyteller. I asked if she wanted a maid to tell her a bedtime story, but that seemed to frustrate her. She said I should know what she meant. That I was connected to the storyteller. The housekeeper came just then, and I was scolded for even talking to the young lady. I was commanded never to reveal our conversation or the nature of the child. That was six months ago, and just afterward I was brought to your company, as you may recall. I'd overheard the chambermaids talking about Rille before that. How she's a witch. I…didn't believe it at first, but now…" He looked at Yeshton. "D'you think she meant Wanderlust? D'you think she saw…the future?"

A shiver ran the length of Yeshton's spine, but he kept his expression implacable. "It doesn't matter what I think. It matters what the Blood Prince thinks and why he ambushed Keep Lunorr. That's our one concern."

"So, what do we do?" asked Brov.

Yeshton downed the last of his ale, slammed the tankard against the table, and rose. "We ride for Sage Province and see what's left. All but you, Kivar. You will return to Kavacos and report what we know. If the Blood Prince has crossed into Amantier, it means open war. We must answer him."

∼

YESHTON TORE HIS EYES FROM THE REMAINS OF HIS lord, drawn and quartered, head on display for any who entered the burnt-out skeleton of Keep Lunorr.

Yeshton and his company had made good time, reaching the keep just as dawn crept over the eastern mountains. They'd taken the old forest road, little used even in broad daylight. Within an hour's ride of the keep, Yeshton had ordered his company to abandon the road and cut through the woods where KryTeer's spies, unfamiliar with the terrain, would become lost if they tried to maintain a vigil.

His caution proved unnecessary. Not a single KryTeer soldier or servant had remained at the keep to claim Sage Province. Not shocking. The Blood Prince wasn't known to creep across the land, conquering territories one by one. Instead he killed the leading lords, bathed in their blood, and moved his mighty forces through the land, burning, raping, murdering, until he reached the heart of the enemy country. Conquered it. Went home. So he had done in Shing. So he had done in Tivalt, Neminar, and Vylam in years past.

The KryTeer Empire was ever growing, swallowing the whole world like a vast, ravenous snake. Amantier was the last bastion to stand against that viper, but Yeshton had known it was only a matter of time. Amantier would become just another province under Emperor Gyath. That vile man's son and heir, Blood Prince Aredel, was like a dread specter, a veritable demon, storming across the world like a thing possessed. And where he struck his sword, the earth bled.

Yeshton picked his way through the rubble of the keep. Brackish blood swirled in puddles of muck. The air was still and hollow. Bodies still littered the reddened earth, though it had been several days since the attack.

Foolish, superstitious peasants. Would they not come to bury the dead? Many their own kin too.

The tower of the keep still stood, but it was a blackened husk. Yeshton sighed. He must resign himself to the fact that the Blood Prince had taken young Rille, or she was dead like her lord father.

"Well, drat," said Brov as he came up behind Yeshton. He halted beside him and shook his head. "What now? We've no master and no money. We're cut adrift, and no respectable lord will take us in without the proper papers. I don't fancy being sold to some no-good second-rate nobleman."

Yeshton shook his head. "It's not up to us, Brov. We ride to Kavacos to meet our fate."

Brov scratched his bristled chin. "Here now, Yesh. I understand your respect for the law. I appreciate your stalwart integrity. But as for me…I just can't abide the notion of starting over. You helped us get far. Maybe we could'a even broke free of our bonds. Been knighted. I dunno. But I just can't abide starting over. Maybe… maybe I'll take a gander at seafaring."

"You would run from your oaths, man?" Yeshton understood the desire to avoid a bondsman's life. He and his company would be snatched up by a middling nobleman in need of foot soldiers and plowed under the enemy cavalry in the first wave of combat. Returning to Kavacos meant death for all. Yeshton was a skilled swordsman, but he wasn't naive enough to think he could survive against the onslaught of KryTeer on the front line. Yet honor mattered more than his life.

Brov rubbed the back of his neck. "Blast it all, yes. I won't be treated like cattle. Lord Lunorr valued us. We won't be that lucky again. Besides, Amantier is finished. I won't give my life up for a lost cause. We can't win, Yesh. We'll all die for nothing. KryTeer's too powerful. And frankly, Queen Bareene's not going to put up much of a fight, for all that she throws around that word, 'sedition,' like it matters to her. There, I said it. Lord Lunorr was right, and we can't dispute that. I only regret we sent that poor, humble storyteller to the chopping block on her say-so. Not sure why Lord Lunorr even cared…"

Yeshton sucked in air. Why would Duke Lunorr send Yeshton and his company all the way to Rose Province to capture a harmless vagrant for the sake of a queen he loathed? Yeshton had been so caught up in pleasing his lord and master, he'd not stopped to ask the question until now.

She sees things. So said Marder. *She inquired after a storyteller*. So said Nallin.

Yeshton scowled at the sky. He'd never know the answer now. Duke Lunorr and his farseeing daughter were long gone. And what did it matter? Brov was right. Amantier was as good as conquered.

"Go, Brov. Take any who would follow you." Yeshton eyed his comrade and smiled faintly. "I *will* report you for running off, but Rose Province is a week away. You'll have time to reach Drea Wharf and charter a boat. Sail to Tivalt. They don't much care there if you're a runaway, so long as you can use a sword."

Brov's jaw tightened. "Come with us."

"No. I can't. I'll die for Amantier before I leave its shores."

"It's a waste," said Brov.

"Honor is never a waste. Farewell, my friend."

They all left. Yeshton couldn't blame them. At first Nallin had said he would ride with Yeshton to Kavacos, but Yeshton ordered him to go with the others. He was too young to waste his life.

Yeshton watched them ride away into the trees, heading northwest toward the sea. Toward freedom, or death if caught. But they wouldn't be. They were all too clever for that.

Turning toward the southern forest, Yeshton swung into the saddle of his own horse. He took up the reins.

Something shuffled in the dense thickets to his right.

Yeshton caught the hilt of his sword and listened.

The thickets rustled.

And again. Nearer.

"Don't kill me, good sir. It would be murder."

Yeshton pulled his hand from his weapon at once. "Who goes there?"

The whisper of leaves drew his eyes to a bush laden with ripening berries. From within that thorny shelter rose a small girl, perhaps as old as ten, though she was so slight and frail it was hard to be certain. Long, pale curls tumbled down her shoulders, and eyes of bright amber considered him with a look of calm far beyond her years. She wore a silken nightgown torn and stained with dirt and blood. Her feet were bare.

Yeshton swung down from his horse and knelt on one knee, head bowed. "My lady. I am your servant."

"Yeshton, son of Yarmir, isn't it?" asked Lady Rille.

"Yes, my lady."

"You will take me to Kavacos. You will take me to the storyteller."

Yeshton's eyes widened. "Yes, my lady. The journey will be hard and dangerous."

"It doesn't matter. We must hurry. The Blood Prince is seeking me. He won't give up. Make haste."

5

THE DUNGEON

"Hold a moment, Sir Knight."

Yeshton brought his horse up short and glanced back at the little girl seated behind him, her thin arms wrapped around his waist.

"I'm a soldier, my lady. Not a knight." He kept his voice a murmur.

"Hush, Sir Knight. Watch."

The road lay beyond the trees. Where possible, he kept within the forest to avoid running into peddlers or the stray armed forces of KryTeer. Though he'd traveled hard at his young mistress's urging, he never spied a single banner to suggest an invading force marched on Kavacos. Eerie silence was all that marked something amiss in Amantier. Few travelers braved the roads at all these days. Yet when Yeshton had dared enter a tavern to secure a warm meal for his mistress, who waited bravely in the woods, no word of KryTeer or even the sad fate of Sage Province wagged on any tongues, though the tavern was full to bursting.

Now, as he looked on, a caravan rolled and bounced on the highway: coaches lit by bobbing lanterns and flanked by knights bearing the heraldry of Aspen Province.

"It is not as it appears," whispered Rille.

The coaches headed for Kavacos, no doubt of that. Yeshton had brought the little girl within a few miles of the city. Night had settled in, and at last the roads were filling up with people, from the gentry down to common waifs. Yet something still felt wrong.

"What is it?" asked Yeshton

Rille said nothing. Yeshton urged the horse onward but kept to the trees as long as he could.

It was near midnight when the trees gave way before the high walls of Kavacos. Pointless walls, for the looming gates were open wide, lit by brilliant torches, to welcome all and sundry into its arms.

"Foolish…stupid…" muttered Yeshton. Had no one heeded the warning from Sage Province?

"I agree," whispered Rille. "We should enter by the main gate. Blend in with the next caravan."

"We're a mess."

"The guards won't notice."

"What will we do after that?"

"Head for the palace. The queen is holding a ball. We should make straight for the dungeons."

Yeshton scowled. Balls at such a time? Was there no end to Queen Bareene's stupidity? "And once we're there?"

Rille offered what she might have thought was a smile. It looked more like a grimace to him. "We will free Jinji Wanderlust from his prison."

PRINCE JETEKESH STOOD UPON THE DAIS NEAR Mother's throne, a goblet of wine in one hand. His third drink this evening, but the night was still young. He had plenty of time to intoxicate himself.

Father's condition was worse. When Jetekesh had entered the king's chamber this morning, he'd found Father tossing in his coverlets, raving like a madman. The court healer pronounced that the illness was nearing its end. Soon King Jetekesh would lose his mind, and the last vestiges of strength would bleed away until he was a mindless, shriveled husk. Then death would claim him.

Yet here Mother sat, gowned and jeweled: radiant before the nobleborn and gentry. Before the knights and their ladies. Before the liveried servants. Before the hunting dogs gorging on bones.

I want to throw up. But that would spoil his looks. Instead, he drank. And drank.

He snatched a fourth goblet from a passing servant and discarded his empty cup. The warmth of the wine cradled his mind and unknotted his nerves. *Much better.*

Father's condition wasn't his only worry. There had been reports of Sage Province toppling beneath a siege. Mother had assuaged the court's fears on that point. Yet last night, she executed the soldier who had ridden from Keep Lunorr with the news. In secret. Why?

Whispers filled the palace. Had Keep Lunorr fallen? Was Sage Province conquered? No one knew. But all day the queen looked so pleased, several chambermaids swore Duke Lunorr was dead. Hadn't Queen Bareene been out for his blood for years?

Jetekesh took another swallow of wine. His vision wavered. Finally.

The gaiety of the ball grew. The music and wine and pageantry of colors wove and glittered before Jetekesh like a menagerie of birds on parade. He smiled to himself and downed his fifth goblet of wine. *There now. I'm so drunk Mother will be furious.* He hardly cared. Was drunk enough, he could *not* care. At last.

He stepped behind the velvet swaths of drapery and slipped through the eastside passage as Mother turned to whisper something to a sycophantic nobleman. Out in a main corridor Jetekesh started for Father's chambers but stopped. Not there. He couldn't see Father now, not tonight. Where could he flee instead? How could he escape the palace and its giggling, flippant, boisterous revelers?

Where can I go?

He turned and trotted north, toward the rear of the palace, where a moldering stairwell took him down into a dank passageway and deep into the ill-kept dungeons of Kavacos, torch in hand.

He had no idea where Jinji Wanderlust wasted away in this foul-smelling cesspit, but he plunged deeper, emboldened by the wine coursing through him. Wouldn't Mother *hate* him being here? She'd banish him to his chambers for a month. But he was the heir, and soon Father would be dead and Jetekesh would become king.

He laughed. *It's not funny. I don't want Father to die.*

Why can't Mother die instead?

His step faltered. Blood rushed in his ears and his heart quickened. He glanced behind him where guttering torches cast shadows up and down the walls. Mother was nowhere in sight. She couldn't hear his thoughts. What a terrible thing to wish. He loved her, didn't he? Of course he did. She wanted the best for him. Wanted to teach him how to be a proper king.

A ragged cough shattered the silence of the dungeon corridor. Jetekesh nearly sprang out of his skin as his heart clattered against his ribs. "Who's there?"

Come to think of it, where were the dungeon guards? Why was everything so silent?

A weak voice drifted from ahead. "Your Highness?"

He gasped. "Storyteller!" He inhaled to slow his heart, tossed his head, and strutted on until he reached what he guessed was the right door. "Jinji Wanderlust?"

"I am here, Your Highness."

Jetekesh held his torch higher to peer beyond the barred window in the wooden door. Within the cramped chamber the storyteller lay across a bed of reeking straw. A fit of rasping coughs broke in the man's chest. When it passed, Jinji rose on one elbow.

"What brings you down here, Your Highness? This is not a fitting place for royalty."

Jetekesh wasn't sure it was a fitting place for anyone. Two weeks had passed since he'd sent the storyteller here. Hadn't Jinji been ill already?

"Are you dying?" Jetekesh's voice quavered. His ears burned, and he turned away from the window. Why was everyone around him dying? First his fencing instructor, executed for tutoring him, then a soldier doing his duty. Now Father.

And Jinji Wanderlust.

"I'm only a little ill, Your Highness. Please don't fret on my account."

Jetekesh scowled. His ears burned hotter. "I'm *not* fretting. If you died tomorrow, I'd not care a whit."

There was a smile in Jinji's voice as he asked, "And if I died tonight?"

Jetekesh jerked the torch away from the window. "I only came to request another story before your execution. Tell me something about Prince Sharo. Quickly now. I can't abide this filth for long."

Another cough. "Of course, Your Highness. Shall I tell you of the time Prince Sharo tamed a dragon? Or shall I speak of the wandering knights who long sought their prince, but lost their way again and again? Shall I tell you of Sharo's quest to seek the rightful prince of Shinac, who was stolen as a young child from that realm of magic by a man darker than all others?"

"I hardly care," said Jetekesh. "Just anything. How about Prince Sharo's quest; tell me that. Why would he seek after someone else with a claim to the throne? Why not keep it for himself? It sounds to me like the child heir is long dead."

"Oh, indeed not," said Jinji. "The seers of Shinac have foretold of his return to claim what is his and bring Shinac back to our world, to return magic to all the countries of Nakania."

Jetekesh laughed. "Oh yes, magic. You really believe in it."

"Yes, Your Highness, I do. Magic is as real as all the other senses we possess. It's just a little more particular about who inherits it."

"Magic gets to choose?"

"Certainly, Your Highness. It's rather like a sword

who chooses its master. To feel that grip and know that it's right, isn't that proof that the sword has chosen you?"

"Ridiculous. How would you know? You said yourself you've never held a sword."

"So I did. Perhaps it is more like stories, who choose their tellers rather than the other way around. I did not choose to speak the tales of Shinac, but rather, Shinac called me to share its stories with those around me. So it is with all storytellers: we don't choose, we are chosen."

"Is that why Prince Sharo went looking for the rightful heir of Shinac? He was *chosen*? Would that be by magic, or by the child heir?"

"I can understand why you mock," said Jinji. He pulled himself up to lean against the damp wall of his prison. His eyes snared Jetekesh. "We're not alone."

Something sharp bit into Jetekesh's back. He gasped and dropped his torch.

"It is good to see you again, Yeshton. You look well, despite the dust of travel." Jinji used the wall to push to his feet. "But do you think it wise to threaten your crown prince?"

The knife retreated. "Surely you jest. No prince would enter this dank place."

Jetekesh whirled, jerking his chin up. Yeshton, was it? A man in his twenties. A rugged face and sharp eyes. "How *dare* you threaten your future king." Where was Tifen? His protector should be here somewhere. He was always close. Surely Jetekesh hadn't given him the slip.

The faint crunch of a shoe against grit drew Jetekesh's eye.

Hands lifted in surrender, Tifen stepped into the light

of the guttering torch lying on the ground. His face contorted in the light, but the scowl was evident.

"We must hurry." From around Tifen poked the head of a little girl, slight with cat-like features. She slid her eyes from the armored man with the knife and turned her gaze on Jetekesh. "Greetings, cousin."

Jetekesh shrank back. "What is this? Who are all of you and what do you want?"

"I too am curious what brings so many people to my dungeon home," said Jinji.

"Sir Knight," said the girl, "we have mere moments. Bring my cousin as well. His life will be spared if we do."

"Yes, my lady. As you wish."

Jetekesh stamped his foot. "By the Driodere, someone tell me what is going on!" He whirled on Jinji still locked inside his prison. "Is this your doing?"

A faint breeze tickled the prince's arm, and he looked down to find the girl mere inches away, peering up at him. He glanced toward Tifen, but the soldier now pointed his sword at Jetekesh's protector.

"This is my doing," said the girl. "We must hurry, cousin, as I've said once before. KryTeer is here. Now. In the palace. Your lady mother has sold out Amantier for her own gain. She plans to wed Emperor Gyath upon your father's death. Already she has murdered my own father."

Jetekesh's limbs were leaden. His head spun. "Your father?"

"Duke Lunorr. Your lord uncle. I am Rille, your cousin." She offered a frigid smile. "It is a pleasure to meet you at long last." She turned. "The keys, Yeshton?" She padded over to her soldier's side. Raising a dagger she'd concealed in the folds of her soiled nightgown, she moved behind Tifen. Yeshton lowered his sword and strode to the dungeon door.

"Excuse me, Your Highness," murmured the soldier. He bowed his head, shouldered past the prince, and lifted a ring of rattling keys.

"You can't do this," said Jetekesh. None of this was right. It couldn't be real. This was a dream. "Jinji Wanderlust is a prisoner."

"Yes," said Yeshton. "My prisoner now." The door shrieked open. "Come out here."

Jinji stepped into the passageway. "Shall I go in shackles this time?"

"No. That would just slow us down." Yeshton turned to the little girl. "Which way, Lady Rille?"

Jetekesh stared at the child. Was *she* the one in charge?

Rille frowned. "There is no safe path from this place. We will have to risk the stables and steal horses for each of us."

"Understood." Yeshton took Jinji by the arm and turned to Jetekesh. "I would suggest coming quietly, Your Highness. Don't make a scene."

"*I'm* coming too?"

"Yes, cousin," said Rille with that quiet smile. "We're kidnapping you. Call it leverage to escape your lady mother's grip."

∽

This was all Tifen's fault. The blasted man was supposed to keep Jetekesh safe, wasn't he? Yet this evening had gone from bad to far worse.

"You can't *do* this to me! Unhand the royal person!" The stairs appeared ahead in the gloom. "Listen to me!"

Yeshton pushed Jetekesh against the wall. Dank cold seeped inside Jetekesh's clothes. "Hush, Your Highness, or I'll have to silence you."

Jetekesh's eyes widened. "You won't kill me, surely."

"Gag him," said Rille as she swept past. Glancing back, she beckoned, "Come, storyteller. Stay near me."

Jinji took her slender fingers in his frail grasp. "I've a cough, my lady. It may hinder our stealth somewhat."

The little girl shrugged. "A risk we must take, it seems."

Yeshton pawed through Jetekesh's surcoat and pulled forth a handkerchief. "Here we are."

Jetekesh pressed hard against the stone wall. "I won't—"

The soldier jammed the cloth into Jetekesh's mouth, then produced a leather cord and wrapped it around the prince's face to keep the gag in place.

Yeshton leaned close. "Don't make me bind your wrists and ankles, Prince."

Heat flooded Jetekesh's cheeks, but his string of oaths was a muffled sea of noise. Yeshton grabbed his arm and yanked him toward the stairs. A dagger in his free hand caught Jetekesh's notice. He stared up at Yeshton's face.

How would this end?

The soldier offered him a grim smile and wiggled the

knife. "Just in case your friend harbors any foolish notions."

    Rille glanced back as the group climbed the steps. "Follow my lead. Do nothing on your own, any of you. And for saints' sake, keep quiet."

6
THE HOLY EMPIRE OF KRYTEER

Q ueen Bareene surveyed the great hall like a preening cat. As the gentry danced the night away, she perched on her throne and waited. Midnight crept near.

Soon she must deliver a terrible shock to the people of Amantier. Terrible and necessary. It was time to accept that alone they stood no chance against the ever-changing tides of the world. KryTeer had tolerated this tiny country only because it could afford to take its time. And Bareene, seeing that, had moved to avoid a great slaughter. Her people should be grateful.

Her move also ensured her son would rule, if not a kingdom, then a province under the grand banners of KryTeer. And perhaps much more.

Bareene glanced toward her son and froze. Where was Jetekesh? Where had he gone?

Tifen was gone too.

The queen leaned back and tapped her fingers against the arm of her throne. Jetekesh had indulged too much in his wine. Perhaps he'd made himself sick. Stupid little boy. Hadn't she scolded him for such behavior in the past?

Bareene stood.

Jetekesh had probably gone to his father's bedside. Why did he always do that? Hadn't *she* always been there for the boy? Hadn't *she* been the one to comfort and rear him, while the king was too busy with affairs of state? Ungrateful fool. Well, it wouldn't last.

Soon Bareene would be free! Free to wed a more elevated man. Stories of Emperor Gyath painted the image of a grossly self-indulgent, fat, greedy man, but that worked well for Bareene. She wasn't Gyath's first, or second, or even twelfth wife. But she would be his favorite before he died of his indulgences. She'd make certain of that. And then she would arrange an accident to end the life of Blood Prince Aredel. *He* was too cunning to woo and win, that much Bareene knew already. But even smart men were mortal, and then her own son would rise up as emperor; and through him, Bareene would rule the entire civilized world.

Would midnight never come?

Bareene glided from the dais to the flock of sycophants waiting below, a smile plastered to her face. A laugh here, a light touch there. Floating and dancing across the hall, basking in this last celebration as a mere queen.

Time crawled by. Finally, Bareene returned to her dais to perch on the edge of her throne. And she waited.

The hour struck. She rose with a whisper of silks. The music faded away and every eye turned to her. Rumors had spread across the city that she would make an announcement at midnight. Guessing, guessing. But they would never guess the truth. Never.

"Gentle lords and ladies, loyal subjects, all. On this most auspicious night, as summer reaches its zenith, I announce with immense pleasure an alliance which shall end this fearful time of dread, when war seems so inevitable. Behold, my people!"

The doors across the great hall boomed open even as Bareene raised her arms in welcome.

"Greetings, High Prince Aredel elvar Gilioth d'ara KessRa, first prince of the blood of High Emperor Gyath elvar Kenn d'ara KessRa of the Holy Empire of KryTeer, Spear of the World and High Heaven's holy portal. Our new liege lord!"

The Blood Prince swept into the chamber, dressed in the strange curved, bloodred armor of his northwestern country.

Jewels flashed and glittered as he strode across the hall, while the nobles and gentry shied back before this demon in the flesh. In procession behind Prince Aredel streamed a dozen fierce warriors, all in the same bloodred armor, though not as grand as the prince's own. Curving tips extended from their shoulders, and their armored shoes pointed and curved upward as well. Arcing blades hung in strange sheaths from their waists. Fearsome helms masked their heads, like grotesque painted faces.

As he neared the dais, Prince Aredel removed his helm to reveal long black hair and keen brown eyes in an olive-toned face. He wore a smile that was neither haughty nor self-assured, but amused. A secret sparkled in his eye. He was more handsome than any reports had said. Indeed, he was a beautiful man; fierce and strong, but not the brute Bareene had expected to find. The queen held her head high as the Blood Prince inclined his own. He stepped onto the dais and whirled to face the room as his warriors flanked him just below the raised platform.

"Amantier is now a province of High Emperor Gyath's mighty Empire. You are blessed by Holy J'Aka to enjoy this great honor. May we live in peace ever after." He turned to Queen Bareene and spoke over the din of distressed voices behind him. "You will take me to your husband now."

"He is almost dead," said Bareene in honeyed tones. "Surely it is best to let him die in peace and ignorance."

"I will view the face of my dying foe. Lead on."

Bristling, she hoisted her chin and led the Blood Prince from the hall and its denizens. A glance back at the door revealed drooped heads and the flash of burning eyes. She tasted fear and defeat in the air like a heady wine. Smiling, she swept from the hall.

As she and Prince Aredel paraded down the corridor, two Blood Knights flanked their crown prince. The silence rang in Bareene's ears.

"How does your lord father fare, Holy Prince?"

"Better than your son's own, I should think," said the prince.

"I do long to meet him."

"That remains to be seen."

Bareene halted and turned to the Blood Prince. "I had understood that word of my beauty intrigued your father, and he is eager to meet me." She lowered her eyes and smiled, then glanced up.

Prince Aredel arched a dark eyebrow. "His Imperial

Majesty is intrigued by a new beauty every day, and I would venture to say you're not as young as some he favors. Best not to count on your legend too much, Lady Queen. Age can be telling, as can be treachery." He advanced down the corridor.

How dare he? Blood ran hot in Bareene's veins. She inhaled several times, drew back her shoulders, and traipsed after the prince.

They reached King Jetekesh's chamber. As Bareene opened the door, she braced against the stench of death. But while the shrouded chamber reeked of stale sweat and corruption, the figure in the bed still tossed in his fever. *Just die and have done with your misery!*

Prince Aredel slipped into the chamber, silent even in his heavy armor. "Leave me."

Bareene stiffened. "I won't leave you alone with my dying husband."

The Blood Prince turned a wry smile on her. "No pretense here and now. For whom do you perform? None here, surely. Leave and seek one of your lusty young lovers. No doubt any will be eager to comfort you." His dark eyes flicked behind her. "Shevek, attend me. Ledonn, guard the door."

One of the armored men moved past Bareene without a glance her way.

Bareene planted her feet. "I demand to know what you intend to do with the king."

The prince's eyes narrowed. His armor glistened like slick blood in the candlelight. "That is not your concern." He neared the bed. "*Traveria*, my lady? A brutal poison indeed. You've administered exceedingly small doses over a great length of time, I presume."

Bareene scoffed. "I don't know what you mean."

The Blood Prince glanced at her. "Ledonn, remove her from my presence. I find her repulsive."

Hands seized Bareene's arms from behind and dragged her through the doorway. "Unhand me! I won't leave my husband to be murdered by this demon! He won't use the king's blood for his evil rites!"

The door shut in her face.

Ledonn unsheathed his sword. It gleamed in the torchlight. "Go, Queen. Before he uses *your* blood to bathe in." A wicked smile curled at the corners of the warrior's lips.

Bareene backed away. Her knees trembled. "You will *not* touch me again!"

He barked a laugh. "You are now a subject under KryTeer. A lowly queen. *I* outrank you, *Majesty*. Show more respect to a Holy Warrior of KryTeer or I may cut out your tongue."

Throwing her chin into the air, she gathered her skirts and stormed down the hallway. They were mad! Vile! She'd not stand for this once she became empress. And she would, no matter what the Blood Prince thought. She would charm Emperor Gyath and become his next wife. Her beauty was second to none.

"Your Majesty!" A soldier ran up the corridor toward her.

"*What is it?*"

The soldier bowed. "My queen! It's your son. He's been abducted!"

7
IN HIDING

Entering the palace grounds and sneaking into the dungeon had been the easy part. Stealing horses and riding past the palace guards was little harder. But tearing through the streets of Kavacos was altogether reckless.

Where before there had been the steady procession of nobles pouring through the palace gates to attend the queen's ball, now the streets flowed red with Blood Knights. KryTeer had reached Kavacos after all, and the soldiers of Amantier had already surrendered. Houses sat dark, silent.

Yeshton's knuckles whitened as he gripped the reins of his horse. Let KryTeer invade. They would *never* get their hands on his mistress. She was all that remained of his oath to Duke Lunorr.

Lady Rille rode in front, with the storyteller behind her on the same horse. Yeshton held the rear, Prince Jetekesh riding with him to keep the boy's protector—in the center on his own steed—from doing anything desperate. But now that the protector had seen the bloodred armor of the enemy, he rode as hard as anyone.

Hooves thundered behind them. Arrows whistled past Yeshton's head as he urged his mount faster along the wending roads of the old city.

He could only pray Lady Rille had a plan to slip past the front gates.

The royal protector—Tifen wasn't it?—craned his neck. "I can get the gates open."

Yeshton nodded. "One wrong move and I'll slit your prince's throat."

Rille's voice rose above the clatter of hooves. "Don't interfere, Tifen! The gates will be open!"

They rode faster. Faster. And there, ahead, the gates of Kavacos began to open.

Yeshton felt the prince's tears against his hands. The trembling of his shoulders. At least he wasn't loud, and he didn't struggle.

They ducked beneath the rising portcullis and charged out into the night. The Blood Knights stopped at the gates. Arrows ceased. The little company galloped on until the break of dawn. Ahead, a tavern appeared in the morning mist, and Rille slowed her frothing horse.

"We must rest." She glanced back. "The storyteller is sick, and the horses are weary."

"Not here," said Yeshton. "A little farther up the road there's a path that leads to a farm. I know the farmer. He's a good man. He'll offer us shelter."

"Very well."

They trotted past the tavern and eventually reached the familiar rutted path. The weary travelers plodded along the trail until the flanking trees gave way to reveal a hut and a large barn. Chickens scuttled aside for them, and a goose flew down from the barn with a hiss and a flurry of feathers. A cow lowed as a maid with auburn hair raced from the barn, milk pail in hand. She beamed up at Yeshton, who smiled grimly back.

"What-ho, Kyella?"

"Heigh-ho, stranger!" Her smile slipped as she studied the ragged group. When she saw Jinji slumped against Rille, she turned and ran to the hut. "Fa! Fa! Travelers! Yeshton brought them! Hurry, one's sick!"

Farmer Drinel appeared in the doorway. He crossed the yard, as strong and large as when last Yeshton had taken shelter here some years ago. He nodded to Yeshton, then turned his attention at once to Rille and Jinji. "Let me help you down, my fellow. Easy now."

Drinel dragged Jinji from the horse and wrapped the storyteller's arm around his neck. "Kyella, boil some water and make an herb broth. He's hot with fever."

"We can't stay long," said Yeshton. He glanced back the way they'd come.

"Running from the Bloody Ones, I'll wager. Fair enough, but this man is terribly ill. Move him too soon and it'll be his death."

"We'll stay until he's mended," said Rille as she dropped from the horse's back and smoothed her nightgown. "Or as long as you'll have us in the meantime."

Drinel inclined his head. "Any friend of Yeshton is welcome here as long as ye need. I owe him my life."

Yeshton nudged the prince. "Wake up, Your Highness."

Drinel and Kyella halted in their tracks. They glanced

at each other, then up at Jetekesh propped against Yeshton's chest. Tifen dismounted and stalked to the horse.

"Give him to me."

"Not until I'm certain you won't run straight back to Kavacos."

The protector scowled. "Prince Jetekesh's life is my only concern. I won't lead him into the maw of a viper. I'm no fool."

"He speaks truth," said Jinji. He hoisted his head. "Yeshton, let Tifen…aid the prince."

"Do it," said Rille. She swayed on her feet. "I'm rather weary myself."

Yeshton handed down the prince and flung himself from the saddle to reach his young mistress. "I'll see you inside. Kyella, once you've tended to Jinji Wanderlust, will you draw a bath for Lady Rille?"

The maiden's eyes had grown wide, but she nodded and trotted ahead into the house.

"Come inside, all of ye," said Drinel. "Seems ye've got quite a tale to tell, and I've a hankering to hear it. But first, ye all need some rest, methinks."

∽

Hunger pains drove Yeshton from a heavy slumber as dusk settled in around the farm. The others slept on. Between mouthfuls of Kyella's hearty cooking, the soldier recounted all he could of the past two weeks. Drinel listened until he finished.

"We saw the Blood Knights come this way, but not along the road," said the farmer. "Strangest thing. They used boats along the river, and a thick fog shrouded them from sight until they were already passing. Thickest fog I've ever seen. Not natural, some say."

"Boats. Makes sense why I didn't glimpse them en route." Yeshton ran a hand through his sandy hair. "I confess, I don't see how there's any fighting against this. If Queen Bareene has sold us out…"

"She wouldn't do that." Jetekesh's voice.

Drinel and Kyella rose to bow to their prince as he approached.

"Your Highness, are you hungry?" asked the farmer.

Yeshton eyed the prince. He'd heard stories about the spoiled youth since the boy was small, and he didn't care much for him. Now the poor exiled fool was heir to a lost kingdom, one he would never rule. He should be pitied above all else.

Jetekesh approached the rough-hewn table, Tifen shadowing him.

The prince sank onto the chair at the head of the table, which Drinel had relinquished to him. "Bring some wine for my supper."

Kyella curtsied and scurried to the pantry. Yeshton resisted the urge to call her back. Let her serve the prince. Though his titles weren't worth much, his blood was still royal.

Drinel heaped a plate with the best fare the humble farm could supply and set it before the prince. Kyella offered a mug of wine. Jetekesh ravaged his portions and downed a second mug before he settled back in his chair.

"Where are we?"

Drinel bowed his head. "My farm, Your Highness. It isn't much, but we help supply the royal army of Kavacos."

"So, we're near the capital?"

"Yes, Your Highness. About ten miles south of the Royal City."

"South." Jetekesh frowned. He turned on Yeshton. "You. Who are you?"

"A knight of my father's house," answered the soft voice of Rille. She drifted into the room, groomed and clothed in one of Kyella's old homespun dresses. Rille took a seat at the table and accepted a plate of food with a warm smile.

"A knight?" Jetekesh arched his eyebrow. "Yet, he didn't know who I was in the dungeon?"

Rille scooped up a spoonful of potatoes. "It was dark, and you were facing away from him, cousin." She turned to Yeshton. "How is the storyteller?"

"His fever is bad. That dungeon did him no kindness."

Rille frowned at her plate. "He must improve. I have need of him."

"What kind of need, my lady?" Yeshton knew the question was unwelcome. The girl had been tight-lipped all along their journey to Kavacos. Why should she answer now?

She plucked up her spoon and prodded her food. "I'm not certain. I only know he's important to me. To us." She looked up. Her eyes swept the room. "All of us."

Kyella offered a plate of food to Tifen. He accepted it and remained standing beside Jetekesh's chair as he discreetly shoveled food into his mouth. If Jetekesh noticed, he said nothing.

"Aren't you supposed to be a halfwit?" asked Jetekesh, eyeing his cousin.

Rille's mouth twisted. "Aren't you supposed to be a clever boy?"

Jetekesh colored. "Look here—"

The girl held up her hand. "Not now, cousin. I think the storyteller is stirring." She glanced toward the loft. "Kyella, will you check on him, please?"

As the maid climbed the ladder to the loft, Yeshton looked at his mistress. "Where will we go once Jinji is mended?"

"South. That's all I know."

"South?" Jetekesh shook his head. "We must head east to Willow Province. There we can muster a force of arms and take back Kavacos."

Rille wrinkled her nose. "Have you no sense at all, cousin? Amantier is defeated. We've lost. Any force of arms won't be enough to drive out KryTeer now."

"So, we just surrender and abase ourselves before the dread empire?" Jetekesh scoffed. "I would sooner die—"

"Then do so. Here. Now. It will do as much good! Maybe more, for I won't have to endure your stupidity a moment longer." Rille stamped her foot under the table. "Be silent unless you can contribute rational thought to our plan."

"Plan?" Jetekesh jumped to his feet, face flushed. "Go south. What sort of plan is that?" He slammed his fist against the table. "I won't run away when my people need me. I won't hide while Amantier suffers under the tyrant hand of Gyath the Gluttonous and the Bloody-handed Prince!"

He won't run away from his dying father. The thought struck Yeshton like a sword. The boy was still young, and despite his flaws, he remained a devoted son and heir. But his wishes were foolhardy and impractical. Yeshton stood. "Be calm, Your Highness. This isn't a decision we need to make right away. Until the storyteller is able to move, we can't go anywhere."

Jetekesh turned blazing eyes on him but said nothing. Huffing, he stormed across the room to the front door. "I need some air." Tifen stayed on his heels. The door shut softly after him.

Rille heaved a sigh. "Just the reunion I would expect from *her* son." She shook her head.

Yeshton sat again. His mind strayed over the events of last night. "If I may ask, my lady, how did you know the gates of Kavacos would open to us?"

The girl shrugged. "The queen has some clout with KryTeer, as she did sell Amantier. And whatever else she may be, Bareene *is* a protective mother. She wouldn't let anything happen to her precious son."

"But how did she alert the gates to his presence before we arrived?"

Rille shook her head. "That, I don't know. But I knew the gates would open to us. I saw that much." She poked at her half-finished supper. "Sir Knight, you'd best grow accustomed to how my gift works. I know things. Not the *why* of things, or the *how* of things, only the *what*. Be patient with me." She tried a smile. "I do thank you for your service thus far. You're a faithful retainer, and I shall reward that someday, saints willing."

Yeshton lowered his eyes. "My reward is your smile, my lady."

She chuckled. "Why, Sir Knight, I do believe you truly feel that way." She knelt upon her chair and reached across the table to rest her small hand on the crown of his head. "Bless you, sir. I…I'm…" She withdrew her hand and returned to her food. Her eyes were lowered, so Yeshton couldn't see them, but he thought she might be holding back tears.

∽

"They let him pass as ordered, my holy prince."

Aredel turned from the high-rising window to consider the kneeling warrior in red. "Was he alone?"

"Nay, my prince. He rode with others: Crown Prince Jetekesh of Amantier, Lady Rille of Sage Province, and a soldier called Yeshton, along with Prince Jetekesh's protector, Tifen, by name."

The Blood Prince turned back to the night view of Kavacos. Torches lit the city, but few braved the streets. All was quiet. He approved.

"He was unharmed?"

"Yes, my prince."

Aredel nodded. "Fate is a strange thing, Muhun. That Jetekesh, Rille, and the storyteller ride together—could it be anything else? Bareene's prize. My lord father's prize. And…" He smiled to himself. What could he call Jinji of Shing? Not a prize, surely. Not a trophy at all. What was Jinji to be called?

"Tail them, Muhun. Do not harm them or interfere. Do nothing but keep a vigil for now. Let us see where they will flee." Aredel's smile stretched. Could it be said that Jinji fled? He was no coward. No warrior. Nothing but Jinji called Wanderlust.

"The queen will want her son back," said the warrior.

"Good. Let her stew and fret. It is the least we can arrange for her."

"Yes, my prince."

The warrior stood. Bowed low. Turned and left the king's chamber.

Aredel paced to the bed where the ailing king of Amantier lay. Silent now, the king slept. Aredel returned his gaze to the window. To the silence of a vanquished kingdom. To peace. He breathed in. A pity it couldn't last.

8
TRAVERIA

Darkness covered the hut like a shroud. Deep breaths drifted up from the bedrolls scattered across the dirt floor. Jetekesh tiptoed around the slumbering bodies and scaled the rickety ladder to the loft where Jinji Wanderlust slept.

He knelt on the straw beside Jinji's makeshift bed and studied the storyteller's wan face. He could feel Tifen haunting the ladder steps.

"I don't understand you, storyteller," Jetekesh murmured. He plucked up a bit of straw and peeled it strip by strip. "You must be a madman. Only a madman could act as you do. Smiling and pleasant with people like...like everyone." He tossed the straw aside. "Everything is a mess. All of this is..." He scowled. "This is stupid. You're not even listening. You're practically a corpse."

"Apologies, Highness. I feel very weak. But I am listening."

Heat crept up Jetekesh's neck and face. "H-how dare you not acknowledge the royal presence before now!"

"My deepest apologies." Jinji's smile broadened. "But I am listening if you wish to unburden your troubled heart, my prince."

Heat scalded the prince's cheeks. "Unburden myself? To you? I'm not so troubled that I would confide in a wayfaring peasant."

Jinji chuckled. "Indeed not. But what of a friend? Would you confide in one who held that title of affection?"

Jetekesh snorted. "A prince has no friends. Only subjects."

"Not so," said Jinji. "Prince Sharo has made many a friend in his travels."

"Stop that. Using mythical princes to argue a point is ridiculous!"

Silence. Had he fallen asleep again? Jetekesh glanced toward Jinji.

The storyteller watched him, brow furrowed. "Your Highness, forgive me, but I must ask, I think, a hard question of you."

Jetekesh tossed his head. "What?"

"Why do you treat others with such meanness? What causes you to think that hard-working people deserve your derision and disgust? Are we not people, too, walking the same path of life, learning and growing and shaping into what, in the end, defines who we are? Am I not a man like you?"

Jetekesh recoiled. "Are you a simpleton? I have every *right* to treat you however I please. I'm a prince. You're a peasant and a foreigner."

"*No*. That is how you *see* me. It is not who I am. Think a moment: consider that you are stuck within that royal head of yours. What you see is limited to what lies within your sphere. But I have traveled from Shing, where *you* would be the foreigner just by stepping over a boundary drawn by *men*. You would be the stranger in a strange land. You are also wrong to call me a peasant. I was a shepherd in Shing, not a beggar. I lived on the side of a hill overlooking a beautiful valley filled with growing things."

Jetekesh folded his arms. "Aren't you a peasant now?"

"No, I am a storyteller. I travel for my trade. I have money enough to get by, and boundaries do not cage me. This doesn't make me a peasant nor a criminal. From where I stand inside my own sphere, I am wealthy beyond measure. Perhaps, Your Highness, I am even wealthier than you."

"Ha! Ridiculous."

"It depends upon your point of view." Jinji struggled to sit up. Jetekesh didn't move to help. The storyteller took several deep breaths before he turned to the prince again. "Your Highness, I am a plain man, without title or rank in this world. I cannot read or write. But I do understand one thing: that which we prize most becomes our wealth. Why is gold precious? Because men covet it. Why are jewels of such value? Because men deem them so. Why are kings revered? Because men choose to bow the knee to a sovereign force. Perspective, my prince, determines the worth of what we crave. For myself, I place little stock in worldly riches but am instead content to view the nesting birds, the gushing waters, the depths of sky, the wet of rain, the cold of snow, the cry of an infant, the bleating of sheep—for these are my treasures. I am a wealthy man indeed."

Jetekesh stared at the meek and ragged man before him. "You're well and truly mad, tale-weaver. I've never seen the like."

Jinji's smile was patient. "If this is madness, my prince, I never wish to be well." He reached out a hand and brushed Jetekesh's arm. "You are worried for your father, aren't you?"

Jetekesh flinched. "Of course I am. He's dying. Don't be daft."

"Of course. My apologies once again. What ails him?"

The prince's shoulders slumped. He shook his head. "His physicians don't know. It's like nothing they've seen. He began at first to be weak over a year ago. Headaches plagued his nights. He couldn't sleep. His appetite diminished. The illness subsided for a time, but then returned worse than before. Nightmares struck in the day sometimes, and he saw things, things that weren't there. Now he's nothing but a corpse, too weak to move, and…mad. He raves like a lunatic, haunted by phantoms none can see." Jetekesh faltered. What was he saying? What had possessed him to admit all this to a lowly beggar?

"*Traveria.*" Jinji's unexpected voice struck Jetekesh like thunder.

"What?"

The storyteller looked down at his hands. "It is a plant originating in Shinac. A poison. You merely brought to mind its effects. It is said to harm those without magic if ingested."

A fire flared within Jetekesh, and he snatched Jinji's

threadbare shirt. "How *dare* you compare my father's condition to one of your fairy stories! Do not make light of my pain!"

Jinji's blue-green eyes filled with compassion. He caught Jetekesh's fist with his hand and gently pried the prince's fingers free. "I do not make light, Your Highness. I do not mock or compare. I am suggesting, my prince, that your father does not suffer from a disease, but from a poison. *Traveria* originated in Shinac, but it exists here, in Amantier, in Shing, and in other countries. It is rare but not impossible to find. Costly, though. Quite costly unless one knows where to look in the deep woods." His eyes focused on a point in the dark, until a harsh cough doubled him over.

Jetekesh squared his shoulders. "You're wrong, Wanderlust. No one would want to poison my lord father. No one." He climbed to his feet. "I'm sorry I've wasted any time with you. You're a mad, babbling fool."

He stalked to the ladder and clambered down to the main floor. He turned to find every soul in the house awake and staring at him.

Cousin Rille stood closest, her pale hair a tumble down her shoulder. "Who is the fool, cousin?"

Jetekesh pushed past her to take the hut's single bed, earlier forfeited by the simpering farmer. He climbed under the coverlets and hid his face.

The knight's voice drifted in from the front room. "*Traveria*, huh? I've heard of it. Nasty and effective. But who would want to poison the king?"

"Isn't it obvious?" said Rille. "Who stood in the way of my queen aunt's ambition more than her king and husband? My lord father spoke often of their unhappy marriage alliance. He once said Queen Bareene lost her mind years ago when she miscarried her daughter. She's treated my lord cousin like a pet ever since, an ever-faithful lap dog. It's revolting."

Jetekesh buried his head under his pillows. How dare they? What did they know about anything? What did any of it matter now?

Poisons. Magic. Madness. None of it mended the simple fact: Father was dying.

9
DEATH

A stampede of flapping chickens brought Yeshton's head up from polishing his armor. His hand fell to his sword. He smiled and relinquished his grip as he spotted Kyella trotting across the yard. Gasping, she stopped before the front step where he sat.

"Any news?" Two days confined to the farm made him feel blind and helpless.

Kyella bobbed her head. "News...of the king..."

"King Jetekesh?"

She nodded again and leaned forward to whisper. "He's dead, Yesh. It was announced publicly this morning."

Yeshton lowered his fauld and polishing cloth. "You're certain? It's not a wild tale?"

Kyella rolled her eyes. "I'm not a simpleton. It's published news. See here." She shoved a parchment at him. "Stole it from the notices myself." She peeked down at it. "What does it say?"

Yeshton sighed. "I can't read any more than you can."

He set aside the fauld and threw a wool blanket over his armor. "Stay here and keep watch."

He stepped inside and found Rille at the butter churn. She leaned against the stick protruding from the barrel and frowned. "No use, Sir Knight. This cream will spoil before I ever finish." Her eyes strayed to the parchment in his hand and she perked up. "What did you bring?"

"I'm hoping you can tell me, my lady."

He bowed and proffered the parchment. She slid it from his hand, and her eyes darted down the column of words. "No, no!" She lowered the parchment. "Oh, Yeshton. He's gone."

Yeshton's heart sank. "So, it's true. Kyella heard the taverners speaking about the king."

Rille's chin trembled. "It's true. King Jetekesh is dead. May his spirit find rest with the saints. My lord father spoke often of him. He said my uncle the king was a good soul, too good to rule a kingdom, for it was slowly breaking his spirit. No wonder, if he was also being poisoned." She sighed. "Where is my lord cousin this morning?"

"Gone with Tifen to the barn. I think they chose to groom the horses over other less savory chores."

The corners of Rille's mouth curved. "They may repent their choice once they discover what mucking out a stable means." Her smile fell. "We had best let the prince know, though I'm loath to worsen his dread mood." The girl unfolded herself from the chair. "To the barn, Sir Knight."

"My lady. I'm not a knight."

"Keep up, Sir Knight."

Yeshton followed her from the hut. They picked their

way across the yard and Kyella trailed after them. Inside the barn, Tifen had taken it upon himself to handle the chores, while Prince Jetekesh sat on a pile of hay and fiddled with a rope he'd found somewhere.

"Good to see you keeping busy, cousin," said Rille.

The prince lifted his eyes. "What do you want?"

Rille hesitated, then marched forward and thrust the parchment into her cousin's face. "We have no reason to believe it's false information. He was very sick."

Jetekesh tore the parchment from her fingers. He looked down and his eyes widened. "No…no… It's not true."

"As I said—" began Rille.

"Don't!" His hands trembled. "Don't talk to me."

The prince didn't look up to see Rille bite her lip and turn away, eyes wet. He read the notice again. And again.

The little girl whirled and hurried from the barn, Yeshton on her heels. In the open air, she swallowed a deep breath.

"Stupid boy. He acts as though he's the only one who lost a father." She let out a little scream. "Those bloody, horrible KryTeer monsters!" She stamped her foot and stalked back to the hut. "Come, Yeshton. We've butter to churn."

∽

It couldn't be true. Not yet. Not when Jetekesh was miles away, exiled from Kavacos, barred from the palace by KryTeer warriors on every street of the royal city.

His vision swam.

Father.

"Your Highness?"

He looked up. The farm maid stood a few feet away, wringing her hands. What was wrong with her? What could be so important that some *peasant* would speak to him in his shattered world?

The parchment was wet in his grip. Why was it wet?

"Your Highness," the girl said again. "I'm so deeply sorry. It's so hard to lose a beloved parent. I know. I lost my mama two winters ago from the fever…and it still aches so. Sometimes I can't even breathe."

What was she babbling about? Why didn't she go away?

Tifen appeared before him to shoo the girl out with gentle words. Why gentle? She was a bother. A leech, trying to curry favor with the prince, trying to worm her way into his good graces… Carve out her tongue and let that be a lesson for speaking to the Crown Prince of Amantier.

Amantier. It had fallen. Father was dead. Mother was a prisoner of the KryTeer Empire.

Jetekesh fell backward. Sank into the hay. It smelled like sweet grass and dirt.

Someone wailed. Wouldn't they be silent? Couldn't they tell his pain was greater? Deeper.

He needed a drink. Needed to numb this pain. It burned him, burned him up inside. Soon there would be nothing left of Jetekesh at all. Soon he would be a husk like his mad father. Dead. Decaying.

Wouldn't that be better?

10

THE VICES OF MEN

He drank. And drank.
Jetekesh sat in the loft, empty bottles beside him, another half-full bottle in his hand. The storyteller slumbered nearby.

No one bothered the prince. They stayed below, except to bring broth to Jinji once that evening. Kyella; was that her name? She pressed the clay bowl to Jinji's lips, and the sick man sipped with an effort.

"Is he dying?" asked Jetekesh, surprised by the slur in his voice. He couldn't be drunk yet. It still hurt.

The young woman bowed her head. "No, my lord. I think he's getting better."

Jetekesh laughed. A short, barking sound. "But of course. Let the peasant live and take the king's life instead. Why would the saints want a peasant in heaven anyway?"

The girl stared at the floor. "Please, Your Highness. Forgive me, but should you keep drinking? You might harm yourself—"

"It's sire." He took another swig. "I'm king now. My lord father is dead. That makes me your king."

"Yes, sire. Forgive me."

A cry sounded below, and someone clattered up the ladder. Rille's head appeared above the rungs. "Come down, Kyella. Leave your drunken liege to drown his sorrows." She turned sharp eyes on him. "Coward. Disgraceful, slovenly. You look more the beggar than the king. Wouldn't your father be proud?"

"Shut up! You know nothing!"

"Don't I? You're not the only one who lost a loved one, cousin. But never mind my pain. Never mind anyone but yourself! Isn't that what selfish brutes do? I hate you. You're just like your mother: a self-indulgent, scheming, cowardly sluggard!"

"Hush, my lady." Jinji sat up. "I think His Highness can be allowed a moment's grief without reproach."

Rille's mouth snapped shut as her eyes flashed. She inhaled. "You're right, storyteller. I doubt I was any less a sight after my father was drawn and quartered. I just didn't choose to drink myself to death."

"To each his own vice," said Jinji.

Jetekesh snorted. "Pray tell, what is your vice, O saintly teller of tales? Let me guess. Lies! You sell lies to simple folk who don't know better than to believe your hogwash."

Rille let out another outraged cry, but Jinji raised his hand. "This is my battle to wage, my lady. Please return to Yeshton and remain below tonight. Thank you, Kyella, for the broth. It was very good."

Both girls retreated down the ladder. Jinji extracted

himself from his bedding and crawled to Jetekesh's side. He rolled aside two empty bottles and sat.

Jetekesh finished the bottle in his hand. "Will you chide me now for drinking too much?"

"You asked what my vice is," said Jinji. "Shall I tell you?"

"Must I care?"

"No. But perhaps you do, nevertheless. I…am a coward."

Jetekesh frowned. "A coward?"

"I have run a very long time from my demons. I have not wished to face them. Pain is difficult to conquer, most especially grief. I feel yours keenly, my prince. I know its kin."

Jetekesh groped for another bottle of wine. Jinji knew nothing. *Nothing.*

The storyteller's eyes followed his hand. "There is no more wine, Your Highness."

"Stop it!" Jetekesh flung his hands over his face. "I don't need your comfort. I don't need empty gestures. You don't know me."

"But I do," whispered Jinji. "It is my blessing and my curse to know."

The emotion in his voice brought Jetekesh up short. He lowered his trembling hands and turned to Jinji. Why? Why was he afraid?

Jinji's clear eyes met his stare. "I see a small child raised by parents in conflict. A good father whom you respect and admire. A fragile mother, arrogant and possessive, whom you try so dearly to please in the hope that you will heal her broken heart. But you cannot replace her lost child. Nor can you allow yourself to be swallowed by her crafty machinations. She wishes to smother her son, leaving only a living doll to obey her every wish. Where once there might have been motherly love and affection, now there is a monster dwelling within her frame, consuming all that she touches. You fear her. Dreadfully. You *want* to love her, but how can you love a creature no longer human? No longer that sacred being called Mother?"

"Stop it. Stop it!" Jetekesh grabbed an empty bottle and hurled it against the floor. Glass exploded everywhere. A shard bit his cheek. He threw his hand to his face. "Oh, no! No. She'll be furious. She'll kill me. She'll kill me!" He lurched to his feet. Staggered and slammed his knees against the floor. His vision swam. Hot tears splashed his knuckles as he hunched forward and retched. Bile burned in his throat. He'd ruined his face. He'd made himself sick. She would *kill* him!

Gentle hands caught his shoulders. "Be calm, my prince. Breathe."

"She'll kill me!" He wiped his mouth with his sleeve. *No!* He'd soiled his clothes. She'd be so furious.

"Hush, Your Highness. She's not here. She can't hurt you. Just breathe."

Jetekesh choked. "She'll know. She always knows."

"Shh. Be calm. I'll help you to clean up. Kyella will patch your face. It will heal soon; it's not deep. Come along, Your Highness."

"Majesty," whispered Jetekesh as he allowed Jinji to pull him to his feet. "I'm your king now."

"Yes, Your Majesty. So you are." Jinji led him to the ladder, climbed down before him, and helped him find each rung until Jetekesh was upon solid ground.

"Kyella, will you bring some salve for his cheek? Yeshton, if you would please, warm some water for a bath. Come, Your Majesty. This way."

When the bath was ready, Jinji helped Jetekesh to scrub himself clean and hauled him from the tub. The farmer produced rough clothing from a chest in the corner, and Jetekesh dressed, then allowed himself to be tucked into bed.

Jinji smoothed back his hair. "Sleep, Your Majesty. Your mind will be clearer tomorrow."

"He'll have a powerful headache," said the man called Yeshton.

"He'll deserve it," said Cousin Rille.

"Hush. Come away."

The voices retreated.

Jinji appeared above the bed. He dabbed something cold on Jetekesh's cheek.

Jetekesh blinked up at him. "For a coward and an escaped prisoner, storyteller, you aren't horrible."

The man smiled. "Thank you, sire."

Jetekesh rolled onto his side. "If you're from Shing, why do you have light eyes? Shouldn't they be black?"

"An inheritance from my father. He was Amantieran."

"So then," Jetekesh laughed, "I really *am* your king."

"Yes, sire. You are."

"Where is your father? Why didn't he speak for you when you were captured?"

"He never cared for me," said Jinji.

"It's rare for an Amantieran to wed a Shingese."

"Yes, sire, it is."

"An arranged marriage? But you're a shepherd, you said." Despite the coarseness of the bedding, Jetekesh nestled into the coverlets and welcomed sleep as it drifted over him.

"There was no marriage, sire."

His tone implied something but Jetekesh was too sleepy and too drunk to comprehend what. Did it matter? Father was dead. Nothing mattered. Tears leaked from his eyes.

"Shh. Sleep, sire. Just sleep. Tomorrow will be hard, and so will many other days, but time will dull the pain. Be brave and endure it. You aren't alone."

"Y—you're wrong," whispered Jetekesh. "I'm alone in the dark. Lost. Alone."

"Hush. Sleep. The dawn will come."

He didn't believe Jinji, but he tumbled into sleep anyway.

⁓

"If you're on the mend, we'd best consider our next step." Yeshton handed Jinji a cup of water.

"I told you," said Rille from where she sat at the table, "we must go south."

Jinji took a seat as Yeshton reclaimed his own chair. The storyteller was still pale, but he moved easier this evening.

"I must go south myself," said Jinji, and took a sip. He set down his cup. "You may come with me if you please or go your own way."

"We ride with you," said Rille.

Tifen hovered near the doorway to the bedroom where Prince Jetekesh slept. If he had an opinion, Yeshton couldn't find it in his face.

"And the prince?" asked Jinji.

Rille scowled into her cup of fresh milk. "I suppose he must come too. To remain here is death. And for my dead uncle's sake, I can't let his son perish at the hand of bloody KryTeer brutes."

"It is best that he come," said Jinji, perhaps to himself. "Is it true the Blood Prince has come to Amantier?"

Yeshton nodded. "It's true."

Jinji sipped his water again. "He is in Kavacos?"

"So the rumors say," said Kyella as she set a plate of food before the storyteller. "Care to try something hearty in your stomach?"

"I do, yes. Thank you." Jinji speared a stalk of asparagus. "It smells wonderful." He nibbled the greens and smiled appreciatively. "The taste does not disappoint."

Kyella beamed and moved to serve the rest of the table.

"If my cousin comes along, we shouldn't supply him any sort of spirits to drown his sorrows." Rille pulled a face. "He's hard enough to handle sober."

Jinji lowered his fork. "A little compassion would serve you well, Lady Rille. He lost his father this day. We each cope with grief differently. While I agree that intoxication is not a wise answer, kindness is our best defense against his habit."

Rille's grimace deepened. "I will tolerate my lord cousin, storyteller, but I will *not* show him kindness when I shall get none in return."

"Is kindness bought or freely given?" Jinji returned to his food.

Silence wafted over the air.

"Do we leave on the morrow?" asked Yeshton.

Rille looked down as she nodded. "Yes. We're much too close to Kavacos for my comfort. Let us leave at first light."

11
A BATTLE OF WITS

At last her husband was dead.

Bareene was not as pleased as she deserved to be. By now she should be on her way to wed Emperor Gyath. How had everything fallen apart?

The Blood Prince was to blame! He'd blockaded all routes in and out of Amantier, and only those with his written permission could come and go at the border. Bareene's request to travel to KryTeer had been twice denied. And the beastly man had refused to see her or explain his reasoning.

A knock sounded on her door. At last! She'd sent a handmaid an hour ago to sniff out news of the Blood Prince. Bareene trotted to the door and wrenched it open, a string of insults ready on her tongue.

Prince Aredel stood at the threshold. Instead of full armor, he wore *sirwal*, a sort of baggy trouser. His chest was exposed, save for a half-length vest lined with gold and gems. He wore gleaming cuffs and jewels on his belt, bracelets along his arms, and a circlet around his forehead. His shoes were of gold cloth, curved upward on the toe.

Bareene's jaw slackened. He looked stunning.

"My condolences on your husband's death," said Prince Aredel. "I know what a trial it must be for you to lose him."

Bareene drew her shoulders back and raised her chin. "I am bearing it as well as I can."

"I've no doubt of that."

"What brings you to a lady's chamber?"

His lips curled upward. "No need to fear. You couldn't tempt me if you used every art you've perfected." His gaze flicked to the bed. "Alone, my lady?"

"Of course. Would a mourning queen be otherwise?"

"I suppose it is daylight for a few hours more. I have come regarding your journey to KryTeer."

Bareene's eyebrow arched. "I thought you had already answered my request."

"So I did. Twice. Yet you sent a third missive with a demand to see me promptly. That was yesterday, I think. What can be so urgent that you required my attention, Lady Queen?"

Bareene turned her back on him. "If we are to be a province under terrible KryTeer, I would know your customs and traditions."

"Not if, my lady. You *are* a province under terrible KryTeer, and by your hand, you may recall. And I do respect your sense to know when defeat is inevitable. Still, I hear you're not a very popular figure to your own people. Your statue upon the steps of your god's cathedral has been pulled down, beheaded, and thence crushed to dust. All save the head. I hear it was mounted on a stick, doused in oil, and lighted on fire. You are called she-demon. That is the correct term, yes? Also, treacherous fiend. Spawn of the two hells. What else? Ah yes, Jevalla, as well. Isn't that a woman in your holy scriptures who sold her soul for a man who was not hers to have?"

Bareene set her jaw and curled her fingers into fists. She longed to run a dagger through the hateful man's heart and *eat* it! But she wouldn't lose control of herself in front of him. Despicable, loathsome creature. He would not have that victory today.

"Setting that aside," he went on, "I wanted to let you know that I will not now, nor ever, approve your request to visit KryTeer. If my lord father requests your presence, that is something else. Write him if you please. Laud your praises. Intrigue the old goat. But it will not be said of me that I unleashed a vixen, however old, upon my own people. Good day."

She whirled to watch him leave and caught the flash of a smile on his lips before he slipped from the room.

That pox-ridden, churlish, dog-headed death token!

She *would* write to Emperor Gyath and entreat him to rescue her from Amantier. She would claim her life was in danger for bringing the kingdom into the arms of his great empire. And once he learned her husband was dead, wouldn't the gluttonous swine crave entrapping a woman so vulnerable and helpless as she would lead him to believe?

Let the Blood Prince think he had won. She would outwit him and become Empress of the world. Then he would bow and scrape for favor whether he liked it or not.

12
THE JOURNEY SOUTH

Rille always felt small. Not because she was, but because others treated her as she looked, rather than how she ought to look. She had never been a child, so far as she knew. She had always seen what others couldn't, and most people viewed her with fear and suspicion. Not her lord father or lady mother. They knew and understood. But they were gone now.

She must be brave. To show her fears and sorrows would cause Sir Yeshton to treat her like a child rather than as his mistress. Already she must contend with her cousin lest he seize command over the party and leave her bereft and unimportant.

I am important.

So she told herself every day, but somewhere inside she doubted. Oh, the Blood Prince sought her. Had murdered her father to find her. Her *gift* was important, but not *her*.

She had hoped Jinji Wanderlust would understand,

but he'd taken her lord cousin's side instead, coddling and protecting the prig like he deserved it. Pah!

I'm jealous. Truly, Rille, are you any less pathetic than Jetekesh?

But she longed to hear kindness from Jinji. To peer into those clear, calm eyes and feel his radiating love, as he bestowed it so willingly on that sopping ninny.

Dawn came slowly. News of King Jetekesh's death had stirred up every tender, grief-stricken memory of her own dear father, and even of her mother. She envied Jetekesh his wine-induced oblivion. Not that she wanted to be drunk. But she did long to escape pain for a brief time.

A floorboard creaked behind her. She'd taken up residence on the porch, away from Yeshton, the snoring farmer, the creepy Tifen near the bedroom. Turning, she expected to find Yeshton. Dear Yeshton was the closest thing she had to a kindly figure in her life, after everything.

She blinked. Jinji Wanderlust stood in the doorway, a steaming mug in each hand, a gentle smile on his gaunt face.

"May I sit with you awhile, my lady?"

She turned away. "If you please." Her heart galloped. Had he come to comfort her? To impart the affection she craved? *Don't let your hopes run away with your good sense.*

He sat near. She could feel the warmth of his body. Jinji set the drinks aside and unfolded a blanket he'd draped over one arm. "Here," he said, wrapping the thin blanket over her shoulders. "Don't catch cold." He offered one of the mugs. "Warm milk with cloves of cinnamon and a drizzle of honey. A childhood favorite of mine."

The creamy sweet taste warmed her like a tonic. She cradled the mug in her small hands and basked in the scent of spices. A bat squeaked somewhere in the woods.

"I must apologize," said Jinji. "In my efforts to aid Prince Jetekesh I've caused you distress."

"Oh, no. No." Had he read her thoughts so clearly? "I was being foolish. Of course he deserves your compassion. With that witch of a mother, what chance had he, really?"

"Exactly my thought. Not much chance until now." He glanced at her. "But that we already know. Let's not discuss your cousin just now. I owe you my thanks for rescuing me from that dungeon, my lady." He bowed his head low. "I am in your debt."

"Nonsense. I—I had to do it."

He smiled. "No one *has* to do anything, Lady Rille. You chose to, and that matters to me. Thank you. I shall do what I can to repay you."

She looked out at the trees. "Let me come with you. You travel south. Let me go with you as far as I must, and we shall call your debt paid."

Jinji fell silent. "It may be dangerous."

"Yes," said Rille. "It may."

"Very well, my lady. You are welcome." He rested a hand on her arm. "I am deeply sorry for your loss, Lady Rille. Duke Lunorr was a good man."

"He and King Jetekesh both," said Rille, voice thick with emotion.

"Yes, King Jetekesh as well." His tone was strange, and Rille glanced at him.

He smiled. "You see the what of things, my lady. That is not my gift." His eyes strayed toward the fading stars. "I see the why."

～

Dawn struck Jetekesh with all the mercy of a battering ram. His head exploded with pain and he moaned as he retreated beneath his pillows. Someone shook him.

"Get up, slug-a-bed. We're losing the day!"

How could anyone lose what had barely begun? He crawled from under his pillows to glower at his cousin. She regarded him with her usual derisive expression, hands on hips.

"Hurry, or you'll miss breakfast."

He hardly cared. His head pounded and his stomach lurched as he sat up. He knew why he felt sick, but his mind skittered away from the memories of yesterday. He was a king now, so he'd claimed last night. But he had no kingdom. Amantier was defeated, and no mustered army would be enough to take it back from KryTeer.

I'm nobody now. I'm nothing.

Jinji Wanderlust entered the bedroom, a clay cup in one hand, his smile brighter than the dawn glow through the open window.

"Good morning, sire. Take a sip of this. The herbs will settle your stomach and help a bit with your headache as well."

Jetekesh accepted the cup. For a wastrel storyteller, Jinji was perceptive. The bitter concoction racked Jetekesh with tremors but he downed the cup in a few swallows. He sighed as he lowered the cup. The light wasn't so bad now. "We're really leaving? Where will we go? It's not safe."

Jinji's smile remained. "Nowhere is safe, but I must go southward."

"Why?"

"Because I must."

Jetekesh arched his eyebrow and glanced toward Rille. The little girl watched Jinji with a light in her amber eyes. He turned away, eyebrows pinched together. "Why does everyone want to go south? There's nothing there but desert." An itch started in his head. "Wait. The Drifting Sands are that way. Is that why you're going? To exhume some evidence of your fairy kingdom?"

Jinji took the cup from his hands. "Hurry and dress, sire. We must go soon, or we'll miss the cool of the morning to start our journey."

Jetekesh scowled. "Won't you answer my questions?"

"There will be plenty of time for conversation as we travel." Jinji left the room, Rille on his heels.

Jetekesh groaned but rose and climbed into the homespun rags provided by the farmer. The clothes were too large, itched like fleas, and smelled musty. *Better this than looking like a prince, with KryTeer's soldiers running up and down the roads.* As he smoothed his hair, he tried not to think of Mother's reaction if she could see him now. There was no looking glass to check the scratch on his cheek. It would heal. Most things did.

But not death.

His heart throbbed. He hurried out for a last hearty meal of cornbread, heaping eggs, and slices of ham before the journey.

Once fed, the party entered the yard, where Farmer Drinel and Kyella bade them farewell. The girl lingered at Yeshton's side until he mounted his horse, and she reached up to brush her hand against his.

"Be safe. And come back sooner than last time, you thoughtless creature. We don't see near enough of you."

Yeshton smiled wryly. "Hard to say what will happen now that we're a province of a heathen nation, Kyella. But I'll do what I can." He looked at Drinel. "Don't remain for long. The pillaging will start soon."

The farmer sighed. "Alas, it's true. We'll be run out if we stay a day or two more, I'd reckon. Don't worry. We know where to go."

"My thanks for your hospitality," said Jinji from Rille's horse. The girl had offered to teach him how to ride as she managed the reins herself.

"Not at all." Drinel smiled, showing his teeth. "You, storyteller, are welcome at my hearth anytime—assuming my home remains when all of this is settled."

Rille shifted in her saddle. "Well," said the girl, "we should get along. Daylight is wasting."

They rode into the trees, leaving the little farm and its family behind. Jetekesh glanced back and saw Kyella waving after them until she disappeared as the trees closed in around the travelers.

Jetekesh rode alone. Drinel had sold Yeshton a fourth horse for a song, despite its good breeding. Jetekesh had been shocked to find the farmer in possession of such good stock. Yeshton took that horse for himself, leaving the royal mounts to the rest. Now the knight rode in front, with Rille and Jinji next, Jetekesh following, and Tifen in the rear. No one now feared

Jetekesh and his protector would steal back to the capital. Indeed, why should they? Returning to Kavacos now would only signify death.

The company held a steady pace. Jetekesh was a good horseman, but Mother had forbidden him from riding this past year. Now his muscles protested the constant jostling motion. He would be sore tonight. He grimaced. No one would heed his complaints, so why voice them? Of all the people in Amantier, he rode now with the most tyrannical, unsympathetic curs alive.

His one comfort was knowing Jinji would feel the same soreness when they camped for the night.

Camped. Jetekesh's grimace deepened. *Don't think about it just now. Endure each trial in their turn, else you'll go mad.*

Perhaps that was Jinji's matter. Whatever evils the man had suffered must have broken his mind. *That's why he's so disgustingly kind and patient.* Jetekesh would much rather carry on sour and proud and *sane*, for it would serve him better as king.

Father is gone.

Stabbing pain doubled him over his saddle.

Tifen's mare came even with his. "Should we stop, my prince? Are you ill?"

Jetekesh scowled and straightened. "Don't harass me. I'm bearing up."

Tifen's mount fell back.

In the afternoon, a summer storm rolled across the sky, darkening the woods. Rain pelted the ground as the wind picked up and thrashed the branches of the trees, ripping leaves from their bows. The fragrance of pine and moss and loam filled the air, rich and deep. Kyella had supplied each traveler with a woolen cloak, and now Jetekesh pulled the cowl over his head, for all the good it would do. He was already drenched.

Yeshton didn't let them stop. No one said anything. Jetekesh pretended not to mind, but resentment festered in his chest, building up as evening crawled closer.

When the knight called a halt, dusk had fallen, and the storm had moved west. Leaves still dripped with rain, and the ground was a muddy mess of puddles and twigs. Yeshton unrolled a canvas and tied its four corners to several trees to make a sort of shelter. He spread a second canvas across the forest floor beneath. That was it. That was the only protection from the elements.

Jinji sat within the shelter and drew his knees up to his chest. He lowered his head to his knees and sank into himself, shaking and wilted.

A pang assaulted Jetekesh's chest. His gaze lit on Yeshton. He stalked to where the knight attempted to make a fire from damp kindling. The man looked up, gray eyes sharp as flint. Jetekesh spotted Rille slink closer from the corner of his eye, and he glared at her, then turned on Yeshton.

"While I realize that avoiding KryTeer soldiers on the road forces us to travel cross country in the woods, and there's some urgency in distancing ourselves from Kavacos, why, pray tell, could we not stop to rest for a midday meal? Were ghosts chasing us? The Drifting Sands are weeks away yet. What haste could there be?"

Rille marched forward. "Are you really that daft? Of course we must hurry. This isn't a pleasure trip or a fox hunt. We're *running* from the enemy. That implies haste, does it not, cousin?" She showed her teeth in a friendless smile.

Jetekesh drew his lips back in a snarl. "Running to the point of exhaustion will *only* slow us down in the long run, *cousin*. And besides, no man looks more guilty than he who runs. If we appear calm and at our ease, we're less likely to draw unwanted attention. That's basic strategy."

"Except," said Yeshton, "we're already being followed."

Tifen moved from where he'd been caring for the horses. "It's true, my prince. Someone has been tailing us all day."

Rille looked between them. "Then that is why we haven't stopped?"

Jetekesh glowered at her. So, she *had* been wondering the same thing, yet she still came to her precious knight's defense. "Why did no one tell us?" He glanced toward Jinji, but the storyteller's head remained lowered. Perhaps he'd fallen asleep.

"And worry you when you're already overwhelmed with grief?" Yeshton abandoned the kindling. "We won't have a warm supper, I'm afraid."

Jetekesh glanced at the damp tangle of twigs. "Is a fire wise? If we're being followed…"

"Then it doesn't matter if we give ourselves away. The Bloody One already knows where we are."

Jetekesh moved away from the center of camp and Tifen shadowed him. The prince looked up into his protector's green eyes. "If one of KryTeer's knights has already tracked us down, why hasn't he attacked?"

Tifen shook his head. "I'm afraid I don't know, my

prince. I had thought the KryTeer demons killed on sight of their prey, but this one must be under orders not to engage for the present. Perhaps he is attempting to ascertain our purpose in traveling southward."

Jetekesh snorted. "Well, I wish him good luck. *I* can't ascertain why. None of us can." He glanced toward Jinji Wanderlust. "I suppose it will prove interesting in the end, whatever the outcome. We follow a madman, Tifen. I wonder what he's truly after."

Tifen shrugged. "I've heard legends of gold hidden in the cruel sands of that vast desert, my prince. Perhaps he seeks that."

Jetekesh frowned. "I doubt it. He appears not to care for money, or he's the finest liar I've ever met." He laughed. "What a thought that is, with all the liars at court. Could Wanderlust really best them all?"

Tifen offered a shrug. "Well, sire, if you know them to be liars, it appears likely." His eyes slid toward the storyteller. "Is he a fugitive from justice in Shing, do you think, my prince? To abandon his home for lands where he is unwelcome—what could have compelled him to come to Amantier when a price is on his head?"

"I told you," said Jetekesh, "he's a madman."

"The mildest of his kind I've ever seen."

"Perhaps." Jetekesh studied the slumbering man. Jinji had called himself a coward last night. Was he on the run from something? His father was from Amantier, he'd said. But there was no marriage. Jetekesh could surmise what that meant.

In the years before Shing was integrated into the KryTeer Empire, Amantier had occupied the country for a time. It was a poor land, full of farmers and shepherds, with a weak government after a century-old revolt against its ancient monarchs from which it had never recovered.

In times long past, Shing had been large, prosperous, powerful. It had also been corrupted, worshiping many gods rather than the One God. Now it was nothing, its heritage fading—the One God's punishment for Shing's wayward traditions. The people were easy to control now. During its occupation, Amantier had sent middling lords to bully the Shingese into submission. Those same lords had enjoyed all the fruits of that lush and strange land, including its women.

Jinji's mother must have been one of them. A lord had his way with her, and then returned to Amantier without a backward glance, leaving the young woman to raise his child alone and without his knowledge.

Jinji Wanderlust was illegitimate by his own admission. Disgusting.

Jetekesh trudged back to Yeshton and Rille in the middle of the camp. "What shall we eat for supper, if we can't cook anything?"

Yeshton untied a knapsack. Bread, cheese, cold cuts, a few apples. "Kyella packed this for us. She said it would rain. She's always right about the weather."

"A happy skill for a farmer's daughter," said Rille as she bent to snare an apple. She brought it to her lips and paused. "Do you fancy her, Sir Knight?"

Yeshton glanced at Rille with a wry smile. "She's like a little sister to me, but I'm aware of her affection. It has yearly grown into something different from my own feelings. But it will pass. Already I saw it waver while we guested in her house." His eyes flicked toward Jinji. "As becomes a farmer's daughter, she is more attached to peaceful men than to men of war."

Rille laughed. "She begins to favor Jinji Wanderlust?"

"And why not, my lady? He's a handsome fellow, if I'm any judge of a man's beauty, though I don't claim to be. And he's a gentle soul, which should suit women best, I think."

"What suits women fully depends on the woman, I should think," said Rille before she bit into her apple.

Jetekesh cast around for a place to sit but found none. He stood instead and ordered Tifen to serve him. The man brought him a large chunk of bread, meat, and cheese. Jetekesh's eyes strayed toward Jinji again. "I should think the girl would want one of her own people, not Shingese filth. Besides, he's illegitimate. She should be more selective. But then, perhaps a farmer's daughter can't afford to be choosy."

Silence fell across the little clearing. Jetekesh looked up from his meager meal to find them regarding him with dark gazes. "What now?"

"You shouldn't accuse a man of what you don't know to be true," said Rille. Heat bloomed along Jetekesh's ears as she went on. "Just because he's half-Shingese and half-Amantieran does not mean—"

"He speaks truth," said Jinji.

Jetekesh stabbed a finger at the storyteller. "There, see? He told me himself."

Jinji staggered to his feet and limped to join the others. He stooped to choose an apple lying on the knapsack, straightened up, and rubbed the smooth surface with his thumb. "My mother raised me in Shing. She never told my lord father of my birth. That is the Shingese way. She was a proud woman, descended from ancient emperors. She did not love me. She did not want me. I was her great shame. I am, as Prince Jetekesh says, illegitimate. If this fact is abhorrent to any of you, you may abandon your journey with me and be on your way. I would not blame you." He bit into the apple.

No one spoke. Jinji returned to his place beneath the canvas and ate his fruit.

Rille stomped her foot. "How silly it is to blame a man for his birth! It's the same as blaming a loaf of bread for not being a cake when the baker chooses its ingredients!" She flew to Jinji's side and sat beside him.

Jinji laughed and ruffled her hair. "I thank you."

She beamed up at him, cheeks flushed.

Jetekesh turned away. He would not associate with filth, even if his cousin found it acceptable. She was a child and not heir to a throne. He mustn't be sullied by his associations.

He stalked across camp and sat on a patch of wild grass beneath a beech tree. Tifen joined him but remained standing.

As Jetekesh ate, his muscles stiffened and his heart ached. So far from home, in company far beneath his station, he didn't doubt every inch of this journey would be misery like the two hells.

13
CHILDREN OF THE EARTH

The next several days continued much as the first, though Yeshton did call for rests. Rille had insisted on them for Jinji's sake. While Jetekesh was irritated that accommodations weren't made on *his* behalf, he chose not to complain. Whatever the reason, a rest was still a rest.

Jinji Wanderlust's cough worsened, and shivers racked his frame as the five huddled each night under the canvas shelter, with naught but cloaks to keep them warm. Rille grew more anxious as Jinji's health declined.

But Jinji insisted he was all right. That the journey must continue. Rests must be few and infrequent. Jetekesh despised his nobility of spirit. Let the man drive himself into an early grave if he wanted, but he shouldn't try to take the rest of them with him! Jetekesh longed for a decent bed, a decent meal, a decent set of clothes. Already his boots, the only remaining articles belonging to him, were caked in mud, and ruined from moisture.

Tifen looked as unhappy as he felt. The man's brown

hair hung lank and matted after several intermittent storms. During each meal he picked at the bread like a fierce beast, trying to remove the moldy bits before he ate the hateful fare.

It grew colder as they pushed southward, away from the pleasant climes of northern Amantier. Jetekesh's tutors had explained that the further one rode from the invisible line they called the equator, the colder it got – except, of course, the phenomenon called the Drifting Sands, where it was hot and miserable even so far south.

Why, *why*, must they go south?

Summer had already reached its summit and would begin winding down. Even at their present pace, it would grow very chilly before they reached that awful desert scape.

He didn't want to go. He wanted to stay in Amantier. He wanted to go home, to crawl onto Father's bed, curl up beside him, and never move again. But Father was dead. Already entombed. Mother must be distraught. Not because of Father's death—way out here Jetekesh couldn't fool himself on that point—but because her precious son was lost to her. But she couldn't imagine how miserable the truth was.

Fourth night on the trail, Tifen whispered the question plaguing both of them.

"My prince, why do we remain with this party? We could sneak away in the night and head east as you wanted. We could reach Peregrine Fortress within a fortnight and muster your forces. Even if we could not attack the KryTeer head on, the fortress is strong; with enough men we could last there for years."

Jetekesh whispered back the answer they both knew.

"For two reasons, you daft creature. First, we're being followed by one of the Bloody Ones, who can't have an interest in anyone but ourselves. If we sneak away from the knight's protection, we'll never reach Peregrine Fortress before we're captured or killed. Second, we don't have the necessary supplies *or* a knowledge of the terrain to survive even should we avoid the Bloody One." He paused. "And third, now that I come to it, there's some doubt we would sneak away undetected in the first place; and I seriously doubt they'd let us go, though I can't imagine what good we are to them."

Tifen didn't argue the point. Why would he? Miserable as this entire experience was, there was no way around it.

The fifth day dawned bright and cheery. Jetekesh despised it. The warmth eased the tension of the others, however, and Yeshton struck up conversation.

"Last time I came this far south, I was in training as a lad. I hunted with Duke Lunorr and his knights to hone my woodland skills."

"Aye," said Tifen, from the rear of their trotting line. "Once I came to these same woods in such a party as well. I was a squire then, with hopes of knighthood one day, before—well, things changed."

"What changed?" asked Yeshton.

Jetekesh glanced back at his servant. "Indeed, what did change, Tifen?"

The man's brow furrowed, and a frown pulled at his mouth. The prince studied that face. He'd known Tifen all his life. The man had always been there, as far as Jetekesh recalled. But this was the first time he'd really *looked* at his protector. Tifen was middle-aged, perhaps in his fortieth year, with hints of gray at his temples. *I didn't know he was so old.* Despite that, Tifen was spry, slender, even youthful in his face and limbs. He'd not have made a very impressive knight, to say the least.

"My father was disgraced, Your Highness," said Tifen. "He lost his lands and titles after a…scandal…and I thence became a servant. My skills with a sword saved me from a life of drudgery, and your Lord Father instead acquired me to protect you, my prince. That was when you were just born."

"You're the son of a disgraced knight?" asked Jetekesh. He'd not have guessed Tifen had any royal blood, yet few outside of nobility were granted the title of knighthood.

"It was Sir Palan, wasn't it?" asked Yeshton. He'd slowed the party's pace to a crawl.

Tifen scowled at the ground before his horse. "Yes. Though I would ask you not to use that name in future, Sir Knight. He is dead to me."

"I can well understand your feeling," said Yeshton. "Though it's a pity, as the knight's reputation was one I deeply admired as a lad. One of the few knights granted his title through skill rather than bloodline in this era."

Tifen snorted. "And lost the same way."

Jetekesh looked back and forth between the two men. "What did he do?"

Silence fell.

"I was young, Your Highness," said Yeshton. "I don't know the particulars…and rumors are always exaggerated."

"It's not spoken of, my prince," said Tifen, his eyes

fixed on some distant tree past Jetekesh's head. "If you please, that's all I'll say."

"It is *not* what I please. I asked a question and I'll have the answer."

"Oh, don't you get it?" cried Rille from her horse. "It involved your Lady Mother. Why *else* would they skirt the issue? Or did you never consider that such a woman could enjoy whomever she pleased while it suited her, and then cast them aside in disgrace when she grew bored?"

Jinji rested a hand on her shoulder. "Lady Rille, please. Delicacy would do you well." He craned his neck to look back.

Jetekesh's cheeks must have been the bright red of a cherry, as hot as they burned. How dare Rille insinuate such vulgar nonsense about his mother? His head lowered and his fingers tightened against the reins.

The company rode in silence.

Jetekesh's mind tripped against Tifen's tale. He too had heard stories of Sir Palan, who twice chased off an entire company of KryTeeran Warriors without losing a single knight in his company. The man was a legend. He was also dead, so the official records stated. But was it possible the knight had been banished for dallying with the queen instead? Preposterous. He wouldn't believe it. How could a *child* know such a thing?

He reined in his horse. Everyone ahead slowed and stopped.

Jetekesh hoisted his head high. "I don't believe you. You're lying, cousin. You're all lying."

Rille shrugged. "Fine, cousin. Order it so. But truth isn't subject to royal decree."

JETEKESH'S HEART LEAPT. STEAM ROSE FROM THE bathhouse near the borders of the sleepy village. Finally, warmth, food, cleanliness. He reeked of pine needles and mud. His stomach rumbled at the prospect of mutton, cheese, ale and, most of all, a fresh change of linen.

"We will visit the village for supplies," said Yeshton before the company rode from the timberline into the field-dotted open, "but we can't stay at the inn overnight, and we must ride cautiously."

"Whatever for?" asked Jetekesh. "We'll hardly be recognized in this forsaken realm. And I shan't move a *muscle* from this village until I've soaked an hour in that bathhouse."

"A bath does sound pleasant," sighed Rille.

Jetekesh glowered at her but held his tongue. For once they were in accord.

"Sorry," said Yeshton. "No bath."

"Why not?" demanded Jetekesh.

"We're travelers, penniless by our looks, and only the rich stop to cleanse themselves in those fancy contraptions. We'll draw too much notice."

Tifen and Rille looked as crestfallen as Jetekesh felt. He protested, but Yeshton was firm. No baths.

"I'll *die* of this filth," was Jetekesh's final effort.

Yeshton sat tall in his saddle. "Well, Your Highness, there are worse ends than that, if you must choose."

Jinji had climbed down from his horse and now walked on toward the village green. Yeshton signaled the rest to commence their ride, and Rille trotted ahead to collect the storyteller. Jinji shook his head.

"I'd like to walk a while." He kept on.

Utterly mad, thought Jetekesh.

Yeshton held the horses to a plodding pace to match the storyteller's gait, and they reached the village far later than Jetekesh liked. It was evening when they passed the first buildings and approached the well in the center of the village square. Peasants glanced their way, looking up from beating rugs, or chasing a wayward duck, or drawing water from the well, but no one inquired after their business. The chime of the blacksmith's hammer rang across the green.

Jinji strolled to the well. "Good day to you, matron."

The woman fetching water nodded back as she sank a dipper into her bucket and offered it to Jinji. "What brings you travelers so far south?"

"I'm a storyteller," he offered, and took the dipper with a grateful smile.

The woman chuckled. "Not much use for tales these days, good sir. Or haven't you heard fairy stories were outlawed by the queen?"

"I have heard that."

The woman glanced behind her. "Heigh-ho, Mosill! We got a tale-weaver among us."

The blacksmith's hammer ceased to ring and a brawny man with a dirt-smudged brow stepped from the shadows of his shop, wiping his hands on his soiled apron. "That so?" He grinned and traipsed over. "I always did love me a good hearth story on a winter's day. But alas, traveler, we've no use of stories in the summer months and into harvest. Days are shortening already, and we can't be wasting no time. You might come back when the fields are bare and the night fires long."

"Don't forget it's against the law," the woman added.

Yeshton dismounted. "We've no intention of staying, good people. We've only stopped to buy some food to carry on our journey."

The blacksmith and his wife looked over the company with wrinkling brows. "A troop of tellers?"

"No," said Jinji, "but we travel together. These are my friends."

Several other peasants gathered to listen.

"From where do you travel lately?"

"Northwest," said Yeshton, his tone light, unguarded.

"Not from Kavacos?" asked the blacksmith.

"Not lately," said Yeshton.

"But you've heard word from there, I'd wager."

Yeshton nodded. "Unpleasant word, too. The king is dead."

The blacksmith sighed. "So, then it's true. And what of the other rumor? Is it true KryTeer is invading?"

Jetekesh stiffened. Invading? But Amantier was already conquered. How had no one heard that if they knew of Father's death?

"I've heard the rumor, but I don't believe it," said Yeshton. "The same rumor spread like a grass fire last spring in Moss Province. KryTeer's always invading, but nothing ever seems to come of it."

The blacksmith chuckled. "True, true. Well, be welcome, travelers. We've wares to sell you if your coin is good enough."

"It's good enough," said Yeshton, "if the price is fair."

"We'd also like a bath," said Jinji.

Jetekesh stared at him. So did the others.

Jinji only smiled. "If it's not too much trouble."

"Sure, sure. No trouble. Looks like you could use it."

"Our thanks for your hospitality." Jinji bowed at the waist with hands steepled and pressed against his chest.

The matronly woman laughed. "You're from Shing, are you? I do love their foreign customs. So pretty." She chatted on amiably as she led them all to the stables adjoining the blacksmith's shop, and from there to the bathhouse.

The woman swept Rille off to a separate bathing room, while the men found their way to a chamber rolling with steam. Yeshton collared Jinji.

"We've no money for this."

The storyteller gently pried the knight's hands away. "Villagers only charge the rich for the use of the bathhouse. Those of their own station are shown courtesy and pay nothing. It is an old custom, begun in Shing many centuries ago. Relax, Yeshton. We are among friends. These are my people."

"You're from *Shing*."

"So I am. And should these humble folks be travelers passing through my own village back home, I would be one of *their* people, as they are mine. Humble farmers, tillers of the earth, workers in the field: we share a common bond that transcends borders or race. We are the earth's children, and as such we are kin to one another." He stripped off his buttonless vest and unfastened his shirt. "Shall we clean ourselves?"

Jetekesh had never bathed in a common bathhouse, nor had he been in company with others when he scrubbed himself—except in Farmer Drinel's hut—yet the experience here was not unwelcome. He sank into the hot water and let out a long sigh. Jinji and Yeshton joined him in the large, round tub. Tifen stood by, waiting his turn.

The storyteller looked at Tifen. "If you wait upon your prince, you will give away his good breeding, and we shall be charged a dear sum for the use of this chamber. Join us, Tifen, or we shall be truly broke."

The servant unhappily obeyed. Jetekesh said nothing. Cleanliness was worth sharing, even if he bathed with a lordless knight, a disgraced servant, and an illegitimate peasant.

∽

Mosill the Blacksmith, and his wife, Breya by name, insisted on the travelers staying in their home for the night. The village was too small to keep a proper inn. Few lords or ladies came so far south, and the next village over had a tavern already.

"We keep the bathhouse, they keep the tavern, and so we split the profits of any noble guests between us," Breya had explained.

Dinner consisted of lamb, warm broth, mulled cider, and a tray of cornbread. Afterward, Breya showed her guests to the loft, where fresh straw served as their beds. Jetekesh hated the notion of insects and mice disturbing his rest, but he was sleepy from his bath and the warm supper in his belly, so he wordlessly climbed under the scratchy blankets he'd been given. He fell asleep almost at once.

Angry voices jerked him awake. It was pitch black. Someone shouted.

A rough knock rattled the door below.

Jetekesh rolled onto his side and dragged himself into a sitting position. Faint light flickered below, lighting his surroundings enough to make out Yeshton's crouched frame near the edge of the loft.

The blacksmith's deep voice shook the rafters. "...the meaning of breaking down my door in the middle hours of the night, Ilim?"

"Just bring him out, and we'll leave right away."

"And if I say no?"

"You can't keep him for yourself, Mosill. We got a right—"

Angry shouts of agreement drowned the man's words out.

Mosill's voice rolled over them. "Don't be daft! You think we'd see a single coin?"

More cries. Jetekesh's heart clenched. Cold sweat pricked his forehead. They were after *him*. They'd discovered that the crown prince slept here, and they wanted the reward money Mother had posted for his safe return. Or perhaps the KryTeer Empire was after him, with or without his head attached to his shoulders.

"You won't have him, and that's final," growled Mosill.

Breya's higher voice joined her husband's at the door. "We don't betray our own, Ilim. Not ever."

Our own? So, it was the KryTeer Empire who sought him.

A hand fell on Jetekesh's shoulder. He quailed and whipped his head around. Jinji's bright eyes were vivid against the dark. A finger pressed against the man's lips. He leaned close.

"They are after me," Jinji whispered. "You are not in danger, my prince. Be at peace."

But of course! These stupid villagers had no idea KryTeer had invaded the kingdom. No idea the crown prince had gone missing. They only knew that a storyteller had two hundred gold kana on his head. And, fool that he was, Jinji had admitted what he was. Why risk himself for his daft stories?

"Return to sleep, my prince. They will not get past the lord of this house."

Jetekesh could hear Jinji's smile in his tone. "You're completely mad," he whispered.

"Perhaps. But no harm will befall us tonight. Sleep."

It was long after the angry voices retreated against the thunder of Mosill's voice that Jetekesh laid back down and sought slumber. Long after Yeshton returned to his own bedroll and began to breathe deeply.

Jetekesh's eyes had grown accustomed to the dark, and as he waited for sleep, he watched Jinji sitting up against the straw. The storyteller rocked back and forth, back and forth. Finally, Jetekesh rolled over.

14
THE MISSING KING

"Wake. Up. Cousin." Yeshton stifled a smile as he watched Lady Rille shake the prince like a ragdoll.

"Hurry, cousin. We need to leave before the village stirs. Get *up*, you sluggard!" She gave a frustrated little cry and sat down on the prince's back. *Hard*.

Jetekesh sputtered and shot up, long hair a tangled mop, eyes like daggers. Rille toppled off him with a faint grunt. She picked herself up and straightened her plain frock. "Good morning, cousin."

Jetekesh glanced toward the tiny hole that served as a window to the loft. "It's still dark out."

Rille followed his eyes. "Yes. After last night's incident, we thought it best to get an early start on our journey. Breya is making us breakfast. Hurry." She flitted to the ladder.

Yeshton's smile won. In his way, Jetekesh was good for his cousin. He brought out the fire Rille had inherited from her father. Duke Lunorr had been a just and exacting man, honest to a fault, and fair to all no matter their station.

The prince slithered from his bedding like a slug. Best leave him to it.

Below, Jinji and Tifen helped Breya scoop up mounds of eggs, fat slices of bacon, and more cornbread.

"Pour ale for everyone," ordered Breya.

Yeshton pushed aside his hair and set to work. He glanced around for Rille as he set the tankards on the table. His heart spasmed. "Where did Rille go?"

"Out to feed the horses," said Tifen.

Jinji set the last plate on the table and glanced toward the door. "Should she have gone alone?"

Jetekesh clambered down the ladder rungs. "What's for breakfast? I'm half-starved."

Breya chuckled. "All growing boys are."

Yeshton sprinted to the door and peeked outside. There! Rille ambled back from the stables, calm as a summer's day, and met his eye through the sliver in the door.

"I don't know any passwords." Her face was grave.

He cracked a smile and opened the door. When it shut behind her, Rille caught his arm.

"Sir Knight."

His muscles tightened. "What happened?"

"The horses are gone. Not just ours. All of them. The stable was wide open when I got there, and every stall had been opened. I would guess someone didn't want us to leave."

Tifen crept close. "What do we do without horses?"

"Is there trouble?" asked Breya across the room.

Prince Jetekesh looked up from his plate.

Jinji continued to break his fast.

"The horses have been set loose. All of them." Yeshton folded his arms. "That leaves us one option. We walk."

"A pleasant pastime," said Jinji. "While I do enjoy horses, I find I prefer my own two feet better still."

"Saints curse those fools," Breya growled. "I'm terribly sorry about your horses."

The color had drained from the prince's face. "We must walk?"

"Afraid so." Yeshton gestured to the food. "Eat, but quickly. We mustn't waste good Breya's cooking." He smiled at the woman. "We got off lucky if the horses are all we lost."

Though Jinji was the first to eat, he was the last to finish, the only figure in the room unperturbed by the danger that dogged them. He set aside his fork at last and nodded. "Our thanks for your service, good woman, and to your husband as well. May the blessings of Shinac and the good earth guard your home."

"Shingese blessings are so pretty," said Breya, grinning. "Good travels to you, storyteller. May the One God guide your feet to safe paths. And to the rest of you."

The party slipped from the house under the shadows of predawn.

Mosill waited near the stables. He guided them behind the shops and houses to the edge of the village where a stream ran. "Carry on along the bank for a time before you rejoin the road. Even so much as a day. It will delay you somewhat, but better that than capture."

"Many thanks," said Yeshton. He pressed several coins into the man's palm. "I wish I could do more."

"If you could, it would mean only half as much. Farewell, strangers." Mosill turned and headed back for the village.

Yeshton slung his pack over his shoulder and started southwest along the stream. "Keep up."

Jinji set the pace. His slow, steady gait kept them from making good time; but then, the company's destination was of little consequence to Yeshton. He only cared that Rille wanted to follow Jinji. In the end, time mattered little.

No one crossed their path as the company trotted along the stream bank. Jinji paused around noon to eat a light meal, and the rest followed his lead. Yeshton settled down beside Rille, who nibbled on a slice of cornbread Breya had provided. Yeshton cut off a chunk of cheese from its wedge and sampled a strawberry.

"'Tis a fair day in Shinac as well," said Jinji, eyes riveted on the sky above. "Even now, Prince Sharo rides east along Araliass Bay, that crystal depth of truest blue, ever hunting for the true king of Shinac: his ancient cousin. In the air far above his head wings the great dragon Taregan, who dubbed the prince Dragonfriend not so long ago when they rescued six maidens fair from the cruel clutches of Lord Peresen."

Yeshton stretched out on the grass and watched the clouds gliding by overhead. He smiled. "What could the lord want with six maidens fair? Most men hardly want one after a while."

"He meant to sacrifice them," said Jinji with sorrow in his tones. "The use of a maiden's blood would be enough to grant a dark wish. But Peresen's wish was too great for only one maiden's lifeblood to answer."

"That's a dark tale, storyteller." Yeshton turned his head sideways to study Jinji. "Aren't your tales for children?"

"The tales of Shinac belong to all," answered Jinji. "And perhaps the darkest of them are most important to hear, for we must know the warning knell of evil before it tolls."

Rille spoke up. "What was Peresen's wish?"

Jinji picked at the leaves of a strawberry. "Not was, my little friend. What *is* his wish? That is your question." He sighed. The pallor of his skin was stark under the sunlight and his eyes sparkled like shades of the ocean. "He wishes to rule Shinac, but not just the human realms. He wishes to enslave all creatures, even the magical. To oppress the dragons, the fairies, the elves, the fae things of the sea. And not only that. He wishes to return to our realm, the world we call Nakania; and here too he desires to rule over all, not as a king or an emperor, but as a tyrant overlord, where none is more than a slave to his every whim."

"Quite a bleak future for us, should he succeed," said Yeshton. "Just the sort of story that belongs to a troupe of players. It's enough to ingratiate ourselves to our present circumstance by comparison."

Jetekesh sat up. "It's just that line of thinking that makes my Lady Mother want your head removed, Wanderlust."

Yeshton sat up as well. "And *that* should be cause to push us along. We've rested enough for one day. Those villagers are likely not far behind."

"They aren't following," said Jinji as he unfolded his handkerchief. Coughs broke in his chest as he held the cloth to his mouth. His body shook against the assault, until he gasped for breath and wiped his mouth. His eyes glinted with tears, but he smiled. "The angry men last night were drunk, and thus became a mob. Today the sun shines upon their shame and they know better than to pursue us. Likely they will try to recapture our scattered mounts and return them to the stable, hoping to make amends, not yet aware that we have gone ahead. Should we return to the village in a few weeks, they would treat us as Mosill and Breya did."

Yeshton shook his head. "That so? Well. Perhaps the storyteller knows best. Let's get moving."

Rille climbed to her feet, Jetekesh just behind her. Tifen hovered near his master. Jinji rose last and stumbled before he righted himself.

Yeshton's eyes narrowed. "You're still ill."

"I will be fine." Jinji squinted at the sun. "We can reach the ford of the Chaos and Minderen creeks by nightfall if we keep a steady pace."

Yeshton started. "You know the names of this place? You've traveled here before?"

Jinji's eyes brightened as his smile deepened. "No indeed, Yeshton. The creek told me so."

Jetekesh snorted. "Of course it did. Answer me a last question about this Lord Peresen who wishes to rule all Nakania, Wanderlust. Is he the man you mentioned before, the one who stole the true king of Shinac away all those years ago? The darkest soul ever known, or whatever you called him?"

Yeshton caught a flash like fear in the storyteller's eyes.

"No," Jinji said in a whisper. "Lord Peresen is not the

Dark One. Perhaps he may be called a servant, though he himself does not know it. The Dark One has many servants in many countless worlds. No, Prince Jetekesh, Peresen is not so dark as that. He is greedy."

"*King* Jetekesh. And that's rather sad, isn't it? Otherwise Prince Sharo would've been close to achieving his goal."

"Yes, Your Majesty. Indeed, Prince Sharo had hoped so. But alas, he was far wrong."

"Where is this Dark One?" asked Jetekesh.

Jinji's eyes drifted heavenward. "He is not upon this world at all, nor in the Realm of Shinac. He is extremely far away from here."

Jetekesh smirked. "What a pity for Prince Sharo. It seems he'll never find his missing liege."

Jinji's eyes twinkled, no longer grim. "Do not say so, Majesty. I never said the true king was still with the Dark One. I never said where the true king is at all."

15
THE HONOR OF BLOOD

There's always a weak link. It took Queen Bareene longer than she'd hoped to locate a man who succumbed to her charm. He wasn't among the more favored of the Blood Prince's men, but he knew enough to answer some of Bareene's questions.

The most important thought on her mind was Jetekesh. Where was her son? Why could no one find him?

HeshAr, the KryTeer knight, knew the answer. "He has fled south with his protector, my lady." The knight leaned close and stared. She pretended not to notice.

"All alone, save one man to guide him?" *Why* would he flee south? His greatest hope of salvation lay in Peregrine Fortress or if that road proved too dangerous, the Keep of the Falls near Nagali River.

"He's in company with a soldier and a vagabond as well," said HeshAr, before he took a sip of wine. They sat together on the terrace of her private rooms. Only her maid servants came and went, accustomed to her habits, and inclined to look the other way.

Bareene twisted her skirts beneath the table. "A soldier and a vagabond? Pray, tell me more. I fear gravely for my son." The prince wasn't prepared for life beyond the palace walls. He was too delicate, too temperamental. Without her, he was helpless.

HeshAr set the goblet of wine aside. "Yes, my lady. Of course. The soldier bears the heraldry of Keep Lunorr, which means he has no lord anymore. It's believed he's a man for hire now, so if he's well paid, your son should remain safe. The strange part is the vagabond. Apparently, he's a storyteller, well known in your kingdom for his skill at his trade."

Bareene stared. "A…storyteller?" Jetekesh had taken Jinji Wanderlust with him? What had possessed him? She nearly laughed. How preposterous! Absurd! She closed her eyes. How could one lordless soldier and a bumbling storyteller protect her son from the cruel world?

HeshAr slipped from his chair and knelt before hers. Taking her hand in his, he kissed her fingertips, her palm, her wrist. "My lady. How may I comfort you?"

Bareene wrenched free of his grasp and leapt to her feet. "Comfort me? How can anything bring comfort? My son, heart of my soul, rides the southern wilds with naught but ruffians as his companions."

"And a little girl," HeshAr said.

Bareene faltered. "A little girl?" Why by the names of all the saints would Jetekesh keep company with a child?

"I believe it's the soothsayer, that daughter of Lunorr,

the one my prince seeks for Holy Emperor Gyath—may his name be praised in song for all time."

The queen's eyes narrowed. She turned to face the Blood Knight. "Little Rille?" The mad child. The treasured heir of that foolish Lunorr. Her dead husband's niece. "I thought all died at Keep Lunorr."

"All but the child. We never found her. But that soldier came from there. It's possible he sneaked her out in the commotion." HeshAr shook his head. "What I don't understand is why my holy prince doesn't just order them brought here." A shrug. "He's always acted strangely concerning storytellers, so I've heard. He sought a certain one for five years. I think this vagabond may be the one he's wanted to find."

How this man did babble on!

Bareene sat down and caught up HeshAr's hands. "My love, tell me more. Tell me about the soothsayer child your holy emperor wants." At last! Now she could bargain with Gyath. She need only capture that horrid little child and at the same time bring Jetekesh home. And if the Blood Prince had a peculiar interest in Jinji Wanderlust, she could use that too.

HeshAr told her all he knew, and much he only guessed. Her smile grew as her mind plotted.

The Blood Prince would regret assuming she was only some silly woman.

∼

"HeshAr has arrived, Holy Prince."

Aredel looked up from the scroll in his hands. He nodded, and Shevek allowed the Blood Knight through the double doors to the private study. Once King Jetekesh had scrawled most of his decrees here. As Aredel lowered his hands from the grand desk of ancient monarchs, the scroll sprang back into its roll.

The knight, a rugged man with sun-kissed skin and dark eyes, cowered before Aredel. He fell to his knees. "My prince, holy son of KryTeer, O mortal god: spare me, I beg you."

Aredel slipped from his wingback chair and rounded the desk to stand before the quavering knight. "From what offense should I pardon thee, Sir HeshAr?"

The knight poured out his sins: dallying with the heathen queen, confiding state secrets with her, disrespecting his liege lord, helping the queen escape the palace to go after her son.

Aredel listened. He already knew each offense. HeshAr also knew that Aredel was aware. So too he must know his fate, for there was no mercy in KryTeer.

"You are a brave and skilled warrior from my homeland, Sir HeshAr dij Aban, and so it is an honor to spill your blood that I may gain your strength."

HeshAr's shoulders slumped. He sobbed without sound.

"Shevek."

"My prince?"

"You will execute Sir HeshAr and drain his blood that I may bathe in it."

"As my holy prince commands."

Shevek pulled HeshAr to his feet and together they left the study.

Aredel smiled to himself. He had known what Bareene would try. He sat again at the desk and unrolled the scroll. Dipping his quill, he let the ink drip back into its pot.

Finally, he began to scrawl:

The lady queen has left Kavacos as expected. She will travel south to obtain both her son and the means of bribing you, my lord and holy father. Thus, it shall be easier to rid ourselves of her by a means which appears natural. She believes herself unequaled in beauty, but rest assured, my holy liege, she is among the ugliest of her sex I have ever beheld. The witches of Lioth are roses by comparison, for their souls are not so withered.

You shall have your soothsayer as soon as I accomplish all that must be seen to in Amantier. I expect to return to the shores of my homeland by next planting season at the very latest. Be well, I pray. Yours faithfully in the blood.

He dripped sealing wax against the parchment just beneath his message and pressed his signet ring against the red wax. A flash of light, red like the seal, erased the message from the scroll, leaving it blank.

He waited. Another flash of red blinded Aredel, and then he saw the return message scrawled against the same scroll face: *I lose patience waiting for my soothsayer. Return by harvest.* The royal seal swirled gracefully beneath the command.

Aredel sighed. He scooted back his chair and rose to his full height. Lord Father was a selfish and demanding old fool, but his word was the law. Harvest wasn't enough time to subjugate the people of Amantier, but Aredel would find a way.

He slipped from the study through a private passage that brought him to King Jetekesh's chambers. Aredel marched to the bed. For a long moment he studied the man lying there.

"Your lady wife travels southward, King Jetekesh, intent to claim your son and heir. I must follow her. Shall you journey with me?"

King Jetekesh's eyes opened. His jaw set. "By all means, Your Highness. I have a debt to repay."

Aredel's lips pulled in a grim smile. "As do I."

~

High Emperor Gyath elvar Kenn d'ara KessRa of the Holy Empire of KryTeer, Spear of the World and High Heaven's holy portal, studied the reports resting upon his golden desk. He sat back and steepled his sausage fingers to tap them against his several chins. For once, in this moment alone, he regretted becoming fat.

Once, years ago, he had been as spry and lithe as his children, but prosperity and gluttony had altered the emperor. He had never minded the change, for it was a sign of endless pleasure and delights, of his wealth and influence. He had never minded the passing years either, for the beauty of youth expired for all, but *he* alone was emperor of the civilized world.

Yet he sensed change upon the wind. Indeed, he *feared* it.

No, not quite.

If he was honest—which was rare—yet if he *was* honest, he must admit to himself that he didn't fear change, but rather he feared Aredel. His own son, blood of his blood. The most dreaded man in all Nakania. None were fiercer, more violent, nor cleverer, than he. Gyath had always been pleased with Aredel's skills, his cunning arts, his merciless sword carving a path for KryTeer across every border in every land. But now a question plagued Gyath's mind. Aredel had conquered the world. What would a man who bathed in the blood of the strong do now that he had no more ground to claim?

There was but one answer. After all, Aredel was heir of KryTeer. He had been toppling kingdoms and growing KryTeer's wealth for more than Gyath's sake these several years, and now he must want to enjoy the fruits of his labor. Could he bear to wait until Gyath died?

No. Gyath had murdered his own father to gain the throne, for the old king of KryTeer, at the time not an empire, never seemed like he would die on his own. Aredel would not wait either. It wasn't in the blood of the KessRa House to wait for death. They were its masters. Death served them until the end, and only a KessRa ever had the skill to destroy a KessRa.

But Gyath was far from ready to die. Despite his physicians' warnings, he felt hardy and well. He would last another forty years or more. He would glut himself on all of life's pleasures for decades yet. No son of his would defeat him and take away his property. His empire. His world.

Aredel must come home, and when he did, when he faithfully obeyed, Gyath must kill him. The man was too powerful, his influence too great. Should Gyath hold back, the Blood Prince would bathe in his essence.

Gyath looked up from the reports. One from Aredel. Another stating that his informant, a man called HeshAr, had been killed by Aredel. The third accompanied a letter from Queen Bareene, that self-satisfied, witless woman.

Gyath's eyes strayed again to the death report of HeshAr. How had Aredel known?

The truth struck Gyath hard: He could not allow Aredel to live, not even until his return to KryTeer. It might be too late then to protect himself from the power of the Blood Prince.

"Bring me Second Prince Anadin." Who better to send against Aredel than his own brother? Anadin would see his chance to become heir of KryTeer. He would seize it. Once the two brothers had loved each other but grown men in KryTeer knew better than to maintain such sappy sentimentality. It could be deadly.

16

THE HUT IN THE WOODS

"On the other side of the world," said Prince Jetekesh, "the farther south you go, the hotter it grows."

"That's ludicrous," said Lady Rille, but her voice rang flat.

"It's true. My tutors explained it. The great scientist Galin set about to prove it, and nearly has. He calls the dividing line an equator."

"Nearly has." Rille sighed.

The cousins stood beneath a drooping tree, trying to defend against the rain, but to no avail. Yeshton stood beneath a nearby tree, his cowl and cloak sopping wet, water running down his neck. Jinji sat beside him, and Tifen stood still as a statue on the storyteller's far side.

Yeshton glanced down at Jinji. "Feel all right?"

Jinji's head rested against his knees. He raised a hand and waved off Yeshton's concern, but otherwise didn't move. Rivulets of water ran around Jinji's feet, cold and muddy. The rain just wouldn't let up. The sky hung low and dark, though it wasn't yet noon. The nearby road had been washed out, and the company had taken high ground to avoid being swept along the raging river.

Thunder grumbled above. Yeshton watched lightning strike over the hill.

Rille stepped from the shelter of the tree. "There is a woodsman's hut nearby." She tripped her way across the uneven ground and Yeshton trotted after her. The others followed. Sure enough, not more than a few hundred paces brought them past a stand of trees to view the derelict shape of a long-abandoned hut.

Upon inspection the interior proved sounder than the outside suggested, except for the piles of debris. Yeshton let the others in, and they collapsed on the dirt floor in sodden heaps.

"I'll never walk anywhere ever again," moaned Prince Jetekesh. He struggled to sit and wrenched his boots from his feet with a wince.

Rille wrung out her skirt. "I cannot say I blame you, cousin." She brushed hair from her face and glanced at Jinji. "Are you well?"

Jinji had flopped down against the wall. He leaned his head back now, pale, and breathless. "I shall be. Tomorrow."

Tifen crouched before him and touched the storyteller's forehead. "He's fevered."

"It shall pass." Jinji crumpled forward as harsh coughs overtook him.

Yeshton stepped close, frowning. "You can't keep this up. We won't be able to move on until you're well."

Jinji looked up with dismay. "There is no time for that."

"Time? Are we pressed for time?"

Jinji frowned and lowered his eyes. "We must reach the Drifting Sands before Lord Peresen succeeds."

Tifen caught Jinji's shoulders. "Lay down." He glanced up at Yeshton. "He's delirious from fever. And his flesh is frail as a bird."

Timid footsteps approached. Yeshton glanced down to find Rille clutching a ragged blanket. "Remove his damp clothes. Wrap him in this. It's better than what he has on now at least."

Tifen peeled away the soaked apparel. Yeshton hung it from the moss-covered rafters. He and Rille then began to dig through the debris. There was no food and no more blankets. Only bones from hunted game, a few broken barrels, and shattered pottery.

"Lady Rille, do you know what Master Jinji seeks in the Drifting Sands?"

The girl shook her head. "I only know he must reach those Sands, and soon. And I know that we must help him do so. He cannot make it on his own now."

That much did appear to be the case. Jinji Wanderlust was a very sick man. "Will he make it that far as he is? Can you tell?"

Rille said nothing.

Yeshton volunteered to go outside and set up traps to catch some supper. The rain turned into a drizzle as he pruned small branches with his boot knife to construct a rabbit snare. He used the strings of his satchel to finish the trap, found himself a comfortable niche in some brambles, and waited for some unsuspecting creature to lope by.

Duke Lunorr was dead. KryTeer had conquered

Amantier, yet the world went on, oblivious, unchanged. Yeshton had a purpose, and for that he was grateful; but it was strange to travel the wilds of southern Amantier protecting a child who chose to follow a lunatic. Yeshton wasn't altogether certain Rille was sane herself. Perhaps the child had a gift. She seemed to, but was it real or was it luck that led her along? Yeshton wanted to trust her. Jinji and even the KryTeer Empire believed she was special, yet that would suggest she had a sort of magic. Magic wasn't supposed to be real.

The trap snapped shut.

He caught two rabbits and cleaned them before he returned to the hut. Rille had scooted the debris into a corner. Tifen had salvaged a few dry logs from behind the hut and started a fire. The hut still felt damp, but it was warm.

Prince Jetekesh sat near the hearth, his back to the room. Jinji slept beneath the musty blanket, shivering, head tossing in a fevered dream.

Yeshton held up the rabbits. "Supper."

Rille flinched and turned away. "Well done, Sir Knight."

While Yeshton cooked the meager meal, Tifen crouched beside him. His green eyes were riveted on the flames. "You served Duke Lunorr?"

"I did." Yeshton glanced at the man. "Is that a problem?"

Tifen shook his head. "Not for me."

Yeshton could feel the prince's eyes on them. He ignored the boy and stoked the flames with a long, stout stick. "Why mention it?"

"I know you."

Yeshton started. Was Tifen threatening him? To claim himself a knight was punishable by death under the law. Yet *he* didn't claim the title; Rille alone did. Yeshton had wanted to inform the rest of the company that he was merely a man-at-arms in service to Keep Lunorr, but the girl thwarted him each time he tried.

Tifen studied his face. "I saw you once as a lad, when you rode through the gates of Kavacos upon the back of a certain knight's horse. You've climbed higher than I had thought possible of common blood. In a way I envy you. But I must be content."

Yeshton let his shoulders relax. With a crooked smile he eyed the protector. "What difference lies between us now, friend? Are we not both sworn servants to a fallen throne?"

"True that. A discouraging thought…but true." Tifen nodded toward Jinji. "What think you of the storyteller?"

"He seems harmless enough, though a bit touched in the head. He really believes in Shinac, doesn't he? I'd heard tales of that fairy realm as a small boy. I even wished I could see a dragon someday. But when I grew up, I grew sense enough to let go of fantasies. Life's troublesome enough without whimsical dreams attached to one's expectations."

Tifen grunted. "Still," he whispered, "stories do have their place." His eyes flicked to Prince Jetekesh and then away.

Yeshton could appreciate the man's unspoken hope. Jinji's mild manner, his kindness, his stories, and morals, might just help the miserable prince value those same qualities, if he'd let himself. Or such gestures might drive the prince deeper into his selfish ways. Too often kindness was mistaken for weakness.

Rille padded to Yeshton's side as he rotated the rabbits.

"Did you know my father well, Sir Knight?" A faint quaver laced her voice.

He frowned at the fire. "Not as well as I should like to have known him, my lady. But he was the very best of men."

She said nothing for a long time. Her skirts rustled. "I'm all alone, Sir Knight."

Two drops of water splashed against the floor.

Yeshton jerked his head up. Her cheeks were wet. He hesitated. Should he comfort her? Pretend he didn't see? She wiped at her face, hands trembling. Yeshton's throat closed as adrenaline surged through his limbs. He straightened into a full kneel and wrapped his arms gingerly around the sobbing child.

Rille threw her hands around his neck and clung to him. She began to wail. Water soaked Yeshton's shirt front, but he didn't move. Tifen had better watch the food, lest it burn.

Yeshton glanced at the prince. Disgust had drawn lines in the boy's face. Yeshton held his gaze, jaw tight. Was he so quick to forget his own loss? Perhaps the same thought dawned on Prince Jetekesh. His eyes flicked to Rille, and he looked away, hunching his shoulders forward to sink into himself.

The sounds of Tifen prodding at the fire were all that broke the stillness of the forsaken hut. Rille's sobs had quieted. The prince sat motionless beside the hearth. Jinji lay tormented by illness. Yeshton held Rille. If only he knew how to ease her pain.

"I know what it's like," he found himself whispering. "I know how it feels to be all alone."

Cold swept through Yeshton like a winter chill. Not a single soul here had parents to claim; not even Prince Jetekesh, despite his mother's existence. Not Tifen, whose father had vanished in disgrace. Not Jinji, whose father neither knew nor claimed him. Not little Rille, a true orphan. And not Yeshton, whose own parents had died of an illness that had ravaged his seaside village when he was a small child. He couldn't even remember their faces now.

We're not so different, any of us. Together, we're alone. His gaze rested on Jinji, and inexplicably he knew that the storyteller would put it a different way: *Alone, we are together.*

The storm redoubled its barrage that night as the company ate supper. Everyone retired early, curling up in damp cloaks, catching what sleep they could against the howling wind and pounding rain that hammered the leaky roof and fragile walls.

Yeshton slept in snatches, stirring now and then to tend to Jinji. The storyteller mattered to Rille, so he mattered to Yeshton.

At dawn Yeshton rose to hunt for breakfast. He pulled the hut door open—and found himself staring out at an imposing figure wrapped in furs, a broadsword clutched in one hand, disheveled length of tangled brown hair veiling the man's face.

"What brings you to my humble abode?" boomed a voice. It tickled Yeshton's memory.

He held the man's fierce eyes. "The hut looked vacant. One of my companions took ill, and so we stopped to wait out the storm."

"Perhaps you're telling the truth, or perhaps you're in league with the Bloody One I slew last evening."

Yeshton's brows flew up. "You slew him, did you? That's no small feat."

"'Tis for me," growled the man.

Yeshton pawed at his mind, trying to place this figure, or his likeness. "Pardon me, but you don't appear to be a woodsman or a trapper. That sword's no trinket."

The man grunted. "You say one of your company fell ill. How many are you?"

"Five, including myself."

"You speak like a northerner. Marsh Province? No, Sage, I think."

Yeshton started. He had never met anyone who could distinguish speech patterns so well. "I did hail from Sage Province until recently, yes."

The man grunted again. "I assume you fled in the chaos created by KryTeer's invasion? Troublesome matter. I'd wager the queen bit off more than she could swallow, the greedy old hag."

Yeshton's eyes widened more. "You speak boldly, stranger."

"I have a recollection," said the man. "Your name wouldn't be Yeshton, would it?"

Yeshton staggered back a step.

The man bellowed a laugh. "Right again, I see! I've not lost my touch. Well. You've grown into a fine young man. A bit stiff, mayhap, but fine nonetheless." He reached up and pushed aside his tangled mane of hair, revealing a much older face, rugged and lined from hard years, but Yeshton knew him.

Torn between falling to one knee before this legend or pulling his sword against a traitor of Amantier, he sucked in a rattling breath. "Sir Palan?"

The knight grinned, showing his teeth. "You're not pleased to see me, I think."

"I heard you died aboard a pirate ship off the coast of Tivalt ten years ago."

"Aye. And others say I died as a mercenary in Lormenway three years before that. Which is right, I wonder?" His grin stretched wider, but lines appeared between his brows. "Don't give me that look, Yesh. Not you."

"I owe you a debt for bringing me as a lad to Duke Lunorr," said Yeshton, "but that debt does not grant me right or desire to rekindle friendship with a traitor."

The grin slipped from Sir Palan's face. "Harsh words indeed. Enough I'd lop your head from your shoulders, but for fond memories of your boyhood and our journey together."

Yeshton squared his shoulders. "Memories do not sponge out sins, Sir Palan." He grimaced. "I shouldn't call you sir. You lost that title when you disgraced yourself."

The man, once a fetching figure, now showed the wrinkles of one approaching his sixtieth year. He took a step forward, eyes flashing. "Tread carefully now, lad. My composure isn't as it used to be, being so long from court life. I might forget for a moment that I like you."

"You don't know me, Palan. It's been over fifteen years."

"So it has." The man's shoulders relaxed. "And so we should let it remain."

Yeshton's hand tightened on his sword hilt. "Your son is within."

"Tifen? Here?" His gaze flicked past Yeshton to the dark space beyond the open door.

Yeshton heard metal scraping as a sword unsheathed. "My father is dead," said Tifen in a rasp. "Sir Palan is no more."

The old knight looked his son up and down, a gleam in his eyes. "What a man you've become. Your mother would be proud."

"Do *not* speak to me of my mother." Tifen pushed past Yeshton. "Leave, old man. Do not return until we have abandoned your pathetic home."

Pain creased Palan's brow. "You have every cause to hate me, believing what I am alleged to have done."

Tifen shook his head. "Do not speak of it. Do not disgrace yourself further."

Yeshton rested a hand on Tifen's shoulder. "Easy. He has killed a Blood Knight. His skill isn't diminished." Yeshton turned his eye to Palan. "You used the word *alleged*. Do you profess that you were falsely accused?"

Palan shrugged. "Not that it matters, but yes. And the king knew it too. Knew his lady queen claimed that I'd forced myself upon her, all because I refused her advances."

"Liar." Tifen spat out the word. "If you were innocent, King Jetekesh would not have banished you."

"He *didn't* banish me, my son. I left. Court rumors called it my guilt-ridden conscience chasing me off, and from there stories of concocted dalliances sprang up like milkweeds. King Jetekesh warned me not to go, but I had to. The queen's influence was too great, her court too corrupt, and I'd had my fill of it all."

Tifen's lip curled into a snarl. "If that is truth, it's little better than rumor. You abandoned me and I became a servant, without lands or titles, forced to lug your soiled memory and the shame of our blood."

"And if I had stayed?" Palan shrugged. "There was no means to exonerate myself. No proof against the queen's testimony. And she expecting the heir apparent at the time. No, I couldn't stay, not even for you, Tifen. The king knew it too. It was best that I disappear. I am sorry that you lost all you had, my son, but without titles you were no target for the queen. I spared you that, at least."

Tifen's eyes flashed the same fire as his father. "Don't make it sound noble."

"Be calm," murmured Yeshton. "Reflect on Sir Palan's words before you pass judgment. There is the ring of truth in his tale."

Tifen turned his head away. "Whatever his tale, whatever the truth, my father is dead to me." He sheathed his sword and stalked away from the hut, out into the shelter of the stately trees. Sunlight glistened against water droplets and birds trilled their morning song. Yeshton watched Tifen's back until the man had vanished against the forest.

He turned back to Palan. "You were never close?"

The knight sighed. "Tifen was always conscious that our blood wasn't noble, and he felt we must therefore prove ourselves better and stronger than any other knight or lord. Our honor meant much to him. I understand his plight, but in my mind a knight should be chosen for his actions, his integrity, not the stature of his house or the past honor of dead ancestors."

Yeshton considered the man before him. Sir Palan, strongest knight of Amantier, born of questionable means, raised as a servant, groomed on the front lines in combat against KryTeer in years past, distinguished by saving the life of King Jetekesh the Third. All before the age of peace established under the hand of King Jetekesh the Fourth. Yeshton had admired him until the scandal fifteen years ago. Despite Palan's unknown parentage and coarse upbringing, he'd been hailed for his honor, his unfailing virtue, his unwavering faith in the One God. Even when news reached Yeshton's ear that Sir Palan had fled in disgrace, he'd not believed it. He'd expected the knight to clear his name and return to his king's side. But he never had.

"You left your family, never explaining your side of what happened. Why?"

Palan sighed again, shaking his head. "Tifen was a grown man even then. Ready to be knighted. He refused to see me before I left, too ashamed to receive his dishonored father. He would not read my letter. Of course, he had hoped that my shame would not destroy his own chance for knighthood. In a just world that might be so. But this world isn't just, Yeshton, and the queen saw to Tifen's misery. But as I said, it spared him her interest, and that has eased my mind these many years."

Yeshton uncurled his fingers from his hilt and leaned against the door frame. "What have you been doing all this time? Not living a woodsman's life, surely. Your strength is as great as it ever was, if your account of the Bloody One's death is true."

"You doubt me?" Palan's grin reappeared. "I've served King Jetekesh these fifteen years. In disguise I've traveled from land to land, even within KryTeer itself, reporting what I see. Keeping trouble at bay..." His smile slipped. "That is, until the king grew too sick to receive my reports. I can guess the why of it. Queen Bareene, always the ambitious vixen, saw her chance and took it. One kingdom isn't enough for a woman so hungry as she. I heard the first hints of an alliance two years ago, but by then King Jetekesh was already ill. *Ill*."

He barked a sharp laugh. "Poisoned; that's my guess. Something slow, lethal, but undetectable by any without the proper knowledge. I imagine the king's physician is already the queen's man. And now it's done. The king is dead. A pity, for he was a good man. Young, and occasionally foolhardy, but strong where it mattered most."

Palan tapped his chest with his large fist. "Much of this you must already know, Yesh. Why else would you be so far south? Whom do you protect? Which nobles have escaped the queen's betrayal?"

His sincerity was the same. Yeshton knew Palan well enough to recognize it. And he *wanted* to believe this knight was as he had always seen him. Yeshton nodded inside. "Come. I'll introduce you."

They entered the hut. Yeshton found Rille first, still asleep inside her cloak, hair tangled around her face. Next his eye fell on Prince Jetekesh, but the boy was wide awake, expression hard. His blue eyes, bright against the sunlight leaking into the hut, shimmered with unshed tears. He hugged his legs to his chest, as though he tried to shield himself from all the world.

"You're wrong," he whispered, voice choked. "My

mother isn't what you say. She wouldn't…betray her people. She wouldn't accuse a knight falsely. She wouldn't…"

Palan looked sharply at Yeshton. "Is this…?"

"Yes," said Yeshton. "This is the heir of Amantier, your crown prince." He faltered. "Your king now, I suppose."

The old knight sank to one knee and clapped a hand to his chest. "My king, I am honored to meet you at last, though these days are dark and uncertain."

Confusion clouded Jetekesh's eyes. He trembled. Reaching a hand up, he wiped at his face with his sleeve. "Are you truly Sir Palan, First Knight of the Rose?"

"Yes, sire. So I am."

A smile haunted the boy's lips, before it fell away. He turned his face from the knight. "Leave me alone."

"As you command, sire." Palan climbed to his feet. "Yeshton, you'd best explain all you can."

"I will. Come away and let the others sleep."

The two men strode back outside.

17
THREADS OF FREEDOM

So, Muhun was dead. That was no small feat.

Prince Aredel studied the scroll. A splotch of red ink signified the death of the party to whom the twin scroll belonged.

No doubt it was murder. Muhun was too skillful a warrior, and too careful a man, to die by accident or illness.

"Shevek. Ledonn."

Aredel's warrior attendants appeared at his side. He rested a hand on the bow of the barge and studied Lily River stretching on before him, southward.

"See to our guest's needs, Ledonn."

"Yes, holy prince." Ledonn bowed and backed away.

"Shevek." Aredel held out the scroll. "Muhun is dead."

"Surprising," said Shevek, taking the scroll to inspect the mark. "An impressive thing for one to accomplish. Do you know the killer?"

"I have only suspicions about his identity."

"Palan?"

Shevek had always been a clever guesser.

Aredel nodded. "Probably, though I had thought he was farther east, near Shing."

"That slippery snake is always where we least want him," said Shevek, rolling up the scroll.

"True." Aredel took the scroll and tapped it against the wooden rail. "Can this great, unwieldy contraption go any faster?"

Shevek sprouted a wicked smile. "With the proper motivation, anything can go faster, Holy Prince." He cantered away, far too pleased by the prospect of intimidating the ship crew. Aredel allowed himself a smile.

He reached into the inner pocket of his red cloak and pulled out a dried crimson flower. "*Rehar vilDoch*, Muhun. Rest in the arms of the Gods of War. Paradise is yours." He tossed the flower over the rail and into the waters of Lily River.

∽

King Jetekesh the Fourth looked up from the maps spread before him on the bed. A Blood Knight stood in the open doorway of the barge's single cabin, a tray of food in one hand.

"I am to see to your comfort, Your Majesty," said the warrior.

King Jetekesh frowned but nodded. "I thank you. What is your name?"

"First Warrior of the Blood, under First High Prince Aredel. I am called Ledonn."

"Ledonn. Very well." King Jetekesh watched the

knight place the tray upon the bed. "Have we passed Crystal Port yet?"

"About an hour ago," said Ledonn as he poured white wine into a goblet. "Will there be anything else?"

"No, thank you."

Ledonn left. King Jetekesh stripped meat off the bone of a pheasant with a relish. For the first time in more than a year he had a healthy appetite, thanks to the last person in all Nakania one might expect. The Blood Prince of KryTeer was not what King Jetekesh had imagined him to be.

When he first woke from fevered madness, Prince Aredel had stood before his bed to explain two facts: Amantier was now a province under Bloody Gyath; and King Jetekesh was recovering, not from disease, but from a poison administered over two years by his own wife. Neither fact surprised the king. What did surprise him was that he yet lived.

Traveria, that deadly pale plant found only in the darkest reaches of the deepest woods, was almost impossible to combat once administered. After it ran through a man's blood, he was never the same. Visions of terror haunted his mind. His body grew cold. Even without a lethal dose, it altered him forever. Yet somehow, apart from weakness, King Jetekesh was now mending. The terrors were gone. Warmth spread throughout his limbs, and he could eat; *wanted* to eat. To stretch his limbs. To stretch his mind. He could face life again.

Strangest of all was knowing *who* had given him back that life. And *why*.

Prince Aredel had explained that too. "I've used a peculiar cure to save your life, Majesty. It is not known in your lands, but the blood of what is magical can counter what *traveria* does to those without magic. Were you fae, the poison could not have done its lethal work. As it is, I have given you a draught of blood taken from a fae creature, and thus your life is spared. This I have done, not from some noble sentiment, but from a desire to know my enemy—and to make use of your mind. You know that your wife attempted to kill you. Indeed, she did kill you. But I have resurrected you, and you have a chance now to exact your vengeance upon that fell beast you once called queen."

King Jetekesh agreed. Bareene was the cause, not only of his suffering and illness, but also of betraying her country. And, most personal of all, she had done her own son great harm while King Jetekesh was too weak to intercede.

Now Prince Jetekesh hid somewhere in the wilds of Southern Amantier, Queen Bareene on his tail; determined to sever the last stubborn threads of the boy's independence; to make him into nothing more than a doll for her amusement. King Jetekesh shuddered to think of all that might entail.

It seared King Jetekesh's soul to know he worked alongside the Blood Prince of KryTeer, but to accomplish his goals it was the smartest place to stand. He would find and execute Bareene. He would rescue his son. And once he had gained his strength back, he would muster a force to stand against KryTeer, even should every soul fall. He would not let Amantier, last free kingdom of Nakania, fade under the corrupted shadow of Emperor Gyath and his barbarism.

Now, within the cabin of a barge headed south, King

Jetekesh lowered his fork to the empty plate upon his tray. He drained the last of his wine. His eyes flicked back to the maps spread around him.

    He thought, and plotted, and prayed. In the end it might make no difference. He might well fail in all his schemes. But he must try; to gain freedom for his brave kingdom, for his suffering boy, for himself. For he was still king of Amantier, a descendant of King Cavalin the Third, hero of Nakania.

18
WHERE DECEPTION ENDS

"The White Death, they're calling it. Now the borders of Shing are sealed. KryTeer has pulled out most of its armed forces until the plague completes its deadly run." Sir Palan sighed. "'Tis a sad affair."

Every eye strayed to Jinji, who slept beside one leaning wall.

"You don't suppose...?" Prince Jetekesh couldn't finish the question. He sprang to his feet and hurried to the door. Panic hammered against his temples and his lungs constricted.

"Where are you going, Highness?" called out Sir Palan in his booming voice.

"*Out.*" Jetekesh shoved the door shut behind him and stumbled away from the hut, gulping fresh air. A plague? Had Jinji carried it out of Shing? Sir Palan alone had appeared undisturbed as he narrated his recent travels through the infested realm while he'd chased after phantom reports. It was there the old knight had learned of Mother's alleged treachery, and he'd hurried back to Amantier, but too late.

The rush of water guided Jetekesh down a wooded slope. There he found a tiny glade where a brook tripped and gurgled over rocks that sparkled under hints of sunlight above the trees. He halted, dazzled by the playing light, until the burning of flea bites, the grime of mud and sweat, the reek of his body, swarmed his senses.

Jetekesh lurched to the edge of the water. His distorted reflection stared back at him, eyes wide. His hair was matted. Clothes disheveled and stained. Face smudged with soot and dirt. He raised his hands and watched them tremble. Ruined. His hands were ruined. Calluses and scrapes riddled his palms and knuckles. His nails were broken and muddied. Mother would weep if she saw him this way.

I look like a peasant!

He sank to the ground. Mud squelched beneath his knees. He leaned forward and plunged cupped hands into the frigid depths. Shuddering, he splashed his face with clean water, again, again, again. Spluttering and gasping, he didn't relent until his reflection in the brook revealed that every splotch against his skin had been scrubbed away.

It wasn't enough. With surging adrenaline, he wrenched the clothes from his body and plunged into the deepest part of the brook. He gasped as his limbs ached in the frigid water.

I won't leave this spot until every speck of me is clean!

His clothes were another matter. They lay in a heap, soiled with sweat and dust. He couldn't put those back on. The cloak he'd slept in was caked with mud at the hem, but otherwise it was the safest stitch of cloth he had. Grimacing, he wrapped himself in the coarse garment and found a rock to scrub the stains and crusted sweat from his other clothes. As he worked, his scraped knuckles bled in the icy water. Tears pricked at his eyes.

Everything was a ruin.

His life had become an endless nightmare, waking or sleeping. There was no peace. No comfort. Sobs escaped his lips as he scrubbed harder, harder. His fingernails chipped as he dragged his shirt across the rough rock face. Up, down. Hair clung to his cheeks. He tasted salt against his chapped lips. All he did anymore was cry. He was nothing but a throneless prince blubbering in protest against all his life had become. But there was no changing it. No means of escape. He could go on bawling—or he could stop.

With a scream he flung the shirt. It slapped against the muddy earth. Jetekesh drew his head to his knees and rocked back and forth. It wasn't fair. Not any of it. Why would Mother betray Amantier? Why would she poison Father? It couldn't be true. Everyone was wrong. They lied…lied…but why? Why lie to him?

Why not? Mother always did. She lied and said she cared about Father when she never had. Not ever. Father had tried to fulfill her endless needs; to give her whatever she demanded; to be a dutiful husband. But it was never enough for the selfish woman.

Jetekesh knew this. He *knew* it.

He sat before the rushing brook, bruised, battered, chilled through, and finally clean. His eyes found their reflection in the water. He held his gaze. *Mother* was the liar. She had murdered Father and allied herself with KryTeer.

She was the reason Jetekesh's world was over now.

Even before this nightmarish journey, even before Father's death, she had been the source of his pain and confusion. She wouldn't let him ride horses for fear of him tumbling off. No hunting for he might grow ill or bruise himself. No fencing for it created calluses. He was delicate, she said. He couldn't strain himself like that.

So he was delicate. Whose fault was that? The horrible woman had never let Jetekesh grow stronger, never let him pick himself up and try again. He'd tried many times to defy her, but she always found out. Like the servant who had always groomed Jetekesh's horse and let him ride in secret; that servant had vanished one day. And the fencing master, executed for teaching Jetekesh on the sly.

Why must she take everything from him?

Why did she murder Father?

Because Father said Jetekesh could be strong. He wouldn't let Mother have her way in all things. Because Mother was a selfish, gluttonous creature who used every man at court to satisfy a hole she could never fill. Mother had been wounded since she lost her second child, the little sister Jetekesh had never met, for the baby was dead at birth. It had almost killed Mother, so the rumors said. Mother could never have another child. That was certain. But was it an excuse to become cold-hearted, selfish, and cruel? Was it the reason why Mother did what she did? Hadn't she destroyed Sir Palan's life *before* that tragedy?

She's always been horrible. The realization struck

Jetekesh like a physical blow. His heart flinched. *She blames other people to escape a guilty conscience.*

I hate her.

He stared at the blisters and calluses on his hands. Hadn't he *wanted* these? It meant he wasn't delicate. He didn't need coddling. He could make decisions on his own without Mother plotting out every course he took. His knuckles were bleeding. *Fine.* He must understand and accept pain or he'd never get back up when a horse threw him.

Too late.

He hunched his shoulders. What did it matter if he learned now? He would never be king. KryTeer had conquered his country. He had no throne and no future.

Jetekesh lowered his head back to his knees.

Amantier was no more. He was nothing. In the end Mother had won.

~

Yeshton followed the prince's retreat with his eyes, but he didn't run after him. Tifen was still somewhere out there in the woods, and it was his job to protect the prince, not Yeshton's. He turned back to Sir Palan.

"Do you think the storyteller carries this plague?"

Sir Palan shook his head. "I don't think so. He's pale enough, to be sure, but fevers don't accompany the White Death. This man is sick in a different way." He studied Jinji's face for a moment. "It's a strange thing, but I'd almost say this man's case is a matter of too much contained within too little; like if all the countries of

Nakania tried to fit within Amantier's borders. Of course, the country couldn't contain all that land; it simply couldn't."

"He's a storyteller true," said Rille, speaking from her bedroll. Yeshton smiled at his mistress. She smiled back.

"A storyteller true, is he?" Sir Palan rubbed the stubble on his chin. "A rare gift, if it is so."

Rille's eyes pinned the knight. "It is so."

He nodded. "I've also heard of you, young mistress of Sage. Emperor Gyath dearly wants your gift for himself."

She lowered her eyes.

The rustle of cloth brought Yeshton's eyes back to the storyteller. Jinji had sat up, shoulders stooped forward, eyes clouded. He raised his head and smiled at Yeshton.

"Where is Prince Jetekesh?" His voice was a whisper.

"Outside." Yeshton inhaled. "Tell me truth, Wanderlust. Do you carry the plague of Shing with you?"

The man was still for a moment, gaunt face blank. He blinked, and a smile twitched at his lips. "Nay, Sir Knight. I do not."

"Can I believe you?"

"As I told you, Yesh—"

Yeshton raised his hand to cut off Sir Palan. "I need to hear it for myself."

Jinji nodded. "Yes, Yeshton. You can believe me. I am ill, but I am not spreading the White Death across Amantier."

"You know this for certain?"

"I do." His eyes were bright even in the dim hut. His face unguarded. If Jinji was lying, he was the greatest liar Yeshton had ever met.

The soldier sighed. "Very well. I'll believe you."

Jinji's smile deepened. "I thank you for your faith." He pulled the blanket from his legs and struggled to rise.

"What are you doing?"

"I must see Prince Jetekesh." Jinji reached his feet and leaned against the wall, trembling.

Yeshton climbed to his own feet. "Is that wise?"

Jinji chuckled. "Wise? That I could not say." He glanced at Sir Palan and inclined his head. "It is an honor to meet you in the flesh, Sir Knight."

"And you, Wanderlust. I've heard of your exploits in Shing. You got yourself kicked out of KryTeer headquarters not long ago if the rumors are true."

Jinji laughed again. "So I did. It seems the KryTeeran Regent of Shing despises tales of Shinac."

"You seem to be unpopular no matter where you go, Master Tale-weaver."

"So I do." Jinji stepped away from the wall, wavered, but steadied himself. "I must find Jetekesh. I will return."

He moved gingerly to the hut door and out into the green world. Yeshton watched his back. Would he make it to the prince in his condition?

"Let him go," said Rille. "Let him do whatever he pleases." She pointed to the smoldering embers of the fire. "I'm hungry, Sir Knight. May we eat something?"

Yeshton stirred up the fire at once. Sir Palan's unexpected appearance had made him forget his duty to young Rille. Instead he'd explained how he and his companions had come to be so far south. Then Sir Palan had taken a turn to describe his own recent adventures.

Rille sat beside Yeshton as he poured water into the cooking pot Kyella had sent along with them. The little girl watched Yeshton's hands for a moment, then she leaned her head against his shoulder.

"Thank you, Sir Knight, for last night. I was...distraught."

He smiled but didn't glance at her. The girl had trouble expressing herself. No need to make her feel more uncomfortable by acknowledging that fact. He broke apart several roots he'd gathered the previous evening and plopped the pieces into the water to brew up a broth for Jinji. Finished, he rummaged in his satchel until he found some hard biscuits and dried meat. He offered them to Rille.

"Eat up. I'll catch fish for the midday meal. I promise."

"This will do." She nibbled the biscuit.

"I'm very grateful for your patience." The sound of scraping feet brought Yeshton's head around.

Sir Palan stood, brushing off his tattered clothing. He grinned at Yeshton. "I'll go hunt us a proper meal. There are also a few nests nearby. We can create a respectable repast for your half-starved company yet. Stay here and protect the young lass." The old knight left the hut, his movements like a prowl.

He'd always moved that way, as long as Yeshton had known him. Despite his age, Sir Palan didn't look stiff or weary. Yeshton had to admit to himself that having the legendary knight here, and keen to help, was an immense comfort.

They might make it through this after all.

19
A STORYTELLER TRUE

Jetekesh's head shot up. His ears thundered with the rapid pace of his heartbeat.

I was asleep? For how long?

He pulled his cloak tight around his shoulders, eyes flicking to the discarded shirt in the mud.

Someone's coming!

Too late to dress. Was it Tifen padding down the slope behind him?

Let it be Tifen.

He leapt to his feet and whirled.

Jinji Wanderlust stumbled to the bottom of the incline, eyes bright under the morning sun. He wore his usual, detestable, cheerful smile, but a question hung at the corner of his mouth. "Sire, are you well?"

Jetekesh scoffed. "That's a rich question coming from you."

The storyteller shrugged. "Nevertheless, I ask it."

Jetekesh mimicked the shrug. "Should you be up?

Aren't you dying or something?" He stiffened and stepped backward. "Stay away! You've got the plague!"

"Nonsense," said Jinji in an amiable tone. "My ailment is different."

"How do you know?"

The man laughed airily. "I know, sire. Healers have assured me. I haven't got the White Death."

"You might be lying."

Jinji's mirth faded. "So I might. And if I am, you are already dying, Your Highness. But you may rest assured in the knowledge that I do not have any catching diseases at all." His lips twitched upward. "I have been accused several times of possessing an infectious smile, if that alarms you, my prince. Though I shouldn't worry if I were you. You've proved immune to its effects on several occasions."

Jetekesh shook his head. What a peculiar creature. For a wild moment, he was torn between laughter and indignation. "You show no respect to your king, you know, Wanderlust."

Jinji bowed his head. "But I do, sire. I also wish to treat you like you are human. I fear too few people in your life have until now." He padded forward and rested a hand on Jetekesh's shoulder. "You have been crying."

"No, I haven't. I've been bathing."

That patient smile didn't slip. "May I listen? Perhaps it would help."

"How could you help? Does your gift of tale telling lend you some supernatural ability to patch what's broken? My father is dead. My mother killed him and sold Amantier to our greatest enemy. And why?" A choked laugh broke from his lips. "I certainly couldn't say. Can you?"

Jinji's fingers tightened against his shoulder. Jetekesh met the storyteller's eyes to find himself snared by their clarity.

"Queen Bareene is a greedy woman, for that is all she has known. Indeed, it is all she had ever experienced until she came to Rose Palace to wed your father. He tried, oh how he tried, to give her the kindness and affection she had never known from her disinterested and self-absorbed parents and a cruel elder brother. Her husband was the chance she needed to learn a new course; but alas, my dear prince, she chose not to follow that course. Instead she hardened her heart and continued in what she knew. It was familiar and safe. She became the very thing she had always hated, for that is what occurs when we choose the easy way. This is the truth of her life, sad as I am to tell you. But that is *her* tale, Prince Jetekesh. It is not yours, and her choices needn't bind you to those consequences."

Jetekesh pulled back. "But I do face those consequences, you half-wit. I am throneless. I am alone."

"You are among friends."

Jetekesh scoffed. "*Friends*? Princes—and *kings*—do not have friends."

"Your father did when he was a prince, and even as a king."

Blood pounded in Jetekesh's ears. "You know nothing of my father!"

"With respect, I know much of your father. King Jetekesh the Fourth has a noble spirit, a farseeing eye, and an abiding respect for life. Just as Queen Bareene harbors selfishness and disdain and gluttony within her, so King Jetekesh harbors love and hope and concern for others. Small wonder that you, Jetekesh, struggle so within yourself under such a heritage. Yet your love for your father abides and strengthens you. It is my hope that you shall choose to walk his ways, rather than Bareene's."

"Silence. Silence! My father is dead. Stop speaking of him like he's still here. He's entombed by now. Encased in rock and buried in darkness. I'll never see him again!" Jetekesh threw his hands over his eyes. "He left me. He left me behind! Why!"

Jinji's cool fingers curled around Jetekesh's wrist. "It is a hard thing to lose a loved one, sire. Words are not enough to comfort you. Time alone may soften your grief into a caressing memory." He pulled Jetekesh's hand from his face until their eyes met again. "You are wet, weary, hungry, and heartbroken. But you *are* with friends, my king, if you will allow us to be such. Then you will not feel so alone. Indeed, you will be warmed a little, and that will ease your suffering. Let us try. Let us relieve the ache if we can." He tugged on his arm. Those eyes were so bright, so inviting, warm and kind, just like Father's.

Jetekesh allowed himself to be pulled toward the hut, toward life and noise, away from the gushing waters that echoed in the hollow of his heart.

He faltered at the foot of the incline. "My clothes."

"I have a clean set of garments you may wear," said Jinji. "After you are safely in the hut, I will return to the brook to clean what you've been wearing and mend the holes. I am not a bad hand with needle and thread."

The inside of the hut was dismal after the brilliance

outside. Jetekesh stood in the doorway, willing his eyes to adjust. Jinji had slipped by him to rummage through his satchel. Soon he returned, a bundle of clothes in his hands. "Try these. They will be too big, but it will suffice until your other clothes are dry."

Jetekesh accepted the wardrobe with a warm thrill. Clean clothes! He watched the storyteller stroll back outside. Despite the humble threads Jinji wore, his clothes were less coarse than what the farmer and his daughter had provided. Jetekesh recalled hearing once that the weavers of Shing were the finest in the world. Perhaps it was true.

He padded inside the hut and found his cousin nibbling on a half-eaten biscuit. She turned her back to him, though whether in disdain or to respect his privacy, he didn't bother to guess. He took the chance to strip off his cloak and slip into the soft clothes. They *were* too big, but he didn't mind. It was good to be clean.

Rille threw something at him. "Here."

He caught a brush. Likely one of that farm girl's contributions. Allowing himself a smile, he attacked the tangles of his long hair while he glanced around the hut. Yeshton foraged through several of Sir Palan's packs.

"Where is the old knight?" asked Jetekesh.

Yeshton nodded toward the door. "Out hunting. He promises a hearty dinner."

"Excellent. I'm tired of being hungry." Jetekesh fought a stubborn snarl, wincing. "The storyteller doesn't have the plague. I asked him."

"So he said to me, Your Majesty." Yeshton set several jars aside. "He appears to be much improved. We should consider continuing on at first light tomorrow."

"I agree," said Rille.

Great. More walking. Jetekesh sighed. "Will we reach a village soon?"

Yeshton nodded as he inspected the contents of a jar swirling with red liquid. "So Sir Palan says. It's two days from here. Lilac Lake, they call it. There is no lake though. Just a pond brimming with catfish."

Jetekesh grimaced. He drew his cloak around his shoulders and leaned against the wall. "I'm going to nap until dinner is ready."

He closed his eyes but heard the faint voices of Rille and Yeshton.

"What is it?"

"It's fruit, Sir Knight. Berries."

"I've never seen the like of it."

"It's mashed berries, boiled and sweetened. A delicacy called fruit preserves."

"It looks revolting."

The girl giggled. "Try some."

Jetekesh turned his head away from the sounds. Why had Jinji supposed Jetekesh would want friends, especially among this party? They were common, even ill-mannered. Despite Rille's royal blood, she behaved like a peasant girl.

He couldn't count these people as his friends. It was preposterous to consider. He wouldn't do it.

∼

"What say you, Master Tale-weaver? Shall we not have a story?"

Darkness had fallen outside, chasing every member of

the company inside the hut. Even Tifen. Sir Palan had been true to his word, providing a feast, at least compared with recent fare. A wild boar was the highlight dish, while strange roots boiled and sliced helped fill in the hollow places in Jetekesh's belly. And to wash it all down, a cup of ale and a piece of flatbread lathered in fruit preserves.

Cleaned and fed as he was, he was content to sleep. But the old knight's request brought Jetekesh's mind from dreamy realms. He glanced at Jinji.

The man from Shing smiled. "I have no objection, Sir Palan, if none would have me refrain." His blue-green eyes flickered in the firelight.

Rille scooted nearer to Jinji, who sat closest to the fire. Yeshton shifted, but stayed where he was, silent. Tifen, who sat cross-legged near the door, made no noise at all.

"I hear no protests," Sir Palan said with a grin. "Methinks you are safe to cast a pleasant spell upon a few weary travelers."

Jinji's smile deepened. He drew his blanket closer as a shiver ran over his frame. His eyes closed, and for a long moment there was only the sound of the glutting flames in the hearth.

"In a time now lost to memory, in a small village near a great wood, there lived a young lass."

Jinji's voice was like a note of music, humming, growing louder. His words brought a rush of windsong. Like the unfurling of a scroll, Jetekesh started as he found himself upon a dirt road crawling down into a village nestled against ancient trees. He smelled fruit blossoms. Heard the tumult of a river running close.

And above him, from a cloudless spring sky, Jinji's words tumbled in a great wind of sound, light, color.

"This lass was sweet of heart, kind as a kiss, but alas, her face was more than plain; it was indeed quite ugly. And true to human nature, most in the village were cruel to her for this unavoidable sin. Nevertheless, she bravely preserved her good nature and wandered the fields and fens, the nearby villages, and walked among the merchants upon the road, to aid where she might as a healer. As she grew into a young woman, her knowledge and skill to heal any ailment became known throughout the kingdom in which she lived, and people would come from far and near to receive relief from their many pains."

As Jinji spoke, the images surrounding Jetekesh shifted like ripples against the sky and earth, to reform as though upon the storyteller's command. Jetekesh saw the lass with her unfortunate visage, but he also saw the kindly eyes, the merry smile, the warm and gentle hands.

"War broke out, and the prince of the kingdom rode with his father to fend off the enemy."

Jetekesh stood upon a battlefield. He recoiled from the gore at his feet, the scents and sounds of death and fear. The rage of pealing swords. The whistle and crack of distant catapults.

There. Lying among the dead and dying, a fair prince with white-blond hair and eyes of deepest green. Eyes that could not see, though he still breathed.

"The kingdom won its war, though not without great cost. The king was killed in the fray. His son was gravely wounded, but he lived, nonetheless. Alas, a wound to his head had stolen his sight from him, and none of the royal healers could cure this ailment.

"But a wisewoman of his court came to the ailing prince and told him of a healer at the edge of his kingdom who, 'twas said, could cure anyone. Daring to try this last of his hopes, the prince commanded that he be brought to this healer of such renown.

"So it was done, and the good-hearted lass tended to the prince both day and night for one week. During this time, the prince felt her gentleness and heard her sweet voice and fell in love with her, though he could not see her face. At last he declared that if she could but heal his eyes, he would take her as his queen, for she must be as lovely to behold as her voice and hands were gentle.

"The lass said nothing but continued to minister to him until at last upon the seventh day he woke and found his eyes mended. With a cry of joy, he bounded from the bed where he had stayed all that week, and searching, found the lass tending to the fire. Mid-declaration of love, he faltered as she turned to face him.

"So plain. So ugly. This could not be. Surely this was another young woman, less deserving, less gifted. A servant perhaps. But when she spoke the simple words, 'It is I,' the prince knew it was his very love.

"He recoiled, denied his oath of love, and fled from the hut where the ugly lass dwelt. He returned to his castle and worked hard to forget his folly.

"But the lass could not forget as he could, for she had come to love the prince too, though she was wise enough to know he would never keep his word when he could see once more. Hurt, despairing, the lass too fled from her hut and into the ancient woods. On she ran, weeping, heartbroken, until she stumbled over the root of a willow tree whose long limbs drank from a great lake. Here she wept the more, and her tears watered the ground and fell into the depths of the great pool."

Jetekesh's heart throbbed as he stood near the willow tree. His cheeks burned. *I would have fled from her too.*

The tree began to glow.

"As must be when the pure of heart cry out in anguish against wrongdoing, magic answers. The fairy of the willow woke from her slumber and heard the pains of the lass's heart. She appeared to the lass, quieted her tears, and bestowed upon her two blessings. The healer's tears turned into gems of pure light as they fell from her eyes. The second blessing was that of truth: it did not change the appearance of the lass, but those who looked upon her and those who were near her, would see the truth of things.

"The lass did not understand this blessing, but she returned to her home as the fairy instructed. As she entered the village where all had been cruel to her, she beheld monsters abiding in the homes and shops. The people were revealed for what they were, and in great fear they fled from one another and lost themselves in the woods and fens.

"The lass also fled until she came to a village where all the people were beautiful, for they were kind. And when they beheld her, they saw a queenly woman of such radiance they begged her to stay. For the first time in her life she was treated as she always ought to have been. Soon her beauty became more renowned than her healing arts, and many came from every corner of the kingdom to see her. When they met her, they loved her for her kindness even more than for her beauty.

"The prince, now king of his land, heard of the lass's

beauty, and he declared that he would win the fair maid's hand to be his queen, for someone of such beauty must be as kind and gentle as her face is lovely. He rode to the village where she now dwelt, but the truth revealed him for what he was: an ugly monster, hideous to behold, frightening and selfish.

"Most of the villagers ran in terror, but a few caught the beastly man and bound him tight. They argued how to deal with him, afraid that he would devour their loved ones if he was allowed to live. The king begged to be spared, but his words went unheeded, for he had been heedless until now.

"The brave men who had captured him decided to end his life, for his words sounded like the cries of a hungry beast, and they were afraid. But before they could strike him down, the lass arrived, having heard his cries; and knowing truth in its whole measure, she recognized the king and threw herself upon him to shield against the killing blow. The men stayed their hand, and she begged of them to spare the monster's life. 'He is only ugly because he does not know true beauty. Let me teach him, and he will be kind,' she declared with earnest strength.

"And so, the men unbound their king and let the lass guide him to her home. And the king, when he touched her hand, saw her as she truly was: the gentle healer with the soul of a queen. Before her hut, he fell to his knees and begged her to forgive him.

"'You cured my eyes, but not my blindness!' cried he in despair. 'I see now that beauty is not what man can behold, but it is the spirit of love which transcends mortal scruples.'

"And in that moment of understanding, the king was

again fair of countenance. He confessed his love for the plain healer with the queenly heart. He took her to be his queen, and she took him as her equal. They ruled together in peace and prosperity, drawing all that is good and magical to their realm where truth is hailed above man's greed. And so began the true line of kings in the land of Shinac."

The rush of windsong ceased and the world grew dim. Jetekesh found himself seated in the woodsman's hut among his companions, breathless and filled with a warmth in his chest that he couldn't understand.

Jinji's eyes opened. He smiled. "I'm a little tired now. I think I will sleep." He curled up by the fire, indifferent to the hush thick upon the air.

No one stirred for a long moment.

Sir Palan's voice was a faint murmur. "A storyteller true. No mistake."

Jetekesh wrapped himself in his bedding though his heart still pounded. It was just a story. Wasn't it?

He's told me tales before. Why could I not see them like I did this one?

20
THE LOST PRINCE

Merchants had set up shop in the square and customers milled and chattered among the wares. Several Amantieran soldiers stood at the well, flirting with a blushing maiden. A herd of sheep clattered across the cobblestones toward rolling hills west of the village green, following their shepherd.

Yeshton hefted his purse. There wasn't much coin left for food.

Sir Palan strolled from stall to stall, studying the wares with a practiced eye. Passing villagers called out to him in friendly tones, and he returned their greetings heartily.

The knight stooped to examine a stall teeming with catfish.

"Do they know who you are?" Yeshton's voice was a cautious whisper.

Sir Palan glanced up at him with a grin. "But of course. I am the village trapper. I sell my furs every spring after the thaw."

Yeshton nodded. It was a clever ruse and an honest living; no doubt the villagers were more inclined to share gossip and news with a humble trapper than they might a dishonored knight.

"Heigh-ho, Timber," called a colorfully dressed man sprinting across the square. He halted before Sir Palan. "What brings you here so late in the season? Any useful hides today?"

"Nay," chortled Sir Palan. "I bring a few lost souls from the woods, in fact. That last storm left them half-drowned and starved. Turns out I know one of them." He waggled his fingers toward Yeshton, who stood free of his armor and feeling very exposed. Sir Palan had urged him to hide his armor in the hut lest he draw unwanted attention so near a keep. "This is Yesh, a woodsman not unlike myself. I trained him from a pup. Thus, for old time's sake I've agreed to act as guide for his wayward band all the way to Keep Falcon and their new refuge from poverty. Lord Milgar will at last have the servants he's long requested."

"That crazy old coon?" The man hooted. "Have you warned your friends against the going? Lord Milgar's as mad as a lark these days. Even claims he sees fairies in the desert."

Sir Palan laughed again. "Hush now. Don't discourage adventuring to the young. They're bold enough, mayhap they won't even mind the old man's crazy ways."

The colorful man nodded sagely. "True, that. Youth thrives on strangeness." He didn't appear that old himself, but Yeshton was no judge of age. The man leaned near Sir Palan. "Did you hear? A barge has come down river. I'm surprised your friends didn't catch it. They'd already have reached the old keep if they had."

"What brings a barge this far south?" asked Sir Palan, disguising the glint in his eye behind a curious tone.

"Dunno. Supplies, some say. Looked to me like the ghost of a barge. Rumors say when it did reach the keep it was empty, save for the crew, who seemed to have no recollection of anything. Not even what happened to the supplies they were meant to be toting."

"Very mysterious," said Sir Palan, rubbing his chin. "Well, I do appreciate the information. As I'm going that way, should I hear anything interesting I'll be sure to bring it back on my return."

The man grinned. "I can always count on you, Timber. Good luck!" He started away but his step faltered, and he glanced back. "There *is* another rumor. One about a small band wandering southward, bringing with them a storyteller." His tone hung low.

Sir Palan grinned. "Aye? And so I heard, but the tale-weaver was headed west from Rose Province, taking the High Road toward KryTeer. Of course, that rumor comes from the northern provinces and might be old gossip."

The colorful man nodded as his eyes swept over the company with interest. Yeshton's fingers twitched toward his sword but he curled them to resist. He glanced down at Rille and softly spoke. "Wouldn't that be something? A storyteller is worth a hundred minstrels, so I've heard."

Rille looked up at him. "I prefer music myself, brother."

The colorful man lingered a moment longer, then skipped lightly away.

Sir Palan's grin remained and he leaned toward Rille,

his hands gesturing like he told some great joke. His voice was a quiet rumble. "That's Hethek, the village know-all. He keeps a weather eye out for anything that might give him extra coin. I wouldn't trust him as far as I can spit."

"I gathered as much," said Yeshton.

"His trade is cloth, is it not?" asked Jinji. "Quite a festoon he wore."

Sir Palan chuckled. "So he did. That's Hethek for you: a bright and inquiring bother."

The old knight stopped twice more to gather what he called rations, though his food purchases filled every available space in every satchel, save Jinji's.

"The keep is a week's walk from here," Sir Palan said. "We should borrow some horses to get there faster."

Jetekesh gasped. "Yes, please!"

Sir Palan led them to the smith on the edge of Lilac Lake, where he bartered for the lend of five strong mounts and gear. Yeshton expected a protest from Jinji, but when he glanced at the storyteller, he found him beside the mare he would share with Rille, chuckling as the horse ate oats from his hand.

Soon the company headed south.

Keep Falcon was Amantier's last defense against the Drifting Sands, though no one ever invaded from the desert. No one lived there, save the salt miners, and they were Amantieran subjects. Long ago Keep Falcon had been built to defend against a terrible enemy, so Yeshton had heard. But the civilization beyond southern Amantier had been destroyed by the One God in his divine wrath, for it had worshiped magic.

Yeshton considered Jinji astride the horse ahead of

him. Jinji claimed the Drifting Sands were the origin of Shinac. Could that have been the civilization talked of in scripture? Was there truth buried somewhere in the Shingese man's tales?

The company made good time through the day and camped beside the road in the early evening. Among Sir Palan's purchases were new clothes for Jetekesh, plain and rough; but the young king didn't protest.

"Save them until after we spar," said Sir Palan before Jetekesh could slink behind a tree to change.

The prince stared at him. "After we what?"

"Spar. I've seen your movements and I know you have some experience with a broadsword and a fencing blade. But not enough. On the road it's dangerous not to know the basic art of combat. Prepare yourself, sire. I am a strict teacher."

Tifen raced over to stand before Jetekesh. "I will not allow a traitor to duel my king."

Sir Palan smiled faintly. "A worthy argument, my son, but I will teach him, nonetheless. Now, unless you favor a licking as in days of old, move out of my way."

Jetekesh pushed past his protector. "I take no issue with this man, Tifen. Let him teach me. I could gain no better instruction."

Tifen looked stricken, but he bowed and moved silently back. It must be difficult for Tifen to reconcile his feelings toward this mighty legend and the accusations laid against him. Yet shouldn't Tifen know the cunning manipulation of Queen Bareene better than most? Hadn't he spent all fifteen years of Jetekesh's life trying to shield him from the worst of her machinations?

Or did he not see the dangers?

Sir Palan and Jetekesh stepped to the edge of camp. Yeshton rounded the fire to stand near Tifen, who watched his king with furrowed brows.

"Is it true, do you think?" asked Yeshton, keeping his voice low. "Was the queen poisoning her lord husband?"

Tifen glanced at him. "Don't you believe so? Why ask me?"

"Because I want to know what you believe."

The protector fell still. "She is not a woman, but a creature born from the two hells to destroy Amantier. I believe her capable of anything."

"Is that why you feel it's possible she seduced your father despite his honor code?"

Tifen's spine stiffened. "Whether you ask to sate your own curiosity, or to act as an agent on his behalf, I would request you keep out of my family affairs. My issues with my father began long before his public disgrace."

Yeshton nodded. "Your message is clear, friend. But I must say one thing: Many years ago, when I was but a small child, my seaside village was destroyed by fever. It claimed the lives of my parents and my two older sisters. None of the neighboring towns would help for fear of catching the sickness. The port was barred, and ships would not sail near. Sir Palan alone braved the town to discover if anyone survived, and he found me.

"I was brought from Marsh Province to Kavacos, and from thence I became Duke Lunorr's man and settled in Sage Province at Keep Lunorr. I was inspired by your father's bravery and his common blood to become the kind of man he is: a knight for his actions, not for his birthright. That speaks to me of an honorable man, and one to whom I owe my life."

Tifen's face hardened as Yeshton told his story. The protector turned a tight smile on him. "I've heard many such tales from other young men. Do not mistake me, Sir Yeshton. I know that my father is an honorable knight, brave and true under the gravest threats. He does not waver. He does not bend. Queen Bareene likely did not succeed, nor did he wound her. That is clear enough. My personal grievances lie not with his knighthood. I despise him as a father. Always he would charge forth to rescue the unfortunate and right the wrongs inflicted upon peasants. But he was never there for me. What you describe is more of a father than I knew in all my life.

"Take him, Sir Knight. Claim him as your kin. Be to him the son he wanted, for I was only ever a disappointment; and in the end, he forsook me and left so that he could spy and skulk across Amantier, KryTeer, Shing, the Clanslands. Anywhere but his own home. All because my birth caused his beloved wife to sicken and eventually to die — so he feels. But I know differently.

"That most honorable and legendary knight broke my mother's heart each time he went questing. Each time he left us behind, dissatisfied with us, eager for something bigger and better than we could offer to a restless spirit. In the end I know this much: Sir Palan sentenced his wife to death from loneliness."

The protector spat the last words like they burned his tongue, then he turned and stalked into the night, away from the road.

Yeshton stared after him. The protector's voice had risen as he talked, and Yeshton glanced toward the duel to find Sir Palan and Jetekesh standing still, eyes caught on the retreating figure. Sir Palan wore a shattered smile.

A cough broke the silence. Jinji climbed to his trembling feet and stumbled to Sir Palan's side. "He gives voice to the anger of a young man he has never quite outgrown. Go to him, Palan. Speak the words you've longed to say."

The old knight shook his head and turned from Jinji. "It is too late to make amends."

Jinji's strange eyes flashed and he caught Palan's shoulder to whirl him back around.

"If your son were struck dead by an arrow on the morrow, Sir Knight, *then* it would be too late. Where there is life, there is a chance. Take it, rather than the coward's easy path. Such has never been your way. *Go.*"

"I cannot!" Sir Palan's voice grew husky. "My son speaks truth. I did prefer the open roads and fierce battles to the quiet of home. I *was* restless. Mad with it! I couldn't stay still when people needed me. I was a weak and ill-suited husband and father. That Tifen hates me is not upon him. I cannot blame the man. This is my burden to carry. I—"

Jinji's quiet voice cut him off. "A knight's calling is to answer a need; that is so?"

"'Tis."

"Where once you were restless and discontented, now age has settled your soul. Whether you were wrong or right to do as you did in years past has no bearing in this moment. Your son is in need, Sir Knight. The only question you must face now is this: Will you answer Tifen's need? Will you fight for him now as you have fought ever for Amantier?" Jinji lowered his hand to his side. "Sir Palan, *go* to your son. Mend the rift. Do not live with regrets, for life is a fleeting gift, and we cannot know what will cause its end for each of us."

Sir Palan stared into the darkness where Tifen had been swallowed in the lengthening shadows. He looked at Jinji. The furrow of his brow darkened his eyes. Jinji nodded, smiling.

The knight sucked in air, sheathed his sword, and strode after his son.

Jinji turned to Yeshton with a gentle smile. "Well done, Sir Yeshton."

"Why am I commended?"

"You provoked Tifen to an anger he has long kept festering in his heart. Such a thing cannot be allowed silent reign. Having laid his soul bare, his tenderest emotions will give rise to the fondness he thought dead. It will bear him up and aid his father in his own quest to comfort both—" Jinji coughed into his hand, face contorted. He gasped for breath. "I think…I shall sit." He limped to the fireside and sat upon his bedroll.

Rille trotted to his side. "Water." She lifted the flask to him.

Jinji gave her his warmest smile and took a deep drink. "My thanks," he murmured and wiped his mouth.

The little girl watched him with a light in her eyes. Yeshton clenched his teeth until his jaw hurt. Lady Rille could care for whom she pleased, and certainly Jinji Wanderlust had earned his place in her heart. Yeshton was a soldier, not the knight she called him. He had no claim to any devotion.

He took his place near Rille and turned his attention to the fish cooking over the flames. He turned them over and threw on more logs. "We must bypass the keep, I assume?"

Jinji nodded. "If we can, I would prefer it."

Rille shifted beside him. "I am not certain that we can. No matter the route I view in my mind, I see Keep Falcon in our path."

Jinji lowered his eyes and nodded. "Come what may, we will endure it."

∾

EVERY EVENING SIR PALAN DRILLED YOUNG JETEKESH in the art of the broadsword. Yeshton cooked supper while Jinji rested from the hard ride, with Rille nearby in case the storyteller needed anything.

What terms Sir Palan and Tifen had reached, none could say. The old knight maintained his cheerful attitude, and Tifen hovered close to Jetekesh as a protector should but said nothing to anyone. He wouldn't look at Yeshton.

On the fifth night, one day's ride from Keep Falcon, Prince Jetekesh was the first to shatter the unspoken rule.

He nibbled his fish for a while, eyes pinned on Tifen who sat beside him. His scowl grew into a full glare, and he flung his fish to the ground. Yeshton stiffened and choked back a protest. What a waste!

"Tifen," said Jetekesh, "you're a fool, and I can't abide to look at you. Get behind me."

The protector's eyes grew wide. "Sire, if I've done something—"

"Can't you think what you've done?" Jetekesh jabbed

a finger at Sir Palan. "I can guess what happened. Your father begged your forgiveness. He probably bowed before you, looking for all the world like a peasant, and you disdained him. Told him it was too late." The prince's voice caught. "You're a stupid fool, Tifen. At least he's alive! I can't stand to see your face. Until you reconcile with the old knight, keep behind me. I can't bear the pain of it, you piggish, self-righteous, pox-ridden clod. I despise you." He snatched up the fish and began to eat again as his eyes glinted with unshed tears.

Yeshton had wondered whether Tifen cared for his young charge, or if he loathed him. The protector's wounded face answered now: Tifen loved the boy. And was that so surprising? Tifen had been with him since Jetekesh's infancy. Had seen the good and bad alike grow and flourish inside that body. Witnessed the struggle against two philosophies and hoped the king's would win out in the end.

Tifen stood and silently moved to stand behind his lord.

Yeshton hid a smile as he ate. He hadn't expected Jetekesh to bother himself on another man's account, yet the boy was the only person here Tifen might listen to. Was it possible young Jetekesh was growing just a little?

Jinji cleared his throat. "Perhaps a story would chase away the cold."

"Go right ahead," said Jetekesh. "Why don't you tell a tale of a stubborn son unwilling to forgive his long-lost father?"

Tifen bowed his head but otherwise remained stationary.

Jinji's eyes lit up as his voice began to weave the

magic of his words. When the storyteller had imparted his first proper tale back in the hut, Yeshton had seen a vision unfold before him as though he were within the story himself. This time was no different.

A castle of pure white, veined with gold and sparkling with crushed glass and diamonds, arose in Yeshton's mind. Delicate towers stretched to meet the clouds.

The Hold of Valliath, so it was called. Banners streamed in a breeze that smelled of wildflowers and fresh clover. A fair woman with hair of palest yellow leaned upon the hold's outer wall, between the merlons, to wave her handkerchief at a horse cantering along the road. The rider raised his arm in greeting, black hair tousled in the wind, eyes a striking pale blue.

Jinji's lilting voice was like a flute, more music than words, as he unveiled a story of two lovers, one the maiden lady of the hold, the other a knight above the skill of others. Theirs was a love as abiding and deep as the old land itself. They were wed, and the knight became king upon the passing of his bride's father. Nothing could diminish their devotion for each other, save death itself. Alas it struck. A greedy, cunning nobleman lusted after the fair queen, and he stirred war in the north to force the noble king away, where assassins paid by the cruel man took the king's life at the very start of battle.

Yeshton heard the cries of sorrow through the realm of Shinac. The queen grew ill in her grief, but she fought for life and gave birth to her dead husband's child: a son, heir of Shinac. The queen soon wed the greedy nobleman, for a queen could not rule alone, and her child was too young. Blinded by heartbreak, she did not soon enough see the corruption of her new husband until he was already crowned. From that moment hence, he revealed his true colors and tortured his new bride out of spite and jealousy, for the fair queen loved no man but her dead husband.

The wicked king also tortured the infant prince, and through the first years of his life, the little boy with fair hair and pale eyes knew no love save that of his gentle and brave mother, until at last she succumbed to pain and sorrow and joined her lost husband in death. The prince of Shinac, so young and sad, was left alone to face the torment of his stepfather, but his pain was cut short, for the magic of Shinac could not long endure the reign of a corrupt king, and the wicked man grew ill.

A single plant could spare the king, and this the tyrant knew, but he was too weak to obtain the plant himself. The young prince was commanded to bring the cure to the king's bed, and thus he did; but then he merely stood above the bed, *traveria* in his fair young hands, and he watched the evil man die.

True night fell. The young prince remained in the king's chamber until the candles burned out, and a shadow crept close. Yeshton reached out and shouted to warn the prince of danger, but no sound escaped his lips. He watched, helpless. The Shadow grew. Stretched. Consumed.

And the young prince of Shinac vanished.

Jinji's musical voice faltered. Yeshton blinked and found he had been staring into the flames of the campfire. Tears tracked his cheeks, as though he cried the tears of the fair queen and her tiny son.

Jinji spoke again, his voice low and sad. "To this day,

those loyal to the heirs of Shinac have sought the rightful heir of that land, but none have found him."

"But Prince Sharo is looking," said Jetekesh. Yeshton turned to find the prince's face pinched with pain. "He *will* find the rightful prince, won't he?"

"I do not know," answered Jinji softly.

Prince Jetekesh scowled. "You should know. It's your story. It's your silly story!"

"'Tisn't mine, Your Highness. I do not craft these tales. I merely see them, and know them, and tell them. What I have told you is past. Prince Sharo is in the now of days, and so I see his search. But I do not know whether he will be the one to find Prince Ehrikai, heir of that realm. I hope so. I dearly do, for Prince Sharo is the last of that ancient line, cousin to the rightful king of all the fae and beautiful. Should he fail, Shinac will lose its magic before Ehrikai's return."

Sir Palan leaned forward to stoke the fire. "Tell me, tale-weaver. What was the shadow that stole him away?"

"A dark thing," drawled Jetekesh. "Not here at all, but upon some distant star. Isn't that the right of it, Wanderlust?"

"So it is," said Jinji, eyes dancing with firelight. "But he escaped that shadow long ago. Still, he is lost, seeking, ever seeking."

"Seeking home?" asked Yeshton. His voice was loud in his ears.

Jinji looked up. "Nay. Seeking self. Lamenting his loss of it."

A fanciful thought sprouted in Yeshton's head. He smiled. "Do you too seek the lost prince, storyteller?"

Jinji turned his gaze to rest on Yeshton. He sat

silently for a moment or two. "I know where he is. I needn't seek him. I must instead await his return." His eyes traveled back to the fire. "…If there is yet time."

Jetekesh sighed. "But if you know where he is, how does Prince Sharo not know? Is it some great secret? Can you not communicate with your stories or something?"

Jinji stared into the flames. "I have not the power to tell Sharo…yet."

Jetekesh snorted. "Of course not."

Against the following silence Yeshton heard the pop and hiss of burning logs and the faint song of crickets. The trees whispered in the wind. Something rustled in the grass near the road. He tensed and darted to his feet.

"Easy now," said Sir Palan. "No shadows will swallow you up, Yesh."

"Something was out there."

"It was Hethek," answered Jinji. "He came to hear my tale."

Every eye speared the storyteller. He just smiled.

"Tomorrow we will likely meet Lord Milgar's men upon the road, and Hethek's purse will be two hundred kana heavier. We had best sleep."

Yeshton started toward the road. He must find Hethek and strangle the pompous peacock before he came near Keep Falcon.

Quick steps sounded behind him. Jinji's hand fell on Yeshton's shoulder. The soldier started. How did Jinji muster enough strength to move so lithely?

"Do not go, Yeshton. Stay with us tonight. With or without Hethek's interference, the road will be well guarded. He is not the only one upon our very heels.

Should he be compensated for his trouble, it matters not to us."

"The little snake," said Rille. She crossed the camp to grab Jinji's wrist. "Let Sir Yeshton go. Hethek doesn't deserve compensation for selling you out. He deserves to have his ears removed from his head for his trouble."

Jinji laughed. "Do not be so thirsty for blood, Lady Rille. Trouble comes to all. We needn't decide another man's fate; we should worry after our own. Come. Both of you. Let us rest."

Yeshton exhaled and relaxed his shoulders. He and Rille returned to the fire. He could feel her sulking, and the knowledge soothed him a little.

He turned to the storyteller. "You're a reckless fool, Wanderlust."

Jinji's eyes twinkled before he laid on his bedroll and turned over.

Not for the first time, likely not for the last, Yeshton wondered what Jinji intended once he reached the desert wastes.

21
FAIRY WINGS

Two dozen knights stood upon the road, lances lowered. Against the noon sky fluttered the banner bearing a falcon in flight.

"Which of you is Jinji Wanderlust?"

"I am he."

Yeshton shut his eyes and choked back a moan. If Jinji allowed himself to be captured over and over, did he have a goal at all? Or just a mad desire to infuriate every noble in his path?

The lances lifted and the head knight inclined his head. "Lord Milgar requests the pleasure of your company at Keep Falcon, Master Teller. Your friends are likewise welcome. We have come to escort you."

"That is kind of you. My thanks." Jinji's smile was as bright as the sky overhead.

The knights rode at a fast gait, penning the little company in on every side, until Keep Falcon lay in sight. It was a high, hulking beast, made of thick gray stone with parapets and two turrets. The design was crude and functional. A moat surrounded the fortress, green with algae.

The drawbridge rumbled as it lowered.

Yeshton and the rest were led across the moat and into the bailey. A statue adorned the center of the sheltering grounds, perhaps a depiction of Cavalin the Great, hero of a long-ago age. His gaze flicked across the bailey, and he found a small contingent hard at work polishing armor, grooming horses, stocking weapons.

Yeshton glanced at the head knight. "You look ready to march to war."

A wry smile twitched on the knight's lips as he dismounted. "Lord Milgar commands us to be in constant readiness in case of any attacks."

Yeshton dismounted as well. "Are you expecting any?"

The knight shook his head. "But Lord Milgar declares that there shall be, and so we are prepared."

"From KryTeer?"

A laugh broke from the knight's lips. "No, young man. From the desert." He leaned close, eyes sparkling. "Haven't you heard? The fairies are coming." He pulled back, winked, and strode to Jinji's horse to help him down. Yeshton followed to aid Rille.

The company was led into the keep proper. The interior was bare, dusty, and poorly lit by slivered windows along a corridor that ended before a high, narrow chamber swathed in the red colors and Crowned Rose banners of Amantier. A long, crude table occupied the center of the room. At its far end sat a withered old man, white hair haloing his head. He stood, smoothed his lordly raiment, and raised his gnarled hands.

"Welcome, Jinji of Shing. I have ached to meet you."

The storyteller strode ahead of the company until he stood before Lord Milgar. He steepled his hands and bowed at the waist in Shingese fashion. "I am honored by your warm hospitality, my lord."

Lord Milgar stooped to grasp Jinji's wrists until the Shingese man straightened. The lord stared into Jinji's face, old eyes darting back and forth as though he searched for some great secret. Finally, he smiled. "It is true. You *see*, don't you?"

Yeshton and the rest came to stand with Jinji, and the soldier glanced at the storyteller to find his expression drawn in pity.

"My lord," said Jinji quietly, "you should sit down, I think."

"Nonsense." The lord pulled away. "I am pleased by your timing, Master Storyteller. Most pleased. Indeed, it could not be better. The delegates arrived just days ahead of you. Just days." He stepped back, wavered. Steadied and clapped his hands. "Bring them in." He looked again at Jinji, a broad smile on his lips. "You will be very glad to meet them."

"Who are these delegates?" asked Sir Palan.

Lord Milgar's smile stretched into the wrinkles of his face. "Why, the fairies, Sir Knight. The fairies from Shinac, of course."

Yeshton exchanged a glance with Sir Palan. What had the old man mistaken for the fae and fantastic? Doors to the far side of the chamber swung open. The rows of banners hanging from the high rafters rippled as the delegates paraded inside. Rille gasped. Blood drained from Yeshton's face. His heart quavered. Hands clenched into fists.

Three men strode across the Hall, bloodred armor glittering against the gloom; skin rich and dark; long black hair adorned in gems. Curved swords hung from their waists. Cloaks of crimson streamed behind them. Blood Knights of KryTeer, admitted into Keep Falcon by the mad old lord.

The three Knights halted beside Lord Milgar, whose eyes danced with the wonder of them.

"Do you see them, Master Jinji?" whispered Milgar. "Magnificent. Behold their wings." He reached out to stroke the nearest cloak.

The middle Knight studied the company, dark eyes sharp as steel. His gaze lingered long on Jinji. A smile slid across his lips and he raised his arms. "It has been a very long time, Jinji of Shing."

Yeshton jerked his head around.

Jinji's face glowed. "Aredel, you look well! It has been much, much too long, my friend." He walked forward and embraced the KryTeeran.

They laughed. Pulled back. Examined one another.

"You've grown so thin. And pale." The Knight shook his head. "Did I not say the air of KryTeer would be best for your condition?" He brushed his ring-bedecked fingers against Jinji's hair. "It has turned so white. You cannot carry on this way."

Jinji laughed again. "But I must and shall. And you will not interfere, as you promised."

The man called Aredel shrugged his hands. "So I did, and so I have not. But tell me, have you found your blessed Shinac yet?"

Jinji's eyes were bright as a fire. "I am nearly there."

Yeshton's fists clenched until his palms ached. Why did Jinji speak to a Blood Knight, calling him friend, laughing with one of the conquerors of his country?

"You *are* a traitor." It was Jetekesh's voice. High and quavering. The prince shoved past Tifen and caught Jinji's sleeve to wrench him around until their eyes met. "You sold us to the enemy! Traitor!"

Jinji's eyes widened. "Sire—"

"Ah. You are Prince Jetekesh," said the Blood Knight. His tone was cold once more. "I have wished to meet you for several weeks now."

Jetekesh's chin thrust up. "I will not acknowledge the Bloody Knights of KryTeer." He turned away.

The Blood Knight gave a low laugh. "A spirited boy. That is good. You will need it when your mother arrives to fetch you." He flicked a hand toward one of his companions. "Arrest them. All but Jinji." He turned back to the storyteller. "You have saved me a lot of trouble, my friend. I thought I would have to chase them across Amantier for a few months, but you've such a way of attracting people."

Nausea writhed in the pit of Yeshton's stomach. His hand went for his sword.

"Please, Your Highness," said Jinji, eyes fixed on the Blood Knight called Aredel.

Aredel. Yes, that *was* the Blood Prince's name! Yeshton had heard Duke Lunorr say it once, like a curse word. This was High Prince Aredel of the Bloodfold of KryTeer. Jinji Wanderlust knew him. They were friends. So Jinji *was* a spy for the KryTeer Empire. He had betrayed them. Brought them all this way, only to hand them over to the enemy.

Yeshton's vision seared red. He started to draw his sword. He would *kill* Jinji for his betrayal. He would rip him apart!

The sword rang out as it clattered to the flagstones. Yeshton's fingers tingled from the force that had struck the weapon from his grasp. The Blood Prince's sword hovered before his eyes, naked, bright against a strand of sunlight overhead.

"None may harm Jinji of Shing," said the KryTeer conqueror in a quiet rumble. "He is under my protection."

Yeshton lowered his empty hands. His eyes sought out Rille. She stood stricken, pale as death, staring at Jinji in a silent plea.

Jinji was speaking, but no one heeded him. Not Prince Aredel or Jetekesh. Not Tifen, red faced and trembling. Not Sir Palan or the two Blood Knights who fought him, swords drawn and flying through the air. Not Lord Milgar, awestruck by some fantasy only he could see in the violence.

Yeshton could hear nothing. All was mute.

It had all been pointless.

Jinji had sentenced them to death.

22
UNFOLDING VISIONS

As Jinji of Shing entered Aredel's appropriated study, the Blood Prince couldn't help but smile. Jinji always stirred affection within Aredel's heart; a rare feeling for the war-hardened man, and a welcome one. He made him feel almost human.

Jinji approached the desk with gravity in the lines of his pale face. He stopped beside the wingback chair intended for guests.

"Welcome, my friend." Aredel gestured to the chair. "Please, make yourself comfortable."

"I will stand," said Jinji.

"As you please."

"I am very cross with you."

Aredel's smile grew. "Not much angers you. It must be quite a thing I've done."

Time had not been kind to Jinji. While he was a comely man, the prolonged illness of his body had marred Jinji. His flesh was ashen, his frame too thin, his hair—

once a glossy black—now streaked heavily with snowy locks. His movements were slower, more ginger.

"You must not keep my friends," said Jinji. "Be merciful and let them go."

"You would say that of any prisoner I possess, I don't doubt. But I cannot adhere to your wishes in this matter. My word to you is unbreakable, and so I will not trouble you or allow any KryTeeran to hinder you. But the others are of Amantier, and I have conquered this land. Prince Jetekesh is a tool too great to release, even for your sake. I'm sorry, Jinji. You may go as you please, but the rest will remain here."

Jinji sighed and sank into the chair. He looked so weak, so delicate, like he might break apart and float away. Not at all like the strong and clever man Aredel had met five years ago near the shepherd's hut in Shing.

Jinji covered his face with his hands. "They think I have betrayed them."

"That is regrettable." Aredel laced his fingers together and set his hands on the desk. "I will inform them it is not so."

"They shan't believe you." Jinji dropped his hands and straightened to meet Aredel's eyes. "You healed King Jetekesh, did you not?"

Aredel chuckled. "As astute as ever. It is true. I healed the king just in time. *Traveria*. That is what almost killed him."

"I know. The queen…" Jinji's soft murmur was nearly indistinct.

Aredel shook his head. "You are the cleverest man I've ever met. I wish you would return to KryTeer with me. You would be revered as a god."

"It is not cleverness that affords me this knowledge, and no such gift should be awarded so. I merely understand people."

"The humble shepherd emerges." Aredel leaned forward. "I beseech you one last time: Come to KryTeer. Let my House care for you until the end. It would…grant some peace of mind. Do it for me, if not for yourself."

Jinji's eyes found the candlelight. Those warm, discerning eyes; so strange in a Shingese; so unsettling in all they saw and all they hid. "I must refuse, Aredel. My quest bids me to enter the Drifting Sands, where I hope to find what I seek."

"The Drifting Sands have been searched for innumerable years, Jinji. There is no hint, no remnant of Shinac. Stronger men than you have tried and died in that harsh climate. Give it up." He knew his words fell on deaf ears. Even above himself, Jinji was the most stubborn creature Aredel had ever met.

"I must go." The light of Jinji's eyes burned like fire. "Come with me. Come to the border of that realm and see if I am not right." He leaned against the wide chairback. "My strength is almost spent. Time grows short. Lord Peresen will soon make his move. I sense it." His eyes closed. His breaths hitched in his lungs.

Aredel studied the storyteller's face. Jinji's disease was a brutal one. Even in KryTeer, where cunning healers discovered cures each day for rare illnesses, this one, so rare itself, yet had no hope. It began in the lungs, much like the White Death, but it stayed contained. It brought fevers. Nightmares. Weakened limbs, as though nutrition could not be absorbed into the body. The strain of it turned hair lank and gray. In a year, or sooner, the victim died of a kind of starvation of body and spirit.

But Jinji was different. He had lived five years with the disease, and something kept him moving. His hair, too, turned white rather than gray, and his eyes had not lost their strength. It was as though something buoyed Jinji up until he reached his goal.

Aredel longed to take Jinji to KryTeer, far from the legends of Shinac, far from the chance to find what he sought. Perhaps it would prolong Jinji's life.

But Aredel knew better than that. Jinji was close to the Drifting Sands. So near to his heart. No one could take him from here now.

"I will come with you," whispered Aredel, though Jinji had fallen asleep.

～

JETEKESH WOULDN'T TALK TO ANYONE.

Yeshton brooded in a corner of the keep's dungeon.

Tifen paced.

Sir Palan paced too.

Rille watched them as she wiped tears from her eyes. It made no sense. Not any of it.

Jinji wouldn't betray them. He would *not*.

She stamped her foot. Against the stone floor, the sound was a mere scuff. "I won't believe it."

Yeshton turned toward her, the only one obligated to listen. "My lady?"

"Jinji wouldn't do that, Sir Yeshton. He only wants to find Shinac; I'm certain of it." Compassion lit in the soldier's eyes as the hard lines of his face softened in the torchlight. She scowled. "You don't believe me."

"I'm sorry, my lady, but the man led us straight into the arms of KryTeer. He *knows* the Blood Prince. They're friends."

She folded her arms. "So are we. We're his friends too."

Tifen spoke up. "We were tools. A means of ingratiating himself to his prince. Don't forget, Shing was conquered by KryTeer several years ago. He owes the emperor of KryTeer his fealty."

"It's just like Mother said." Jetekesh turned from the wall. "She said he was a spy of KryTeer, selling sedition. Making up those horrible stories about lost princes and ugly peasants. And fairies who live in willow trees. Ha!"

"But they weren't horrid stories." Rille stalked across the small dungeon room, clapped her hands to Jetekesh's face, and jerked his head up to face her. "They were beautiful tales. So beautiful I could *see* them. Couldn't you? How could a spy of KryTeer conjure such a thing? Jinji didn't betray us. Just because he knows the Blood Prince doesn't mean he meant to lead us to him. How could Jinji possibly know he would be here ahead of us?"

"The lass has a fair point." Sir Palan's voice.

"Don't you start," Tifen growled. "Your allegiance is also in question."

Yeshton moved from the corner. "Now is not the time for us to lose our tempers. We need to think rationally and try to escape."

The soldier's voice struck a familiar chiming note inside Rille's head. He had triggered a vision, as voices sometimes did, when a Keyword was spoken. Not unlike

Jinji's unfolding stories, an image formed in her mind's eye, and Rille saw clouds of sand billowing before her. She tasted salt. Wind stroked her hair. The banner of KryTeer and the banner of Amantier stood side by side, while between them rose a great tree.

Rille sank to her knees. Yeshton crouched at her side.

"My lady?"

"Never fear, Sir Knight. I think we will not be long in this dungeon." She smiled. "Jinji will yet take us to the Drifting Sands. I have seen it."

23

THE CURSE

Queen Bareene stepped down from the coach and looked up at the looming fortress before her. Soldiers flanked the path that led to the oak door of Keep Falcon, their armor brilliant in the morning sunlight. She smiled and allowed Foan, a capable and lovesick knight who traveled with her, to guide her up the few steps.

Here at last. A source had told her that her son hid within the keep. Thank the saints he'd had the sense to hole up here, though it was a strange destination to be sure. The Amantieran flag above the keep assured Bareene she had gotten here before any KryTeer Knights. She would show the Blood Prince that she was every bit as clever as he. Perhaps even more clever.

Old Lord Milgar waited inside. "Fair as the fae princesses of Shinac, my lady queen," he crooned.

Bareene offered a tight smile. She had outlawed all mention of that blasted fairy story! But Milgar was senile and couldn't help himself. *Keep your temper, Bareene.*

"You are too kind, my lord." She glanced around the Hall. "Where is my son? I've come to bring him home."

Milgar's vacant smile stretched. "I have no sons here, Lady Queen. Only the fairies."

She fought to keep her expression composed, but her voice sounded strained even to herself. "Of course you have no sons, but mine came to see the fairies, Lord Milgar."

Steps echoed across the Hall behind Bareene.

"He is not with the fairies, Your Majesty."

That voice! Bareene whirled to find Jinji crossing the room. The Shingese peasant stopped before her and bowed.

"Jinji Wanderlust. I'd heard you would be here."

"Your Majesty, you look well."

That was more than could be said for the storyteller. He was so thin and haggard Bareene feared he might drop on the spot, gasping his last breaths.

"Never mind myself," said Bareene. "Where is Prince Jetekesh? I've come for him. He fled before he understood the situation in Kavacos." She smiled, showing teeth. "And you will return with us, Wanderlust. I believe you missed your trial."

Jinji shook his head. "I cannot return to the capital, Lady Queen. Nor shall you take Jetekesh back with you. He will come with me to the Drifting Sands."

Bareene tilted her head to one side, fingers flexing. "Your impudence will be your death, taleteller. What right have you to keep my son from me?" She drew near to Jinji. He wasn't tall; she barely had to look up into his eyes. "I understand now. My son didn't flee; he was taken. You kidnapped the Crown Prince of Amantier. You will burn for this, Jinji of Shing."

"He will *not* burn for any reason, Bareene."

The authoritative voice was like a stab wound in Bareene's chest. She spun, skirts rustling, to find High Prince Aredel standing beside Lord Milgar. What was *he* doing here? Why had none of the guards alerted her to his presence?

Foan's hand went for his blade, but he hesitated. Bareene could understand why. Amantier was a conquered nation; to defend his queen against the heir of KryTeer was now treason.

Aredel strode forward and halted a few feet from her, his tall frame imposing in the dimly lit chamber. "You were not allowed to leave Kavacos, yet you disobeyed me."

"I came for my son." Bareene's mind reeled. Why would Aredel be here? How had he gotten here ahead of her? The barges, of course! She had refused to ride in one, for it was filthy. But the Blood Prince wouldn't bat an eye; the people of KryTeer loved boats of any kind.

"You won't have him." Aredel's tone was frigid.

"You can't keep my son from me."

"I can keep anything and everything from you. You are a lowly queen of a KryTeer province now, my lady. I owe you nothing, but you owe me everything you wear, eat, breathe, or even think. That you live is proof of my tolerance. That I do not allow you to see your son is my prerogative."

Heat swept through Bareene's body, burning her eyes, perspiring on her brow. Her limbs shook. "You will *not* keep my own son from me!"

"But I will." Aredel's lips curled in a wicked smile. "Will you not ask me my reasoning?"

Her teeth clenched. "Why then?"

"'Why then, Your Imperial Highness'—that is how you will address me, Queen."

"Why then, Your Imperial Highness?"

"That is better. It is for two reasons. The first is your treatment of Jinji, who is my friend."

Bareene's eyes widened. "That ill-bred waif?"

The ice in Aredel's eyes glittered. "Just so. My second reason is *traveria*. While I can understand discontentment within the institution of marriage, I find it offensive to murder one's own spouse. Should I discover such plotted treachery in my own harem, I would consider it cause for severe punishment."

Bareene threw out her chin. "How *dare* you accuse me again of such an act! And to compare me to a KryTeer harem—"

The Blood Prince laughed. "I do so enjoy your display of piety. Never fear, my lady queen. You are not compared to a KryTeer harem, for your own habits are not so exclusive as that, and I would not sully the women of my House so. Ledonn."

From the shadows stepped Prince Aredel's armored attendant. He bowed. "My holy prince?"

"See that the queen is escorted to the dungeon. For Jinji's sake, allow Bareene to bid her son farewell. On the morrow, Lady Queen, you will die."

A chill swept from Bareene's head to her toes. "B-but I've done nothing to warrant—"

Prince Aredel raised his hand. "We will not discuss the ways in which you have warranted my decree. Suffice it to say, I have had others executed for lesser sins." His eyes were cold. Glacial. As impregnable, as heartless, as a great fortress. The finality of his tone crumpled Bareene to her knees.

"Holy Prince of KryTeer, do not condemn me to death. I will serve you faithfully. I will please you—"

The prince's attendant pulled her to her feet. "This way."

Jinji pushed past her. "Aredel, you cannot kill her like this. Consider mercy."

The prince's voice carried across the room. "I did, for your sake. But it was not enough, Jinji. Not even your pleas will spare her. Keep your strength for better fights."

Bareene wrenched against Ledonn's arms. Bruises formed against her flesh; his grip was a vise. She threw her head back and screamed: "Curse you, Blood Prince! Curse you to the deepest depths of two hells! The One God will smite you!"

Laughter rang in her ears long after she was dragged from the Hall. Along a stone corridor. Down a flight of narrow steps. Into the rank passage of a dungeon.

"This way, Lady Queen." Ledonn pulled her through another short passage to a rotting wood door. He pushed her against the filthy surface and slid open the eye portal to let her see into the cell.

Five figures huddled within the straw-strewn chamber. All raised their heads to study the door. There. Jetekesh leaned against the far wall.

He leapt to his feet, eyes wide. "Mother?"

"Jetekesh, my son!" She tried to slip her hand between the bars of the tiny window. Only her fingers could reach inside.

He stumbled past his fellow prisoners and hovered near, but he didn't stretch for her touch. "Why are you here, Mother?"

"I came to take you home." Tears pricked her eyes. "Jetekesh, my little boy, the Blood Prince has sentenced us to death."

Ledonn chuckled. "Not the prince, Bareene. Only *you*."

Jetekesh's eyes widened more. "Death? But why? You sold Amantier to KryTeer. Why would he kill you?"

Tears rolled down Bareene's cheeks. "Because I wouldn't give you up, Jetekesh. Because he knew I would make you emperor of KryTeer. That was my plan all along, you see. You do see, don't you? I did all of this for you, my baby boy. I groomed you to be the greatest ruler in all Nakania. Not just a king. Emperor, Jetekesh! You would rule all!"

Jetekesh searched her face. "Liar. You foul, greedy liar." He took a step back. "*You* wanted to rule *through* me. You would do anything to control the world. You murdered Father because he was in the way. You don't love me, Mother. You only love you. What of me you do profess to love is what you crammed into me. I hate you. *I hate you.*" He turned away. "I'm glad you're going to die. I'm *glad.*" His shoulders trembled.

Bareene stared. Tears dripped down her cheeks. For a moment she thought of lying, of telling him all the things he wanted to hear, but anger teemed inside her stomach. "Fool. You foolish, foolish boy! Just like your father. I could have given you the world, but you chose to run — run away from all I offered. Yes, I would use you. Of course I would. What else is a child good for? But you could have enjoyed the fruits of my labor. All you had to do was let me lead you. Stupid child!"

His shoulders hunched. He shrank into himself. How ugly he looked in the weak light. How filthy, bruised, battered. He'd grown so thin. So feeble. Nothing of herself remained in that fragile creature. How disappointing.

"My daughter would not have failed me," she whispered.

Jetekesh whirled. His eyes flashed like lightning. *"Your daughter is dead!"* The fury died. Pity swelled in its stead. Horrid, humiliating pity. "And so are you," he said in tones too calm to be right. How could he be calm? She had been sentenced to death. Would he let her end this way?

Traitor. Fool. Her tool was broken.

"It seems you've lost, Bareene."

That voice.

She tore her eyes from Jetekesh. There, older, careworn, but still the cut of a strong man. "Palan?"

The knight smiled grimly within his dungeon cell. "Your son will be king, Bareene. I will see to that. But he will not rule beneath your thumb. He will be greater than ever you could make him, and he'll do it without subterfuge or treachery."

He dared to mock her? Oh, how he had always mocked her! That noble-hearted, saintly, pious man. The only man she'd ever wanted and never obtained. With a piercing scream, she lurched at the door. Splinters stabbed her fingers as she clawed at the wood. "Let me in there! I will not let him treat me so! I am queen! I AM QUEEN!"

Ledonn held her. She hollered and shrieked. How had it come to this? How had she lost everything on the very threshold of gaining all?

That storyteller! Everything had gone well until he appeared in Amantier. First her husband and then her son had fallen under his spell. Even the Blood Prince wished to protect that wretched peasant. She would *kill* him!

She sank against the Blood Knight. He sighed and bent to lift her in his arms. She shoved hard against him. The man stumbled backward.

Bareene bolted down the corridor.

The next corridor.

Up the stairs.

She had always been a swift runner. She could outstrip most in a contest. Though she heard the thundering of boots against the stones behind her, she smiled to herself. She would reach Jinji before Ledonn reached her. Bursting through the doors of the Hall, she sought the Blood Prince. There, still speaking with Jinji. Triumph rolled through her like a strong drink. She sprinted forward, feet light in her slippers, nails raised like claws, torn and bloodied.

Die. Die, Jinji!

His spell must break! Jetekesh would be hers again. The Blood Prince would see reason. The world would right itself.

Jinji trotted toward her. The Blood Prince looked on, calm, heedless of danger. The fool!

The storyteller was so near, so very near.

His eyes danced with pity, just like Jetekesh.

"Curse you, curse you!" She reached up to choke him, claw out his eyes, tear him to shreds.

Pain bloomed in her chest. She looked down. A blade protruded from her dress, red with blood. A sword. But how? She had beaten Ledonn. The Blood Prince was still yards away. Jinji stood before her, unarmed, eyes wide. He reached out and caught her, eased her to kneel against the floor.

"Hush, shh."

Tears burned her eyes. Looking up, neck craning, she found the second Blood Knight, Shevek, just behind her, the sheath at his hip empty. The blade in his hand dyed red.

"I'm dead?" she whispered.

Jinji stroked her cheek. "You are dying, Lady Queen."

She reached up and wrapped her fingers around his throat. Squeezed. He gently pried them loose.

"No need, my lady. I will die soon too."

She gasped for air. "Good."

"I am sorry for you," he said in such gentle tones, like a murmuring brook.

She coughed a laugh. "Why?"

"Because you didn't mean to become what you are. But you realized so late what you were becoming, and you thought it was impossible to change. You were wrong to think so, but no one told you as much."

The pain was fading. She could hear him still, but Jinji's voice was far away.

"Stay away from…my son…"

"I cannot promise that. But I do promise to aid him, my lady. To save him from your fate if he will let me."

She tottered. The ceiling lay before her now. Darkening.

"Be at peace, my lady."

"I hate you," she whispered.

"I forgive you for it."

She reached for anger, but numbness answered. She couldn't lift her head. Couldn't find his eyes. "Curse you."

"That has already been done." A warm hand caught hers. Gently squeezed. "Rest. You will soon leave this world."

Her eyes burned hot. Blurred. "Not yet."

"We cannot choose our time. But I understand your fear. I cannot promise your end will be sweet. But you must go just the same. Do not linger, Queen. This world is not meant for the dead."

She spat out a bitter laugh. It tasted like iron. "This world is not meant…for the…living either…"

She closed her eyes. Felt herself falling. Falling.

Fallen.

24
THE DRIFTING SANDS

"You truly know the art of making enemies, Jinji." Aredel strode forward to stand above the dead queen. He smiled. "I confess I feel better about her death this way. Execution is far too formal and far too public, and I face enough of that in KryTeer. I had hoped she would be foolish. In the end, she did not disappoint."

"So I thought," said Ledonn, as he moved from the back of the Hall. "And she looked so furious, I suspected she might wish to vent."

Shevek laughed. "Chivalrous as Cavalin of old! Are you certain you were not simply careless, Ledonn?"

The other man smiled. "She was clever, but not clever enough. To presume she could outrun a Blood Knight if he wished to catch her? Ignorant sow."

Aredel knelt beside Jinji, prompting his men to lower themselves to the floor. The Blood Prince rested a hand on the storyteller's shoulder and felt it tremble. "Jinji, my friend?"

The Shingese man lifted his head. Aredel started. Tears tracked down his face, and his smile looked broken. "I weep for this woman, as I wept for my mother, Aredel. Both were selfish, ambitious, loathsome creatures, incapable of love or kindness. Who could be more pitiable than they?"

"No one," said Aredel to soothe Jinji. Personally, he found such creatures undeserving of pity or mercy or any other tender feeling this peculiar, kindly soul could give. Yet that's what set Jinji apart from Aredel. He wouldn't want the humble man to be any other way. "Come, my friend. You've wept long enough for her damned soul. Let me introduce you to someone who deserves your smile. I believe the two of you will be friends, though it may cost me something to allow it."

He offered his hand and pulled Jinji to his unsteady feet.

The storyteller's eyes shone through his tears. "Did you bring King Jetekesh with you then?"

Aredel chuckled as he shook his head. "Never can a man surprise you, O astute one. Could you not pretend ignorance now and then?"

Jinji laughed. "My apologies, Aredel. But I recall well the price of deceiving you."

Memories flickered in Aredel's mind, warm with nostalgia. "How you grate upon a man's patience. I wished at that time to skin you and wear your strange eyes for jewels."

Jinji's laugh was like the crystal chimes of Rahajardaj Temple back home. "Do you not now wish the same upon occasion?"

Aredel shrugged. "The thought does cross my mind in your stubborn moments. I suppose you expect me to honor your word and let Prince Jetekesh attend you in the desert?"

Those bright eyes glittered with nothing short of cunning. Had circumstances been different, had fate not made Jinji live the life of a shepherd, Aredel almost feared the course the storyteller might have taken. Surely their paths would still have merged, but under far uglier conditions than what they'd been. And that was a feat.

The Blood Prince led Jinji from the Hall, Shevek and Ledonn following. The procession strode up into the west tower of Keep Falcon, and to the westmost chamber. The King of Amantier sat upon his bed when the Blood Prince stepped into the room.

"How do you feel this morning, Your Majesty?"

King Jetekesh shrugged. "Your Imperial Highness, I am better. And my son?"

"Brooding, I suspect. I am here about another matter, though it does relate to your son."

King Jetekesh arched his eyebrow. "Indeed?"

Prince Aredel stepped aside and allowed Jinji to slip past him into the room.

"Greetings, Your Majesty." Jinji touched his hands together and bowed at his waist.

The king's faint smile broadened until his teeth showed. "It has been too long, Jinji."

Aredel blinked. "You know each other?"

Jinji nodded. "We met once when King Jetekesh visited Shing at the end of the Amantieran occupation. He and his guards reined in at the lake near my home, on their return to Amantier, and I told them stories while they camped for one night."

"Quite the tales they were, too," said King Jetekesh with a chuckle. "I dearly loved to hear of the poor lost knights." He shook his head, smiling at his own thoughts; but the smile slipped, and his eyes flicked between Jinji and the Blood Prince. "It appears, Master Storyteller, you are acquainted with all the great powers of this world. Most impressive for a shepherd. My wife, alas, does not care for your stories; she won't be pleased to see you when she reaches the keep."

"She already has, Your Majesty," said Prince Aredel as Jinji's smile fell. "Upon her arrival, your late wife attempted to murder Master Jinji, and so my men dispatched her. I would offer my condolences, but I doubt you perceive my news as a loss to yourself, except perhaps in the matter of justice. But you will understand when I say that my orders dictate none shall harm those under my protection, and Jinji is my friend."

The king stared at the Blood Prince for several heartbeats. Disbelief lined his eyes and set his jaw. He bowed his head and fingered the fabric of his travel tunic. "She is dead. You're certain?"

"Quite."

"And my son?"

"Alive. He has given me no cause to alter that yet, and Jinji speaks on his behalf."

King Jetekesh's brow drew together. "Why would you speak for my son, storyteller?"

Jinji's gentle smile returned. "You have a good-hearted boy, Your Majesty. He is confused, but he wishes to do right. He believes you are dead, and his grief has been terrible. So too has been the depth of his torment upon learning of his mother's treachery. I want to help him in any way that I may."

The king nodded, eyes lowered in contemplation. He swallowed and looked up. "What happens now, Imperial Highness? I've long wondered what you intend in all this. I had thought to confront my own wife concerning all she's done, and I'd spent the week coming here planning my strategies. It seems, however, that you have your own schemes, and I must ask what fate you would weave for my son and myself? It must be something grand to spare our lives."

Prince Aredel cupped his hands behind his back. "It is true that I have been scheming. I always scheme, Majesty. In truth, my purpose in keeping you alive was to spite your lady wife, but as I nursed you, my desires deepened. I have saved you, and thus you owe me *shamalheer*—a life debt, you would call it, I think."

The king's eyes narrowed further. "Go on."

"I require one service of you, King Jetekesh, and then I shall call your debt repaid. But it is a matter to discuss at another time. Tomorrow Jinji must enter the Drifting Sands and your son will attend him per the storyteller's request. We too will go and wait upon the border of the desert."

"Everyone within the dungeon must come with me," said Jinji. "They will not be left here to sicken in the dark below."

"They think you've betrayed them, Jinji. They won't want to go with you."

Jinji shook his head. "It matters not. Let them come."

"I told you no once before."

The storyteller's lips tugged in a smile. "This time say yes. It is really that simple."

Aredel laughed and shook his head. "Only you, shepherd of Shing, can persuade the Blood Prince of KryTeer to undo what he commands. But I will accede because you are my friend—and because I am curious. We shall all attend you to the border of the Drifting Sands, and there we shall learn what you are all about."

The light in Jinji's eyes brightened into a twinkle. "Do not presume so much, Friend Aredel. You shall see only what you shall see."

~

Subterfuge was no longer necessary, and so the flags of Keep Falcon were replaced. Amantier's banners were folded and stored, and the Winged Sword of KryTeer was raised to stream in the wind. The soldiers around the keep removed their silver armor and donned the bloodred of the Empire. Keep Falcon had been the southern torch of KryTeer since it was taken three years before by the Blood Prince's men under the very nose of the snooping Sir Palan. It pleased Aredel to at last reveal his handiwork.

Queen Bareene was buried behind the keep without pomp or ceremony. Aredel denied King Jetekesh's request for a stone to mark her grave.

His reason was simple. "In KryTeer an unfaithful woman is drawn, quartered, and burned into ash to then be mixed in bitter wine and imbibed by the men with whom she dallied. Be thankful I haven't the time to spend on formalities."

Aredel also oversaw the execution of Queen Bareene's traveling companion. Sir Foan was buried beside the queen, having been spared the aforementioned formalities himself.

Shevek saw to the organization of a caravan for the journey to the Drifting Sands. They would leave the next morning and travel through the heat until eventide, when they should reach the border of the wastes. Aredel found himself annoyed that the journey must be delayed, but preparation was important. There was always risk near the desert, and especially now. He could taste the approaching army on the cool winds tonight. Lord Father had sent Anadin at last.

"You are grim," said Jinji, coming up behind Aredel on the keep's outer wall.

Aredel glanced at him. "And you are pale. You should be resting."

"I have rested all day." Jinji leaned against the nearest raised merlon. "What troubles you this night, Prince Aredel?"

"So formal." Aredel tried a smile, but it felt heavy and he let it fall. "My father is sending Anadin to kill me."

Jinji's brow drew. "Will he reach the keep soon?"

Aredel shrugged. "You're the one with true sight. You must tell me if anyone knows."

"That is not how my vision works. I'm afraid I am not useful in this matter."

Aredel turned from the storyteller and leaned against the crenel to stare out into the growing shades of night. For a time neither man spoke. Wind danced with the banners overhead. The murmur of the watch floated in the air. Torches guttered against the keep's imposing face.

"Are you afraid?" Aredel asked at last.

"To die? No." Jinji pushed free of the merlon and moved to Aredel's side. He sagged against the crenel and stared down at the moat. "Not anymore."

"But you were?" Aredel glanced at Jinji to study the man's profile. "Why? You of all people have no cause to fear death. What sins have you committed?"

Jinji's faint smile was wry. "A coward's sin, perhaps. I have been running."

"You had no choice."

"That isn't what I mean. That I've made powerful enemies does not frighten me. My own feelings do. Aredel, sometimes…" He drew a deep breath. "Sometimes I feel so angry. So *resentful*."

Aredel turned away and fought against a laugh. "Oh, Jinji. How human you sound. You condemn yourself for the very thing that makes you so endearing to me. If another man harbors the same anger or resentment, you soothe and comfort him and tell him all will mend itself in time. But you aren't allowed these same feelings? And all this time I've thought you a humble man."

"Not so," said Jinji. "I am a proud creature. I demand much of myself, and it is a torment."

"You *were* such a man on the day we met, but not now. Now you are caught in your memories as you look back upon your life, aware that it is winding down. But you conquered your demons long ago, my friend. These feelings you have fled from—they don't exist any longer. The wrath in your eyes has burned away. Only injustice reignites that long-ago fire, and only in the matters of those around you. Do you still hate your father?"

Jinji sighed. "No. No, thank the spirits of the earth. I reconciled with him at his graveside."

"He is dead?"

"For two years now."

"*Hashab* keep his tainted soul," spat Aredel.

Jinji laid a hand on his shoulder. "No need to speak ill of the dead."

Aredel laughed. "So you also said that day in Shing. But your tone is kinder now. How we've both grown. You, into the meek lamb of summer days. I, into the ice-crusted fortress of bloody conquest. We could not be more different from one another than we are."

"And does that matter?" Jinji leaned further out on the crenel and pointed at a distant dark line. "There, Aredel. The southern road. My path is straight before me. And, as you promised yesteryear, we shall go the last stretch together. I had not thought it possible at the time, for I'd just learned you were the high prince of KryTeer with a separate destiny upon your broad shoulders. But destiny is a strange thing: not set in stone like the works of man, but vast and endless, like the distant stars whose guiding flames endure long after death." He turned his eyes skyward, but the heavens were cradled in clouds that hid the stars from view.

He sighed. "This night seems endless."

∽

JETEKESH SHIVERED AS HE AND HIS COMPANIONS stepped out into the chill breeze of early morning. He exchanged a glance with Rille as they were left to stand beside a wagon. A long procession of wagons, soldiers, servants, and a large, screened palanquin lined in gold gleamed in the dawn light. Jinji stood beside the palanquin, speaking with someone hidden beneath a heavy cloak. The storyteller broke from his conversation to look toward the prisoners, and Jetekesh jerked his head away.

The crunch of footfalls against the gravel drive came near. Jetekesh resisted looking until curiosity drove his gaze back toward the palanquin. Sure enough, Jinji strolled toward him, eyes smiling.

"My friends, I am glad you are free of the dungeon."

"No thanks to you, traitor," said Tifen.

Jetekesh nodded his vehement agreement.

Jinji's smile softened. "I do not blame you for your feelings, Tifen, son of Palan."

The protector stiffened.

"Easy now," said Sir Palan, stepping forward. "No cause to squabble. It will only harm us." He looked down at Jinji with a grave frown. "You deceived us, Jinji."

"That, I never did."

"Jinji speaks the truth," said Rille. "His friendship with the Blood Prince did not cause our capture. I know it."

Jetekesh snorted. "You guess it only, cousin."

Footsteps crunched behind the party. Jetekesh glanced toward the sound to find the Blood Prince striding their way. He was dressed in bloodred armor and his dark eyes appeared the same red color under the morning sun.

"Jinji of Shing speaks true, Amantierans. He did not expect me to be here ahead of your company, nor did he wish me to keep you imprisoned. It is at his behest that you will travel now with us to the Drifting Sands."

Jetekesh whirled back to face Jinji. "Why? Why have us come?"

The storyteller's eyes filled with something like pain. He opened his mouth to answer, but coughs broke through his words. He doubled over and sank to his knees, gasping between fits.

Jetekesh stared, alarm ringing in his mind. The Blood Prince trotted past the party and knelt beside Jinji. He murmured soothing words until the fit passed. When Jinji lifted his head at last, Jetekesh was startled to find his hair whiter than before; indeed, it was more white than black now.

"We must move," said the Blood Prince. He pulled Jinji to his feet without any effort. "Shevek, Ledonn, get the prisoners into the wagon."

Jetekesh allowed himself to be herded. Mother was dead; he'd been told so the day before. She had tried to kill Jinji, and for that she'd been cut down. Now Jinji was dying. That was no longer in question. It was only a matter of when it would occur.

Just as well. Jetekesh slumped down in the wagon and buried his head in his hands. He envied them. Why must everyone leave him behind?

Feet thumped past him into the wagon, and he glanced up. Rille sat nearby. Tifen took Jetekesh's other side. Sir Palan claimed a place across from him, along with Sir Yeshton. Jetekesh buried his face again. Another set of boots sounded against the heavy wood of the rocking wagon-bed.

Would Jinji ride with them after all?

Jetekesh looked up.

The cowled man stood before him, outlined by the golden sky above. "Kesh?"

Jetekesh recoiled from the familiar nickname. His back slammed into the wagon's high wall. Who would dare to use Father's pet name for him?

The man knelt and Jetekesh could see into the shadows of the cowl. A man's face. Father's face. Impossible.

The ghost smiled. "Hello, Kesh." A finger lifted to his lips. "Don't react. Few know of my presence here, and Prince Aredel insisted it remain that way for now. But I'm here, Kesh. It's really me. The rumors of my death were false."

"Impossible."

Father shook his head, a smile on his lips, color in his skin. "Not so, son. I'm better now. The Blood Prince saved my life."

"Your Majesty," whispered Tifen, and he shifted to drop into a low bow.

"None of that for now, Tifen," said Father. "Formalities will give me away. I am merely a foreign guest of the Blood Prince at present. Best to call me Setwesh, as Prince Aredel does in company with others."

Jetekesh reached out. He caught the cloak in his hand and tugged. Father reached up and took his hand. Squeezed it. It was *his* hand. *His* smile. *His* blue eyes.

With a cry, Jetekesh threw himself against Father's chest and sobbed. "I thought…"

"I know," whispered the king, wrapping his arms, so strong and steady, around Jetekesh. "But I'm here now,

Kesh. I won't leave you again, not for many years to come. Shh."

The wagon rolled forward with a jolt and a shout from the driver. The caravan was underway.

Jetekesh didn't care. He could go anywhere now, be anywhere, even in the very heart of KryTeer, and he wouldn't fear or complain. Father was alive. Jetekesh wasn't alone. The dearest man in the world was here, holding him, soothing him. Alive.

∽

THE DESERT SHONE LIKE GOLD IN THE SUNSET. Jetekesh had never seen its like before. When courtiers back home mentioned the southern wastes, the prince had always pictured a barren land, cracked and dead. But the Drifting Sands were dazzling beneath the red-streaked evening sky.

A Blood Knight herded him and his companions from the wagon. Already High Prince Aredel and Jinji stood at the border into the desert, where wild grass ended all at once and sand began. The wind too was strange. A faint breeze stirred in the grassland, while within the desert high winds howled and thrashed, lifting the sand to dance against the sky.

"I would venture to call this more than mere drifting sands," murmured Sir Palan. "Why not raging sands or a desert tantrum?"

Yeshton grunted his agreement.

Lord Milgar wandered nearby. "The fairies are unsettled."

Jinji spoke to the Blood Prince, but his voice was too soft for Jetekesh to hear.

Prince Aredel nodded and turned to face the caravan. "Set up camp here."

"What happens now?" asked Sir Yeshton of the old knight.

Sir Palan shook his head. "'Tis any man's guess."

A faint moan brought Jetekesh's attention to Rille, who stumbled as she held her head.

Sir Yeshton stepped to her side at once. He caught her arm to steady her. "My lady?"

"Sir Knight, I saw a force of great strength descending upon us from the northwest. It will soon be here."

Sir Yeshton looked up in alarm. "Should we tell the Blood Prince?"

Sir Palan's face was lined with worry. "I'm unsure."

"He is coming toward us," said Tifen.

Father stepped from the concerned circle and approached Prince Aredel.

"Trouble is coming this way," Jetekesh heard him say.

The Blood Prince nodded as Father's voice lowered until his words were indistinct. Jetekesh stared. Was Father bespelled somehow? To warn the Blood Prince, to confide in him Rille's secret sight, was ludicrous.

The king and the high prince approached Rille.

"How far off?" asked Prince Aredel.

Rille shook her head. "I don't know. But close, or I would not have seen it just now. I most often see threats when they are very near."

The Blood Prince nodded and moved away, steps firm

even in the tall grass. "Jinji, when must you enter the desert?"

"Near noon tomorrow, I believe."

"Very well." Prince Aredel moved away to bark orders at his soldiers while servants pitched great tents in bright colors. Fine foods were unloaded from the other wagons and toted into the shade of the tents while musicians unpacked instruments.

It was like a royal outing back home, and for a moment Jetekesh could almost pretend nothing had changed since then. But the banners flirting overhead were the red and black of KryTeer, rather than the gold and red of Amantier, and the music was the strains of foreign lands, unfamiliar and peculiar. The food was a mixture of Amantier and KryTeer cuisine.

Jetekesh, Father, and the rest of the prisoners were permitted to sup with the Blood Prince, his two attendants, old Lord Milgar, and Jinji Wanderlust in the largest tent. The canvas doors had been tied aside, and strange, lightweight netting hung in the doorway to keep away insects and invite the breeze.

Seated upon plush cushions over an ornate rug, Jetekesh ate with a relish, despite his wariness in company with the enemy. He avoided any food he didn't know, after Tifen reacted strongly to a dish he described as terribly spicy. Father too had a healthy appetite, and Jetekesh's heart soared as he watched the king put down several heaping platefuls.

Jinji was solemn where he sat at the head of the tent, at a long table set on short legs over an intricately woven rug. Jetekesh watched the Blood Prince try to converse with the storyteller several times, but while Jinji answered softly, his eyes always returned to the desert view beyond the screen. As Jetekesh studied him, Jinji blinked and turned his head. Their eyes met. The storyteller smiled. Jetekesh looked away. What did it matter to him if Jinji was lost in his own thoughts? Why should he care if the man looked downcast and afraid?

"Shall we have a story?" asked Prince Aredel.

A murmur of pleasure sounded from the KryTeeran attendants and soldiers throughout the tent.

"I should like one," said Father.

"Aye," agreed Sir Palan.

Rille beamed at Jinji.

Yeshton and Tifen held still, and Jetekesh joined them in their silence.

The storyteller tore his gaze from the desert wastes. "A story? This night?" He shifted. "If you so wish it, I must comply."

For a long while Jinji sat so still, Jetekesh wondered wildly if the storyteller had died of his illness. But Jinji moved then, a smile spreading across his face, lighting his eyes, coloring his cheeks. His voice was the light, lilting music of birds in flight as he spoke of the two lost knights of Shinac.

"Years ago, they served Prince Sharo faithfully, until the day Sharo's father, King Darint, banished his son and heir from the kingdom. Devastated by the decree, the knights set out to reunite with their prince and serve him once more, for they could not abide the corruption of the wicked king.

"Alas, King Darint perceived their desire and called a witch to him. He commanded her to keep the knights away from their prince by whatever means necessary.

The witch was promised great wealth if she did so; thus, she agreed. The knights were cursed to forget what they wanted most to find, and thus they would search forever but never discover their prince, even should they meet him upon the road.

"Pleased, the king ordered the witch to depart from his court, but he would not pay her. In anger, the witch secretly altered her curse. She could not undo its magic, for it had already been woven, but she could weave into the spell a means to overcome its magic. Forever would the knights seek what they could not remember; and if upon finding their prince, they again faithfully served him for his own merits, then would the curse be lifted. They would remember him once more.

"And so, the knights traveled hither and thither, unaware of their curse, unable to recall their quest, but determined nonetheless to see it through. For many years they served those they encountered along their journey, but always they just missed crossing the path of their beloved wandering prince. Until this very night. Tonight, they meet their prince upon the road, though they do not yet know him for who he is." The imagery of the two bright-eyed, aimless knights in broken armor faded away. The storyteller bowed his head.

A heavy silence followed. No one moved until the Blood Prince waved his hand.

Musicians struck up a song. The evening slowly passed into night. Two servants entered the tent and handed out blankets to each prisoner.

"You will sleep here," said Ledonn as he approached the rug where Jetekesh and the rest sat. Guards stood at the door. The night air was cool, but not cold.

The Blood Knights moved off to their sleeping quarters.

Jetekesh heard the distant cry of the desert sands. Even before he shut his eyes, he began to dream of the two Shinacian knights walking side by side along a forest path, lost, forgetful, but boldly striding on. Just ahead, a white-haired, youthful, tall, and comely man came around a bend in the path, and he stopped to smile fondly at the knights. Waiting.

25
BEYOND THE ARCH

Jetekesh's eyes fluttered open.

Soft breaths rose around him in the dark.

He sat up. Brushed his hair back and glanced around. What had awakened him? A faint light danced in his peripheral vision, and he craned his neck to find a candle against the black night.

"Your Highness." It was Jinji. The candle bobbed closer, and the storyteller's face became visible. "Will you come with me?"

Jetekesh recoiled. "Where?"

"To the Drifting Sands."

"Tomorrow?"

"No. Now."

"Why?"

Jinji fell still. "Please."

"Go, cousin." Rille's voice was a faint murmur.

Jinji moved toward the tent flap where a figure cloaked in shadows waited. What could the storyteller intend to do in the dark? Jetekesh grabbed his blanket and wrapped it around his shoulders. Slipped on his worn-out boots. Picked his way through the sleeping bodies scattered across the tent floor.

He passed the cloaked figure and stepped out into the night. His jaw slackened. A myriad of stars, larger and brighter than any he'd ever seen, filled the velvet darkness. The stars weren't all white in this place, but red and blue and purple as well. White dust sparkled around the brilliant spheres like a stream of diamond dust.

"Your Highness."

He tore his eyes from the heavens and stumbled through the tall grass after Jinji. Footsteps behind him brought Jetekesh's head around. Prince Aredel followed, visible under the full moon and bright starlight.

The Blood Prince offered a wry smile. "You'll find no man more intriguing than our mutual friend."

Jetekesh scowled. "He's not my friend."

Prince Aredel raised his brow. "No? Then you're a fool."

Jetekesh turned forward again and found Jinji on the edge of the desert, waiting, the candle still in his hand, its flame extinguished.

"Thank you for coming with me, my friends," said Jinji. "Aredel, I lied concerning the time when I would enter the Drifting Sands. It must be when the sands are still. That is only at night." He tilted his head toward the desert. Jetekesh froze.

The sand, golden bright in daylight, now glowed white beneath the slivered moon. It shone and sparkled like moonlit water. A faint wind breathed over the grains of sand, and they lifted in a lethargic dance, glittering, flashing like the stars overhead, white, red, blue, purple.

His lungs constricted. The sands danced around themselves to form twisters that rose upward like flanking pillars, lining a pathway running deep into the crystalline desert.

"It is time," whispered Jinji. "Aredel, Jetekesh, come." The storyteller stepped over the border. The pillars of twisting sand halted in place, tall and proud as sentinels.

Aredel followed at once.

Jetekesh hesitated. Sucked in air. Stepped onto the sand and found it warm even through his boot. Another step, and a breeze ran through his hair like fingers. He glanced back.

The camp had vanished. Only a vast desert stretched behind him, bright and white under the moon.

"Come, Jetekesh. Come."

Jinji's voice was no longer somber or weak. A laugh followed the beckoning.

Jetekesh scurried after the two men now far ahead. He caught up, and the three followed the path lined by the pillars of sand. Jetekesh paused before one pillar and reached out to touch it, half afraid it would collapse against his fingertips. His hand slipped between the grains, and a tremor spread up his spine as his fingers tingled. That was all. No collapse. No torrent of wind. He pulled his hand free and jogged to Prince Aredel's side.

Neither of them spoke. Somehow it seemed wrong to converse in this place. Only Jinji was immune to the feeling, for he urged them twice more to hurry along.

Ahead lay a different structure of sand: An arch, silvery white, glowing brighter than fire.

"Here," said Jinji. "This is it, Aredel, Jetekesh. This is Shinac."

Jetekesh stared. Was it possible? Was it real?

"Here I must leave you." Jinji smiled, and his eyes were full of starlight.

Jetekesh started. "Leave us?"

Prince Aredel nodded. "I understand." He bowed his head. "It has been an honor, my friend. I shall miss you greatly, but this is as it should be. You do not belong in Nakania. Perhaps you never did. Shinac is your true home and should be your final rest."

Jetekesh looked between them, chest tight. "But we—we aren't going through? We can't see Shinac?"

Jinji laughed. "It is not that you are forbidden, or the sands would not have let you reach the Arch. You may come if you choose, Jetekesh. But those who pass beneath the Arch into the bastion of magic rarely return to the world of Nakania; for once you are a denizen of Shinac you are banished from the mundane realm."

Jetekesh lowered his head to hide his disappointment. His shoulders slumped. "I see. Well then, I suppose I mustn't pass through." He swallowed, worked his face into something approaching indifference, and raised his eyes. "Why did you bring me here?"

"To let you see what you would see," answered the man from Shing, "and feel what you would feel." His eyes radiated the same strength and virtue as the sands. "Jetekesh, if you turn from here and never think of me again, I would not blame you, for while in my company you have suffered great pain. But please do not forget this place and how you feel within it. Know that only those with noble hearts may enter the true Drifting Sands and reach this point.

"You can do amazing things, my prince, if you will strive to do so. Do not be as your Mother, proud and selfish. Let your father guide you to something greater, and you shall stand as a mighty king in deed and memory. I shall miss you." He set his hand on Jetekesh's shoulder and squeezed, then turned to Aredel. "Farewell, my friend."

"May the gods of valor attend you," answered the Blood Prince.

Jinji's eyes twinkled as they flicked between Aredel and Jetekesh. "So they have." He turned to face the Arch. His shoulders quavered. "I am going now."

"You will be safe, won't you?" asked Aredel. "Shinac is a harbor of safety, yes?"

The storyteller didn't turn around. "Go now, Aredel. Take the young prince, take him home. I must go on."

Jetekesh glanced at Aredel and found him frowning.

"*Jinji.*" The Blood Prince's voice was a low warning.

The storyteller stepped into the Arch. Vanished in light.

The sands twisted in their slow dance.

Gone. Jinji had left him for Shinac, for the lost prince, for the dragons. Jetekesh started. "No! Wait. He's gone to stop Lord Peresen from sacrificing maidens and conquering Shinac and Nakania both. I remember—"

Aredel cursed. "We cannot enter Shinac. You heard him. We'd never be allowed to return home." His eyes narrowed. "Drat the man! He must go this alone. We cannot help him this time. I can't help him anymore." He turned away.

Jetekesh glanced toward the Arch one last time, stomach churning. He'd barely known Jinji. Had mocked him. Shouted at him. And in the end Jinji had shown him something unbelievable—something real. More real than Mother and her endless revelries. More real than court squabbling. More real than clean hands. Now he was gone, and all his tales with him.

"He never said goodbye to the others. Rille and Sir Yeshton. Tifen and his father."

"He's never been good at bidding people farewell. Come on."

Jetekesh started to follow.

A voice, faint, indistinct, called from within the Arch. Jetekesh whirled back around. Moved toward the Arch. "Do you hear that?"

The voice returned, high and panicked. A girl's voice, raised in a plea. A shriek followed. Jetekesh stepped back. He mustn't enter. He glanced at Aredel, who stood beside him, eyes riveted on the portal.

Another piercing scream.

"Stop!" cried Jetekesh. His voice rang above the pillars and across the white sand. "Don't hurt her!"

"*Who are you?*"

This voice was different. Male, young.

Prince Aredel approached the Arch. "Do you hear us? Who are *you?*"

"*I am called Sharo, Blood of the Woods. Will you answer me now, stranger?*"

"I am Blood Prince Aredel of KryTeer. I stand with Prince Jetekesh of Amantier beyond the Arch."

"*Ah.*" The Arch flashed with light as a note struck the air. Jetekesh threw his hands over his eyes until the sound ceased. When he lowered his arm, he found a hand protruding from the undulating storm of light.

"*I offer my greetings, royals of Nakania. I have waited long for you. Come, and be welcome.*"

Aredel shook his head. "We cannot cross, or we will be unable to return home. So Jinji of Shing has told us."

"*That is unless you are invited as guests into Shinac by its rightful rulers. And so, I invite you. Come, if you will. Great is my need of you. Come.*"

Jetekesh glanced at the Blood Prince, heart hammering. Aredel was frowning, his brow furrowed.

"I'm going." Jetekesh jumped at his own voice. *What am I saying? Aren't there enough troubles in Nakania? I have no time for Shinac!* His feet took him to the light. He grasped the proffered hand. It clasped his fingers and pulled him through the Arch.

∼

THE AIR FELT STRANGE, ALMOST MISTY, THOUGH THE day was clear and bright. The sky was a blue color more alive than any hue he'd ever beheld.

He stood upon an old highway, surrounded by tall, thick trees, where the road cut a sliver between them to disappear around a bend. The woods felt hallowed somehow, and a breeze whispered like a lullaby as it swept through the creaking limbs.

Ahead upon the unkempt path stood a young man, tall and comely, with snowy locks pulled into a ponytail atop the crown of his head to tumble past his shoulders and halfway down his back. His eyes were the blue of the ageless sky, lit with humor. He wore the shabby remains of once-fine raiment, and his boots were in desperate need of replacement.

Jetekesh's jaw fell. Prince Sharo was just as Jinji had painted him.

"So, you are the prince of Amantier." The prince of Shinac bowed. "It is quite an honor to meet you at last." The blue eyes traveled past Jetekesh. "And you are the infamous Blood Prince of KryTeer. You do not disappoint, good sir."

Jetekesh spun to find Aredel upon the same road.

The Blood Prince smiled dryly. "You must be Prince Sharo."

The young man's laugh was light and clear. "So I was, once upon another age. Now I am merely Sharo Wanderer, for so I am called in present days." He gestured down the road behind him. "If you will accompany me, I will direct you to my humble encampment and present you to my companions, one of which you know." He started down the forest road.

"Jinji?" Jetekesh flushed at the excitement in his voice.

Sharo laughed. "Indeed, yes. He will be delighted to see you, once I have explained you are not trapped within this realm." His step faltered. He glanced over his shoulder. "I fear that in my haste I did not explain what may befall you in Shinac. We are not in the peaceful times that once we claimed. Dark things have invaded our land since the capture of our rightful prince. Foul things. Shinac is a poison to the heart of any man who seeks power."

"Like King Darint and Lord Peresen," said Jetekesh, nodding. "Jinji told us."

"Did he? I am glad to hear it. That makes this easier. I am traveling now to the lair of that same Lord Peresen. Once already I have thwarted his efforts, but now he intends to try again on the night with no moon. He stole three fair maids from the fae woods, and the fairies alerted me to his plot. I came to this point in company with my charger, Amaranth, and the lovely Ashea. Now I am joined by two princes of Nakania, along with two of my own former knights, and the renowned Jinji of Shing."

He rounded the curve, and Jetekesh followed to find a tiny trail leading from the old road into the woods. The scent of wood smoke lingered on the air. Birds sang strange music overhead. He followed Sharo along the trail, Aredel on his heels. A few moments more brought the threesome into a clearing where a fire blazed and several bedrolls adorned the forest floor. Two men stood near the flames, conversing in quiet tones. There. Jinji lay upon a bedroll beyond the fire, his eyes closed, chest rising and falling.

"Ho the camp," said Sharo cheerily.

The two knights at the fire lifted their hands in unison.

"Hail, Sharo," said one. "What bring you now to our camp? We already have one storyteller, finest in all the realms of Shinac."

"Perhaps vagabonds then? Ruffians? Thespians?" asked the second.

"Princes," answered Sharo.

Jinji's eyes snapped open, and he sat up. "Aredel? Jetekesh?"

"Do not fret," said Sharo. "They were invited. There is a way home for them, and so they chose to come and aid us."

Jinji stared a moment longer, then sighed and smiled. "You never cease to surprise me, Aredel." He turned to Jetekesh. "I *am* glad you are allowed to see Shinac. I wished it could be so, but I hadn't the power to invite you myself."

"They are grander even than their stories."

Jetekesh stumbled backward at the sound of a woman's voice, so near yet invisible.

Sharo laughed. "My deepest apologies, Prince Jetekesh. What you hear is the voice of Ashea, my fairy friend, lady of the willow. Look down just a little."

Jetekesh's eyes dropped, and he found the tiny, winged thing flitting and darting in the air before him. She was hardly the span of a man's hand, delicate and fair. Her hair was the pale lavender of flowers, and she was robed in filmy sheets of delicate, pale gold, long and flowing. Her tiny hand reached out. He lifted his own to let her rest her little fingers against his finger. The fairy tilted her head, hair rippling against her back, wings beating so fast they were a blur. Her eyes met his. Molten gold. Shining like the sun. Her delicate lips lifted in a fond smile.

"I like you, Prince of Amantier. There is a fire in your soul." She released him and flitted to the Blood Prince, where the same scene played out. He extended his hand, and she took a finger in her little grasp. They regarded each other. "You smell of blood and power, Great One.

But you smell of honor as well, and that matters most. I am glad of it." She darted backward, fleet as a hummingbird, and landed upon Sharo's shoulder. "I like them both, Sharo."

The Shinacian prince beamed bright as a sunrise. "I am glad, Ashea. Then I made the right decision." He gestured to the two lost knights. "These are my companions upon my quest: Sir Chethal, the elder, and Sir Blayse, the younger. We met last eve upon the road, and it seems our purpose is the same."

"So it is," said Sir Chethal. He was a man of fifty, dark haired and graying, of average height and stubble-chinned, just as Jetekesh had seen him in Jinji's tale. His armor was old and mended in several places, his scabbard dented. Wisdom lent strength to his declining stature.

Sir Blayse was still growing into his full height and likely to remain lanky. He was plain of face and absent-minded in his nature, with unruly hair of copper brown. His armor, too, was worn and bent. He carried himself well, despite his height, and the sword at his belt was comfortable there.

Jetekesh started at his own thoughts. How could he know so much, see so much, *feel* so much about these men? He had barely met them.

He found Jinji, still seated on the bedroll. Was the storyteller responsible? Had the images conjured by his stories permitted Jetekesh to understand these men? Did stories allow that to happen?

I'm one of them now. I'm part of the tales.

The idea warmed him through.

"Supper is almost ready," said Sir Blayse.

Sir Chethal nodded as he stirred the cauldron

simmering over the flames. "Just need to add the chestnut sauce." He poured in a milky liquid.

Jetekesh's mouth watered.

"Come," called Ashea. It took a moment to spot her on a rock near the fire. "Sit near me, both of you. You will discover you are very tired from your passage through the Arch. Time flows much differently here, and your bodies will find that strange."

As though her words held magic, Jetekesh staggered as he moved toward the flames. Aredel steadied him. They sat beside the fairy.

Am I dreaming?

Ashea cleared her throat quietly. Jetekesh glanced at her twinkling eyes.

"Not a bit of it, Princeling. You are truly in the realm of Shinac."

26
THE SECOND PRINCE OF THE BLOOD

"But where did they go?"

Yeshton watched the servants of the Blood Prince run around, searching for their lord. Searching for the storyteller. For Jetekesh. But Rille sat in repose under the shade of the tent, watching with those knowing eyes. Yeshton remained with her.

Tifen was another matter. The protector searched with the others, going from wagon to wagon, tent to tent, even sneaking a glance inside the palanquin.

There was no explanation. Jinji of Shing, Blood Prince Aredel, and Prince Jetekesh had all vanished in the night.

"Sir Knight." Rille's tone was sharp.

She pointed at the fabric of the tent behind them, as though she could see through it to something beyond. He rose at once and sprinted outside to stare northwest. In the distance, thick clouds of dust rose into the air. Yeshton returned to the tent.

"An army is coming. It will be here within fifteen minutes, I would guess."

Sir Palan stepped into the tent, with the cloaked King Jetekesh beside him. They too had joined the hunt for the missing princes and storyteller.

"We've got company," Sir Palan said. "KryTeer banners."

"Yes," said Yeshton. "We know."

"We will be unable to escape," said Rille. "Best we not start a fight that will end in death."

Yeshton glanced at her. "If we don't…"

"We will go to KryTeer. Yes. I do not think there is any helping that now." Rille sighed. "I wish I could have gone with them."

"With whom, my lady?"

She turned a scornful look at him. "You cannot guess?"

Yeshton colored. "You mean Jinji and the two princes. But where did they go? Into the desert?"

Rille sighed and stood to brush off her skirts. "They have gone to Shinac, Sir Knight. Do you still not believe in it?"

He frowned. "I'm…uncertain, my lady."

"It is a hard thing to accept," said King Jetekesh, his tone careful. "But it would explain their disappearance. There is no trace at all."

Sir Palan shook his head. "No tracks. And I would deem that impossible. Unless—" He shrugged. "It is a wonder, I will grant."

A shadow fell across the tent opening. Tifen stood there, torment written in his brow. "Forgive me, Your

Majesty. I cannot find your son." His voice was tight with grief.

King Jetekesh strode to him. "Come in, Tifen. Out of the sun. You've done all you can for the moment." He turned to Rille. "While we cannot resist the might of KryTeer, I cannot leave my son here."

Rille shook her head. "But he's not here, Lord Uncle. He's in Shinac and might not return at all. I'm not certain how it works."

Shouts sounded outside.

Sir Palan glanced toward the door flap. "It appears the KryTeer army has been spotted."

"But isn't this part of KryTeer's army?" asked Yeshton. "Why would they be alarmed?"

"It's Prince Anadin's banner," Sir Palan said. "His forces are only mobilized to destroy undesirables, and long has Emperor Gyath feared the strength of his son and heir. It's just possible Prince Anadin has come to dispose of that threat if he possibly can."

"But," said Tifen stiffly, "the Blood Prince isn't even here."

"That he's not," said Sir Palan, nodding. "Which bodes ill for us. I've heard Prince Anadin's temper is explosive. Should he not claim what he seeks, we may all suffer for it."

"What can we do?" asked Yeshton, looking between Rille and King Jetekesh.

The king shook his head. "Should we run, one or the other KryTeer force will cut us down. We can do nothing, as much as I'm loath to admit it."

"You'll be killed, sire," said Tifen.

"Not necessarily. None in KryTeer knows my face. Remember that my name is Setwesh, and you do not know me well, and perhaps I will not be drawn and quartered."

Yeshton glanced at Rille. The words might have stirred memories of her father's death. But the little girl was staring at the tent wall.

"I cannot see the future, Sir Knight. I cannot see it at all."

The thundering of hooves rumbled in the air. The dread forces of Prince Anadin had arrived. Yeshton caught Rille's arm and pulled her close.

The thunder ceased. Horses whinnied.

"Brother!" cried a voice. "Brother, it is I, Anadin. Come forth to greet me!"

Yeshton raised his brow. "That doesn't sound like a man at odds with his brother. He sounds friendly."

Sir Palan nodded, brow drawn. "So he does but be on guard. I've heard many strange reports of KryTeer's spare, and feigned friendliness would not surprise me. What second brother doesn't feel tempted to stab the heir in the back?"

"Mine never did," said King Jetekesh.

Rille firmly nodded her agreement.

Voices carried from beyond the tent, formal and reverent.

"Holy prince, your brother is lost! We cannot find him. He vanished in the night."

A muddled chorus followed, and words were lost in the din.

A command rose above the rest. Silence fell.

"What say you, Shevek?" Anadin's voice.

"My lord prince. My master has gone beyond this

world, following a path of pillars made from sand. I beheld it at full night from where I kept watch. If I am not mistaken, my lord, the High Prince has entered the fabled land of Shinac."

Silence again. A faint laugh followed. "He found it? Truly? He found that ancient place? Then his storyteller wasn't mad?"

Murmurs rose. Protests. Accusations. Mockery.

The command came again, sharp as a cracking whip.

"When will he return?" asked the amiable voice of Prince Anadin.

"I...I am uncertain, my lord prince."

"Well." A pause. "There is no sense in waiting around. If and when he returns, he'll have a grand tale to tell, I'm certain. We had best return to KryTeer forthwith. Lord Father will be furious, but when has that ever prevented Aredel from doing as he wished?" He laughed. "Dismantle the camp, or however you call it."

"My lord prince?" Ledonn's voice, if Yeshton didn't miss his guess. "We do have prisoners belonging to the Blood Prince. Shall we bring them or release them?"

"I will assess for myself. Bring them hither."

Yeshton and Sir Palan backed away from the tent flap, and Yeshton turned to catch Rille's arm. "You are my sister, not Lady Rille."

She nodded as the flap swept aside and Prince Aredel's two Blood Knights slipped into the tent, hands on their sheathed blades.

"Come with us."

Sir Palan led the procession outside. Yeshton guided Rille on his heels, and Tifen came next, with King Jetekesh in the rear, shadowed by his cowl. Against the sun towered a black-clad figure atop a war charger of the same deep black. Yeshton squinted against the halo of sunlight to study the second prince. Anadin was not a well-built man like his brother, but rather slim and lithe, with angular features against black eyes and long, straight black hair. He was garbed, not in armor, but in the traditional apparel of KryTeer nobility: billowing, and open to reveal his chest, though he lacked the turban about his head.

The prince's eyes traveled across the prisoners as they lined up before him. When those eyes reached Yeshton, their gazes locked for a heartbeat. Anadin turned his attention to Rille.

"Why are these people my brother's prisoners?"

Shevek stepped forward. "They traveled with the storyteller, my lord prince. All but the cloaked man at the end. He traveled with the Blood Prince from Kavacos. What his reasons are, I was not told."

Prince Anadin nodded and looked them over again, one by one. "Significant or not, I doubt my brother would thank me for releasing them. So, on to KryTeer they will come." His black eyes flicked to Rille. "I will call them my guests for now." He pointed to Yeshton. "You, is this child your daughter?"

Yeshton blinked. Did he look the fatherly sort? "No, my lord. My sister."

The royal eyebrows shot up. "Sister? She looks nothing like you." He shrugged. "It hardly matters. Let's move along. I grow impatient."

The sounds of the servants' packing grew louder, though the camp had been half dismantled already, and they could go no faster than they went.

Anadin nudged his horse to the last standing tent just as two servants began to take it down. "Hold fast. I'll need the two of you to stay here and wait for my lord brother to return. Let him know I was here and took his prisoners for myself. Ask him kindly to return to KryTeer, or he'll miss them."

The servants exchanged startled looks. "My lord?"

"I won't change my mind." Anadin wheeled to face the wagons. "Unpack enough food for these two to live on for two weeks."

The wagon was swiftly unloaded again.

Shevek approached the war charger and bowed low. "My lord prince, can the servants not wait at Keep Falcon? I'm certain that is where Prince Aredel will head once he returns."

Anadin tapped his chin with a finger. "An excellent point. Reload the wagon. Dismantle that tent. Quickly now. Hurry. We've not got all day."

The orders were obeyed at once. Yeshton eyed the prince, trying to weigh the man's disposition. Was he addled or cruel? He seemed pleasant enough, but Yeshton had known cruel men in his life who hid behind the kindliest smiles.

At last the wagon was repacked, the last tent stowed, and the two servants were on horseback cantering toward Keep Falcon to await their prince's return from fairyland. No one said anything as Anadin organized the remaining servants to begin the long march to the west coastline, where a KryTeeran ship awaited the second prince's return. When he'd gotten everyone facing west, one distressed servant bowed and spoke.

"What of the palanquin, my lord prince?"

"Should we send it back to Keep Falcon, Your Highness?"

"Nonsense. We'll use it for my new guests." He gestured toward Yeshton and the rest. "Can't very well have them walk, can I? And a wagon will jostle the sense from their heads. Get them inside the palanquin and organize men to carry it."

Yeshton found himself ushered inside the luxurious contraption. The interior was all silks and gold twining over plush cushions. Rille settled back, quite at her ease, while Tifen sat rigidly beside her. Yeshton felt his discomfort well as he tried to find a way to sit back and not scuff the fragile cloth. Sir Palan kept clearing his throat and shifting.

King Jetekesh melted against the cushions, accustomed as Rille was to the luxuries of royal living.

Soon the palanquin took up a swaying rhythm that eased the tension of Yeshton's shoulders despite himself. Tifen too began to slump back and enjoy the ride. Sir Palan alone remained tense, and Yeshton realized that the knight might not be uncomfortable with the grand interior, but with the situation. West to KryTeer. The king of Amantier bound for enemy lands. Rille, the gifted child and target of Emperor Gyath. It wasn't good, and Yeshton cursed himself for letting down his guard, even just a little.

"What do we do?" he asked in lowered tones.

Sir Palan glanced at him. "Nothing for now. In the port of Kilitheer we stand the best chance of escape. It's a busy place. Crowds milling to and fro. We might slip away unseen along the wharves."

Yeshton nodded. "That's a few days from here, isn't it?"

"Three, at our present pace. Five if I guess rightly about our host."

"Is he mad?"

"Eccentric, so they say. Not at all a stickler like his elder brother. Whimsy leads his daily life, so we may… stray from our course a little."

Yeshton crooked a smile. "Well, it will be at least interesting."

"Oh, yes. No doubt of that."

∽

It was two hours to sunset when Prince Anadin called a halt. Camp was arranged with practiced swiftness, and Anadin ordered his new guests brought to the head tent where he lounged upon a pile of cushions behind the same long, low table Prince Aredel had used the previous evening.

Yeshton kept Rille close as he and the others were led by a guard to the table and commanded by their guide to sit beside the prince.

Anadin lifted his eyes from the goblet of wine in his hand. A smile spread across his lips, and his dark eyes danced with private mirth. "Come. Sit. Eat."

Servants poured into the tent and placed tureens and platters of food across the long table. Steam rose from dishes Yeshton had never seen in his life. There was no sign of Amantieran food; only the strange, spicy delicacies of a far away land. Warily he prodded at a white cream, while Rille reached for a kind of meat in a translucent red sauce. The little girl nibbled, and her eyes lit up.

"It is rather tasty, Sir—" She cut off. "Try some, brother."

He sampled the meat. Flavor exploded in his mouth. Strange, but juicy, rich, and robust against his tongue. He swallowed and speared another strip of meat, but a faint gasp from Rille stopped him cold. He dropped his utensil and whirled to find Rille red-faced and teary-eyed.

"H-hot. My mouth is burning up."

Fire leapt across his tongue, as though to prove her right. Tears seared his eyes and leaked down his cheeks. Merciful saints! Was it possible to die of a scalded tongue?

Tifen was gagging. Sir Palan spooned dollops of the creamy white sauce into his mouth, as red-faced as the rest.

"I forgot," the knight gasped. "I forgot how spicy it is."

Laughter resounded from the stack of pillows near Yeshton. He craned his head to find Prince Anadin in a fit of humor, his hand pounding a pillow beside him as he watched the Amantierans. "The yogurt. Eat the yogurt, as your large friend is doing. Go on." He waved a hand, like they needed his permission.

Rille knocked over a goblet to reach the nearest dish of creamy white sauce. Yeshton got to it first and brought it closer, while a servant appeared and leaned in to mop up the puddle of liquid.

"Dip the flatbread in it," said the prince. He broke off a strip of bread and plunged it in the yogurt. "See? Like this."

Rille ate the yogurt straight, as Sir Palan was doing. Yeshton managed to snare a piece of flatbread and doused it in the yogurt. Shoved it into his mouth. The fire smoldered on his tongue. Another bite of bread, a heap of yogurt, and the fire became embers.

The second prince of KryTeer was in stitches of laughter. The KryTeer soldiers, scattered throughout the tent, looked on with silent mirth, eyes bright, though none laughed aloud.

The rest of the evening meal passed at a crawling pace. Rille would only eat the yogurt, and Yeshton couldn't blame her. He managed to sample several spicy dishes between mouthfuls of yogurt to fight the heat, while Sir Palan did the same. Tifen refused to eat at all, but instead nursed a goblet of wine while tears seeped from his eyes from his single bite. King Jetekesh alone appeared unfazed by the foreign fare. He ate steadily, a smile of appreciation on his lips.

Finally, Prince Anadin set aside his utensils and clapped his hands. Servants slipped from the shadows to clear away the food in a matter of moments, and a handful of sparsely clad women moved to the center of the tent and began to dance while musicians played merry tunes.

Had the second prince of KryTeer truly brought dancing women on his campaign?

Rille yawned. Yeshton shifted to let her lay her head on his lap, and she curled up at once.

Eyes watched him. He looked up to find Prince Anadin staring between him and Rille, rather than the dance.

"She looks nothing like you."

Yeshton's shoulders tensed, but he nodded. "So you've said."

The prince's eyes glittered. "She's rather dainty. You're not."

Yeshton nodded again. "True, that."

"If you were her father, I'd understand. I'd think she had a pretty mother to give her slight features. But brother and sister? I don't quite swallow the idea."

Yeshton shrugged. "You don't have to, Your Highness."

The prince propped his chin on his palm and studied Rille for a long moment. "I know her name."

Yeshton prayed his face remained calm as his heart missed a step. He said nothing.

Prince Anadin nodded and took up his goblet to drain the last drops of wine. "*Sahala*, in my tongue. The girl who sees true. I believe you call her Rille." He turned and motioned a servant to fill his goblet again. "Send the others away. I wish for privacy."

The servant finished pouring from a large jar, then backed away to whisper to a second servant, who raised his hand and struck a golden gong. It rang out through the tent, and the men seated on cushions around the interior rose at once and slipped out through several openings.

Yeshton watched them leave, senses taut. His fingers twitched, yearning for his sword, but that had been taken by Prince Aredel's men in Keep Falcon, along with his boot knife, his dagger, and the bit of twine he always kept. Here he was weaponless and powerless.

Drawing a deep, quiet breath, he turned to the prince.

"Is that what her name means?" He was glad he sounded politely interested.

The prince nodded as he sipped his wine. He lowered the goblet and licked his lips. "I will call her Sahala. It is the old tongue of KryTeer. Only the scholarly know its meaning. I'm confident my holy father would not recognize it for what it is…unless he were told by someone, of course."

Yeshton laid a hand over Rille's head. "And *would* someone tell him, I wonder?"

Prince Anadin flashed a smile. "That would depend on whether someone was provided a reason to speak or not."

"Money would probably persuade a man, but I know how light a purse can be."

"Oh, money wouldn't interest the scholarly sort."

"What would?"

The prince leaned across his pillows. "Information."

Yeshton set his jaw. "What sort of information?"

"The kind that can only be gleaned by speaking with Sahala directly." He leaned back against his pile of pillows, content as a cat. "What say you, soldier?"

Yeshton wasn't surprised that Anadin had sniffed him out for what he was. Soldiers had a certain scent, that ageless, iron badge of blood, as well as a certain air. But how had he known who Rille was? Even if Prince Aredel had sent word from Keep Falcon to KryTeer of Rille's capture, Anadin had already been on his way southeast and likely wouldn't have waylaid any missives. Unless…

Rumors claimed that the magicians of KryTeer used spells to send messages from great distances in mere seconds. Was it true? If so, the Blood Prince could have alerted his brother to Rille's capture at once, and even told Emperor Gyath that she was on her way to him as a gift. But would the Blood Prince do so? Hadn't Anadin been coming this way in search of his brother? Why do that if the empire believed their crown prince was returning with Rille in his grasp? And why would Prince Aredel instead drop everything and run off somewhere with Jinji and Prince Jetekesh?

"You're wrong, you know."

Yeshton met those black eyes.

The prince was still smiling. "I know what you're thinking, and it's not true. My holy father doesn't know a thing about Sahala's presence here, nor do I intend to tell him…if we can reach an accord."

Yeshton rested his hand on Rille's back. Her body rose and fell beneath his touch. "She can't tell you your future like some soothsayer."

The prince snorted. "I don't need some fortune told to me. I know my fate. I've always known it."

"What then do you want?"

"Only to understand."

"You can do better than that, Your Highness. Surely."

Prince Anadin's smile turned crooked. "Let me speak with her. No more, no less. I'll not harm the little girl. I recognize her worth."

"Her worth to me or to you?"

The prince laughed. "So suspicious. What is your name, soldier?"

"Yeshton."

"Son of whom?"

"Yarmir."

The prince's eyes traveled past Yeshton. "Sir Palan I

already know. He's been an elusive thorn in the side of my brother for a long while. One of few who can genuinely grate upon his nerves. I commend you, Sir Knight."

Sir Palan inclined his head. "You're most gracious, Your Highness."

Prince Anadin's eyes sparkled. "I am, aren't I?" His eyes slid to Tifen. "This one I don't know."

Sir Palan rested a hand on Tifen's shoulder. "This is—"

"Tifen, a servant. That's all," Tifen said for himself.

"My son," Sir Palan said over him.

Anadin's mouth formed a silent O, and he winked at Yeshton. "Family feuds are familiar to me. I well understand." His eyes flicked to King Jetekesh, still cloaked, sitting slightly apart from the other prisoners. "That one intrigues me, but he appears not to speak. Do you speak, cloaked man?"

King Jetekesh took a long drink of wine.

Prince Anadin shrugged. Set aside his goblet, stretched luxuriantly. Moved lithely to his feet. "Tomorrow evening I will spend one hour alone with Sahala. You will allow this for her sake, Yeshton."

Yeshton frowned. "And if I refuse?"

"You know the result. I made myself plain enough."

"But you won't tell me *why* you want to speak with her?"

The prince shrugged. "If she trusts you, perhaps she will tell after we converse. Goodnight, each of you. Pleasant dreams." He slipped into a second chamber of the tent, behind an airy swath of curtains.

"Strange man," murmured Tifen.

Sir Palan nodded. "Agreed. What will you do, lad?"

Yeshton looked down at Rille, sound asleep on his lap, her pale hair tumbling down his leg and across the cushions. When it came down to it, he had no choice but to comply. The alternative was death for himself and exposure for Rille. Whatever Prince Anadin's interest in the child, it could not be worse than Emperor Gyath's.

Yeshton looked up and met the knight's eyes. "I suppose we must go along with the prince's wishes for now. If there's the slightest chance of making him an ally, we must try." He smoothed Rille's hair. "And my lady here may be the one to accomplish such a feat."

"True enough." Sir Palan grinned. "She's as odd as he is."

27
THE SHEPHERD OF SHING

A remarkable dinner was followed by the two lost knights performing a delightful array of folk music.

Jetekesh had never heard the songs before, but there was a familiar air about them. Ashea sang the last song of the night, her small, high tones giving voice to the stars overhead as she wove words in a tongue Jetekesh couldn't understand, yet the meaning was plain. It was a love song, achingly tragic, filled with longing and regret. It climbed higher, higher, crescendoed—and stopped all at once. Jetekesh felt as though he stood upon a star, overseeing the vast heavens, dazzled.

A laugh brought him back to the world, strange and dazzling in its own right. The wind held music; otherwise, a hush lay over the woods, like the reverence of the cathedrals back in Kavacos.

"You appear to have enjoyed my ballad, Princeling."

He bobbed a nod. "Very much. Though calling it a ballad feels belittling somehow."

"Oh, indeed? That may be so." The fairy sat beside him, atop a large rock placed there for her particular use. Against the firelight she glowed, though not the amber gold of flames, but an almost silvery purple hue. He blinked and wondered only now if she herself was glowing. She beamed up at him, her delicate features fair beyond words. "'Tis an old song of my people, when first we woke from the flowers and trees. 'Twas the second song I learned."

Jetekesh tilted his head. "What was the first?"

Her smile grew, and the light around her heightened. "I will sing it to you some other evening, Princeling. I think it will be better heard another night." Her eyes darted to Jinji, who laid upon his bedroll and stared into the flames of the campfire. He looked pale as snow.

"I thought…" Jetekesh hesitated.

"You thought that he would be healed if he transcended Nakania for Shinac?" asked Ashea.

He nodded.

"So he would, except that Shinac is not as it should be. And there is another factor as well. Though Jinji longed more than anything to enter this realm, yet he maintains a claim on Nakania even now. Between the growing taint passing between your world and this, and Jinji's own torn heart, he remains ill and will soon die unless something can be done about both." The fairy's eyes flicked to Aredel across the campfire. Her voice lowered. "I believe this is why yon Blood Prince came into this realm; he owes Jinji a life debt. Did you know this?"

"Truly? The storyteller saved his life?"

Ashea nodded. "It was five years ago. They met in Shing."

"During KryTeer's conquest of Shing." Jetekesh nodded. "It was Emperor Gyath's last campaign."

"Just so." Ashea's eyes lifted to the stars. "Just after the country issued its formal surrender, Emperor Gyath left Shing's southern hills for the warmth of the north. Prince Aredel was charged with dispatching the last pocket of the south's resistance, but his father had not provided him enough men or provisions for the task. Those who did remain with the prince were disobedient and self-serving. They pillaged and raped every village they came to, and Prince Aredel struggled to stop them. Finally, his own men turned on him and, vastly outnumbered, he was beaten senseless and thrown in the Tindo river to drown.

"As you might easily guess, Jinji lived near the Tindo, and from the hill where he watched his flocks, he spotted Aredel's limp form floating out toward the south sea. He raced to the bank, dove in, and fished the Blood Prince out. Aredel was half dead, but Jinji revived him."

Jetekesh's gaze flicked toward Aredel over the flames. The Blood Prince was listening to Sir Chethal's description of a mighty fortress nearby, heedless of his own story told so near. Jetekesh glanced at Jinji. His eyes were closed now. "And thus, the Blood Prince of KryTeer became indebted to a shepherd."

"It was not just one incident," said Ashea. "While Aredel recovered strength after his beating, a group of villagers from nearby came to Jinji's hut, demanding he turn over the dread prince."

"But how did they know Aredel was even there?"

"Alas, Jinji did not live alone. His mother, once a great lady of Shingese nobility, now an outcast like her own unwanted son, had come to dwell with him when Shing was conquered by KryTeer. In her thirst for vengeance, she told the villagers of her son's deed. Now the villagers had come to demand recompense. Jinji attempted to reason with them. Show a man mercy, he said, and he will learn mercy. Show a man hatred, and he will likewise hate. So reasoned the wise shepherd. None listened. The villagers beat Jinji with sticks until he could not move, and they set fire to the hut wherein Aredel lay sleeping."

The fairy's voice faltered. "Do you know how ugly mobs become, young Princeling? Jinji learned it that day. Angry, drunk with it, humiliated by Amantier and KryTeer in turns, bruised by both, the mob of villagers raped Jinji's mother and killed her. He watched, helpless, held by two men he had once called friend. Aredel emerged from the hut amid the flames, wielding nothing but two kitchen knives. He killed three villagers before they scattered, leaving the ruins of Jinji's home, the corpse of his mother, and the two wounded men of vastly different worlds: a great prince and a humble shepherd."

The little fairy tilted her head. "Do you know, Master Jetekesh, Jinji should have been a prince himself? Had Shing not been occupied by Amantier, his mother, Princess Linglia, would have wed her cousin, heir of Shing. Had Jinji been born legitimate, and had KryTeer not invaded, he would have been the heir of a once-grand nation. But his mother was used and abandoned by the selfish man who once pledged his love to her.

"When Jinji was born, he was sent away to grow up

among other discarded souls unwanted by their noble mothers. He lived in poverty and fought for his bread on the streets of a port city far from his mother's house. Princess Linglia was not disgraced, but she did not wed the heir of Shing either. Her younger sister gained that privilege instead.

"It is to Jinji's credit that, despite his hardships, he owns a poet's soul, and he molded it into a power. Among the Shingese he became known as a storyteller after the fashion of ancient times. He left the streets and was groomed and sponsored by a pretty young noblewoman to present before the court of Emperor Majinglee.

"During his stay with the noblewoman, Jinji and the beautiful lady fell in love. Her name is Naqin. She desired to wed him once he was accepted at court, but alas, Jinji's mother learned of his origin and feared for her own honor. Upon his appearance before Emperor Majinglee, Lady Linglia accused her son of theft and of playing with the heart of Naqin. The crime of such was the removal of his hands, but the lady Naqin pleaded for mercy before the emperor. Jinji was banished from court and allowed to live the life of a shepherd, but he was never to see Lady Naqin again.

"It is a wonder that Jinji did not thenceforth feel bitter. You see, he fought against such feelings, knowing well the ugliness such begets. A year after Jinji's banishment, he heard of his beloved's marriage to another. His heart broke. It is said *that* is when his illness first fell upon him.

"It was a few years after that when he fetched Prince Aredel from the waters of Tindo. Days later, while his hut burned and his treacherous mother lay dead, Jinji fell ill once more and, fevered, called a curse upon Nakania in his grief. It is my suspicion that Prince Aredel has since put it upon his own shoulders to conquer the world for Jinji's sake, to end the tyranny of kingdoms, including his own. But that is my own feeling. I do not understand the mind of the Blood Prince."

Ashea softly sighed. "Alas, poor Jinji feels that his grieving heart did indeed call a curse upon Nakania, and it may be so, for that world has long been sick. A cleansing, I would call it, and none should fault him for his feeling. Would you, Prince of Amantier, knowing all that he has suffered?"

Jetekesh sat still. What did he feel about Jinji now? What *should* he feel?

"No," he whispered, half to himself. "I couldn't fault him. Only pity him. It's horrible how he's been treated."

"So it is." Ashea shook her head. "When Majinglee was overthrown by KryTeer, and a magistrate ruled instead, Jinji was invited back to the court. There he saw Naqin once more, and she begged him to forgive her. Of course he did, for he loved her still."

"I'd not have forgiven her," said Jetekesh, ears burning. "She betrayed him."

"She had no choice. Her marriage was arranged to keep her from following after a humble shepherd."

Jetekesh fell still again. "It isn't fair."

"No, prince. It is not. Bear such in mind, for one day you too will have such power to lift or condemn a man. Choose well the fate of another, for it impacts more than the one standing before you." Ashea stood and fluttered her delicate wings. "I bid you goodnight. I must find the hollow of a tree for my rest. I shall see you upon the morrow." She leapt into the air and flitted off. He watched her until she vanished in the darkness.

He felt eyes upon him and turned to find Prince Sharo.

"Now you have heard truth, Prince Jetekesh. Here in Shinac Jinji is honored as the prince he ought to have been. Not because he has noble blood, but because he wields a noble heart."

Jetekesh lay down on the blanket he'd brought from Amantier and stared up into the glittering night sky. His mind played out the fairy's story over and over. What ill had Jinji ever done a living soul? Even his mother, cruel as she was, had been allowed to live with him when no one else would take her in. Mercy was always Jinji's way. It had cost him all, yet still he kept it. Was Jinji a fool? A madman? Or was Jinji the only man not afflicted with one or the other disease?

Jetekesh rolled onto his side and studied Jinji's sleeping face against the firelight.

I just don't understand you. I would hate everyone who made me suffer. I'd want to tear them to pieces.

He turned away from the storyteller, heart clenching. Disgust burned inside him. But was it directed at Jinji or himself?

I don't want to know.

28
THE WAY OF THE ELDERS

"The fortress is three days from here," said Prince Sharo, who led his charger ahead of the walking party. "If we do not rest, we may cut it down to half that and arrive well before the moonless night."

"I approve of that idea," said Sir Blayse.

"If Jinji can keep up," said Prince Aredel, glancing at the storyteller who walked beside him.

The storyteller smiled. "I will manage, my friend. No need to slow our pace on my account."

Jetekesh walked behind them. His eyes danced between the Shingese shepherd and the KryTeeran prince while he thought of what Ashea had told him. His gaze fixed long on Aredel. For the past five years, Jetekesh had heard horror stories of the Blood Prince of KryTeer. He and his Blood Knights were invincible, like a great tidal wave sweeping over the countries of Nakania, leaving nothing untouched. The Blood Prince was said to be as strong as the KryTeeran gods; his people called him a mortal deity: one who had condescended to take mortal form and convert the world through force of arms.

Yet Ashea's tale made Aredel sound human.

He was defeated by his own men and thrown into a river.

The thought gnawed at Jetekesh. He wanted to ask the man how strong he really was. Had rumors exaggerated the magnitude of Aredel's skill?

The sun was climbing above the trees, lighting the path in patches. The company around Jetekesh conversed as they kept a steady gait along the root-rutted forest road. No one heeded his silence. Perhaps they didn't notice.

He tried to watch his feet as he walked, but that made him dizzy. Looking ahead brought his gaze back to Aredel. He lifted his eyes to the sky above the branches. His toe caught a rock, and he stumbled into Jinji.

Aredel snatched the storyteller before he crumpled. "Are you all right, Jinji?" He glowered at Jetekesh. "Be careful how you step."

Jetekesh flushed. "Don't order me about."

The Blood Prince raised an eyebrow. "It was a word of caution, Your Highness. But next time it might be something else."

Jetekesh's hands curled into fists. "You're not as frightening in person as you're made out to be. I'm not afraid of you, Blood Prince. I've heard you were even beaten by your own men in Shing." *What am I saying?* He took a step back as ice raced through his blood. Even if Prince Aredel *wasn't* as strong as he looked, he could still pound Jetekesh senseless. He was a warrior, not some pampered prince whose mother wouldn't let him ride a horse, or use a blade, or learn to swim, for fear he'd damage himself.

The Blood Prince regarded him with an expression cold as the southern climbs. "That's a dangerous tongue you've got, Highness."

Jinji rested a hand on Aredel's shoulder. "It is all the weapon he has been allowed to use, Aredel." The man from Shing turned to Jetekesh. "Your words are used like a blade, and yet Aredel gave you no cause to unsheathe your weapon."

Jetekesh opened his mouth to protest, but Jinji raised his hand.

"Let me finish, Your Highness. I feel that you have misunderstood something especially important. I assume Lady Ashea is she who told you of the incident in Shing to which you've just alluded?"

Jetekesh lifted his chin. "Yes."

Jinji nodded. "It is true that Prince Aredel was overpowered by his malcontent and hungry men: a number exceeding three hundred in whole. Over a dozen were responsible for torturing their own prince, while the rest watched and did nothing." He glanced at Aredel, then back at Jetekesh. "Alas, not one of those 331 men lives today. Upon his return to KryTeer, Prince Aredel exposed their cowardice and treason and executed every last one."

Jetekesh folded his arms. "I'd always heard the Blood Prince could singlehandedly take down a force two thousand strong."

Aredel barked a laugh. "My reputation has turned me into a god."

Jinji smiled at him. "You are a modest soul at your

core, Aredel. In truth, Prince Jetekesh, with great cunning the Blood Prince has done just that. It required a mountain path, an avalanche of rocks, the illusion of a greater force than he had, and a fair bit of running about atop the very heads of his enemy. Alone in that mountain pass, Prince Aredel did indeed cause an army of two thousand men to turn tail and retreat back into their own country."

"Clever," said Sharo, who had leaned against his stallion to watch the exchange unfolding upon the road. "That isn't a story I've heard about you, Blood Prince. I did hear about the betrayal of your men whilst in Shing, though. A lesser man would have died."

Heat crawled across Jetekesh's cheeks. Of *course* everyone would take the side of Prince Aredel. Apart from his own father, no one in Jetekesh's life cared about him or worried for his feelings. Not even Mother, now dead and buried, had shown him concern for his sake. She'd only cared about appearances. Vanity was the very air she breathed, and Jetekesh was an extension of her, thereby important.

He turned from Jinji, nails digging into the flesh of his palms. "I apologize for my rude comments, Prince Aredel. I was thoughtless." The words stung. He didn't believe them himself, but he and the Blood Prince were traveling together, and he couldn't allow hostility to isolate him from the few people he knew in this strange land.

"You may say what you please, Prince Jetekesh," said the Blood Prince. "Just expect that I might retaliate accordingly. If you can hold your own, I have no issue contending with you in any matter. Just be certain of what you say first and ponder if it is worth the saying." He swept his hand toward Sharo. "Please, continue on, Your Highness. I regret causing a delay."

"Not at all," said Sharo with a bright smile. "Onward we go."

The company began walking again. Jinji fell back to stride beside Jetekesh. "You must feel unjustly used, Your Highness, and perhaps undervalued. Please know that, for my part, I dearly appreciate your companionship."

Jetekesh gritted his teeth. "Don't lie."

"I'm not," said Jinji softly. He fell silent for a while. "Your Highness, I cannot help but feel that we are similar. Do I assume correctly that Lady Ashea also told you a little of my own history?"

"She did."

"Then you know of my mother."

"…Yes."

"When I met your own mother, I could not help but notice a certain…aspect…that each had in abundance."

"Such as?"

"They were very selfish creatures."

Jetekesh's shoulders slumped. "So they were. What of it?"

"Perhaps you don't know it, for you have long been sheltered against life beyond your palace walls, but most mothers are not as ours were. Most are loving, selfless, strong. There is nothing so inspiring, so laudable, as a mother who loves her children above herself. Most children are reared by such venerable women. We were among the unlucky few. And so I feel a kinship to you, my prince. I feel as though we harbor a secret pain, one we might heal from, perhaps together."

Jetekesh glanced at the storyteller and found those strange, light eyes on him. Heat scaled his face again. "You and I are nothing alike."

"We are different in many regards, it is true. I was not raised among riches, but upon the streets of ChinWan. But in feelings, I suspect we are much the same. At your age, I felt the same anger, despair, confusion, longing—all those raw, haunting emotions—just as you do now, if I am not wrong." He caught Jetekesh's gaze again. "Am I, Your Highness?"

Jetekesh looked away. "…No. But how can that possibly help me? Or you?"

"We might be friends, Your Highness. I know it is a presumption on my part to even say it. But still, I ask once again."

His cheeks burned like fire. "Why would you want to—?" He bit his lip hard. "You say the strangest things, Wanderlust."

Jinji laughed. "I cannot dispute the fact. But I will not let you alter the subject, my dear prince. What say you? Will we be friends? For my part, I should like it very much." A leaf drifted from an overhead branch, and Jinji reached out to snare it between his fingers. He twirled the leaf. "Do not consider what propriety or tradition might think. Choose only what *you* desire, for feelings should never come second to opinion. What do you wish, Your Highness?"

Jetekesh bowed his head as loneliness washed over him, nauseating, cold. "I…should like a friend, I think. I-I'm not familiar with how to, to be one."

That laugh sounded again. "Each friendship is different, my prince. It is the act of kindliness one toward another. What your kindliness is, only you decide. So it is for me." He halted on the road, turned to face Jetekesh, and held out his hand. "Friends, Jetekesh?"

Jetekesh hesitated. But an impression of hope washed away the fear, the disdain, and he clasped the frail hand in his fingers. Jinji cupped his other hand over Jetekesh's and squeezed.

"'Tis done, my prince. We are friends."

A different warmth spread over Jetekesh, strange and welcome. A smile tugged at his lips, and he allowed it. He blinked back tears and pulled free of those fragile hands. "Well, we should keep walking."

As Jetekesh moved now, there was a lightness in his step. A flutter in his chest. The world was brighter, warmer. He had a friend. Someone cared, like Father. But Jinji wasn't obligated. He simply *wanted* it.

I like friends, he thought to himself, and his smile deepened. The weight on his shoulders had fled.

∽

"Off the road. Hide." Sharo's sharp tone struck Jetekesh's ambling thoughts like an arrow to his chest. The knights dove right, into the thick foliage, and Jetekesh followed Jinji down an incline, and up, into the treeline while Aredel and Sharo took the rear and came last, scrambling into the sheltering forest.

Jetekesh crouched beside the storyteller just as the hooves of horses sounded ahead on the road.

The riders whipped past, black helmed, astride dark

mounts. Over a dozen black knights, cloaks billowing in their swift canter.

Jinji inhaled a sharp breath.

Jetekesh looked at him with alarm. Was he in pain?

The storyteller's eyes stared after the passing knights. "Lord Peresen's men," he whispered, tone so soft Jetekesh read more than heard the words on his lips.

Jetekesh jerked his head back around to inspect the force of arms, but it had moved on, and he saw only the winging cloaks and horse tails streaming far down the road. What were they doing here? He glanced at Jinji, hoping the man would recognize his silent question.

A mild smile stole over Jinji's face. "Lord Peresen knows I have come. He can guess which road I would take, and in whose company." His eyes flicked to Prince Sharo.

The party climbed to its feet. Jetekesh rose with Jinji.

"Lord Peresen knows of you?"

"Oh yes. We have known of each other for several years now. It has been a kind of race: Would I reach Shinac first, or would he escape from it before I found the way here?"

"But how does he know what you're doing? I thought your gift was unique."

Jinji's smile flickered. "There are many ways to See, my friend. After all, this is Shinac, citadel of magic, where the gifted are more abundant than the mundane; and Lord Peresen is not above heartless tactics to gather information. Were your cousin here, she would be dearly sought by many such men as he."

Prince Sharo crept near. "We will wait a moment

more before we return to the road. How are you faring, Master Jinji?"

"Well enough. Thank you, Your Highness. I shall manage." Jinji reached out and rested a hand on the fae prince's shoulder. "You didn't sleep last night, I think. How fare you?"

Sharo laughed and batted away his hand. "I see you are the worrying sort. Never fear, Master Teller; I could bear up for many more days than this and still outwit Lord Peresen in his own estate. I have before."

"So you have, with the aid of a dragon." Jinji cocked his head. "How is Taregan?"

Sharo's eyes glowed like sunlight upon an ocean. "Much improved. He shall be wheeling about once more in the sky before much longer."

Jetekesh started, looking between them. "What happened to him? Was he injured?"

Sharo grinned. "Oh yes. He's enormously proud of himself. He had a tussle with a sea dragon bewitched to swallow me. Taregan doesn't well tolerate such behavior and took it upon himself to break the spell. He won, too, but his wings were battered in the fray, and he's mending now. Should not be much longer, and he'll be right again. He's a sight better than the sea dragon, I will tell you."

"Did he kill him?" asked Jetekesh, riveted.

Sharo laughed again. "No, no. Nothing so horrible. He just put the fear of the elders into poor Kethalas, which caused the witch's spell to shatter. Come to that, the witch shattered too. Thus, all her bound souls were freed, and Lord Peresen is frightfully angry about it. The witch worked for him, you see."

Jetekesh realized his mouth hung open. "A witch? Elders? Who are the elders?"

Aredel strode closer to the three conversing, his hand draped casually over his sword hilt. "I, too, am curious about these elders. Jinji hasn't mentioned them before."

Jinji shrugged. "I would need to spend every waking moment of my life explaining Shinac to share even half its aspects, Aredel. It is, after all, a world unto itself." He motioned to Sharo. "Will you explain the elders, Your Highness?"

Sharo's eyes twinkled. "Must I keep insisting that you leave off my title, Master Jinji?"

"Only when you have ceased to call me master," was Jinji's patient reply.

Sharo laughed. "Fair enough." His blue eyes fastened on Jetekesh. "The elders are the firstborn of any magical race. The fairies have elders, the elves have elders, the dragons have elders. It is the last of these to whom I refer. Taregan is an elder of his kind in Shinac. He bows to no other dragon, save the Rokahns of Sirinhigha. That Kethalas provoked him was proof of bespellment and cause for Taregan to invoke his full strength, until the very ocean rose in torrents beneath his rage." The twinkle in his eye brightened. "It gave the mermaids quite a scare."

Jetekesh sucked in a sharp breath. "Mermaids?"

Sharo winked. "Indeed, Prince Jetekesh. Mermaids. Fair and treacherous in equal parts."

"Oh, hush," said Jinji. "They are only treacherous when you've stolen their hearts unrequited."

The prince of Shinac blushed crimson. "It was never my intent. I had no notion…"

Jinji chuckled and looked at Jetekesh, a glint in his eye. "Prince Sharo is a clever man, bold and brave against dragons, dread lords, and great armies. But where women are concerned, he is a lost cause. He does not know just how many hearts he has broken in human villages, elven vales, and underwater cloisters."

The blush on Sharo's cheeks brightened with every word. He ducked his head, cleared his throat, and pushed past Jetekesh to march toward the road. "We should not dawdle. Quickly, my friends."

Jinji and Aredel exchanged a look.

"He reminds me of you, Jinji," said Aredel quietly.

Jetekesh followed Sharo's back as the man called to his horse. Now that Aredel mentioned it, there were distinct similarities between Jinji and the Shinacian prince. Not physically, for Sharo was taller by several inches, and his hair was long and fully white, his eyes clear blue rather than the blue green of Jinji's, and there was a vitality in his step—but their presence and mild manners were much the same. Even their laughter held that soft, watery lilt of someone containing magic within themselves.

Jinji's meek smile mirrored Sharo's as well. He offered that smile now. "I have long watched Prince Sharo from afar, and if I resemble him in any way, I am glad of it. I confess that he is my hero."

Jetekesh glanced back to the road and found Amaranth trotting toward the Shinacian prince. Somehow Jetekesh suspected Sharo would say the same of Jinji if he were asked.

On impulse, Jetekesh moved away from Jinji and Aredel, drawn to the prince of this magical realm. A prince who strove to find the rightful ruler of Shinac, rather than take the throne for himself. What caused a man to feel such loyalty toward another?

Sharo looked up from stroking Amaranth's coat, an easy smile on his fair face. "You wear a question, young prince."

A thousand questions leapt up in Jetekesh's mind, clawing for attention. But none raged louder than one. "Do you hate your father for banishing you?"

Sharo stroked Amaranth again, brow creased. "No, Prince Jetekesh. Of all things he might be hated for, that would be the least profitable or just."

"That doesn't stop hate."

Sharo tilted his head and bobbed a nod. "True enough. I admit I was wounded by his actions. But I have never hated my father. He is a blind, narrow thinking, arrogant wretch, and so I pity him for all that he has become; but his father was no better, nor his father before him. I began that way myself, but by the blessed spirits, I was spared. 'Tis my mother I thank most, for she is my salvation."

"Where is your mother?"

"With her people."

Jetekesh blinked. "Oh. I thought she might be—"

"Dead? No. Nor did she remain with my father, once I was exiled. There was no need, so she left with me and returned to the forest fae. I visit her when I'm able."

"Your father must have been very angry."

"No, he wasn't. It is much more likely he was relieved. Long had he feared my mother, when he knew what she was; and he is married anew to a woman well suited to his sour disposition."

"Married? But your mother is still alive!"

Sharo chuckled. "You look dumbfounded, my friend. Their marriage contract was magically bound, and thus breakable under the proper conditions. It was annulled by my fae grandsire once proof was obtained that my fair mother was forced into matrimony by the tyrant Darint, and there was no love between them."

Jetekesh stared, certain he had never heard anything so shocking, not even when he'd learned Shinac was a real place. "What has love to do with marriage?"

Sharo pulled back. "What a question. Do your parents not love one another?"

Jetekesh shook his head. "Not at all. I mean, they didn't. My mother is dead now. It—It was an arranged marriage."

"Ah," said Sharo. "I had heard Nakania's traditions are strange. Here, within Shinac, a marriage is contracted and magically woven together by a covenant of love. Without it the magic cannot stick, and all will know it is a farce. To force another to wed you would not be binding, and therefore not legal. Magically, that can harm the offender. It is why dark witches rarely wed. Years ago, my lady mother agreed to wed King Darint, and so the magic bound them, until she said aloud how she felt."

Jetekesh grimaced. "But that's horrible. It means that should anyone fall *out* of love, they can simply break the magic contract and walk away? What sort of promise is that? What is the point in marriage if it doesn't last? Why marry at all?"

Sharo laughed. "Why indeed? For love, of course. And what I've said does not mean it is an easy thing to break a marriage vow. A man and woman will many times fall out of love, but we do not mock magic by breaking such a covenant for so petty a grievance. Love is action, always. It is the agreement to strive together even, and especially, in challenging times. The covenant cannot be broken on a whim or by one half of a partnership wanting escape from momentary difficulty. The covenant is studied by one of the magical, usually an elder, who determines the truth of their love and commitment one to the other, and a judgment is made. But this is rare in Shinac. Marriage is sacred, Prince Jetekesh. None take it lightly, save those who are greedy like my father."

"But why did your mother ever agree to wed him?"

"He gave her no choice," said Sharo softly. "Let us leave it at that."

Jetekesh bit his lip and nodded, lowering his eyes. "I'm sorry for my outburst. It's just…so strange."

Sharo rested a hand on his shoulder. "Just as I find your customs. Questions are always welcome. Do not keep silent." He pulled his hand back. "Ah, so the rest of you have decided to join us on the road. Shall we recommence our exercise?"

"Your Highness," said Sir Blayse, "Lady Ashea has returned."

Jetekesh turned in time to see a little orb of light flit from the lost knight's shoulder and dart across the air, past him, to light upon Sharo's outstretched palm.

"How went it, my lady?"

The light around the fairy dimmed until Jetekesh could make out her delicate form. "A great force of arms has gathered outside the fortress, Sharo. Dark clouds hang close. The air is poisoned with bloodlust. Foul things have been summoned by Lord Peresen, that he might unleash them upon Nakania with his sacrifice." She turned to face the others. "It appears he intends to hasten his goals, Master Jinji, now that you have come. He is not taking any chances. The sacrifice will be tonight, by dark arts that may hide the moon. He need not wait for the natural moonless night."

"Tonight!" cried Sir Chethal. "We cannot possibly make it by then, my lords."

Sharo's eyes darkened as he turned his gaze to the ground. "Not using our present route, no, Sir Knight. But we may chance another way." He caught up Amaranth's reins and led the horse off the road and back into the breathing woods. The rest of the company trailed after him, curiosity burning in their eyes as clearly as Jetekesh felt it pounding in his chest—all but Jinji, whose knowing look vexed him far less now than it might have yesterday.

Friend.

Jetekesh smiled to himself.

Prince Sharo led them deep into the forest, only stopping when the road was hidden, and the sound of the birds and the wind above enveloped them. "I trust each of you as I trust no other creature, save my fae people alone. Thus, I bestow upon you knowledge only the wise and ancient keep written in their hearts." His blue eyes stopped on Jinji. "Come, friend. I will show thee the pathway of the elder fae."

Jinji's eyes were like lightning in a storm. He strode forward, not the frail man Jetekesh had seen until now, but straight and ethereal. He belonged to this world, this fairy country, where souls harnessed powers beyond a mortal shell. He stood beside Sharo, who turned his attention west with a wave of his hand.

"Step betwixt yonder holly trees, Master Jinji, and thou shalt see the old path."

Breathless, Jetekesh watched Jinji move toward the two trees. As he passed between them, nothing at all changed. He merely disappeared beyond them into shadow.

Sharo turned to the four remaining men. "Who enters yon wood next?"

The knights held back, eyes darting between Jetekesh and Aredel. The Blood Prince glanced at him. Jetekesh shook his head. "Go first, Your Highness. You came to protect Jinji."

Sharo laughed. "Where Jinji stands now, none would harm him."

Aredel nodded. "Go, Prince Jetekesh. I think Jinji would wish you to join him next."

Inhaling, Jetekesh turned and padded to Sharo's side.

The fae prince waved his hand at the berry-laden trees. "Step firm, be courageous, and all shall be well with thee."

Chewing his lip, he rubbed his hands over his pant legs to wipe away the sweat and walked forward until he stood before the holly trees. Against the deep green, the red berries glistened under the light and shade of the sun beyond the limbs swaying overhead. He held his breath as he passed between the two trees and felt the branches against his sleeves.

Before him stretched an aisle columned by tall dark trees, crawling beyond sight. His step faltered, but a hand caught his wrist and pulled him forward as he uttered a protest.

"Do not fear, my friend." Jinji's voice. Meek, soft. Laughing.

Jetekesh followed the shadowed figure of the storyteller, grinning. The air felt thick against his lungs, and the scents of green and damp filled his nostrils. His heart hammered in his ears. The trees leaned close, confining. Water gurgled somewhere nearby, out of sight, beyond the arcing trees.

"Here, Jetekesh. Behold."

He looked past Jinji and saw light. Golden. Radiant.

Jinji pulled him free of the constrictive trees. He found himself standing in a glade surrounded by tall redwoods outlined by molten light. The forest floor was clear of underbrush, and the trees stood wide apart. The air was wet with recent rain.

Jinji's eyes glistened with dancing shadows from the swaying sunlight. "We are in the fae lands, Jetekesh. Look." He pointed, and Jetekesh spotted a wide path wending through the tall trees. Strange blue lights flickered along the pathway. "Fairy lights," the storyteller whispered in awe.

"You are quite at home," said Aredel behind Jetekesh. The young prince whirled, heart bounding into his throat. He scowled at the Blood Prince. Aredel didn't seem to notice. His eyes darted around the glade, just as Sir Chethal and Sir Blayse stepped from the channel of trees, eyes wide and mouths open.

"An elder path," whispered the younger knight. Sir Chethal hushed him with a look.

Prince Sharo appeared from the column of trees last,

leading Amaranth, Ashea on his shoulder. "This path only appears under certain rays of sunlight. If we hurry, we will catch the path to Lord Peresen's fortress and arrive by nightfall."

"Fleetly, friends, or we shall lose the light," said the high voice of Ashea.

Sharo nodded toward the fairy-lit path beyond Jinji. "Go ahead, storyteller."

Jinji moved at once, a spring in his step. Jetekesh followed. As the company stepped onto the pathway, a tingle trotted up his spine. Eyes watched from some hidden place. He glanced back but saw no one.

"They are watchful," murmured Jinji. "Come along."

Jetekesh obeyed. The pathway bent north, and soon the glade vanished behind them. Mist crept in from the tall trees, shrouding the pathway but for the fairy lights. Jinji pressed on, and Jetekesh stayed as close as he could. No one spoke. They barely breathed.

Was that music? Jetekesh paused and tipped his ear to listen.

Jinji tugged on his sleeve. "Do not stray. Do not heed the call."

Jetekesh tripped along, and the music faded away, though the melody haunted the back of his mind. What was the call? He didn't dare ask. Not yet, not here.

The company carried on for several hours before Sharo slipped past Jetekesh and Jinji to take the lead. "We should rest a moment." He sighed and ran his arm across his face. "We barely made it, but we managed somehow. The fae paths are fickle and fleeting for humans, but we were granted passage."

Sharo caught Jetekesh's questioning look and smiled.

"Of myself, I am allowed to use the paths we've taken, but in company the fae do not wish it, unless my need is dire. Today it is, and so I was allowed to cross land by a swifter course than any human road. But as I said, the paths are ever changing. We might have become lost in a land unwelcome to humans, and that would prove ill for all save myself, the lady Ashea, and Master Jinji. It is fortunate that our timing and plight were as they are."

He hesitated. "Though I'd rather we had no plight so great as this to warrant the risk." He whistled, and Amaranth trotted forward. Sharo swung onto his bare back. "I shall go ahead and scout a bit. I will return in time for nightfall. Do not stray into the woods, else you shall be claimed by a more mischievous fae." He winked at Jetekesh. "They should like you best. Keep close to Jinji."

Alarm sprinted through Jetekesh. He looked at Jinji. "Why me?"

Jinji laughed. "You are young, fair, bold, and temperamental. All these things attract trouble in fae woods. That music you heard was an invitation, but it would have ended badly for you."

Jetekesh's eyes widened. "Are the fae dangerous?"

The mirth fell from Jinji's face. "Very dangerous, Your Highness. Do not think fae are all gentleness and wisdom. Some are dark. Even wicked. Most such things do not dwell in the elder woods, but some may pass through. Others mean no harm to humans, but their play is too much for a mortal man to handle."

Jetekesh shuddered. "I thought we were safe here. Sharo said—"

"Sharo meant what he said. Stay near to me and you

shall remain safe." Jinji lowered himself to the forest floor and leaned against a tree. "Sit, Your Highness. We should rest, as Sharo said. It shall be a long and perilous night."

Jetekesh knelt and leaned against the trunk. His eyes strayed heavenward. "What good will I be in a siege against a fortress?"

Jinji didn't answer. Jetekesh glanced at him and found the storyteller's eyes closed. His breathing was deep, but troubled. Jetekesh frowned. Danger lay ahead, and Jinji was so frail. Would he last the quest?

Would Jetekesh lose his only devoted friend so soon?

It wasn't fair.

He shut his eyes and tried not to think. It only made him angry and afraid.

29
THE SNAKE

The caravan remained halted until half past eleven in the morning. Three hours into the day's march, Prince Anadin called another halt and commanded camp be set up for the night.

The servants who had attended him from KryTeer carried out his orders in stride, accustomed to his antics. The servants from Keep Falcon grumbled, but very softly. By four o'clock in the afternoon, Yeshton found he and his companions seated in the second prince's tent, partaking of a foreign meal and entertainment. Prince Anadin applauded the dancers and singers that appeared before his table in turns.

The meal stretched on until the sun began to set. A haze settled over Yeshton's mind, but he tried to press it down and stay alert. He had explained the prince's proposal to Rille this morning. Her response had been a single nod, which alarmed Yeshton, though he knew as well as she did there was no choice but to adhere to the prince's request.

Now, as the rays of a red sunset crept into the tent, Prince Anadin clapped his hands, halting the music of a wild dance. The dancers faltered, bowed, and backed away, while the musicians lowered their instruments and slipped into the shadows of the tent.

Prince Anadin rose. "Come, Sahala. Join me outside."

Rille stood, smoothed her coarse dress, and walked with the prince to the open flap of the tent. Yeshton stared after them, a lump swelling in his throat. His hand felt for a sword he didn't possess.

Sir Palan offered him a pitying smile. "Easy, lad. Take a breath and wait for now."

Yeshton bowed his head and let out a long breath. "She's a capable girl. I must trust her."

King Jetekesh pushed to his feet. "So you should. She's nothing short of clever. Come along. I suspect we are free to return to our own tent."

Tifen climbed to his feet and followed the king outside, where a guard waited to guide them back to the prison tent.

Yeshton hesitated. "I think I'll remain here a while."

Sir Palan nodded. "As you should. I'll go on ahead." He downed the last of his wine, then prowled outside.

Yeshton watched servants clear away the food, while a tightness grew in his chest. She would be fine. She must be fine. He would destroy Prince Anadin if anything happened to her.

∼

THE EVENING BREEZE CARESSED RILLE'S FACE. SHE welcomed the cool sensation, for her nerves were taut and sweat stuck to her dress. She took care to keep her expression unperturbed as she followed the second prince of KryTeer across his large encampment to a stand of leafless trees jutting like naked bones against the red sky.

Prince Anadin traipsed over the roots of one tree, caught its trunk, and swung himself around it until he faced Rille. He leaned his cheek against the trunk, black eyes intent upon her. She halted under that gaze and said nothing.

"You're the sorriest looking child I've ever seen. Forlorn as death," he remarked as though he spoke of a pleasant day.

She lifted an eyebrow. "Is that so?"

He nodded. "It is."

They considered each other for a long moment.

"What do you think of me?" he asked.

"I honestly don't know."

"Come now. Something must come to mind."

She hesitated a heartbeat. "Odd."

A smile crept over his lips. "Oh? Well." He pulled himself behind the thin tree trunk, back facing her, and raised his head skyward. "I'm glad of your honesty. Thank you for being blunt."

"Will you be blunt in return?"

He turned his head to view her from the corner of one eye. "In what regard?"

"Tell me what you want with me."

A smile caught the corner of his mouth. He gripped the tree trunk and swung back around to face her. "I am told you are special."

Rille shrugged. "And so?"

"I was often told *I* was special too. I've come to realize that word is very dangerous." He sighed. "You've had a trying life, I quite imagine."

"Do you?"

Prince Anadin's shoulders slouched. He flopped to the ground and folded his legs before him to rest his palms against his knees. His smile was friendly and patient. "Do not be so cold, Sahala. Can we not set aside the animosity of our two peoples for one conversation?"

She folded her arms. "Give me a reason to do so. A good one. Not mere whimsy."

He bowed his head and chuckled. "A good one, hmm?" He lifted his head. His eyes held vivid pain. When he spoke, his voice choked with emotion. "I am afraid, Sahala. I need your help."

She took a step back, and her hands dropped to her sides. "I…don't understand."

He shrugged and laughed without humor. "How could you? We are both special, but your parents cared for you, did they not?"

She nodded.

He lifted a hand in a helpless shrug. "My father cares only for himself. That he finds me useful keeps me alive, yet the cost is unbearable to me." His brow furrowed. "At least, I think it is."

"Explain," said Rille as a headache throbbed against her temples. "You make little sense."

The second prince of KryTeer blew out a breath that stirred the long, dark hair around his angular face. Against the growing shadows of evening he looked small and very, very young, like a child trapped in a man's body. Prince Anadin leapt to his feet and began to pace, hands cupped behind his back. His black robes dragged across the dirt, but he paid them no heed.

"I am being poisoned, Sahala." His voice hung low and thick.

She blinked. "Poisoned, Your Highness?"

He didn't pause to look at her but kept pacing back and forth. "Behind you, near the flap of my tent, you can see a man, tall and stately in his priestly robes. That is Javanti, my personal guardian priest. He oversees the state of my soul."

Rille resisted an urge to look toward the tent. She would find the man later. "Is he the one you believe to be poisoning you?"

"It is more than mere belief. I know it as surely as I know my own name."

"You said your father finds you useful, so he is not aware of this poisoning?"

"Oh, he is." The prince ran a hand over his face. "It is not a fatal poisoning. It is…to another purpose. I must remain alive, you see."

"Why?"

He exhaled. "I must kill my elder brother."

She frowned. "I still don't follow."

"I am being driven insane." He spat the words out. "There. I said it. It's said. It's fact. I cannot escape it any longer. Each time I go to the priest to pray and cleanse my spirit, each time I am enveloped by the scent of incense until my mind wanders whithersoever it will. When I come to myself, I am told I've had a fit and have been taken to my own bed. This has gone on for years, and while I have no distinct memory of what occurs when I've been drugged, yet I know the purpose. Stray words and sensations well up now and then, and I know my father's fear. My elder brother is dear to me, and I to him. Our holy father wants Aredel dead, and I am the only one who may come close enough to do the deed. As I am, as I think freely, I would never go through with it. But Javanti is here to see it through. Even now he urges me not to return to KryTeer, but to wait for Aredel's return from Shinac. The emperor will not abide my failure. If I do not succeed, if I return empty-handed, I will be gotten rid of. This I know in my heart."

He pressed his fist over his chest. "I want to return to KryTeer instead. Let my life end now, before I can harm Aredel. I do not think I can kill him, even should some other piece of me awaken to try. Aredel is strong. Stronger than any other. I will fail, and I would rather die now as a traitor to KryTeer than as a traitor to my brother. I have no love for my country. My people. My father. Let them all rot; it matters little to me. Now or later, I will die. When Emperor Gyath's life runs its course, his harem, his servants, and his spare shall all meet our end anyway. I just wish Aredel to be the one to destroy my father and let his reign of terror end. That would be justice, yes! Ah yes." He laughed.

Rille studied the panic scrawled across his face. Her throat tightened. She caught his arm. He started and looked down at her, and she tried a smile, though it trembled on her lips.

"Be calm, unfortunate prince. If your brother cares for you as you say, he will soon return, and he shall not let you perish." The smile grew easier to wear as she studied the lonely black eyes in the narrow face. She reached up and ran her hand along his cheek. "Fear has long consumed you, Anadin. Let it out with a breath, and inhale only the calm of a setting sun. In this moment, you are safe."

Tears welled in his eyes. He pulled back. Cleared his throat and turned toward the naked trees. "Is this your gift? Do you see what you speak?"

"No. I only feel it. But your brother is with Jinji, and none knows better than he what ought to be done. All will be well."

"For some, perhaps."

Rille tentatively reached out and caught his billowing sleeve. "You believe there is hope, or you would not ask for my aid. How can I help you, Anadin?"

"I, I don't know. I had hoped you could tell me my course. Tell me what might revise my fate. I don't want to die..." He turned to her. "What can be done?"

Her smile grew. "Come with us, Anadin. Run away with my friends and me. Do not return to KryTeer. Hide in Amantier until your brother returns, and we shall fight your father, all of us together."

He blinked. A single tear wended down his cheek. "Run away? Could I?"

"And why not?"

The prince shuddered. "Oh, no. Father's magicians would know. They would find me."

"You're afraid."

His nod was fervent. "Oh, yes. Terribly afraid. I cannot escape my fate." His eyes lost their focus.

Rille caught each arm and shook him hard, until he blinked and stared down into her face. "Listen to me," she said. "You will let us go. You will come with us. We will hide until the Blood Prince returns, and then we shall do something to end your father's reign. We must. For your sake, for mine, for everyone's. Do this thing, Anadin. It is hard, and frightening, and perhaps it will end badly. But if your fate is already set, if death is your path, take the more meaningful way to meet it."

Anadin's eyes slid up from her face, widening. "Javanti is coming. We must not speak further. I, I will consider your words."

"Tonight, Anadin. We must act tonight, or we cannot possibly escape."

He nodded and wrenched free. At once a smile flitted to his lips. "Ah, Javanti. Do you see my little sparrow? I call her Sahala. I think I will take her home as a pet."

"That is wonderful, my prince," said a deep, cold voice.

Rille turned and found herself staring up at a snake in men's clothes. The priest was a plain man, in ornate robes twice as fine as Anadin's apparel. Javanti was tall, reed-thin, bald, and ornamented in jewels that flashed like blood against the last rays of the day.

Rille curtsied. "Shall I return to my companions?" she asked in a sweet voice.

"Certainly. Goodbye, little sparrow," said Anadin, waving a hand.

She traipsed back to the tent as airily as she could manage, careful to keep her smile in place until she slipped inside. Yeshton stood waiting. She scurried to him and caught his hand. He held hers tight. Neither spoke as he led her to the prison tent where the others dozed.

"How did it go, my lady?" asked Yeshton once they were inside.

Rille leaned against his shoulder and found herself trembling. "We must help that man, Sir Knight. He is a very sorry prince. If we do not save him, he will be eaten up."

30
WITHIN THE FORTRESS

"Here. Take it."

The curved dagger gleamed in the moonlight. Jetekesh grasped it, breathless, heart pounding. Its hilt sparkled with bloodred jewels. He looked up at Aredel. "Thank you."

"Use it well, and stay alive," said the Blood Prince. "That is my price." He rose from his crouch.

Jetekesh tracked the man as Aredel joined Jinji and Sharo beneath a tree beyond his hearing. The three conversed softly, Sharo's brow drawn; Jinji's jaw set; Aredel, hooded in secret thoughts.

Sir Chethal stirred beneath a tree nearby and shook his companion. Sir Blayse moaned and blinked sleep away.

"Where are we?" asked the younger knight.

Sir Chethal shook his head. "Somewhere on the elder path, remember?"

The fog cleared from Sir Blayse's face. "Ah, yes. We

travel with the horseman and his fellows. And that pretty little fairy."

Sir Chethal nodded. "Yes, so I recall."

The younger knight pushed to his feet and checked his armor and sword. "Shouldn't we be heading off to pursue our own quest soon, Sir Chethal? We've delayed long, I fear."

Chethal sighed. "If only we could recall what that quest is. T'would help."

Jetekesh opened his mouth to tell them Prince Sharo was the very man they sought. That there was no cause to wander off. But he stopped himself. Sharo would've told them already if it would lift the curse. *They must choose to serve him on their own, or never regain what they've lost.* He sighed and used the trunk to hoist himself to his feet. He brushed the dirt and leaves from his clothes and moved toward the three men in counsel.

Sharo's voice reached him first. "It is a terrible cost, Master Jinji."

"Nevertheless, I would take it, should no other course be found," was the reply.

"Let us view the situation and attempt another route before we accept a desperate measure." Aredel's even tones.

Jinji lifted his eyes and speared Jetekesh with a look. His face softened. "Your Highness. That's a handsome dagger."

Jetekesh smiled. "I only hope I wield it well."

A tinge of sorrow lit in the storyteller's eyes. "I pray you need not use it at all, but it is better that you are armed against our foe, come what may."

Sharo stirred. "It is time we leave the elder path. It will fade soon."

The faint glow of Ashea flitted from the treetops to land on the fae prince's shoulder. "The way to the fortress is open."

"Thank you, Ashea." Sharo's light eyes danced between each man before him. "I ask none to come with me. It is dangerous, and there is little chance any of us shall make it out alive, except by some miracle."

"Say no more." Jinji rested his hand on the prince's unoccupied shoulder. "I, for one, believe in miracles."

Sharo smiled. "As do I." A wind rose and brushed through his snowy hair, revealing the prince's ears. They lifted into a point. Wonder rushed through Jetekesh like dousing water. Fae indeed.

The prince of Shinac took the lead. They traveled the old pathway for another hour, then crested a hill, and finally trudged down into a fair valley that started where the redwoods failed. A prickle ran down Jetekesh's spine as he crossed the forest boundary, and the wind gave a shriek. Shadows fell before him, and he faltered, blinded.

His vision returned in a single heartbeat, but the valley had vanished. Before him rose a mighty fortress like jutting spikes from the broken earth. Louring clouds hung low, while thunder cracked and drummed within the celestial shroud.

Jetekesh's mouth gaped. His throat ached. Before the great fortress spread a concourse of campfires. A veritable army had formed, not made up of armored men and horses. This foe was a thing of nightmares. Jetekesh quavered and stumbled backward. When Ashea had described the hordes of foul creatures, he had imagined the trolls and ogres described to him by his childhood tutors and servants. These were nothing like those hulking, brutish monsters.

Sleek, winged, shadowed figures prowled around the flames, dancing in slow, deliberate, circling clusters. Tall. Graceful. Deadly.

It wasn't supposed to be like this.

Fear had pulsed through him when he thought he might have to flee from a filthy, blundering troll. Stave off a hive of wicked pixies. But this…this was something else.

"Spirits save us," whispered Sir Blayse beside him. He kissed the first knuckle of his left hand and pressed it to his forehead. "*Unsielie*. Of all dark fae, why must it be they who gather here?"

Ashea's wings hummed like a flitting bird. "It is a contract. They have agreed to enter Nakania with Lord Peresen to enslave the mundane world."

"Why?" asked Sir Blayse.

Ashea shook her head. "To wreak ruin, I suppose. They hate humans and love to spill blood."

Jetekesh looked between his companions. "What can we do?"

Sharo stepped forward. "We go on. Amaranth, remain here, my old friend." He drew his sword. It throbbed a note as he raised it high and strode forth. Lightning seared the sky and thunder rolled. The sword caught the light and flashed with color. Even after the lightning vanished, the sword maintained its luster.

A great hiss welled up from the dark fae army. Every eye followed the small company, but the tall, winged creatures parted before them. Jetekesh caught sight of the pale faces, the fair features, the black thoughts behind ethereal beauty. Men and women both. Strange black armor flashed and glittered in the storm-light and embers. His heart beat against his throat. Sweat trickled down his face. He flexed the fingers of his left hand, while he clutched his dagger in his right fist.

Why weren't the dark fae attacking? Why let them by?

The pathway closed behind them as they moved toward the fortress. The *Unsielie* followed, delicate black wings lifted like nets to catch their prey should they turn and flee.

"Lord Peresen is letting us pass," whispered Sir Chethal.

"So he is," said Prince Aredel. "All the better, for it saves us time."

The earth sloped upward until it touched the start of a stone bridge arcing high above ground to end at the fortress gates. Sharo took the bridge, sword still lifted above his head, and the rest of the company followed. The *Unsielie* halted at the base of the bridge.

Fingers of fear clawed against Jetekesh's throat. His shoulders ached.

The gates loomed ahead, but the bridge spanned forever. Why weren't the fae creatures following to tear them to shreds?

An eerie dirge rose behind them. Jetekesh willed his ears to stopper the noise, but the piercing voices cleaved through his frame like a sword.

"Heed them not," whispered Jinji.

Jetekesh started. Jinji walked beside him. When had

he moved from his place behind Sharo? Jetekesh looked ahead, flushing. "I'm fine."

"That's a brave lad," said Sir Chethal behind him. "Courage is proved in lands like these."

Jinji coughed into his hand.

"Are you all right?" asked Jetekesh.

Jinji waved his free hand, keeping the other pressed to his mouth. He nodded and kept walking. A ragged cough tore from his throat. He bent forward as a harsh fit seized his body. Aredel dashed forward to catch his shoulder.

Sharo stopped and turned, keeping his blazing sword aloft. "We cannot stop. It will be our deaths. Can you carry him?"

Aredel nodded and hoisted Jinji into his arms. The storyteller didn't protest but wiped his hand across his lips. A smear of blood marked his face and hand. He stared at the stain on his fingers, then looked wide-eyed at Aredel.

"*Run.*"

The dirge ceased. The flutter of wings welled up below the bridge.

Jetekesh glanced back. His breath caught in his chest. The *Unsielie* had taken flight, and the sky darkened against the gossamer lace of their black wings. The pitch-colored eyes had turned into a searing white.

Sir Blayse shoved him forward. Jetekesh stumbled, righted himself, and scuttered toward the fortress.

Sharo stayed his ground, sword raised against the airborne foe. "Keep going!"

The others pushed past him. Aredel took the lead, cradling Jinji.

"What made them…made them act?" gasped Jetekesh.

"Blood," Sir Chethal answered. "Causes a frenzy. Makes them want more."

Heart ramming his rib cage, Jetekesh urged his legs to move faster. He could hear the teeming hordes like a swarm of wasps. Sharo must be dead now. He couldn't defend against so many! Against his will, Jetekesh glanced back. Tripped. His knees struck stone as he bit his lip hard. From the ground, he saw Sharo still standing, his sword pulsing with a light that drove the horde back hissing and crying.

Sir Blayse caught Jetekesh's arm and hauled him back to his feet.

"Come on!"

Jetekesh staggered against the lancing pain in his knees. He still clutched his dagger. Panted. Ran on. Hair clung to his sweat-drenched face. The gates loomed nearer. So close.

What comfort was that? The gates belonged to Lord Peresen. There was no safety here. No light to run toward.

Jetekesh stumbled again. Go. Run. Flee. And then, fight.

The gates rumbled open as Aredel reached them, Jinji in his arms. Jetekesh stumbled to a halt. The two knights stopped beside him, gasping.

Between the two swinging gates stood a man. He moved forward, arms extended. He was a powerful man, built like his fortress, with black helm and armor, cloaked in dark velvet. A close beard lent strength to his jaw and dark hair curtained his face. Sharp eyes of deep green peered down on Aredel, gleaming in the light of myriad torches.

A lightless smile touched his lips, and he spoke in a rich voice. "Welcome, Jinji Wanderlust of Nakania. I have long anticipated our meeting."

Jinji lifted his eyes, pain lining his face. The smear of blood against his cheek was a dark blotch in the torchlight. "Lord Peresen. I cannot say I am honored, for I try not to lie."

A crack of laughter broke from the large man's chest. "Come within. Bring your companions." Those green eyes flicked beyond the party at his gate. For a moment, he watched Sharo fend off the dark fae. "*Quii dac*!" The command rolled like thunder across the long bridge and the *Unsielie* withdrew at once back into the sky, leaving Sharo alone with his sword. The fae prince lowered it and turned. Jetekesh watched him sprint toward them, still gripping his sword.

Lord Peresen waited until Sharo reached the gates.

"Hello, Lord Uncle."

The man's smile was contemptuous. "I claim no *Sielie* as my kin, young Sharo. The forces of light shall fall before much longer, and you shall fall with them." Lord Peresen turned his back to the party, cloak billowing. He marched into the fortress.

Aredel followed, at Jinji's quiet urging. The rest trailed after, with Sharo in the rear.

"I did not realize your foe was your own kin," murmured Sir Blayse.

"I did not mention it," said Sharo. "He is my father's brother."

"Ah."

Jetekesh glanced back to find Sir Blayse's troubled expression as he tried to remember what he could not. Jetekesh looked ahead again. The interior of the fortress was shrouded in deep shadow, despite torches set in sconces along the wide corridor. He looked up but saw nothing above him to suggest a ceiling. Only black nothing. He shuddered. Something breathed in that void.

Lord Peresen spoke from the front. "I can guess that you intended to stop my blood sacrifice this night, but you did not anticipate the *Unsielie*. Is that not so, Sharo?"

"I informed him of their presence," said the lilting voice of Ashea.

The dark lord grunted. "Ah, yes. The lady of the willow. Still traveling with the foolish half-fae prince? Fairies are very sentimental, I suppose." He halted before a great stone door and pushed against it. The stone gave and swung inward, rumbling and grinding, stone against stone.

Beyond lay a great throne room, where the throne itself stood upon a high dais overlooking the wide empty hall. Ancient banners hung from the rafters of inscribed wood. Swathes of cobwebs plumed around the banners, reflecting eerily against the lighted torches across the expanse.

Lord Peresen crossed the flagstones, steps echoing, mail clattering. He reached the center of the chamber, whirled around, and extended his thick arms. "Welcome to the Fortress of Crevier." His gaze speared Jinji. "It seems your life will expire soon, storyteller. Set him upon my throne. Let him survey all within my sight, come." He moved toward the dais.

Aredel remained still. "I would not mock Jinji, were I you."

Lord Peresen turned and smirked. "I mock all of you by my every action. What are you to me, stranger? Merely a mule, carting the last treasure of Nakania. Behold the fading life in your arms. A rare man indeed, so he is. Yet Nakania rejected him and called his stories only fables."

Aredel studied the dark lord. "You ask who I am? Shall I tell you?"

The looming man's lips curled into a wicked smile. "Do, please."

"Come here a moment, Sir Blayse."

The young knight trotted to Aredel's side and took Jinji from him. The Blood Prince stepped forward, hand on the hilt of his jeweled sword. Sharo moved nearer, his own blade still ablaze.

"Shall we answer him together?" asked the fae prince. "Or would you alone prefer the honor?"

"You came to save lives," said Aredel. "Allow me to claim one."

Sharo nodded. "I understand. Thank ye." He turned from the dark lord. "Lord Chethal, let us find his prisoners."

Lord Peresen laughed, a deep, booming howl. "You think to leave my sight, O fair prince of light? I will not allow it."

"You shall have your hands too full to bother with them, Milord Giant." Metal scraped and rang across the room. Aredel leapt forward, swift as a lightning bolt against the sky. Lord Peresen drew his blade in time to deflect the slash. An echoing clang filled the chamber.

Aredel fell back. Lunged again, motions light, fluid, tripping, and dancing across the stones beneath him as though he barely touched ground. Lord Peresen was powerful, but slow by comparison. As Jetekesh looked on, he recognized the difference in their skill. Lord Peresen could not win this bout.

The dread lord parried, blocked. Blocked. Again.

Aredel danced in. Out. Spun, for no better reason than to show off his speed against the man-giant. In his billowing white clothes, he looked like a small dove against a great vulture, yet he would not back down as he drove Peresen toward the dais.

Jetekesh glanced toward Sharo, but the fae prince had vanished, along with Sir Chethal. Something soft landed on Jetekesh's shoulder. He started and glanced down. Ashea.

She smiled up at him, a finger to her lips. He turned back to the struggle.

Lord Peresen bellowed. He swung hard, caught Aredel's blade, and knocked it from the Blood Prince's hands. It flew and landed with a clatter.

Aredel pulled a shorter blade from a second sheath.

Lord Peresen wiped sweat from his brow. "What are you?"

"I am called the Blood Prince of KryTeer. Let that be enough." A fire burned in Aredel's eyes. Mockery. Amusement. Pleasure.

Understanding dawned in Peresen's face. His lips parted. "So. You've come after all: the dread prince who bathes in the blood of his enemies to gain their strength. Not a myth at all, but a being of flesh and sinew. Well." His basso laugh rang from the wooden rafters. "What an honor I face this day! I shall not withhold my strength any longer. I have found an equal at last."

Aredel tossed his head. "Has not one Sharo, prince of Shinac, bested you before?"

"He and a dragon outsmarted me, 'tis true. But against my brute strength, Sharo alone stood no chance. You, however, are a challenge worthy of my venture."

Aredel's lips rose. "Let us hope your boasts are not empty."

Lord Peresen unstrapped his cloak and let it drop to the stone floor with a thud. He unlatched his breastplate, removed his gauntlets, laid aside his helm, and stood before Aredel in his chain mail. "Shall we begin anew, Prince of the Blood?"

"Let's." Aredel slid his legs apart, short sword held before him at an angle. He sprang forward. Lord Peresen caught his blade against his own, and Aredel rebounded. He leapt again. Peresen deflected him.

Aredel's speed quickened. He seemed to vanish before Jetekesh's eyes. Lord Peresen spun in time to fend off the Blood Prince, but Aredel ducked. Aimed for the man's leg. Lord Peresen kicked him, and Aredel stumbled backward. He wiped his chin. His eyes blazed, and he wore an open grin.

Jetekesh glanced at Ashea. "Who will win?"

She shook her head. "I could not say. Both are skilled. Both are clever. Neither likes to lose nor play fairly when the stakes are high."

Jetekesh frowned. "Aredel will win. He's the strongest. No one can best him in combat."

"Very likely, you are right," said Ashea.

"I'm useless here," said Jetekesh. "I want to help. But how?"

The two men swung at each other, dodging, dancing. Aredel narrowly escaped a fatal stroke. He drew a dagger and slashed toward Peresen's face. Nicked skin. The man-giant hissed through clenched teeth.

"Jetekesh."

Jinji's voice.

Jetekesh hurried to Sir Blayse's side and looked into the storyteller's pale face. "What is it?"

The storyteller smiled weakly. "Take me *up*." His gaze lifted. Jetekesh followed it until he spotted a flight of narrow steps carved against the east wall of the throne room; mere slats of stone jutting from the wall to make each step. It climbed gradually up to a door mostly hidden against the limp banners.

He turned back to Jinji and nodded. "Sir Blayse."

The knight lowered the storyteller to his feet. Jetekesh wrapped Jinji's arm around his neck and they crossed the throne room by inches. Sir Blayse hovered close, sword in hand, eyes riveted on the fight. At last Jetekesh reached the hewn stairs, and he hauled Jinji up, step by step, breath by breath. Sweat trickled down Jetekesh's skin. Jinji was lighter than he should be, but he grew heavier each passing moment.

"Wh—where does this lead?" gasped Jetekesh.

"A tower. There we will…find the prisoners…" Jinji's tone was strained and feeble. Jetekesh glanced at him and found a trickle of blood at the corner of his mouth.

"Shouldn't we let Sharo—?"

"Sharo…is too far…away." The urgency of Jinji's voice made Jetekesh shut his mouth against further protests. He concentrated on hauling Jinji up each step, while the storyteller hugged the wall and did his best to lift his legs. Jetekesh wobbled a few times, perched on the ledge as he was, but he refused to look down and make this harder. He could do this. He wasn't useless.

Mother would faint to see me like this.

The thought made him smile grimly.

Halfway. Keep going.

The clash of swords continued below. A deep shout suggested Aredel had gotten in another slice. Jetekesh resisted an urge to glance down. He took another step, pulling Jinji with him. His foot slipped. Biting his lip, he leaned inward, but felt the clutch of gravity fight against him. A hand pushed him upright.

He glanced back. Sir Blayse was on the step below, smiling. "Keep going. I'm here. You won't fall."

Warmth spread through Jetekesh's body. "Thank you, Sir Knight. If you weren't already honored so, I'd knight you myself."

Sir Blayse laughed. "Go on with you."

A howl rang through the air.

Jetekesh halted and looked down. Had Aredel dealt the killing blow?

No. Lord Peresen stood above Aredel, who lay sprawled across the flagstones. But the man-giant's eyes were clasped on Jetekesh's, sending a shiver up the boy's spine. Peresen drew a dagger from his belt. Raised it high. Pitched it.

The gleaming blade flew. Jetekesh threw himself forward. Dragged Jinji with him. A heavy weight fell across his back, and he heard Sir Blayse hiss as his body tensed. Jetekesh twisted to catch the knight before he could tumble from the narrow climb. A dagger jutted from the young knight's back where the armor was weak from rust.

Sir Blayse gritted his teeth, face contorted. "Leave me. Take the storyteller and go on. It's not so bad as it looks."

"Or as it feels?" growled Jetekesh. He ripped his sleeve and pressed the cloth to the knight's back. "I can try to remove the dagger..."

Sir Blayse snatched his wrist. "Don't bother with me. *Go on.*"

"But—"

"*Go.*"

Jetekesh pulled back. He pushed his hair aside, set his jaw, and took Jinji's arm to drag him up. A glance back confirmed his greatest fear. Lord Peresen had reached the bottom of the stairs. He was coming after them.

Sir Blayse struggled to his feet, leaning heavily against the wall, sword clutched in his hand. "Go on now, both of you. I'll hold him off."

Jetekesh swallowed. Nodded. Turned and hauled Jinji up the next step. The next. Keep going. Don't look back. A lump formed in his throat.

Almost there. A few more steps.

He heard a cry behind him. A crash as swords met. Someone screamed, and an eternity later, Jetekesh heard a sickening thud far below.

Jinji let out a sob. "Poor Sir Blayse. So noble. He served his lord well in the end."

Jetekesh ground his teeth as fire flooded his body. He trembled beneath it. The lost knight had served Sharo in the end, but he hadn't known it. Hadn't remembered what he'd lost and what he sought. It wasn't fair!

The door was close. Two more steps. He dragged Jinji up, and up. Here. Jinji leaned against the door, gasping. He caught the knob and pushed as he turned it. The door gave way and Jinji stumbled inside, Jetekesh on his heels.

A short corridor. A door on the other end. Jinji staggered ahead and Jetekesh grabbed his arm. He wrapped it around his shoulder again and led Jinji to the second door.

It opened.

Six maidens knelt within, chained by their wrists to the walls of the circular tower room. They looked up, wide-eyed.

Jetekesh faltered. Finding them meant nothing. They were all stuck here, cornered, Lord Peresen right behind them. Aredel was dead. Sir Blayse was dead. Prince Sharo and Sir Chethal were too far away to help.

Where was Ashea? When had she left Jetekesh's shoulder?

"My friend."

He looked toward Jinji.

The storyteller smiled meekly. "You have been brave and true. I thank you from my soul."

Jetekesh narrowed his eyes. "What are you plotting?"

Jinji's smile grew. "You must go home, my friend. I have made arrangements."

"What do you mean? I don't understand."

Jinji caught his shoulders and spun Jetekesh around until they had traded places. Jetekesh's eyes widened.

Lord Peresen loomed beyond Jinji, charging, sword pointed straight.

"Jinji! NO! NO!"

The sword slid through Jinji's back and out his chest. Blood dripped from the point. Jinji wore a smile. That infuriating smile!

Lord Peresen bellowed with laughter. Cut off. His eyes widened, and he howled as wind rose, warm, caressing. Light stretched from Jinji's body. Brilliant, pure. A song whispered upon the wind, and Jetekesh found himself caught in the memory of the tales Jinji had told upon their journey. The ancient willow, where the ugly lass had cried until a fairy took pity. Ashea. The fairy had been Ashea. He saw the young king, humbled by the sight of true beauty. Their wedding party. The start of the country of magic.

He saw a child, fair and bright, swallowed by darkness after the death of his mother. And there, against the glow of memory, he saw the fair child again, but he was grown now. Tall, regal. Comely as morning light but bearing shadows as though he had enslaved the darkness to his will.

"Do you see?" gasped Jinji. "Do you see him, Jetekesh? Sharo? Aredel? 'Tis the rightful king of Shinac."

"I see him," said a voice, distant. Sharo's. A sob sounded in that voice. "He is yet far away."

The wind breathed again, lifting Jetekesh from the ground. He saw only white now. Smelled a green and growing world. Rich loam. Sea brine. Ancient trees. The wood scent of a campfire.

Thunder rumbled. A howl rose above the wind, above the thunder. Raging. Wild with anger.

The world settled around him, gritty earth beneath his feet. He opened his eyes and found himself standing in a desert beneath a burning sun. Jinji still stood before him, sword lodged in his chest. Behind him Lord Peresen wavered on his feet, staring at his own chest. There too stuck a sword.

Jinji sank to his knees, and the man-giant followed to his own. Behind Lord Peresen stood Aredel, eyes ablaze. He wrenched the sword from Lord Peresen's chest and rushed to kneel beside Jinji.

"You fool. Why did you sacrifice yourself?"

"To take Peresen out of Shinac, of course, but alone, without his armies." Jinji laughed. "I am dying, Aredel. It made sense to use myself. A willing sacrifice is far more powerful than any other, and thus I was granted a request." He turned to Peresen. "Behold Nakania, land without magic, home of your final rest." He coughed up blood. "And so, it is mine as well." A tear tracked down his cheek. "Alas, I would like to have stayed in Shinac until the very end."

Jetekesh trembled and collapsed to his knees. "You... you can't die. It's not fair."

Jinji turned his eyes to him. "Oh, Jetekesh, friend of my soul. How much pain you have met upon this quest. I am sorry to add to your suffering, but I could not hope for a better way."

"What of Sharo and his companions?" asked Aredel. "They are lost within that fortress."

"The contract between Peresen and the *Unsielie* ended once the former arrived in Nakania," said Jinji. "The dark fae will return to their woodland homes until another greedy master summons them forth."

A hollow scream rent the desertscape. Lord Peresen tried to stand, but he staggered and tumbled back to lay in the sand. "You cannot…best me this way."

"But I have already, Lord Peresen." Jinji leaned against Aredel's arm. "I feel the life draining from my body, my friend."

Aredel shut his eyes. "I saw him, Jinji. The true king of Shinac. He was magnificent."

Jinji's eyes closed as well. "So he was."

Jetekesh looked between them. "Can we not do something to save him?"

Aredel lanced Jetekesh with a dark look. "We are in the middle of the desert. We have no supplies. No transportation. If I move him, he will only die faster."

Jetekesh bowed his head. "But…" He curled his hands into fists and bit back a sob. *It's not fair. It shouldn't end this way!* Shuddering, he leapt to his feet. "It isn't fair, do you hear me, King of Shinac? He's only ever served you! What sort of king abandons his greatest knight! DO YOU WANT HIM TO DIE LIKE THIS?"

"Hush, my friend. I did not serve the rightful king of Shinac so that he might spare my life as it expires. I served him because I love him." Tears rolled down the storyteller's face. "I love him as all liegemen love their just and mighty lords. It is reward enough, and yet he granted me a chance to see Shinac before my end. I am satisfied."

"*I'm not.*" Jetekesh's limbs shook. Heat scalded his blood. "Don't you dare just give up! Stand. Live. Breathe. You can't just lie there. Has your king asked you to end your life? No! So you can't die yet. Rise, and fight to the finish."

A deep, gurgling laugh reminded Jetekesh of Lord Peresen.

"Foolish child. Jinji died long ago. 'Tis only his soul that wanders now, chained by his grief."

Jetekesh's eyes widened. "You're wrong. That's not true."

A chill ran the length of his spine. A presence, great and terrible, towered behind him. He couldn't move.

"You're correct, Prince Jetekesh," said a rich and silken voice, lilting as a song, terrible as a storm.

Jetekesh staggered around. Standing in majesty and torrential light was the true king of Shinac, not like a memory, but a man of flesh and sinew...yet so much greater. Clothed in black, crowned in light, pale haired, and fair, just as Jetekesh had seen in the windstorm.

"My lord and king," said Jinji weakly.

"Ah, Jinji." The king's tone was fond, and his pale blue eyes softened. He moved past Jetekesh and knelt on one knee before the storyteller. "Brave, foolhardy man. Could you think of no other path?"

Jinji laughed. "Alas, my king, I am only mortal."

"So you are, and so you shall remain. I have not finished with you yet." The king reached a gloved hand to the point of the sword in Jinji's chest. At his touch, the blade vanished. The stain of blood against Jinji's shirt-front disappeared. Surprise fluttered across Jinji's face and he drew a deep breath. A cough seized him.

The king rose to his full height. He was slender, yet well muscled. Tall. "You are not healed of your illness, but nor shall you die of a sword wound."

Jetekesh bit his lip. "Why won't you heal him? Can't you?"

The pale eyes found Jetekesh. Held his gaze, until Jetekesh broke away to stare at the ground.

"I could," said the man of silk. "But Jinji does not wish to be healed, and I will honor his wishes, except in the matter of this sword. Jinji has not yet finished his task."

Jinji inclined his head. "So I have not. There is yet another palace I must be banished from; is that not so, my lord?"

A dark chuckle. "It is. I look forward to seeing Emperor Gyath's face. If you hurry, you will reach the caravan heading toward KryTeer, led by Prince Anadin." He gestured westward, and Jetekesh found himself staring at three strong horses, one laden with packs and water flasks.

"Go now," said the king. "I must leave you. It is not yet time for my return to this world."

Disappointment flashed in Jinji's eyes, but he said nothing. The king turned back to Jetekesh. "You have much to learn, young prince, but I do enjoy your spirit."

Jetekesh blinked, and the king was gone.

Aredel pulled Jinji to his feet. "Can you ride?"

"Yes. I think so." Jinji glanced at Lord Peresen. "He is dead?"

Aredel nodded. "He is. He did not see the king."

Jinji looked away. "Then let us be on our way. The desert buries all."

The three moved toward the horses, sights set westward to KryTeer.

31
A THREAD OF SMOKE

A storm grew with the sunrise, out of the east. Rille watched it at the door flap. "Something comes this way."

She kept her voice soft, but Yeshton's head shot up, and he looked around until he spotted her at the tent entrance. He climbed from his bedroll. A few long strides brought him to her side. The guard outside the tent straightened his spear and tossed Yeshton a warning glance. Rille was able to wander as she pleased, perhaps because she was a child, but the KryTeer guards considered Yeshton and Sir Palan dangerous, if their furtive glances were any way to judge.

"Is something wrong?" asked Yeshton, keeping his voice low.

"Aside from our present circumstance?" asked Rille, glad her voice carried the level of playfulness she'd intended. Emotions were so hard to convey.

The soldier quirked a smile. "Aside from that."

She pointed eastward. "We will have company soon. I

dreamt of three horses holding aloft a banner: a strange golden cross, whose arms split into three points against a divided field, half white, half black. I have never seen its like. Yet the heralds who bring it signify power, for they carry the storm forth."

Yeshton's eyes sought the horizon. His jaw tightened as he eyed the far-off dust riding the high winds. "The storm comes from the southeast. Perhaps from the Drifting Sands. Is it Jinji?"

Hope flooded Rille's heart, warming her, and she hugged herself. "Perhaps that is so. The banner *feels* like magic. Perhaps he has returned." The warmth died as she thought of Prince Anadin, sent to murder his brother. On impulse, she raced from the tent. The guard protested, and she knew Yeshton had tried to follow, but she couldn't stop now. Across the parched earth she kicked up clouds in her wake as she flew to the prince's tent. The guards stationed at its entrance swept aside the flaps.

Within, she flitted past silent servants and impassive guards, through a second, voluminous swath of cloth and into a dark chamber whose furniture crouched like great black beasts in the shadows. She faltered, fear chilling her bones, but squaring her shoulders she pressed toward the largest beast-like shadow, guessing it was the prince's bed.

Patting the surface assured her she'd guessed right. Rille slipped onto the bed, crawled across, and patted around for the prince's form. A soft sound brought her up short. Was someone crying?

"Anadin?" Her voice was so soft, she doubted he'd heard her, but the crying stopped.

"Sa...hala?" The voice was faint, young, and definitely Anadin's.

She crawled across the wide cushion until she touched Anadin's arm and followed that until she could feel his shoulder, neck, tangled locks of hair. Face. His cheeks were wet. "There you are. Why are you crying?"

"Aren't you mad at me, Sahala?"

She sighed. "No. I understand why you couldn't come last night. You were frightened and carefully watched by that snake."

"Snake? Oh, you mean Javanti." He chuckled. "You seem a fair judge of men, my Sahala."

"You haven't answered my question. Why were you crying?"

"Oh, I...had a bad dream." He sniffed.

"What about?"

"My brother. He was lying in a dark room, bleeding out. Something dreadful towered over him, and I feared to find its face. I feared I would see myself."

A shiver raced up Rille's spine. The Blood Prince's face flashed before her eyes. He rode upon a stallion, holding a banner. "Up. Get up. Your brother is coming. He isn't dead. You've not killed him, but if word reaches your snake guardian that he approaches, you might live out your dream. *Up*, Anadin."

The prince climbed from the bed, threw a robe over his dark undergarments, and lit a candle. "Is he coming? Has he returned from Shinac?"

Rille considered the prince's face. Nothing sinister tinged the color of his earnest devotion for an elder brother. She nodded to herself, satisfied. She had done right to tell him, to get him *outside* before he could be influenced by Javanti.

"Come. Hurry."

She took his wrist and led him across the rug-strewn chamber, through the swathing curtain, and out into the larger chamber. Servants dropped to their knees in respect, surprise bright on their faces. Anadin was likely never up so early in all his life.

Rille guided the prince to the tent flap and out into the early morning glow. The sky was pink and gold. The storm drew nearer, but its strength had diminished. The great black cloud was now a faint gray haze. Rille glanced toward the prison tent, and found Yeshton, King Jetekesh, Sir Palan, and Tifen outside, watched by half a dozen armored guards.

Prince Anadin looked around, eyes shining. "Where is he?"

"Not here yet. Be patient." She sifted through the milling servants.

There. Javanti approached, his pace rapid, eyes intent. "Your Highness!"

Anadin pulled against Rille's grasp. "What can I do?" he whispered, terror threading a quaver in his voice.

"Stand steady," she murmured as she relinquished her grip. Mustering all her courage, she plastered a smile to her face, let out a laugh, and ran to Javanti with outstretched arms. "Holy priest, holy priest!" The man came up short, alarm lining his face, brows creased. Rille threw her arms around his waist as tight as she could, then pulled back and peered up into his wide, wondering eyes. "Prince Anadin has told me that I may convert to the faith of KryTeer. I do so wish to worship a goddess!"

He said I must be incredibly good and to promise *you* I would be, and so I do."

A scowl deepened the lines around Javanti's eyes, and he shook her off. "Away with you, pestilent child. My holy calling is above mere conversion. You must speak with lesser priests."

"B-but…" Rille squinted her eyes, hoping it would lend the desired effect of shimmering tears. "But, holy priest!" Her voice rose in a wail. "I want to worship a goddess! Aren't they beautiful? My mother was beautiful. Is *she* a goddess now?" She wrapped both hands around his arm and tugged. Hard.

He wavered and growled. "Let me go, child. I am busy." His eyes darted toward Anadin. "Take your little sparrow."

Anadin started forward, and Rille bit back a dismayed whimper. How could she rescue him if he obeyed the priest's commands? Drawing a breath, she took the only path she could see. Swinging her leg with all her might, she kicked Javanti's shin. He yowled and whipped out his hand to strike her. Rille flinched, but another hand snatched the priest's wrist mere inches from her face. She looked up. Found Anadin beside her, a sneer across his lips, black eyes lit like coals.

"Do. Not. Harm. Sahala." He twisted Javanti's arm, and the priest grunted, but didn't retaliate. Didn't struggle. His eyes lowered to the ground.

"Forgive me, my holy prince," whispered the priest.

Anadin shoved Javanti back before he released his arm. In this moment he was neither young nor weak but looming and seething with ruin and power. Now Rille could see the resemblance between this man and his elder brother. If Aredel was the Blood Prince of KryTeer, perhaps Anadin was its Shadow Prince, cloaked in innocence, forged in sorrow, rooted in darkness. She saw now the tendrils reaching up like chains from the earth, binding his limbs, keeping him caged for nefarious deeds. A great specter, vast and wicked, loomed behind Anadin, bearing the key to those heavy chains.

A shout jolted Rille from the vision. She whirled as soldiers ran from the eastern edge of camp. "Your Highness," cried a burly man, hand pointing behind him. "The Blood Prince is coming."

A hissing breath turned Rille's eyes toward Javanti. He'd known. He'd seen them coming. And Rille had kept him from squeezing those chains so that Anadin would turn on his brother. For now.

The shadows fell from Anadin's face. He let out an exultant call and dashed past the soldiers. "Aredel! Aredel!" The soldiers and servants followed, mixed shouts and cheers rising to the sky.

The storm was now just a strong wind blowing sand from the nearby desert. Rille raced through the crowd, dancing between swinging arms, to catch up to Anadin before Javanti could try anything. She didn't know *what*, but she wouldn't take any chances.

Horses. Three. One was just a packhorse, while the other two—

Rille's eyes widened and warmth surged through her, exhilarating, triumphant. Here was hope!

Her cousin looked wonderfully haggard, smudged, tangled, ripped, bruised. And leaning against his back atop one noble horse was Jinji Wanderlust; pale, sweat soaked, tattered, but alive. On the second horse, sitting proud, as disheveled as the other two, and blood-stained, sat the First Holy Prince of KryTeer.

"Aredel!" cried his brother again, and he threw his arms around the man's leg. "Brother, I'm so glad to see you."

"Greetings, brother," said Aredel. The fond smile on his lips was all Rille needed to see. He would help her to rescue Anadin. And perhaps in exchange, he would release her and her friends. They could go home. Muster a force. Ride against KryTeer.

She shook her head. That was for another day. Now, this moment, was all that mattered. Her gaze flicked back to Jetekesh and Jinji. Both careworn and bone weary. Her cousin's eyes roved, half dazed, until they collided with hers. To her shock, he smiled. *Actually smiled*. It was a faint expression, probably unconscious, but it was real. He murmured something, and Jinji lifted his head from Jetekesh's back. He searched and spotted Rille. His smile was deep but fleeting. His head lowered again, and he clung to Jetekesh as though his effort was all that kept him upright.

"Bring my guests into your tent," said Aredel.

"Of course, my brother." Anadin barked orders. Servants sprang into action.

Rille lost sight of the KryTeeran princes, her cousin, and Jinji. She also lost Javanti in the hustle and bustle. Someone caught her shoulder. She whirled—and blinked up at Yeshton. "How did you—"

He shrugged. "We were forgotten in all the hullabaloo. Alas, we can't slip away. Not with your cousin in his present predicament." He nodded toward something Rille couldn't see at her height.

"What is happening?"

"He's being escorted along with Wanderlust and the Blood Prince to your Anadin's tent."

Her Anadin. For some reason, the words made her smile.

Just which of us is the sparrow?

"We must go there too," she said, and pressed through the waning crowd of armored bodies. Soon she could see the tent again just as the royal persons and storyteller slipped inside. Her pace quickened and she glided into the dim interior, Yeshton on her heels.

"Out, out. Everyone out." Anadin's tone was clipped. Commanding. "Javanti, bring my physician. Go on, man. Are you deaf?" He barked a command in KryTeer's formal tongue, and the priest moved toward the flap. Rille slinked aside, blending with the darkness. He moved past her, past Yeshton, never noticing, face frigid.

She took Yeshton's wrist and moved forward as the clingers-on reluctantly retreated.

Anadin's black eyes flicked her way, at first tense with irritation, but widening as he recognized her. "Sahala. Ah, and your protective *brother*. Come, come. You were right, Sahala. My brother has returned." Rille's eyes followed the motion of his hand, and she spotted the three newcomers seated on the surface of the crouching head table. Jetekesh held Jinji up, but he looked ready to drop himself. Aredel sat straight but pressed a swab of blood-soaked cloth to his waist. Perspiration on his brow glistened against the candlelight. His brown eyes darted between her and Yeshton, and a wan smile haunted his lips.

"So, you've become Anadin's prisoners now?"

Rille felt Yeshton stiffen, but she squeezed his wrist and nodded. "So we are."

"No," said Anadin, tone wounded. "She is my Sahala."

Aredel's eyebrow arched. "Your sparrow?"

Yeshton's arm strained against Rille again. She glanced at the soldier to find his eyes narrowed on Anadin, sharp as daggers. "You said it meant the girl who sees true. You said it was an ancient word for *Rille*."

A sheepish grin crawled up the second prince's face. "Ah, that. Yes. I lied. I'd already heard all about Rille from both my father and from Aredel, so I fibbed to read the truth in your face. Sahala simply means sparrow. The closest Old KryTeeran word for Rille would be *Lah'al*, which means *beauty*. I don't even know a single word that means *the girl who sees true*." He shrugged.

"*Kalakeeridwa* would be the closest." Aredel's voice. Rille and Yeshton turned to him. The Blood Prince shrugged. "It's not exact. The most literal translation is *one who sees far away*. It is a word not used since the ancient days of King Cavalin the Third."

Jetekesh's head rose, as a thrill raced through Rille's body.

"My ancestor," Jetekesh said.

"And mine," said Rille. She too carried the blood of that great-hearted soul.

Jinji's eyes opened. "A more noble king never has lived upon Nakania since Cavalin, for not long before his death a great evil rose up from the sea and tainted the land. It caused the inhabitants to turn greedy; and thus it was that an army marched upon Shinac, and the land of magic fled into a space outside man's mortal reach.

Cavalin fell defending Shinac before it vanished." He gasped for breath and coughed into his hand. Jetekesh held him steady until the fit passed.

Horror shivered through Rille as the storyteller lowered his hand to reveal flecks of blood against his palm. His face, ashen.

"Oh, Jinji." Her voice was barely audible.

"So, tell us," said Anadin above her. His tone was nonchalant. "Did you truly see Shinac, brother? Was it grand?"

The Blood Prince turned from watching Jinji. "It was both grand and horrible, for I saw the elder paths and a fortress of evil."

Footsteps sounded behind Rille. She turned to find Javanti approaching, a white-robed man behind him.

"Thank you, priest," said Anadin. "You may go."

Javanti didn't move.

Aredel's eyes narrowed on him. "Did you not hear my brother, priest? Leave us."

The priest bowed and backed away, while the physician strode forward, a cloth bag in hand. He knelt before the table and peeked beneath the roll of cloth Aredel held. He murmured something in KryTeeran. Aredel nodded, and nothing of pain showed on his face while the physician set to work cleansing the gash.

Anadin's hand found his throat and he pinched his skin. "You'll be fine, yes, *shaqin*? This is nothing to you."

"I am well enough, *shaqel*."

Rille's nose itched.

"I had a dream," said Anadin. "You were sprawled across the ground. You were dying, and a great dark thing reigned over you, deeply satisfied." His eyes were wide and unfocused as he spoke. His tone was edged with panic.

Aredel reached out and snapped his fingers before his brother's face. Anadin shuddered and blinked rapidly.

Rille sneezed.

"What you dreamt did happen," said Aredel, gently. "But as you well see, I am quite alive. The towering figure you saw is dead now and rots in the Drifting Sands. None live who harm the first prince of KryTeer. This you know already, *shaqel*." He gestured to Jinji. "We have defeated the tyrant lord of Shinac; have we not, my friend?"

Jinji's head moved in a vague nod.

Jetekesh gripped his shoulders and glared at Anadin. "Can't he lie down?"

The second prince stared at Jetekesh without comprehension.

Jetekesh's face reddened. His voice rose as he asked, "Can you not hear me?"

Anadin shook his head as though to clear it. "No, sorry. What did you say?" He reached up and pressed a hand to his temple. "I'm quite dizzy. I think I need to…lie down…" He turned and stumbled.

Rille made a sound and released Yeshton as though she could catch the prince. Yeshton moved for her. Two long steps brought him to Anadin's side as the prince slumped.

"He's cold. Ice cold." Yeshton studied Anadin's face. "His breathing is erratic."

"Healer," barked Aredel.

The physician was already trotting toward Anadin.

Rille's nose itched again. The air was thick. Sweet.

She spun around. There. A lean figure retreating through the tent flap. A flicker of light against the shadows. A thread of smoke rising. She raced across the canvas chamber, caught up a stick of incense burning on a silver tray, and threw it to the ground edging the rugs that littered the room. She stamped on it until the flicker died. Smoke danced around her foot.

She looked toward the head table. Every eye, save Anadin's, rested on her. "Prince Anadin has been poisoned by incense," she said. "I, I'm not certain what will happen." Her eyes fell on Aredel. "He's meant to kill you." She pointed toward the flap. "The priest just escaped."

Aredel nodded. "So it is. Anadin must be ready, then."

Rille stared. Her heart quickened. "You mean…you already know what has been done to him?"

Aredel nodded again, calm. "My father has been grooming him since his infancy, in case I grew too independent. It appears the time has come: either Anadin or I must die."

32
ENVY AND REVENGE

Jinji lifted his head from Jetekesh's shoulder. "Aredel, do not mislead everyone. You appear not to care."

The Blood Prince glanced at the storyteller and exhaled. "I have long known that Anadin—"

The hiss of a drawing sword cut him off. Aredel sprang up and drew his blade in time to knock Anadin's strike off course. Rille cried out. Where was the physician?

There. Standing calm as could be, an empty sheath in his hand, a triumphant smile on his lips.

"Sir Knight!" Where had Yeshton gone? He'd been supporting Anadin. Where—?

Yeshton slipped from the shadows behind the physician, a candlestick gripped in one hand. He raised it. Swung. Struck the back of the man's head. The physician crumpled.

Yeshton smiled at Rille. "I'm all right. He thought he hit me hard enough, but he thought wrong." He wiped a streak of blood from the side of his head. "I've now instructed him in the proper method, my lady."

A clatter tore Rille's focus from the soldier and back to the struggle between royal brothers. Aredel was pressed against the table, spine straining. Anadin leaned over him, their swords crossing at Aredel's chest. Teeth gritted, Anadin pushed harder. Leaned closer.

His eyes held no light.

Rille sprinted to the table. "Anadin, stop. You don't want to hurt him. Fight this, Anadin!"

"Stay back. He will use you if he must," barked Aredel. His foot lifted and slammed into Anadin's ankle. Aredel twisted as his brother stumbled, knocked the sword from Anadin's hand, wrapped his arm around the second prince's throat, and spun to stand behind Anadin in an arm lock. Both brothers panted. Aredel's eyes blazed.

"Don't kill him," said Rille.

"He has never been my target. But until the incense is out of his lungs, he will try to kill me." Aredel squeezed his brother's throat, tight. Tighter. Anadin's eyes bulged. He gasped for air. His body slumped and his eyes dimmed.

"You're strangling him!"

"Be calm." Aredel lowered Anadin to the floor. "I know the moment to stop. He is unconscious." He straightened and flinched. His hand moved to his wounded side. "Long has my father feared my strength. I suspected he would try to use Anadin, but I was kept away so I could not interfere. I have conquered the world," his eyes flicked to Anadin, mouth twisting, "while my little brother has been brainwashed and drugged into this inhuman state, whereby he might be useful in killing me.

"Should he fail, my holy father believes I will kill Anadin, and that way at least there will be no extra to worry about. Spares can cause trouble in a royal house. The purpose has always been to let one of us kill the other." His attention turned to the physician sprawled across the ground. "Is he dead?"

"I hit him very hard," said Yeshton, hefting the candlestick. "If he's not, he's stronger than he looks."

Aredel stepped from the table, crossed to stand over the physician, and pressed the tip of his curved sword to the man's chest. "He's breathing. Barely." Aredel thrust the blade into the man's heart.

Rille looked away.

"What now?" asked Yeshton.

"Now?" Aredel turned to Jinji. "Now we let the storyteller rest, and tomorrow we travel on to KryTeer."

Yeshton glanced at Rille.

"All of us?" she asked.

"All but the physician—and Javanti." Aredel moved toward the exit.

"Why?" asked Yeshton. "We've done nothing to warrant imprisonment. Isn't Amantier now a province beneath KryTeer? We serve the Holy House of KessRa. Let us go."

Aredel paused at the door and looked back, a glint in his eye. "And miss the opportunity to use young Rille as bait? My holy father may not desire me to live, but he will also allow me into the throne room of KryTeer so long as I have something he wants." He slipped through the flap.

"So, we remain prisoners." Yeshton sighed. "In the end, are we any better off with the Blood Prince than the Emperor?"

"He's not an evil man." It was Jetekesh who spoke.

Rille stared at him. "Have you become ill or simple-minded, cousin? I can't quite determine—"

"Don't mock me," said Jetekesh. "Just help me get Jinji to a bed. He's had quite an ordeal, and we rode through the night."

Yeshton pulled Jinji to his feet. He and Jetekesh carried the storyteller between them, slipped through the curtain swath at Rille's behest, and laid Jinji upon Anadin's bed. Jinji curled up as Jetekesh pulled a colorful blanket over him.

"Tell us what happened, cousin," said Rille. "Please."

He described pillars of white sand and singing stars. He spoke of Prince Sharo, the fairy, and the lost knights. Of the elder paths. Of the dark fortress and Lord Peresen. His voice caught as he recounted Sir Blayse's death. Last he explained Jinji's plan, the return to the Drifting Sands, and the visit from the rightful king of Shinac. His voice caressed each word with reverence. A light danced in his eyes; something Rille couldn't quite name. Perhaps the residue of magic. Jetekesh had been touched by it, after all. Infused with it.

Rille studied his face as he lapsed into silence, struck by the alteration in his countenance. He wasn't quite—well, quite *human* anymore. An otherworldly quality had settled on his shoulders.

Her heart throbbed. She looked away. Why had Jinji chosen him to travel between the sand pillars? Why had she not been invited?

"Where is my father?" asked Jetekesh.

The ache dug deeper. "Outside, I expect. Sir Yeshton, will you seek him?"

"Of course, Mistress." The soldier bowed and retreated.

Rille tried to smile. "He's been very worried about you."

Jetekesh turned his gaze to Jinji. "As I have been for him. But I'm glad I went."

Rille looked away again as her breath hitched. Jetekesh still had his father, while hers was dead. Jinji had chosen Jetekesh to enter Shinac. She had no one, except for Yeshton, who served her out of loyalty for her father, not through any merit of her own.

She backed away from the bed. Away from her cousin, who had everything she wanted. She slipped through the airy curtains, back out into the main chamber of the tent. Anadin lay on the ground, while the Blood Prince's men, Shevek and Ledonn, guarded him. The physician's body had been removed.

Yeshton slipped inside the room, King Jetekesh, Tifen, and Sir Palan trailing behind him. She smiled at her lord uncle, but he hurried across the rugs and into the bedchamber beyond. Alive. Breathing.

Not like Father.

The Blood Prince had killed him.

Her lungs constricted, and she hunched forward. Back then, he'd been a thing of nightmares. A foreign, black entity, looming and untouchable. Father had died by the will and cunning of a monster. It wasn't until now, this moment, understanding dawned like a blinding sunrise. Aredel. Aredel had killed her father. He had ordered him tortured, drawn, quartered.

Her limbs shook. Tears spilled from her eyes. Her throat tightened, choking her.

Murderer. Murderer!

How could Jinji call him friend? How could Jetekesh say he wasn't evil? Were they blind?

"My lady?" Yeshton stood at her side.

She sucked in a quaking breath. "Sir Knight…" A sob caught in her voice. "Sir Knight, I want my father."

He crouched before her and rested his hands on her arms. Their eyes met. "I know, my lady. I…I'm so sorry."

"Sir Knight…"

"Yes, my lady?"

"I need a dagger."

He became still. "For what purpose, my lady?"

Her eyes strayed to Anadin. "I intend to kill the Blood Prince. Do not stop me."

She watched Yeshton's struggle in the strain of his mouth, the crease of his brow. Felt it in the tightening of his grip. His desire to protect her weighed against her command.

He sighed. "As my lady wishes." He pulled something from beneath his tunic and placed it in her hand.

She looked down. A steak knife from dinner last night. "I knew you'd have something."

He smiled. "I intended it to protect you."

"I'm grateful." She held the knife to her skirts. "I'm going to find the Blood Prince now. Don't come."

Doubt flickered in his eyes; he thought she would die. He was probably right. This was foolishness. She inhaled, moved past Yeshton toward the door, outside, past the guards. No one stopped her. She was a child. What could she do to anyone? She licked her lips, paused and, from her vantage point, searched the cluster of tents, the tethered horses, the supply wagons.

Her eyes flicked toward the bare trees that looked so much like bleached bones.

There he stood. At his feet in a heap lay the dreaded priest Javanti, soon to be as bleached and naked as the trees above him.

She trotted across the encampment, heart thudding against her ribs, loud in her ears. Her legs shook. Palms clammy with sweat. She walked on. The hardness of the earth jolted through her. Soon. Soon, she would meet her enemy.

Aredel heard her. Turned. The fierceness in his eyes brought her up short. He was a wild animal, tense, full of bloodlust like a gnawing hunger. Like Anadin.

Rille's heart faltered. Like Anadin. So much alike. Two princes raised within a powerful, lustful, over-reaching empire.

She moved again, fingering the knife. *You can do this. You must try. He is a monster and he must be destroyed.*

"I hate you," she whispered.

Aredel watched her, shoulders tense, a flash in his eye. She was food to him. Nothing else. But then he blinked. Drew back and glanced down at his feet, to the corpse of Javanti. His eyes flicked back to her and a strange smile slid across his lips. "You plan to kill me, little girl?"

She held up the knife. "Let me. You are more beast than man. You murdered my father and countless others.

In the end you will probably kill Jinji, though he calls you friend."

He scoffed. "If I killed Jinji, it would be *because* he is my friend and his suffering is more than I can bear to watch. But I understand your words, perhaps better than you yourself do. Long have I known the beast within me. The wanton creature spurred on by blood and conquest. I had hoped once to still it, for if the world is conquered, there should be no reason it must awaken." He looked skyward. "I know better now. I *am* a beast, harnessed by Emperor Gyath to sate his greed. But I shall use what he has bestowed upon me, and I shall end *him*. For Anadin. For my sins. And then..." He looked at her sidelong. "And then, I shall let you kill me. Is this fair?"

She studied him. The resolve, the reason. His eyes were clear, and he knew her. She lowered the knife. "It is fair. But in the end, Prince, you must die."

"The Blood Prince shall die," said Aredel quietly, "once he has ended the line of his blood. It is just and right. And, though it matters little against such scales, I should like to die when Jinji does. Evil like mine should not endure, if his goodness must be snuffed out."

She scowled and looked away. "He is not goodness if he calls you friend."

"You do not believe what you're saying. You want to, but you do not. He called me friend before I became what I am. I became so on his behalf, and so he blames himself. He calls me friend still because he hopes to save my soul, foolhardy as his desire is. I am grateful and humbled. Strange emotions for me, I confess." He laughed but sobered at once. "Tell me, Lady Rille, would you ask a man like him to be less than he is?"

She shook her head. "No, I wouldn't ask that of him. But..."

"Ah." The Blood Prince nodded. "You wonder why he chose me and your cousin, rather than you or King Jetekesh or Sir Palan or your faithful Yeshton. One would, I suppose. That is a simple matter: none of you needed the journey. Your faith is sufficient. Do you need to see Shinac to know it exists? I think not. Does Yeshton ask why he must serve you? Does King Jetekesh rule his people in tyranny? Did Sir Palan defile Queen Bareene? Your honor, your faith, your integrity—these are what define the paths of Shinac. Your spirits are like Prince Sharo's: ever right and true and good. For myself, I had to see what true strength was. And your cousin had to witness loyalty and friendship."

He smiled as though something amused him. "Already, Lady Rille, you walk the path of white sands and starlight. So do your companions. Jinji didn't *need* to show you what you already know and feel."

She dropped the knife. It stuck in the earth as a tear slid down her cheek. "Perhaps...you are right. I, I was foolish to forget."

"A weakness you are allowed. Are we not all human?"

33
A PLEA FOR HELP

The hustle and bustle of Kilitheer's wharves overpowered Jetekesh. The sickly odor of sweat and rotting fish, the taste of brine, the deafening shouts of merchants, the ringing bells of the anchored ships, the colors, the jostling, the clattering carts, the peals of laughter, the overbearing sun high overhead—all made his insides churn and his mouth dry. How could anyone handle so much *chaos*?

He needed water. Shade. Quiet. His stomach rumbled. He needed food, too.

He stood with his companions, surrounded by KryTeeran guards. Waiting. Seething, as he stood beneath the noonday sun, sweating, stinking, *starving*.

Overhead, bold as the sky itself, danced the banners of KryTeer atop the masts of great warships. No one seemed to notice, or if they did, no one cared.

Jinji stood beside Jetekesh, a hand on the prince's shoulder. It trembled, and Jetekesh turned to his peculiar friend.

"Do you need to sit down?"

The storyteller nodded as his knees buckled. Jetekesh caught him and set his jaw as he struggled to hold the man up. Father stepped to Jinji's other side and hefted him until Jetekesh held none of Jinji's weight.

"We need shade," Father said. His blue eyes sifted through the guards around them. "You. Tell your princes that the honorable storyteller of Shing cannot abide this heat any longer."

The guard scowled but moved to obey. It had been made clear upon Aredel's return to camp that Jinji was to be granted every possible comfort. None could harm, mock, or even *look* at the storyteller unless they wished to join the many souls Aredel had used in his bath rituals. No matter how weak their skills might be, he assured them, he would make a well-deserved exception. The last few days of travel had been slow, so that Jinji could rest undisturbed in the swaying palanquin.

Prince Anadin, too, had been kept apart. Aredel was careful to stay away until it was certain Anadin's senses had returned. He had no recollection of his attempt to kill his brother. Now, in Kilitheer, he and Aredel had gone off to arrange for passage to KryTeer aboard one of the warships.

The guard returned and motioned down the wide, portside street. "This way. There is a tavern where we may wait."

The crowds drifted aside like the tide for the Blood Knights, never changing the flow of their motion down and up the street. The lopsided tavern cleared quietly as the troop entered, and Jetekesh followed Father and Jinji to a corner table that leaned hard on one leg. Everything felt *soggy*. Dirty. Dim. A stale odor tickled Jetekesh's nose.

"Do you want any spirits to perk you up?" asked Father, lines etched around his eyes.

Jinji shook his head. "No, only rest. Thank you." He folded his arms across the table and slumped his head against them. His back rose and fell lethargically with each breath.

Jetekesh frowned and glanced at Father, who smiled back.

"He's still strong of heart, son. Merely exhausted. Let him sleep." He moved close to Jetekesh and wrapped an arm around his shoulders. "You've been very brave these many weeks, Kesh. I'm proud of you."

A warm flush spread across Jetekesh's face and raced down his spine. The past few days had been spent traveling under heavy guard, and few words had passed between father and son. For some reason, the Blood Prince hadn't yet revealed Father's identity to the bulk of his troops or servants. But neither had he allowed anyone to return to Amantier. What his ultimate plan was, Jetekesh couldn't guess. Surely his reasons to bring Rille to KryTeer didn't mean the rest *had* to come. Still, in a way Jetekesh was grateful, if only because he could care for Jinji en route.

Perhaps that was Aredel's intent as well.

"I'm sorry about your mother," said Father, very softly, dragging Jetekesh's mind back to the present.

Jetekesh hesitated. "I'm not. I mean, I *am* sorry, but not about her death. She, she deserved it. I'm only sorry she did. Deserve it, I mean." He grimaced. Why all the stammering? Why the lump in his throat? He didn't miss the woman who had raised him for her own gain. Never with real love or affection, except for her own traits passed down.

"It's all right, my son," said Father, a gentle lilt in his voice. "You can still love her. There were traits in your mother worth honoring, though they lessened over time. You can love what was good and keep those memories forever. No need to banish them."

Something stabbed Jetekesh's heart. "But she was *horrible*. I hated her."

"She *was* horrible, and likely you did hate most of her. But you can love her too. No one would fault you."

"*I* would."

"Kesh."

He turned to face Father. The king smiled at him with all the affection of a true parent. "I would rather you tried to love what was good, than focus on hating what was bad. We both know there was much of both inside her at separate times. But, for *your* sake, try not to dwell on the bad. Forgive her if you can. She cannot harm you any further." Pain lit in his eyes. "I'm only sorry I let her hurt you at all."

There was no chance Jetekesh would ever forgive the dead queen for poisoning her husband, for imprisoning Jetekesh in a stainless world, for trying to discredit and destroy Jinji—and, most of all, for selling out Amantier to the enemy. But he would hold his tongue. Father was tormented enough.

Jetekesh squeezed the king's wrist. "I'm all right, Lord Father. She didn't do any lasting damage, I think."

A gasp brought his head around. Tifen stood near the tavern window, eyes fastened on the street. He turned, found Jetekesh. Pointed. "Forgive me, but I just saw someone we know. I think her name is Kyella."

Jetekesh trotted to the window. "You mean the farm maid near Kavacos?"

Tifen nodded and jabbed a finger outside again.

It took a moment against the milling crowds, but sure enough, there stood the lass, intent upon the guarded tavern, lips pursed in concentration.

Jetekesh looked back to call Yeshton, but the man was already coming, searching the sea of bodies.

His gaze rested at last on the girl, and his brow furrowed. "What is she doing in Kilitheer?"

"Perhaps she came to save you," said Rille as she slipped in front of Yeshton to see the girl for herself. "You did mention she was fond of you."

"Ridiculous. Uh. My lady. She couldn't possibly know we're here." He strode to the guard in the doorway. "That girl across the street. The young one in the peasant garb. Bring her in here."

The guard turned a sneer on Yeshton. "You not be giving orders," he said in a thick accent.

Yeshton squared his shoulders. "Bring her. For the storyteller. They're friends."

"No chance," replied the guard.

"Oh. It's Anadin." Rille's voice.

Jetekesh turned from Yeshton and found Prince Anadin in the street talking with Kyella. His hands stretched and waved as he spoke. Aredel appeared from the crowd to stand behind his younger brother, and the three conversed for a long moment. Yeshton was back at the window, leaning against the frame.

Aredel motioned toward the tavern. Anadin caught

the girl's wrist and dragged her across the street. The guard pulled away from the door, bewilderment stamped on his face.

"Ah ha," said Anadin as he entered. "As you can see, we have all those you described here in our company. Isn't it wonderful?"

Kyella's eyes danced between faces until they fell on Yeshton. "Oh, Yesh." She broke free of Anadin's grasp and sprinted across the room to throw her arms around the soldier's neck.

"Let me guess," said Anadin, "another sister?"

Yeshton shot him a scowl, and gently pried Kyella's arms free. "What's wrong? Is it your father?"

She nodded as fresh tears leaked from her eyes. "They took him, Yesh. He's gone to KryTeer as a slave. I...I didn't know what to do, until I saw you outside." She glanced toward the KryTeeran princes. "Are you a slave too, Yesh?"

"Something akin to one," he murmured, a faint rumble in his voice. "When was he taken?"

"We were on the road. It was just after we left the farm. They brought him here, and he was sold at auction to KryTeer like some animal. Oh, Yesh. What can I do?"

Yeshton looked grimly toward Aredel.

Jetekesh moved across the tavern room to approach the Blood Prince. "What *can* we do?"

"Nothing," answered Aredel. "If he's been sold to KryTeer, it will be impossible to track him down. He's one slave among a million. Best the girl considers him dead. His loss will be easier to bear that way. Slaves in my father's empire are worse than dead."

Kyella moaned and leaned against Yeshton, eyes

lowered. "Merciful God above, spare him." She tensed and her eyes widened. Slowly, very slowly, she lifted her gaze to Aredel. "Your father?"

"Oh, didn't we mention it?" asked Anadin. "This is High Prince Aredel, and I am his younger brother. Our father is Emperor Gyath."

Kyella made a strangled sound and pressed hard against Yeshton. "I thought…I thought…"

What she thought, she didn't say.

Jetekesh caught Aredel's arm. "There's nothing you can do?"

"Nothing, as I said."

Jetekesh grimaced and yanked his hand away. "Some High Prince you are."

"Tell me, Jetekesh. Could you do better, were our roles reversed?"

"I will never know. Amantier has no slaves."

"Aredel."

Everyone turned to Jinji, who had lifted his head from the table. His skin was ashen white. His eyes appeared sunken. But his voice was strong.

"The ships will have logs. The slavers will have records. He can be found if we reach KryTeer soon. When do we leave?"

Aredel sighed. "You don't understand, Jinji. Not even a prince can free a slave. I haven't that authority."

A light sparked in Jinji's eye. "Does the reputation of the Blood Prince mean *nothing* to your own people, Aredel? If you demanded one slave freed, or ten, or one hundred, would the slavers, the nobles, the soldiers *dare* say no?"

"You wish me to use my influence to steal a slave?"

The light in Jinji's eye dimmed. "Can a man be bought or stolen? He is not property owned by another. There is no moral ground for slavery, and therefore you cannot steal one. The very idea of enslavement offends my soul." He shuddered and bowed his head. "When do we leave, Aredel?"

"This afternoon at high tide."

"Very good. It is growing late."

Jetekesh flinched. It was true; every moment was a struggle for Jinji, as though his spirit wished to shed itself of its own mortal flesh. Like it was imprisoned there against its will.

"Not long to wait," said Father, near the window.

Jetekesh wondered if he meant the wait for high tide, or if his words were somehow prophetic. Best not think of it. He must aid Jinji as long as he could.

34
SEA BELLS

At first glance the southern shores of KryTeer looked no different than the northern shores of Amantier. Jetekesh shifted his feet as his scalp prickled. Rille wrinkled her nose where she stood beside him at the ship rail.

Soon the buildings of the seaside Royal Capital became distinct, and Jetekesh relaxed, though he couldn't say why. Perhaps it was the alien sight of the arches and bulbous turrets; they set KryTeer apart as a strange and horrible place, nothing like the peace loving, quaint lands of Amantier. The spicy scents were also peculiar. He tasted curry on the wind, rather than the brine of further south.

"I don't like it," said Rille.

"Nor I," said Jetekesh with a disdainful sniff. "But it's no wonder they can eat what they do. The very air is like fire."

Footsteps fell behind the cousins. "As are our

sunsets." Aredel came to the rail and stooped to lean his forearms against it, hands cupped together. His brown eyes burned with the flames of his homeland. "Indeed, in this arid scape, most everything is a fire." He gestured to shore. "Vast deserts, tangled jungles, quarries of hard stone, paved roads, gold and gems, the mighty Blood Knights—all are born from a great fire unlike any other. KryTeer is the flame of Nakania; it keeps the world vital. Alive. It is the very heart."

Jetekesh looked away. "If KryTeer is Nakania's heart, I wonder what Shinac was."

"The true heart," Aredel said at once. "In its absence, KryTeer rose like a great lion to keep the world from wilting away. I do not say KryTeer is the greatest of any country. But it is the fiercest. Perhaps one day, if Shinac is returned to this sphere…perhaps KryTeer will be content at last."

"If KryTeer is a lion's heart," said Rille, "then Amantier must be a great bird's heart. And Shing, the heart of a lamb."

"Not so," said Aredel. "Shing has a long and varied history. It is no lamb. Perhaps it is like a stallion, such as our thoroughbreds that ride the desert dunes. Wild, free."

Rille pouted. "Jinji is a lamb, Your Highness."

Aredel smiled. "I disagree. He is a stallion."

"I must agree with Aredel," said Jetekesh, almost to himself.

Rille shot him a hard look. "Why?"

"Because…because I know his past. A stallion suits him more."

The girl sighed and turned back to the approaching shore. "He's a lamb."

"Who is?" Yeshton's voice.

Rille turned, triumph in her face. "Which do you think Jinji more resembles? A sweet lamb or a wild stallion?"

The soldier hesitated, looking between each face. "Uh, well. I always thought him a fox, myself. He seems gentle, but he's cunning and even manipulative when it comes down to the heart of matters."

Rille made an indignant sound. "You're all blind. He's nothing but meek and gentle."

"Who is?" asked Anadin as he strode across the deck to join them.

"Jinji," said Rille with heat.

The second prince of KryTeer paused in his step. "He struck me as sickly and timid. Like a mouse."

The girl stamped her foot. "Now you're being ridiculous. A *mouse*?"

Anadin shrugged. "A sickly mouse. Yes."

Aredel chuckled. "I wonder how Jinji perceives himself if each of us sees him so differently. Perhaps I will ask." The man in the crow's nest shouted down to the captain. Aredel looked toward the approaching city. "But later. I welcome you officially to the waters of KryTeer's Royal City: Bahadronn."

~

SWARMS OF PEOPLE MILLED ABOUT THE PORTS OF Bahadronn, but that only lasted until the Blood Prince descended the gangplank of the warship *Rahadreth*. Like magic, the crowds parted; men in bloodred armor formed two columns, and Aredel glided between them, Jinji close at his side. Jetekesh and the rest of his companions followed, with Shevek and Ledonn taking the rear. A hush had fallen over the people of KryTeer in their bright colors and heavy jewelry.

They're afraid, thought Jetekesh. *It's fear and respect that keeps them still.*

Aredel led the company past the columns of Blood Knights, where a train of large palanquins came to a halt, carried by servants donned in bright red and gold silk. These palanquins were grander than the one at Keep Falcon. Golden threads and tassels glittered while jewels lined the silken fabric of the enclosed transports; they flashed and sparkled under the high sun. Aredel helped Jinji into the first palanquin and slipped in after his friend. Jetekesh and the others were led to the next contraptions.

The crowds never moved. Never murmured. Only the sound of sea bells and the cry of gulls overhead severed the stillness. Jetekesh shivered. It was eerie.

He climbed into the roomy palanquin and sat beside his father, listening to the tinkling chimes against the breeze. He had heard of KryTeer's sea bells from his tutors. They'd used hushed tones when they spoke, like the servants always did when they told ghost stories around the kitchen hearth. As a child, Jetekesh had sneaked from his room on several occasions to hear them.

Before KryTeer had become the war-seeking behemoth of the present age, it had been a country largely made up of seafaring explorers. The dainty sea bells were hung on sticks along the shores of KryTeer to welcome the boats each time the seafarers returned home.

Jetekesh had heard countless tales of lost boats trawling a lover home to the sound of the bells. It was said the bells chimed, even on a windless day, when someone lost at sea returned and let his lover know his fate. Sentimental drivel, Jetekesh had always believed.

But now, hearing the cry of the bells against the lapping waves, feeling the reverence of KryTeer's people like he could almost drink it in, Jetekesh imagined the lost souls at sea coming home to end their wandering.

Jinji. Ice gripped Jetekesh's heart. What if the storyteller heard the bells, and somehow, *somehow* his soul slipped from its mortal cage to return to his home in Shing? To his own lost love?

A hand fell on his shoulder. Father's. Jetekesh looked into the hollowed face and the warm eyes.

"Be brave," Father whispered.

Jetekesh pressed a little nearer to the thin body, and his heart thawed. Father was here, and Jinji was not far away. It was possible none of them would escape alive from KryTeer; but here, with those he loved, Jetekesh must be strong. Too long he'd been weak and frustrated by Mother's stifling protectiveness. Now, surrounded by enemies, frightened for good reason, helpless to escape or triumph, he could prove she'd been wrong to cage him: he was stronger than she ever thought.

Rille and Yeshton joined them inside the palanquin. The transport swayed as it began to move. The rhythmic motion calmed Jetekesh's nerves a little, and he closed his eyes to shut out the ornate interior. He could smell the fragrance of hot spices. Sweat. Salt. But it all became distant, like a hovering dream. This half-conscious, comfortable distance remained until Jetekesh lost track of time. There were only spices and chimes and rocking forth, back, forth.

The motion ceased. Jetekesh jerked forward, heart in his throat.

The curtain door lifted aside, and a Blood Knight glowered into the large compartment. "Out."

Father climbed out first, Jetekesh next, followed by his cousin, and last her knight. The palanquin behind them released Sir Palan, an irritated Tifen, and a trembling Kyella, who hadn't intended to come to KryTeer, but who came nonetheless at Prince Anadin's insistence. Apparently, he was quite taken with her.

Jetekesh turned from them. His lungs hitched. Stairs. Such stairs he'd never beheld in his life. They climbed upward for ages; white marble veined with silver, wide and high, until the palace stretched above it, blindingly white, straight, and proud, topped by a dome of brilliant gold. Four spires surrounded the dome in a perfect square, while the face of the palace itself was made up of archways and peculiar, elaborate carvings of great elephants, wild stallions, fierce lions, mighty birds, and the heathen symbols of their gods and goddesses.

It was obscene, Jetekesh tried to tell himself. But he was riveted by its alien beauty.

The Blood Prince approached, a circlet now resting on his brow. He inclined his head toward Father, offered a faint smile to Jetekesh, then pinned his eyes on Rille.

"You will remain at my side as we enter. King Jetekesh has agreed to assist me in presenting you to the Emperor. If anyone should try to spare you, I will remove his hand." A quick glance at Kyella. "Or her hand, as it may be."

Kyella looked too pale and shaken to attempt anything, thought Jetekesh. But he said nothing aloud. Here, Aredel would reveal his true intent, whatever it may be. He owed only Jinji, and his loyalty remained to KryTeer. Amantier was but a province in his mind, conquered, insignificant. And he was right. Why then did he treat everyone civilly?

A fleeting time ago, Jetekesh would've presumed it an act to keep them complacent, and he'd not have bought it. Nor would anyone else. Yet now everyone remained still and allowed Aredel to do as he wished. Was it trust in the Blood Prince? Surely not. Jetekesh and Jinji alone should harbor any such feeling; and even Jetekesh's trust was parchment thin. Yet Father had come along willingly, and he agreed now to aid in Rille's presentation before the dread emperor.

There must be more to this. Jetekesh hoped against hope Aredel intended to slay Bloody-handed Gyath and take over as KryTeer's ruler; but was that possible? Wouldn't the Emperor be surrounded by his own force of Blood Knights and priests? His own great entourage so close, so loyal, not even his children could come too near? So Jetekesh's tutors had always painted in his mind.

Aredel was clever. But Emperor Gyath knew it.

The company started up the steps. Jinji rode upon an open, single-seat palanquin carried by four servants. Had the storyteller's hair turned whiter since the docks? Jetekesh bit his lip and watched as he strode beside the palanquin. Despite his growing weakness, Jinji's strange eyes drank in the view of the gaudy palace.

The ascent took longer than Jetekesh had feared. A servant had come up beside the palanquin and opened a silken parasol to shade Jinji from the hot sun. Jetekesh dearly envied the storyteller, as sweat poured down his back. Now, as he crested the last step, dragging in gasps of air, Jetekesh's heart fell. There was still a lengthy path to the palace's front doors. The walk was flanked by two long, clear, rectangular pools reflecting the palace stretching overhead. Jetekesh ached to douse himself with water, but he buried the urge. First of all, it was heathen water. Second, it was sacred to KryTeerans, and Jetekesh preferred to keep his hands attached to his arms.

At least up here, on a hill overlooking the capital city, a faint breeze stirred. Not cool, but not quite hot. It felt good against Jetekesh's brow, and he sucked it in gratefully as he trudged on. He could taste spices each time he inhaled. More than once, he sneezed.

At long last the doors of the palace loomed a few yards ahead. Four guards in golden armor stood before the carved wooden doors, swords raised to cross at an angle over one another. As Aredel marched forward, the swords lifted until they pointed heavenward, and the guards bowed their heads in unison.

One spoke strange words that flowed like a chanting song.

Aredel cupped his hands, pressed them to his chest, and inclined his head in a slow, deliberate nod. The guards moved, two on the left turning right, two on the right turning left, and they backed away from the doors. A great crashing boom sounded within. A gong, Jetekesh thought. The doors pushed outward to admit the High Prince of KryTeer.

This was it. Jetekesh's heart swelled in his throat, and he wheezed for breath. This was real. He was going to stand before the dread Emperor of KryTeer.

He couldn't wake up.

It wasn't a dream.

35
BEFORE THE EMPEROR

Never had Jetekesh seen so many jewels, so many gold surfaces, so many rugs and tapestries. Amantier was a prosperous country, but frugal in its fashions. Even the royal treasury, with its wealth of gems and artifacts dating back to Cavalin the Third, was nothing to the pomp of KryTeer's enormous throne room.

Jetekesh gaped, but he knew he wasn't alone. Only the two princes of KryTeer and their servants could be underwhelmed by the grandiose display of wealth. Even Jinji, climbing from his palanquin, stared in open admiration.

The chamber was vast, and long, gleaming. At the far end, elevated high above the floor, perched a man of great girth. A table had been placed before his golden throne, spread with heaps of steaming food on platters and in tureens of solid gold. He ate heartily, licking his fat fingers between each succulent bite, a dribble of grease trailing down his several chins; but his eyes fixed on his sons. His brow wrinkled.

Dancers bowed low as they backed away from the open space below the high throne. The chamber was crowded with people dressed in ornate costumes and intricate headpieces. Women draped silk across their faces to hide all but their dark eyes. Earrings and bangles flashed as they turned to murmur to their neighbors when Aredel strode forward. Rille trotted beside him. Jinji and Father went next, and Jetekesh scurried to join them. The others came last.

"Aredel, my firstborn of the Bloodfold," boomed a voice that rattled Jetekesh's bones. It was deep and mighty; not at all the whining, mincing tone Jetekesh had anticipated from the fat man seated above.

Of course not. He might be slovenly, but he's still the Emperor of KryTeer. Hadn't Jetekesh heard a thousand stories of this man's strength on the battlefield? Hadn't Gyath been a demon in the minds of all his foes? Not like Aredel, perhaps; but his reputation was well-earned. While Emperor Gyath had taken to glutting himself, he still maintained the air of a powerful figure.

The Blood Prince reached the rug below the throne; he fell to one knee, bowed his head, and pressed a fist to his forehead. "Holy Emperor, I have returned bearing a great gift."

Jetekesh's stomach lurched. His eyes darted to Rille standing beside Aredel. Was he really going to give the girl over to the emperor? Hadn't it been just a ploy to get in here? Was it all a trick? Did Aredel intend to hand them over to the Holy Empire, thereby proving his loyalty to Gyath and sparing his own life? All so he could finish conquering the last corners of the world?

Bile burned in Jetekesh's throat. Lightheaded, he swayed.

"Present your gift," Emperor Gyath rumbled.

"May I first—"

"Hello, Holy Father." Anadin's amiable voice.

The emperor's face turned red. "Silence, you useless fool!"

Anadin's smile remained, but he shrugged and held his tongue.

Aredel glanced at his brother, then still bowing, swept his hand toward Father. "My Holy Emperor, may I first present unto you King Jetekesh the Fourth of your newest principality, that ungrateful and self-righteous country, Amantier."

Jetekesh bristled but bit his lip. *Remain calm. Do not become angry. He's merely performing.*

Father took a single step forward, keeping his eyes lowered. He knelt upon the tapestry, rested his palms against the floor, and bowed forward until his head touched his hands. "Most holy and venerable emperor, it is the dearest honor of my life to bow before you."

The murmurs of the gentry—could they be called gentry?—grew louder. Heat climbed Jetekesh's cheeks as his limbs shook. He had never felt so humiliated, not ever in all his life. To see his father bow and scrape before a heathen tyrant—!

"Well, well," boomed Gyath. "I am pleased, my son. Most pleased. Long have I craved this moment. Long have you, O throneless Jetekesh the Fourth, withstood my invitations to allow your tiny country to join itself to my empire. But now, here you are, a pebble beneath my shoe." He let out a bellowing laugh that shook the ornate lamps above. The sound grated on Prince Jetekesh's soul like grit in his teeth.

"That is not all, my holy emperor," said Aredel. "He has also bestowed upon you a gift. The very gift you sent me to claim for you in Amantier."

Jetekesh risked a glance at the face above him. Emperor Gyath's eyes gleamed, and a hungry smile lifted the flaps of his cheeks. "So." The man's voice cracked like thunder. "This child is the gifted one?" He leaned forward, sausage fingers gripping the arms of his throne. "You could not find her on your own, Aredel? Perhaps your skill diminishes."

"Amantier is a strange land, Holy Father," was the Blood Prince's curt reply. "Who better to lead me through its winding provinces than its own ruler? Besides, he had something to gain by assisting me if your magnanimous will finds no fault in the idea. Would you grant unto Jetekesh the right to maintain his reign, acting as governor of Amantier beneath your mighty banner, Most Majestic One?"

"Oh-ho?" crowed the massive man. But his eyes narrowed. "Do you take me for a fool, O son? Do you think I would not see your secret desire? You and this stubborn, ungrateful man have formed an alliance. To whom shall he be more loyal? You, who speaks on his behalf, or me, for whom he blames our conquest?"

"You are wise," said Aredel, bowing his head. "Yet this is not our intent, my father. Behold, Rille, the child you have long sought. Do you think I would try a cunning ploy with this new weapon in your arsenal? She, whose gifts I have seen along our journey home?"

"A fair point, yet I have no proof this is the very child. How can she reveal her gift to me?"

"I shall show you, if I may be allowed to speak for myself." Rille's voice rose like lark song. The emperor's eyes speared her, but she stood with chin high and shoulders back.

Gyath chuckled. "So you say, tiny one, yet your eyes smolder with defiance."

"I am no man's, that he may gift me to another."

The emperor's smile lifted in a lopsided smirk. "Yet you would prove to me your gift? Why?"

"I hold no fealty to Amantier, for the kingdom is no more, my father is dead, and my uncle betrays me. Should I not use my gift within your court, I am no better off than a waif in the streets of a heartless city. If I *do* serve you willingly, you shall bestow upon me every luxury my talent deserves. Is this not so?"

Gyath slapped his large hand against the arm of his throne and let loose a laugh like a wild storm. "What a child!" More bellowing laughter. "Clever. Very clever. It is true: if you please me, I shall give you riches and prestige the like of which none other may know, not even my sons. Prove yourself unto me. Show me your gift!"

The echoes of pelting laughter died against the distant, muraled ceiling. All fell still. Rille stood alone beneath the throne of KryTeer, fearless, proud. Jetekesh's heart galloped. She must be afraid, though she didn't show it. He was terrified, even though Gyath had no use for him...

Maybe that's why I have cause to fear. Throneless, weaponless, I'm nothing anymore.

Not so. Jinji calls me friend. His breath snagged. He

glanced toward the storyteller who stood close by, pale, perspiring, but riveted on Rille. Jetekesh reached out to him and caught his sleeve. Jinji turned, startled. He blinked and smiled gently. They both shifted back to Rille.

The little girl considered Gyath for a long, long moment. A faint breeze whispered from the open windows flanking the walls of the chamber, and strands of Rille's hair drifted in a lazy dance. She breathed.

"*Well?*" Gyath's voice cracked like a whip. "Do you *see* anything?"

"Hush," said Rille. "If it were as easy as shouting, anyone could do it."

Prince Anadin laughed—the only one who dared.

Time pressed on. The heat of the day grew and sweat trickled down Jetekesh's temples and back. Despite the perfume of the courtiers around him, the onion odor of hot bodies haunted the air. Rille was so still she might have been carved of stone.

A fly hummed overhead. Jetekesh cringed as it flew nearer.

"I See," stated Rille. Though her voice was quiet, her words traveled through the silent chamber. "Your reign is troubled by a fear of betrayal. Long have you heard the whispers of those who should love you best; and even now you expect daggers in the dark. Be at rest, O Emperor, for you shall reign until a man, crowned by chains, shall appear and give unto you immortality in payment of all you have given."

Gyath's eyes widened. His tongue darted out to lick his lips. "Immortality?" A grin stretched across his face until his teeth bared. "I shall truly be a god!" He turned toward a cluster of men in robes near the base of his raised platform. "You see? She is a true Seer! Yet you doubted me. Doubted my wisdom! I shall be a god in the flesh! Ha!"

Jetekesh resisted an urge to roll his eyes. Rille had given no proof of anything; she had merely told him what he wanted to know. And even then…wasn't it subject to interpretation? Was the man so blind, so deaf, he couldn't detect the risk in her words? Might not immortality also mean death?

With a clap of Gyath's hands, music struck up again. He commanded Prince Aredel to stand. "You've done me proud this day, First Prince." Gyath's gaze roved the remaining party behind his children. "Who else do you bring? More gifts?" An edge of greed guttered his voice.

"No gifts, but one among them is honored throughout all the eastern kingdoms for his talents." Aredel swept his hand toward Jinji. "Behold, my lord father: the storyteller of Shing gifted with the tongue of ancient bards in spoken form. If it pleases you, Holy Emperor, he shall weave a tale in celebration of your triumph over all the civilized world."

A dark light flickered in the emperor's eyes. "Granted, surely. I look forward to measuring the worth of my son's boast, storyteller. Welcome to KryTeer: paradise upon this world."

Jinji stepped forward, and pressing his palms together, he bowed. "Venerable Emperor of KryTeer, it is a privilege to stand upon this ancient stone in the hall of long ages, and present to you my art. If you will allow, I beseech you to stay your music and give heed unto my tale."

With a gesture, Gyath silenced his musicians. The courtiers and gentry hushed again, and the stillness was broken only by the tinkle of chimes swaying in the open windows. Smoke from incense curled across the beams of light from those windows, and Jetekesh held his breath, waiting, aching for Jinji's story.

"A shroud drapes over the world of men," said Jinji in somber tones. "Ever there is bloodshed and war, greed and sorrow. But ever is there light; and that which I speak of this day is of light. Shinac, it is called; most ancient word. No man recalls its meaning. It is not important now, except to know that its meaning grants a spell of protection for all who dwell worthily in its hallowed lands."

"This Shinac," said Gyath, cutting Jinji's spell as he might sever a spinner's thread. "I've heard tell of it. Is it not the realm of merfolk and sprites spoken of at the hearths of Amantier? Bedtime stories, they are called, yes?"

Jinji nodded. "So they are called. And so within Shinac dwell all the fae of this world."

Gyath chuckled. "I thought so. But it is no realm of light, as you claim. Aren't *Unsielie* also inhabitants of this *hallowed* land?"

Jinji's shoulders tensed as Jetekesh's spine stiffened. How did Gyath know of the dark fae?

"You know of the *Unsielie*, Your Eminence?" asked Jinji.

Gyath's eyes gleamed. Jetekesh could swear a mantel of darkness settled across the emperor's shoulders. He leaned forward in his throne, teeth flashing a wicked smile. "I know many, many things, Master Teller. I know a great deal about *you*. Indeed, I knew your mother. I knew her very, *very* well."

Jinji's face lost the last of its color, and his frame trembled beneath the sinister figure above him.

"Then, it was a lie," whispered Jinji so softly Jetekesh could hardly hear him. He swayed on his feet. Jetekesh snatched Jinji's arm to steady him. He could feel the penetrating, gleeful eyes above, but he didn't look. Why bother? Who was the tyrant Gyath next to the meek and gentle Jinji?

Jinji tried a smile, but it fell at once.

Jetekesh smiled in his stead. Squeezed his arm to reassure him.

"What child is this who dares to aid you before the Emperor of KryTeer?" rumbled Gyath.

Jetekesh faced the throne and held his head high. "I am Jetekesh, son of Jetekesh, prince and heir of Amantier's throne. I am a descendant of Cavalin the Third, and I see no emperor before me. Only a pig. If this world were not broken, it would worship and serve meek souls like Jinji rather than gluttonous, self-serving peacocks such as you or I."

Aredel moved in from the shadows and laid a hand on Jetekesh's shoulder. "Enough, Your Highness. If you wished to die, you had but to ask."

"Leave him, Aredel," barked Gyath. "I am not angry but intrigued. All word of this boy was that he would amount to nothing but his mother's lapdog. Spineless, fragile. Weepy like a woman. Yet I see before me a budding man, the kind any father should be proud to sire.

There is strength and virtue in true Amantieran tradition. My, my. It does me good to see that the diluted bloodline of Cavalin yet has hope. I will spare him for now."

Fire rolled through Jetekesh. He curled his hands into fists. "Do not make it sound so noble. You want my life for sport alone. But I won't serve you or bow to you. I may be a prince without a country, but I still have pride—and honor, what's more. The latter cannot be said of you."

Gyath threw his head back and roared with laughter. "Well, King Jetekesh. What say you concerning your insolent son? Shall I whip him to bind his tongue, or let the harmless pup alone?"

Father's voice held strong and steady. "Whip him, Holy Emperor. It will do him good. I've long been tired of his insolence myself. He gets it from his mother, bless her rotting corpse."

Laughter broke over the courtiers. Gyath chuckled. "Let him alone. Young men should be free to express themselves, and I cannot fault a prince, even if he is throneless." Gyath's mirth dimmed. "But now, the matter of Jinji of Shing."

His smile darkened again. "It is a strange life you have led, O crownless one. Marked by meetings and partings of all the great souls of Nakania. You have slept in dungeons and supped with kings. Wandered the byroads and fields. Sailed the open seas. Loved well. Hated deep. And mostly, you have preached. But preached what? Peace? Tolerance? Faith in that which is unseen? What good has this journey done you? You're dying. That is obvious. No power in this world can save you, and the powers of your precious Shinac *will not* save you. What is left?"

Jinji lifted his eyes from the floor. His body shook, but his gaze, that stalwart, blue green gaze, held Gyath's stare. "I must tell you one last story, and then…then I may finally rest, Lord Father."

36
FIVE SPEARS

Silence spilled over the chamber. Jetekesh couldn't believe his ears. He'd heard wrong. Jinji had misspoken. But as Jetekesh turned toward the throne of KryTeer, as he looked into the face of Gyath, tyrant-emperor of Nakania, he saw the truth. There was no indignation in Gyath's expression. No confusion, fury, wonder. *He smiled.* Acknowledging truth in the triumph of his squared shoulders, the tilt of his head.

Desperate, Jetekesh looked for Aredel. The Blood Prince stared, horror and wonder written as clearly as script across his brow. His wide eyes darted between Gyath and Jinji.

"You must be confused, Jinji," said Anadin, the only one in all the throne room who would dare to fracture the silence. "You called the emperor your father. Don't you mean Lord Emperor? Or Divine Eminence? Or a thousand other titles?"

Jinji shook his head. "I am not confused, nor am I mistaken. Is this not so, Lord Father?"

Gyath leaned back and folded his hands over his immense belly. "She never told you, did she?"

"No. But now I better understand her shame," said Jinji, bowing his head. "There is much that I better understand." His head lifted. He found Aredel. His smile was like a dove's wing. "Aredel, my brother."

The Blood Prince stiffened and stepped back. Blinked and shook his head. "Jinji…? I don't…"

"It's not that challenging a concept, boy!" Gyath scoffed. The lamps above trembled. "This lowly shepherd's mother pleased me, and she was glad to do it, too! Never let her later efforts to play the victim fool you. She knew what I was, and all I would become, and she offered herself to me. She wished to be empress. Ha!"

Jetekesh shivered as Gyath's laughter chased warmth from the chamber. It still made no sense. Shing had been occupied by Amantier for years before KryTeer ever invaded, and that had been *after* Jinji was born. Before Gyath had been an emperor. How had he made such an impression upon Jinji's mother or even crossed Amantier to visit Shing?

"You all appear perplexed. Why not enlighten them, my long-lost son?"

Jinji weakly shrugged. "Which question shall I answer first? My lady mother always led me to believe my father was a man of Amantier, for it explained the color of my eyes. Yet always I felt uneasy with that answer, for I sought the man who sired me, and when I found he whom she had named as such, he could not—or as I thought, *would* not—claim me. He had been in Shing during the Amantieran occupation, and even some years preceding that, but not as a loyal Amantieran citizen. He worked for another, stronger force. Long before Amantier entered our borders, KryTeer held a presence there. We were, in all but name, a province of this mighty land many years longer than history recounts."

He sighed. "Gyath, called king aloud, was already an emperor, and by my own mother's admission, he frequented court often, attended by his Blood Knights and his agents from Amantier. One of these was the man I had thought my father. It is only today I have learned otherwise, yet I feel the truth of it within my breast." He placed his fist over his heart and gazed up at the throne. "What I do not understand is *why*. Why you know of me. Why you openly declare my lineage. Why allow me to live all these years in ignorance, yet today, within your own court, reveal a secret none living but you were likely to know?"

The emperor's smile stretched until Jetekesh's mouth ached to see it. Gyath flexed his neck from side to side slowly, lazily. His fingers drummed against the arms of his throne in a drawling rhythm.

"*That*," he said, "is simple. I discovered who you were when my son met you in Shing five years go. He returned to KryTeer to, shall we say, *discipline* those men who beat him and threw him in the river. He also carried a story of *you*, and the strange creature you are. Strange men alarm me, and so I sent out spies to learn about you. Your history was not hard to discover. I even had the pleasure of corresponding with your lost love — Naqin, isn't she called? She was very forthcoming in all she knew, for she hoped to curry favor with the emperor of KryTeer, that she might gain you back. Of course, she didn't know your true bloodline, but I learned enough of your life to fit the pieces together myself. You are my own seed. Why acknowledge you, you ask? Why not? You *are* my kin. Illegitimate, yes. Unworthy to sit upon a throne, true. But I do not forsake what is mine. I always gain, never lose.

"Let all my court, all my lands, know the truth! Jinji called Wanderlust, born of a princess of Shing and the Holy Emperor of KryTeer, raised on the streets of a seaport city, cultivated in the courts of ancient philosophers, favored by a noblewoman, exiled to a shepherd's hill, and lastly donned in the mantle of an outcast storyteller with delusions of a fairy kingdom, soon to die of a lingering illness—this, my son, has come home at last, where his most holy father claims him as his own. Is it not a grand tale?"

Gyath leaned forward. "You have done me much service in the world, my son. By your efforts I have shaken the foundations of all countries in Nakania."

Jinji's brow drew together, and he shook his head. "How can that be? I've done nothing to influence the world so greatly. I do not understand you."

"Doubt, my son. You have planted doubt in the minds of miserable people. Paranoid fools such as Queen Bareene latched onto your drivel and wasted time and coin on capturing *you*. And so, she formed an alliance to supplant your efforts, as fear drove her thither. You have also planted discontentment within the common folk of pastoral Amantier and Shing. Such has led to rebellions, enough to chip at the last pockets of resistance in my empire. By your words, Jinji, you have handed me the world as fluidly as Aredel himself. After all, you inspired my heir to begin his deadly work. Brothers, working together. Is it not a touching concept? The day you met was fate; indeed, the gods themselves moved mobs and soldiers to bring you together."

Jinji was trembling.

Jetekesh gripped the man's arm tighter as his anger boiled over. *I will let him say no more.*

"Liar! Fool!" His voice rang throughout the chamber, rolling over the strafing laughter of the tyrant. "You think, just as my mother did, that this man plants sedition and doubt and unhappiness among the peasants of every country—but that isn't true! He brings hope. Faith. Joy! But how would you know? You've never heard his stories. You've never witnessed what happens to those who do listen. I, I may not be the best example, but I *want* to be better, all because this peculiar man *believed* I could be, and showed me how to try." Tears shimmered in Jetekesh's vision. He swiped at his eyes with his free hand and met the dark, glinting depths of Gyath's. Haughty disdain flickered in his gaze, but there was something else.

Jetekesh laughed. "I see the truth in you, *Gyath*! You're afraid. Jinji of Shing frightens you witless. Of course you must claim him. If you don't, if you keep silent, he will *destroy* you; for he stands for everything you are against. He will buoy up your oppressed people, inspire them, make them think and hope for themselves. He will preach liberty. Friendship. Loyalty. Love. Faith. Faith in something greater than you or your gods, for he does more than mollify and degrade. He lifts by example.

If you disown him or allow him to run free, untied by blood and oaths, he will stand as a banner by which others may rally against your tyranny. So, you claim him, and soon you will call him mad, as you do your spare.

"If you can just make Jinji bow his knee and call you liege and force him to swear an oath to his kinsman, you can quietly undermine his work. This you *must* do, or he'll overthrow you. You cannot kill him, certainly not that! A martyr lends unmatched strength to the masses: so history has taught us. It is the mortar to fill in the cracks of newfound faith. This you know. And so, you chain him with your blood claim and hope it's enough to stem the tide before it rises up from all your provinces."

Jetekesh panted as he finished, his face hot with curdled blood. He knew he'd been babbling. Had he made any sense at all? Everyone was staring. Even Jinji stared. A black fury scarred Gyath's round face, and he looked for all the world like an *Unsielie*, though fat and looming, wingless, and garbed in the colorful silks of KryTeer.

"You have crossed the threshold of my patience, young prince," rumbled a voice like glutting flames. Gyath rose, lifting his bulk until he towered above Jetekesh.

Trembling servants shoved the table aside, and Gyath took the steps that led from his high dais. When he descended, he stormed forward and stood before Jetekesh, tall—not as tall as Lord Peresen, but wide and powerful nonetheless. Gyath's skin was splotched from too much drink, and the wrinkles of his face were deep crevices. But there was nothing aged or weak about his eyes: two dark, sharp spears, fastened on Jetekesh, wrathful and murderous.

"My lord father," Aredel began, his tone one of warning.

"Silence." The emperor's command tolled low, edged. Aredel fell still.

Jetekesh's knees had grown weak, and his mouth was like sand. If this man struck him with his hand, surely Jetekesh would snap in two. *Will I die here?*

He drew himself up, urging his hands to be still. *Be proud. Be brave.*

Gyath lifted his hand. Father shouted as Aredel reached out. So slowly. Too slowly. The hand flew down. Jetekesh flinched. Why? Why couldn't he keep his composure in the end?

The blow never came. Cries and murmurs hummed through the air. Jetekesh pried his eyes open. Who had intervened? Who had dared?

Oh no! Jinji?

Jetekesh found Gyath standing several paces back, clutching a bleeding wound on his arm. At his feet, writhing beneath the hafts of four spears, lay Tifen, a discarded steak knife near his hand. Invisible, forgettable, loyal Tifen. Beside him, a spear jutting from his back, knelt Sir Palan. Had Sir Palan tried to save his son, while Tifen protected Jetekesh?

As Prince Jetekesh stared, blood rushing through him like icy water, the old knight reached for his dying son and pulled him near. Tifen cried out but raised his shaking hand and caught Sir Palan's fingers in a clasp.

"F-Father, I…"

Sir Palan leaned forward until his ear was near Tifen's

lips. His son spoke, words lost in the murmurs of the crowd. But Jetekesh knew what they were: *Father, I'm sorry. Forgive me.*

Tifen gave one last heaving gasp. His eyes flattened. Sir Palan slumped over the body and joined his son in death.

37
CAUGHT IN A TRAP

I killed him.

Jetekesh crashed to his knees. Jinji sank with him.

"Quite a spectacle," said Gyath, with a chuckle. "Bring my physician. This wound won't stop bleeding."

Someone sobbed. Jetekesh tore his eyes from Tifen and his father to find the source of the alien noise. Rille. She clutched Yeshton's arm, face turned away, shoulders shaking.

I killed them both.

Jetekesh turned his eyes to the rug beneath him.

Why had he not held his tongue? Why? *Why?*

The murmuring of the courtiers and gentry had grown from an angry hum to an energized buzz. Tifen's death had revenged their wounded feelings, feelings not even their own; but what the emperor felt, so too felt his sycophants and lackeys. These preening, mindless peacocks were for display alone; they had a collective mind. Jetekesh well knew their sort. He'd been raised to rule them.

He'd been *one* of them.

Disgust cushioned his guilt, easing his pinched heart. He couldn't look at the bodies of Palan and Tifen as KryTeeran guards dragged them away. *Think about it later. Grieve later.*

If there was a later.

The emperor's physician had arrived.

While Gyath was being treated, he gestured to the company brought by Aredel. "We are indeed blessed this day. Two less Amantieran dogs plague the world."

Cold laughter flooded the chamber.

Jinji's fingers twitched against Jetekesh's arm. The prince looked at his friend and sucked in a sharp breath. Jinji's expression was one Jetekesh had never seen before on the mild man's face. His eyes blazed, leeching the blue until only vivid green remained. Color dusted his face. He released Jetekesh and staggered to his feet, hands fisted and shaking.

"*Gyath.*" His voice was sharp as steel. "Do you regard common life so little? You, whose line once dwelt in squalor? You, whose ancestors are no more royal than the fishermen of your market squares?"

The laughter faded. Gyath eyed Jinji. He shook off his physician's probing hands and took a single step toward the storyteller. "Say no more, insolent *jutik.*"

"I *will* speak." Jinji's entire body shook. His breath caught as he panted. But he remained standing.

Jetekesh pushed to his feet and took Jinji's arm to support him.

The storyteller breathed in. "Gyath, son of DulShil,

descendant of one who unleashed darkness from the sea and thus banished Shinac from Nakania. Hear me all who stand here now: hear me and know truth. Long ago, when Nakania cradled Shinac on its southernmost shores; when this warm desert clime was a scape of winter, and the farther south you traveled the warmer it became—at that fair time, fairies and mermaids and elves roamed our many lands in peaceful years. Cavalin the Third reigned over the middle free lands of Nakania. He supped with the fae and sang their songs.

"I cannot say all was light and good, but people strove for it, even by the sword if necessary. Alas, not all were content with peace. A young man, Tallat by name, hungered for power. He was naught but a fisherman who dwelt near the southern shore of KryTeer, but he longed to become a knight of Cavalin's court so that he might earn fame and fortune. Such feelings attract foul things, and a great darkness read his heart and whispered to him many promises. And so Tallat took his boat out in a storm as the whispers directed him, seeking those promises. The storm worsened, and the boat sank, taking Tallat with it to the bottom of the vast sea. It was there, beneath the crushing waves, that darkness took him. Possessed him. And Tallat emerged from that raging sea with power unlike any mortal man.

"He swiftly earned his right to serve as Cavalin's knight in the free lands of Nakania, but that was not enough for the yearning hunger of Tallat. He returned to KryTeer, murdered the king of his own country, and claimed the throne for himself. At first, he thought himself content, but Shinac—pinnacle of magic, pillar of light—began to plague his thoughts, and the darkness of his heart thirsted to conquer that flourishing realm."

As Jinji spoke, just as in times before, imagery unfurled like a scroll before Jetekesh, and he saw now a vast army of dark fae amassing under the banner of KryTeer. At their head, astride a great war horse, rode a man whose visage resembled the Blood Prince. Greedy men joined the ranks of *Unsielie* and marched upon Shinac.

Cavalin the Third mustered his army to oppose the dark force, and there he was slain on the battlefield by Tallat, who then advanced upon Shinac. But just as he reached the border, the country of magic vanished, and all the dark fae disappeared with it, leaving Tallat with only his human force of arms. Furious that he had lost his conquest, spurred by the darkness within, he advanced upon the free lands of Nakania to conquer what remained of Cavalin's kingdom.

But Shing, then a great eastern empire, came to the aid of fallen Cavalin's people, and Tallat was driven back to KryTeer, wounded and humiliated. There he nursed his wounds and strengthened his lands and allowed the darkness inside of him to fester and grow. Upon his death, Jetekesh watched in horror as a black vapor slipped from Tallat's lips and into the mouth of his son and heir.

"So it has been, becoming the root of KryTeer priestcraft and the foundation of your monarchy," said Jinji. He drew a wheezing breath and leaned hard against Jetekesh. "The darkness from the sea has possessed the line of rulers from Tallat down to you, Gyath. Upon your death, it will descend upon your heir. But I cannot abide it. Aredel is a fearsome specter, strong as those before him; but while you are greedy in thought and deed, Aredel serves his people, for he believes *that* to be right. I will not watch the wickedness of Tallat possess my friend...my brother..."

A cruel grin slid over Gyath's face. "Assuming all you have said is true, it sounds to me that you can do nothing but watch. But do not fret, Jinji of Shing: I shall yet live a long life. Aredel need not swallow darkness yet." He laughed. "Your stories are amusing; I shall not dispute this. But you've entertained us enough. You have told your story. We are reunited, father and son. The evening is upon us, and it is time for feasting and song! Let us celebrate the arrival of my brave three sons, each back from a battle unique to his skills. Bring wine! Bring dancers!"

Music struck up. Women draped in colorful silks stepped onto the rug and began to sway and twirl, twinkling with jewels and golden baubles. Jetekesh drew Jinji away from the revelry, and the others of their party followed, including Aredel and Anadin.

The Second Prince of the Blood stepped to Jinji's side. "So, you are truly our brother?"

Jinji smiled wanly at Anadin. "So I am."

"But your eyes are so light." Anadin cocked his head. "How?"

"Can you not guess?" Rille pulled Yeshton by his hand to join the group. "It is because he Sees true. It is because all his life he has walked with the princes of Shinac. He is their kin, as much as yours."

Yeshton frowned. "The real matter is what happens now, my lords? Mistress?" He glanced at Gyath, who had climbed the steps of his throne to watch the dance. "If Jinji's words are fact, we cannot slay Emperor Gyath. The darkness would then enslave Prince Aredel, and I for one would rather not encounter *that* scenario."

"Nor I," said Rille and Anadin in unison.

"Gyath knows this," said Father, brow furrowed. "As Jinji spoke, I saw the emperor's countenance change. He feels that he will be safe, so long as we try to protect Aredel from that fate. But how…?" He glanced toward the throne. Jetekesh followed his gaze. Gyath was enraptured by one of the dancers. The guards stationed around the chamber were too far away to listen. Father turned back to the group. "How can we possibly defeat this… this darkness? Jinji?"

Jetekesh looked at his friend, but the storyteller's eyes were closed, and a thread of blood trickled from the corner of his lips. Father moved toward Jinji as Jetekesh reached up to touch his friend's face.

Jinji's eyes fluttered open, but he slumped forward, and Jetekesh held him up with gritted teeth. Father took his other side. Aredel stepped before Jinji and wiped the blood from the man's lips.

Aredel looked at Father. "Let me take him. He needn't stay here for the feast. Prince Jetekesh must come with me. The rest of you will remain here. Stay close to Ledonn and Shevek and say nothing. Eat. Try to rest as best you might. I will return when I can."

"Take care of my son," said Father.

Aredel swept Jinji up into his arms. "Your son has a bad habit of speaking his mind, Your Majesty. He will be safest in my company."

"What about me?" asked Anadin, a pout in his voice. "Jinji is my brother too."

"Stay near Rille," Aredel commanded. "Protect her."

Anadin hesitated but nodded. "Sahala shall be safe with me. So will Kyella." He smiled at the farmer's daughter, who looked pale and weary.

The Blood Prince turned away. Jetekesh followed, aware of many eyes on his back. Was one of them Gyath? He'd angered the emperor, and now two good men were dead.

Why am I so foolish?

Aredel led him through a door to the throne room's side, and beyond, into an arching corridor of white stone and marble. Ornate lamps and tall sconces had been lighted along the corridor. Evening had descended across KryTeer. Jetekesh's steps echoed along the vast space.

"You have caused a great deal of trouble, Jetekesh." Aredel never looked back as he spoke.

Jetekesh scowled at the man's back. "I spoke truth. No one else would defend Jinji. I thought you, at least, would stand up for him against your father. Isn't Jinji your friend?"

"Of course." The Blood Prince halted and turned enough to glance at Jetekesh. "I owe Jinji everything. Thus, I kept my peace. If I were to defy my lord father openly, it would be Jinji's end, even after all the truths you spoke. Gyath does not want a martyr on his hands. He *is* afraid. He knows this, and he knows that I know it. But my defiance is yet a greater fear. He would risk all else if I gave him cause to believe I stand against him." He began to walk again. Jetekesh trotted after him.

"Besides," Aredel said after a moment, "Jinji came

here at the behest of the rightful king of Shinac. I trust that my friend knows what he must do. I don't wish to interfere with his purpose."

Jetekesh looked at his feet, cheeks burning. *I'm a fool. Of course Aredel knew what he was doing. Why do I never think? Tifen's death is my fault. I killed him.*

∽

Aredel pushed open the door to his bedchamber, careful to keep his arms steady. Jinji had grown so thin, he was light as an adolescent girl. Aredel's arms barely ached, even after carrying him up four flights of stairs to reach the eastern wing and the blood heir's private suite.

Jetekesh slipped into the room behind Aredel and barred the door.

The Blood Prince marched to the wide, plush bed, and laid Jinji across the coverlet. The storyteller moaned and rolled to his side, where he curled into himself. His hair was whiter now than it had been this morning.

A pang throbbed in Aredel's chest. This man, his friend—and all this time, his brother. If only Aredel had known. Not that knowing would increase his affection; how could he love Jinji more than he already did? That wasn't it. Perhaps he'd not have done anything different, for Jinji had gone his own way, as he always would. But Aredel could have called him *brother*; could have thought of him so, not just wished he were so.

Aredel stooped over the bed and rested his hand on Jinji's hair. A few days more, perhaps a week or two, and Jinji's life would expire.

"He's so pale," whispered Jetekesh, hovering close.

Aredel looked up and read the concern etched in the young prince's face. How much the boy had grown, just since Keep Falcon. How would he fare when Jinji was gone?

No better than myself. We are much alike, Jetekesh and I. Two self-centered children, craving affection. And Jinji gave us what we desperately needed. Will we survive without him?

Aredel pulled his hand from Jinji's head, trembling. He had always seen Jinji as a fragile man whose soul was greater even than Cavalin of old. "Elder brother" was a term Aredel had never dared to think, yet it was truth.

Too late to say it aloud.

Aredel retreated a few paces from the bed. "We must let him rest. There is much to be planned."

"Like what? How can we do anything at all?"

What, indeed? Aredel had thought of one solution, but he loathed it. The simplest course was to end the royal line of KryTeer, but that meant taking his own life, and poor Anadin's, before Gyath could be killed. And now Jinji too was at risk. Could the darkness from the sea possess the storyteller? Likely not, but there was always the chance. It was not a path Aredel wanted to take: especially for Anadin's sake.

Upon Gyath's death, there would already be a problem. It was KryTeer law to execute the deceased ruler's entire harem, along with his sired spare, to avoid messy successions. Even should Aredel not become possessed by the darkness, he could not be crowned until the law was satisfied; and without the title of emperor, he could not rescind the law. Such had always been Aredel's greatest trouble and his reason not to kill Gyath long before now. He had intended to use King Jetekesh's life debt to request that Anadin escape with the Amantierans to their homeland, and there hide until Gyath could be dealt with.

But things had grown beyond Aredel's control.

Motion caught his eyes, and he turned to watch Jetekesh walk to the open balcony. Outside the sky glowed red and purple.

The prince of Amantier leaned over the railing and stared down into the faraway courtyard. "Rille said one crowned by chains would gift Gyath with immortality. I can guess what she meant by the last bit: someone will kill him. But who is the one crowned by chains? You, a slave of your father? Anadin, likewise? Jinji, chained to his illness? Or someone else?" Prince Jetekesh sighed. "She said nothing about what follows, or the darkness, or how to stop it." He turned to meet Aredel's eyes. "What can we do?"

"It is a question my lord father ponders as well. He is no fool."

Jetekesh's eyes widened. "But he was thrilled when she told him what she Saw."

"Of course. There is the chance he will be granted such a gift. But he knows better than to believe his perception alone is the only possible meaning of her words. He knows *we* at least would prefer to translate it another way. He will be cautious, and he will try to kill us all. Tonight, if he possibly can."

Jetekesh moaned. "You make it sound impossible! Why hasn't he killed you before now, if you're such a problem?"

Aredel allowed a smile to flit across his lips. "Did I say he has never tried? I am not so simple to kill as you seem to presume. Consider the lengths he has gone to control my younger brother."

Jetekesh folded his arms. "Very well. What makes him believe he can kill you now, tonight, where all other times he has failed?"

"Because he is desperate, and because he is greedy."

Jetekesh shook his head. "Why? What's changed?"

"Are you familiar with the succession of kings down to Gyath in KryTeer?"

"I am since the time of Cavalin."

"Can you tell me the common correlation between each generation?"

Jetekesh was silent for a moment, fingers flexing as though he counted. "Well, the obvious theme is that each king always has two sons by his queen: no more, no less. An heir and a spare. Beyond that—"

"That will do. You've made my point. My pet theory is that the darkness saw to it that it could continue forward through the royal line since Tallat; an heir to possess, and a spare in case the heir died. Would you agree it's possible?"

"Well, yes." Jetekesh's eyes widened. "You're proposing to end your line? But that would mean Anadin too—and what about Jinji?"

"Relax. That is only a worst-case solution. I would rather not die, but I'll thank you for your concern."

The prince flushed. "What's your point then?"

"My father has considered another theory. I am less than convinced of its effectiveness, but there is always the risk…" He cupped his hands behind his back and paced the large rug beneath his curled-toe shoes. "Rille said that one crowned by chains would gift Gyath with immortality, yes?"

"Yes." Jetekesh's voice was cautious.

"What happens if there is no heir? Nor any spare? No one with the proper claim to succeed the KryTeer emperor? Where does the darkness go should Gyath die?"

The prince of Amantier stared at him, brow wrinkled. "Go? But—" His brow shot up. "Gracious saints preserve us! Do you think the darkness would *stay* inside Gyath? I mean, indefinitely? You believe it would make him immortal?"

Aredel shrugged. "It doesn't matter if I believe it possible or not. My *father* is likely to consider it."

"B—but even if he killed both his rightful heirs... how could he possibly test the theory to see if it's true?"

"He likely believes Rille would tell him."

"He trusts my cousin a great deal without knowing her."

"She argued a good point. Amantier, as it was, is no more, and your mother's feud with her father is well known in KryTeer. But that's not important now. Rille has played her part, and our struggle is how to survive long enough to destroy the darkness before Anadin or I become its host."

"It's not possible! This isn't Shinac. None of us is fae. Your own country's magic is most likely derived from the darkness itself. No one possesses the knowledge of how this threat can be conquered—except perhaps Jinji. But he's too weak to help anyone now. We're as good as doomed."

Aredel tilted his head. "I didn't know you were such an optimist."

Jetekesh's scowl was impressive. "Show me a ray of light in all this mess and I'll seize upon it at once!" He ran a hand through his hair. "I want a drink."

"There is white wine in that jar on the stand." Aredel gestured to the bronze bottle. Jetekesh sprinted across the room and poured himself a goblet. Aredel resisted the urge to join him; he must keep his wits sharp as daggers.

Jetekesh's words echoed through his head. *As good as doomed. It's impossible. Doomed.*

There must be an answer. Why come here otherwise? Why would the true king of Shinac appear to Jinji and spare his life, only to have him imprisoned or executed? Then, was Jinji the key? Could he somehow slay the darkness? But how? Jinji was gifted to see into Shinac itself, but that was the extent of his power. He wielded no magic spells, no great sword, no talismans, or charms, not even the authority of a church to exorcise evil, such as the priests in Amantier.

He halted his pacing and turned to Jetekesh. "Would your priests be able to destroy this darkness? They use the authority granted them by your One God, yes?"

Jetekesh lowered his goblet. "Well, yes, possibly. But Emperor Gyath banished all Amantieran priests from KryTeer two years ago."

"What of a former priest of your faith?"

Jetekesh shook his head. "Impossible. If he's no longer a man of the cloth, he has no authority from the One God to exorcise spirits or demons."

Aredel cursed under his breath. "What use is that? You cannot tell me spirits or demons *only* appear when priests are present to dispose of them."

Jetekesh's cheeks colored, but he said nothing as he took another drink.

Aredel began to pace again. There must be another way. The priests of KryTeer would never help. The Shingese believed in spirits of the earth, and their tenets didn't include exorcism, as far as he knew. Not that he knew much of Shingese faith. Jinji had rarely spoken of it.

There were other, less known mystic faiths, but Aredel suspected many of those would only summon more darkness rather than banish what had already gathered.

If he only knew the nature, the origin, of this darkness.

Caught in a trap. Now that he had theorized Gyath might become immortal if he and Anadin died—if there was even the most remote chance of that—he couldn't risk killing his brother and then himself. Which meant Jetekesh was right.

We truly may be doomed.

38
ALMOST DAWN

It must be nearing dawn by now.

Jetekesh rolled over to check on Jinji, who lay beside him on the giant bed. Still sleeping, breathing deeper now. Good.

All was quiet; all but the distant sea bells.

Jetekesh sat up. He'd slept off the influence of several goblets of wine, and fear had returned to stab his insides like shards of ice. He shivered despite the warmth of the arid night.

Aredel had left hours ago, probably to prowl the hall outside and keep Jinji safe. Or perhaps he'd gone to check on Father and the rest.

Not all the rest. Not Tifen and Sir Palan.

Tears pricked Jetekesh's eyes. He batted at them. All he did anymore was cry, and what good did it do? He'd never realized just how weak he was until he was taken from Kavacos. Taken along with Jinji across Amantier, into Shinac, and out again into KryTeer. Never had he dreamed of anything so wondrous and so harrowing as this journey.

His vision shimmered and tears burned his cheeks. Mother. Tifen. Sir Palan.

He sat up and drew his knees to his chest. Sir Blayse too.

Jetekesh had dreamed just now of Sharo. The fae prince had stood over a grave, eyes dark, shoulders hunched.

Was that my fault too?

A gentle hand fell on his back. He looked up and stared into the kind eyes of Jinji Wanderlust.

"Be at peace, my friend," whispered the storyteller. "Tifen and Palan are both far beyond the reach of tyrants or pain."

"I…killed them…" The words scoured his tongue. The tears fell faster.

"Not so, not so," murmured Jinji. "Gyath is the man to blame for their deaths. Do not rob him of reproach, my prince."

Jetekesh unfolded himself and leaned against Jinji's shoulder. "What can we do, Jinji? Gyath will kill us all—and if we kill him first, Aredel will be possessed by that terrible darkness. I can't imagine the horrors he would do under that influence."

Jinji's fingers stroked Jetekesh's hair. "Do not fear or fret, Prince. The vapors of night cannot long withstand the call of day. What shadow could conquer the sun?"

Jetekesh stirred and looked up into Jinji's face. The light was back in his eyes, burning like a candle's flame.

Anger stabbed Jetekesh like a dagger through his ribs. He recoiled from Jinji. "You dare try to soothe my fears, but you don't understand them! How could you? You're dying. You don't care what happens to us. You *want* death! You welcome it! I—I hate you! I hate that you want to leave us behind. You'd rather die than stay. I hate you!"

Jinji stared at him, lips parted. His brow creased and he bowed his head. "Your words are just, my friend. You have great cause to hate me. Five years ago, I cursed this world for my pain—and since that time, I have watched that curse give birth to terrible acts and unmentionable cruelty. Prince Aredel took it upon himself to carry my curse to every country upon this continent and in lands beyond the sea. The tragedy of Amantier, of Shing, the horrors in Tivalt…all are due to my hateful cry for justice. I should be despised above all other creatures…"

Jetekesh gaped at the storyteller. The man thought he was responsible for the actions of Gyath and Aredel? For the witch-hunts in Tivalt? The fall of Amantier? Hypocrite! Hadn't he just told Jetekesh not to rob from Gyath's reproach? Hadn't Mother made the choice to sell out her country? And Aredel acted under the banner of Gyath—not to avenge Jinji's wrongs. Surely Aredel *knew* Jinji would resent world conquest; and if at first he did act in Jinji's name, later he must have come to recognize the man's nature.

Jetekesh opened his mouth, but his words strangled in his throat.

He won't listen to reason. He has a martyr's spirit.

But he also harbors the soul of Shinac.

"You're right," said Jetekesh. "This is your fault. Everyone is dead because of you. Nakania will fall into chaos and ruin. You called this curse upon the world, and now you're running away at the most crucial moment. Your cry for justice woke the darkness within Gyath, and that creature is now going to swallow everyone—me, Aredel, Rille, Sir Yeshton—we're all going to become that darkness. Unless…" He paused until Jinji's eyes lifted from his wringing hands. "Unless *you* do something to remedy what you've begun."

The storyteller shuddered. His eyes flickered. "What can I—"

"You told me there is still hope. *You* said the sun conquers the shadow. *You* tell *me* what can be done. What you can do. Because otherwise this world will end, Jinji Wanderlust, and it will be upon *your* soul."

A sob broke from Jinji's lips, and he bowed into his hands. "Ancient kings of Shinac, guide me!"

Jetekesh looked away, limbs quivering. Face flushed. His stomach writhed. What if he had pushed too hard? Jinji was so weak…

His sobs fell away.

Jetekesh jerked his head back around.

The storyteller knelt upon the bed, hands in his lap, gaze riveted on the door across the chamber. "Jetekesh." His voice cracked. "Will you please aid me? I know that I am a burden, and you may refuse—"

The prince scowled. "Oh, be silent, Jinji. Of course I'll help you." He wrapped Jinji's arm around his shoulders and pulled him from the bed. "Where are we going?"

"To Gyath. We must end this now."

39
BETWEEN TWO PILLARS

Most of the revelers slept on the floor. A few worthy souls swayed on their feet near tables laden with remnants of food and drink, singing rowdy songs in the tongue of KryTeer. Yeshton didn't need to know the words. Drinking songs were all the same; boundaries never mattered.

Prince Aredel stood sentinel nearby, sober, and solemn, eyes fixed on Gyath's throne, where the fat emperor whispered to a blushing dancer seated upon his expansive lap.

Rille and Anadin had fallen asleep hours ago, heads propped on each other, bodies slumped against a pillar. King Jetekesh sat close to them, cross-legged. Awake. He'd refused to sleep when Aredel suggested it. Kyella sat beside the king of Amantier, half asleep, eyes glazed over.

Yeshton turned to the Blood Prince. "Will Jinji and Prince Jetekesh be safe by themselves?"

Aredel arched an eyebrow. "I sent Shevek and

Ledonn back to guard them. I will be alerted should anything happen."

Yeshton wanted to ask if anything *would* happen, but he held his tongue. The night was almost over; just an hour or so left until dawn, unless Yeshton had misjudged the passage of time. It was possible, for though his mind could tally the hours, his soul felt a hundred years older, like this night was lost to the annals of time.

Aredel's eyes darted toward any sound, hand draped over his curved sword. Yeshton could feel his tension like a mist rising from his body. It was all that kept Yeshton awake; if the Blood Prince was ready for anything, he must be ready too.

It would conclude before dawn.

The thought wasn't Yeshton's own. No one spoke it. It was an impression, thick as fog, suspended upon the air. When would the fog part to reveal the spell that had conjured it like a player's curtain? Could he fend against the threat, or was the unknown, creeping thing born of supernatural power? He was a mere soldier; how could he battle against magic? How could he protect Rille?

Servants wrapped in turbans entered the throne room, carrying candles to relight the snuffed-out lamps. Yeshton watched them, his hand itching to hold a blade. If only he'd been able to claim Tifen's knife from the floor before the guards confiscated it.

Yeshton bowed his head. He'd come to respect Tifen on their journey together. And Sir Palan, his childhood hero and benefactor, had fallen in the halls of KryTeer.

The soldier's heart lurched, and he willed his mind to flee from pain, from regret. This was a battlefield, no matter how strange; there would be time to grieve the fallen later.

A commanding voice called out behind Yeshton in the KryTeer tongue.

He spun. So did Aredel.

Jinji stood in the center of the long chamber, supported by Jetekesh, flanked by Ledonn and Shevek. The man from Shing was pale, thin as a reed. His hair was completely white. But his eyes, always light-filled, shone now like jewels. He took a step away from Jetekesh, wobbled, but steadied himself and strode forward. His movement was graceful and firm like a king's strong steps. His stance, erect and commanding.

Not a fox or a mouse. Not a horse either. He's something else. Something ethereal. Awe coursed through Yeshton's frame like a warm spring breeze. He felt that he stood not on marble, but soft grass. He breathed in and tasted sweet air.

Jinji's eyes lifted to the throne high above him. He opened his mouth and spoke. The words were foreign to Yeshton, like Shingese or KryTeeran speech, though separate; yet he understood what Jinji said.

"In the name of Shinac's rightful king, by the grace of the fae, through the strength of brave Cavalin, I stand before thee, Gyath of KryTeer, and denounce thee."

Gyath laughed and pushed the dancing girl from his lap. She stumbled down the steps and fled into the shadows of the room. The emperor lifted himself from his throne and raised his many chins to look down his nose at Jinji, grinning.

"*You* denounce *me*, my son?" He laughed again. "Should this wound me, pray tell? Have I lost my title by your words? O great tale-weaver, spare me this hurtful action!" He threw his head back and roared until the lamps swayed. The drunken revelers stirred and climbed to their feet, already laughing, though they didn't understand their emperor's amusement.

Yeshton stared at Jinji. What was he doing? He stood before the tyrant—fearless, it was true; but what power could he wield against Gyath's strength? A glance at Aredel told him nothing. The Blood Prince crouched like a tiger prepared to pounce upon its prey. But he waited, watchful, eyes narrowed.

A small hand slipped between Yeshton's fingers. He started. Looked down to find Rille. She smiled grimly, then turned her attention to Jinji.

Prince Jetekesh had followed the storyteller and stood behind him.

Yeshton glanced back and found King Jetekesh upon his feet, his gaze lighted on his son. Waiting. Quiet. Kyella had risen with him, mesmerized by Jinji.

Anadin alone slept on, oblivious to the exchange that would likely be the death of all.

Come now, Yesh. Have you so little faith in this man? Has he not proved himself wise?

But Jinji was dying. He was in pain. Perhaps this was his answer: execution would be the end of his suffering.

No. He wouldn't do that to the rest of us. He's too selfless for that.

What then did Jinji intend to do?

"Watch," whispered Rille.

Jinji stood against the emperor's laughter, a man of slight frame, powerless, dying. He had no titles, no claims, no prestige. Yet Yeshton saw now a man who might have been a prince. He was regal enough, graceful, even kind, as a benevolent ruler ought to be. All these things Yeshton had always admired in King Jetekesh and Duke Lunorr.

In another life he might have been emperor of KryTeer. Or the ruler of Shing.

But he's just a shepherd.

Jinji's voice carried above the mirth of Gyath's court. "I have no power to stop you, Gyath. I cannot take your title, nor can I destroy the darkness that abides within you." He raised his hand, as though he beckoned to the emperor. "If only you had chosen not to feed the darkness. Not to let it grow. It would not have consumed you without your consent; and thus, I know that you will not be spared."

"Ooh." Gyath rumbled a laugh. "You *frighten* me so, my son. What shall you unleash upon me? The *Unsielie* of Shinac? Do not forget, they once sided with my forebear!"

Jinji's eyes flashed. "I do not forget, Gyath. I see true! It is *you* who have forgotten: it is not darkness which defeats itself, but light. Behold!" His hand lifted. "Sharo, son of light, prince of woods and fields, protector of the fae, I beseech thy help!"

A humming note struck across the chamber like harp song, and the air split with a burst of light. White sands spiraled up from that great crack to form two pillars.

As the light dimmed, from between the two pillars stepped a tall, ethereal man. Chains twinkled against his wrists and trailed back into the space beyond the pillars, connecting him to what lay beyond. Long white hair tumbled down his back. He was dressed in silvery-blue cloth of rich embroidery; and he held in his hands a broadsword of magnificent workmanship, gold, bronze, silver metal twining up the hilt, while the blade shone unblemished.

Yeshton knew him: Prince Sharo of Shinac, last of the true line of fae kings, cousin to the lost prince.

Trembling, Yeshton sank to his knees, but he couldn't lower his eyes.

"Gyath of KryTeer," called Prince Sharo in clear, commanding tones. "By the song of the fae, by the light of the sun, I purge thee of thy plague. Begone, *Erisyrdrel.* Return to the depths and to thy slumber and wake no more until thy last stand against thy foe, Lord Ehrikai, True King of Shinac!" Sharo bounded impossibly high, blade flashing.

Gyath bellowed and drew his sword. Swung. It struck air, and he stumbled. Sharo's sword plunged into Gyath's chest.

Silence.

Sharo wrenched the sword free. Gyath gurgled and slumped back in his throne. His eyes stared heavenward, and a vapor of black sand rose in writhing particles from his lips.

"I said begone!" cried Sharo, and his sword burst into white flames. He swung it. The black sands hissed and contorted until they formed a vortex and shot up and out through a high window.

"Imposs...ible..." gasped the emperor. His head dropped. His body slackened. Sharo turned from the throne and jumped down to the floor below. He wiped his blade with the hem of his silver cape and sheathed the sword.

Yeshton caught movement from the corner of his eye.

The Blood Prince raced to the throne, climbed the steps, and tore the circlet crown from Gyath's head. He turned to face the chamber, hefted the crown, and placed it upon his own brow. "I am Emperor of KryTeer! All my subjects *will* bow!"

His voice thundered through the throne room, and all the KryTeerans slumped to their knees, eyes darting between their new ruler and the fae prince of Shinac whose chains sparkled in the growing light of dawn.

A shiver rushed down Yeshton's spine. "Has Prince Aredel been possessed?" he whispered.

"No, Sir Knight," said Rille. "The shadow from the sea is banished. Aredel is acting before Anadin can be executed as the spare. I hope it will work…"

"Sharo!" Prince Jetekesh ran forward, incognizant of everyone else.

The fae prince lifted his hands. "Jetekesh, my friend." He clasped the boy's arms and smiled. "How good to see you once more in the flesh. How fare you?"

"I…I'm all right. Is the darkness gone? Did you truly banish it?"

Sharo's smile flickered. "For the time being. I have not the power to destroy it, but it will be long beyond your lifespan before it stirs again, spirits willing." He lifted his eyes. "Jinji."

Jetekesh turned around. Yeshton followed his gaze and found the storyteller kneeling on the ground, shoulders slumped. White hair hung in his face and his breath came in gasps.

Prince Sharo stepped across the marble floor and

crouched before the man from Shing. He murmured too softly for Yeshton to hear.

Jinji raised his head. His smile was radiant.

"I have done all that a man can do," he said in a voice stronger than it should be. He shut his eyes and tumbled forward.

40

THE MAN FROM SHING

The white sands sparkled under the light of the ancient moon.

Jetekesh stood shivering in a blanket, but the cold didn't matter. His vision swam. A flute played nearby, soft and sorrowful.

That didn't feel right. Jinji would want something full of life, not death.

Warmth tickled his arm. He glanced left to find Aredel beside him. The new emperor of KryTeer.

King. He's just a king now.

Aredel had relinquished all the lands he had conquered during Gyath's reign. It had been a simple, irrevocable decree; his second, following the abolishment of the law that would have claimed Anadin's life. No one had disputed the orders of the Blood Prince. No one ever did.

The journey back to the Drifting Sands had taken over a week to start, for Aredel first had to solidify his reign. A purging of the palace had begun at once, and the former Blood Prince appeared to relish it. Perhaps it was his way of coping with Jinji's death.

Jetekesh's lungs pinched. His heart recoiled. Jinji.

The storyteller gave the last of his strength to summon Sharo to Nakania from the country of magic. As he took his final breath, the fae prince had disappeared, along with the white sands and the gaping crack of light.

I'll never see either of them again.

The thought was unbearable. Jetekesh wanted to rail against it, to scream until it wasn't true. But Nakania was not a world of magic, and the last shard of it had been taken with Jinji of Shing. Even Rille said so. She had assured Jetekesh and Yeshton that her gift to See had departed with Jinji's soul.

It wasn't fair. Not any of it.

He drew a shuddering breath. Blinked back tears. Stared at the plain coffin Aredel had constructed with his own hands. Jetekesh understood why he'd done so. Jinji wouldn't want ornate decoration or fanfare.

It was a small party that gathered on the edge of the Drifting Sands to honor the passing of their friend. Not Tifen and Sir Palan, of course; but everyone else who mattered had come. Father, Rille, Sir Yeshton—truly knighted now for his valor—and Kyella, reunited with her freed father, along with Ledonn and Shevek, King Aredel, Prince Anadin, and a dark-haired beauty draped in embroidered silks: the Lady Naqin of Shing. She had already been on her way to KryTeer when Ledonn and Shevek were sent to fetch her, brought by a dream of her lost love.

"When you are ready, Jetekesh," murmured Aredel.

He inhaled and, clutching the stick tighter in his

hands, moved to the border of the desert and stabbed the stick into the earth. The tiny silver bell fastened to the stick chimed. "May you find your way home to Shinac, Jinji, friend of my heart." His voice caught. His chin trembled.

He pulled back.

Aredel came forward to rest a fistful of soil over the coffin. "Do not forget Nakania, brother. We shall never forget you."

Lady Naqin came forward last. She laid a white lotus from Shing over the soil. "My love, my soul."

No one moved for a long while.

"Lady Rille." Aredel's voice drifted out like the sand beneath his feet.

"Yes, Blood King?"

"You may avenge your father now, if you wish."

Jetekesh glanced at his cousin.

The girl considered Aredel with her strange amber eyes. "No, Aredel. I think not. We've both lost what we best loved. Your anguish is enough." Her gaze drifted to the sea bell. "I think Jinji would want you to live."

Rille took Sir Yeshton's hand and led him back to the small encampment. Others trailed away. Soon Aredel and Jetekesh alone remained.

The night grew colder. Jetekesh let the tears track down his face, while the lump in his throat swelled.

A faint breeze danced across the desert floor, stirring the sand. The sea bell chimed.

Jetekesh looked up. He gasped. Aredel stiffened beside him.

There, glowing bright as the heavens above, between two pillars of white sand; there stood Jinji beside Prince

Sharo. The man from Shing lifted his hand and waved, a smile of purest bliss on his face. He was free of pain, free of guilt. Free.

Jinji turned away and traveled with Sharo beyond sight. The light vanished.

The sea bell chimed one last time and then it sang no more.

Return to the worlds of Nakania and Shinac in the sequel trilogy launching Soon.

To stay in the know, sign up for my newsletter at www.mhwoodscourt.com!

DEAREST READER

Thank you for picking up *Crownless*! I've had this story in my head since I was fourteen years old and to finally send it out into the world is my dearest joy.

If you've enjoyed Jinji's warmth, Jetekesh's lessons, Rille's honesty, Yeshton's loyalty, and the world of Nakania, please consider leaving an honest review online where you purchased this book and/or Goodreads. Reviews help writers gain exposure as well as feedback on what's working and what isn't.

You can also sign up for my newsletter via www.mh-woodscourt.com to receive updates on new releases, special sales, free short stories, and lots more!

May all good things attend you.

Sincerely,
M. H. WOODSCOURT

ADDENDUM

People

Amaranth [*am-uh-ranth*] – Prince Sharo's horse.

Anadin [*ann-uh-din*] – Second prince of KryTeer.

Aredel [*air-uh-del*] – High Prince of KryTeer. Also called the *Blood Prince*. His full name is **Aredel elvar Gilioth d'ara KessRa** [*air-uh-del ell-vahr gill-ee-auth duh-arr-uh kess-raw*].

Ashea [*aw-shee-uh*] – Prince Sharo's fairy companion in Shinac.

Bareene [*buh-reen*] – Queen of Amantier.

Blayse [*blay-ss*] – A lost knight of Shinac.

ADDENDUM

Breya [**bray**-uh] – A villager in Amantier.

Brov [*brawv*] – A soldier in Duke Lunorr's service.

Cavalin the Third [*cav-uh-linn*] – A legendary hero from a past age.

Chethal [cheth-**all**] – A lost knight of Shinac.

Darint [*ðair-int*] – A king in Shinac. Prince Sharo's father.

Drinel [*ðrinn-**ell***] – A farmer of Amantier. Kyella is his daughter.

Drioðere [*ðree-oh-ðeer*] – An ancient word for *Death* or the *Grim Reaper*.

DulShil [*ðool-shill*] – Deceased father of Emperor Gyath of KryTeer.

Ehrikai [***air**-ih-kye*] – The lost prince of Shinac.

Erisyrðrel [*eer-iss-seer-ðrel*] – A water demon from Shinac.

Foan [fo-***onn***] – An Amantieran knight loyal to Queen Bareene.

Frebe [*freeb*] – Captain of the guards at the Rose Palace of Amantier.

ADDENDUM

Galin [*gal-inn*] – A famous scientist in Amantier.

Gyath [*gye-uth*] – Holy Emperor of KryTeer. His full name is **Gyath elvar Kenn d'ara KessRa** [*gye-uth ell-vahr ken duh-arr-uh kess-raw*].

Hashab [*hash-obb*] – The KryTeeran Devil.

HeshAr dij Aban [*hesh-arr deej ah-bawn*] – A Blood Warrior of KryTeer.

Hethek [*heth-ek*] – A villager from Lilac Lake.

Ilim [*eye-lim*] – A villager of Amantier.

J'Aka [*juh-aw-kaw*] – A god of war worshiped in KryTeer.

Javanti [*juh-von-tee*] – A priest of KryTeer.

Jetekesh [*jet-eh-kesh*] – Crown prince of Amantier.

Jetekesh the Fourth [*jet-eh-kesh*] – King of Amantier.

Jevalla [*jeh-vall-uh*] – A woman in Amantieran scripture who sold her soul for a married man.

Jinji [jin-jee] – A wandering storyteller from Shing. Also called *Jinji Wanderlust*.

Kethalas [*keth-uh-loss*] – A dragon of Shinac.

ADDENDUM

Kivar [*kee*-**vahr**] – A soldier in Duke Lunorr's service.

Kyella [kye-**ella**] – Daughter of Farmer Drinel.

Ledonn [*leh*-*dawn*] – A Blood Knight of KryTeer. One of Prince Aredel's personal aides.

Linglia [***ling***-*lee-uh*] – Jinji's mother in Shing.

Lunorr [*loo-nor*] – Duke of Keep Lunorr and Rille's father.

Majinglee [*mah-jing-lee*] – Emperor of Shing.

Marder [*mar-dur*] – A soldier in Duke Lunorr's service.

Milgar [***mil***-*gahr*] – A lord of Amantier dwelling at Keep Falcon.

Mosill [moss-ill] – A blacksmith in Amantier.

Muhun [*moo*-***hoon***] – A Blood Knight of KryTeer.

Nallin [***naw***-*linn*] – A young soldier in Duke Lunorr's service.

Naqin [*naw*-***keen***] – A noblewoman of Shing.

Palan [***pal***-*inn*] – A disgraced knight of Amantier.

Peresen [***pair***-*eh-sin*] – A dread lord of Shinac.

Addendum

Rille [*rill*] – Daughter of Duke Lunorr.

Setwesh [*set-wesh*] – A mysterious guest of Prince Aredel.

Sharo [**shawr**-oh] – A fae prince of Shinac.

Shevek [shev-**ehk**] – A Blood Knight of KryTeer. One of Prince Aredel's personal aides.

Tallat [*tuh-**lot***] – A fisherman from KryTeer in the age of Cavalin the Third.

Taregan [***tair***-*eh-gen*] – A dragon of Shinac.

Tifen [***tee***-*finn*] – Prince Jetekesh's protector.

Yarmir [***yar***-*meer*] – Yeshton's deceased father.

Yeshton [**yesh**-ton] – A soldier in Duke Lunorr's service.

Places

Amantier [*aw-mawn-**teer***] – A kingdom in Nakania where fairy stories are against the law.

Araliass Bay [*uh-**raw**-lee-ess*] – Located in Shinac.

Aspen Province – A province of Amantier.

Bahadronn [*baw-haw-drawn*] – The royal city of KryTeer.

ADDENDUM

Chaos Creek – Located in southern Amantier.

ChinWan [*chin-wan*] – A port city in Shing.

Clanslands – A country to the northeast of Amantier.

Fortress of Crevier [*kreh-**veer***] – Lord Peresen's fortress in Shinac.

Hold of Valliath [*voll-ee-auth*] – The castle of Shinac's lost prince.

Ivy Province – A province of Amantier.

Kavacos [*kav-uh-k**ohs***] – The royal city of Amantier.

Keep Falcon – The southernmost keep in Amantier.

Keep of the Falls – Located in Moss Province of Amantier.

KryTeer [***cry***-*teer*] – The conquering empire located to the northwest of Amantier.

Lilac Lake – A village located in southern Amantier.

Lormenway [***lor***-*men-way*] – An island country located southwest of Amantier.

Minderen Creek [***min***-*ðer-inn*] – Located in southern Amantier.

ADDENDUM

Nagali River [*nuh-**gall**-ee*] – A river running from the Clanslands into Amantier through Moss Province.

Nakania [*nuh-**kahn**-ee-uh*] – The mundane world.

Neminar [***nem**-in-ahr*] – An island country north of Amantier.

Peregrine Fortress – Located in Willow Province of Amantier.

Rahajardaj Temple [*raw-haw-jar-dahj*] – A KryTeeran temple.

Rose Palace – The royal palace of Amantier.

Rose Province – The province where the royal city of Kavacos stands in Amantier.

Sage Province – A province in Amantier.

Shinac [*shee-**nok***] – A legendary fae kingdom.

Shing [*shing*] – A country to the east of Amantier.

Tindo [*tin-doh*] – A great river in Shing.

Tivalt [***tee**-vault*] – An island country north of Amantier.

Vylam [***vye**-lum*] – An island country north of Amantier.

Addendum

Willow Province – A province in Amantier.

Terms

Blood Knight(s) – The elite knights of KryTeer.

Dragonfriend – A term used to honor those befriended by dragons.

Jutik [*joo-tik*] – KryTeeran word for *filth*.

Kalakeeriðwa [*kal-uh-keer-iðð-wah*] – KryTeeran word for *one who sees far away*.

Lah'al [*luh-all*] – KryTeeran word for *beauty*.

Quii ðac [*koo-wee ðawk*] – Unsielie speech for *fall back* or *retreat*.

Sahala [*ʃaw-haw-luh*] – A KryTeeran name meaning *sparrow*.

Shamalheer [*ʃhaw-mal-heer*] – A KryTeeran life debt.

Shaqel [*ʃhaw-kel*] – A KryTeeran term of affection meaning *younger brother*.

Shaqin [*ʃhaw-kin*] – A KryTeeran term of affection meaning *elder brother*.

Sielie [*ʃee-lee*] – Light fae in Shinac.

Traveria [*truh-**vair**-ee-uh*] – A rare poison.

Unsielie [*un-see-lee*] – Dark fae in Shinac.

Witches of *Lioth* [***lee***-*auth*] – A cluster of wisewomen in KryTeer who perform dark magic for the Holy Court of Emperor Gyath.

ACKNOWLEDGMENTS

This labor of love has been possible only with the support of my beautiful family, without whom I'd likely get more writing done—but none of it would have any heart. It's our loved ones who show us the purpose of life.

I wish to thank my beta readers for your tireless efforts to help me improve my prose: Laura Barton, CJ Farley, Mandi Oyster, Heidi Wadsworth, and Tawnee Wadsworth. Thank you for believing in Jinji as much as I do.

A *huge* shoutout to Sara B., my epic editor, friend, and slayer of plot holes. I'll never let you slip back into retirement.

My eternal gratitude to Cac Stiner of www.cactheproofreader.com, who caught those last minute typos and word inconsistencies—as well as encouraged me to get this book out there!

Most importantly, I humbly acknowledge my Father in Heaven for gifting me with an overactive imagination and the drive to harness it into something tangible and timeless.

ABOUT THE AUTHOR

Writer of fantasy, magic weaver, dragon rider! Having spent the past 20 years devotedly writing fantasy, it's safe to say M. H. Woodscourt is now more fae than human. *Crownless* is her fifth published novel.

All of her fantasy worlds connect with each other in a broad Universe, forged with great love and no small measure of blood, sweat, and tears. When she's not writing, she's napping or reading a book with a mug of hot cocoa close at hand while her quirky cat Wynter nibbles her toes.

Learn more at www.mhwoodscourt.com

facebook.com/mhwoodscourt
twitter.com/woodscourtbooks
instagram.com/woodscourtbooks

ALSO BY M. H. WOODSCOURT

RECORD OF THE SENTINEL SEER
Science-Fantasy/New Adult

Prince of the Fallen

Rule of the Night

∽

WINTERVALE DUOLOGY
High Fantasy/Young Adult

The Crow King

The Winter King

∽

PARADISE SERIES
Portal Fantasy/Humor/Young Adult

A Liar in Paradise

Key of Paradise

Made in the USA
Columbia, SC
21 August 2022